P9-DYJ-438

SHOW
WORLD

ALSO BY
WILTON BARNHARDT

Emma Who Saved My Life

Gospel

SHOW WORLD

A NOVEL BY

WILTON BARNHARDT

ST. MARTIN'S PRESS
NEW YORK

SHOW WORLD. Copyright © 1998 by Wilton Barnhardt. All rights reserved. Printed in the United States of America. No part of this book may be used or reproduced in any manner whatsoever without written permission except in the case of brief quotations embodied in critical articles or reviews. For information, address St. Martin's Press, 175 Fifth Avenue, New York, N.Y. 10010.

Design by Maureen Troy

Library of Congress Cataloging-in-Publication Data

Barnhardt, Wilton.
    Show world / Wilton Barnhardt.—1st ed.
       p.   cm.
    ISBN 0-312-18684-3
    I. Title.
    PS3552.A6994S48   1998
    813'.54—dc21   98-3035

First Edition: July 1998

10 9 8 7 6 5 4 3 2 1

To Jean Kostelich, Kate Sparks,
and Mary Stark,

CAREER GIRLS

SHOW WORLD

JOURNAL ENTRY,
MAY 25, 1998

Dear Mimi,

   With mixed feelings about it, I'm mailing you my journal and an accordion file that has everything I've ever written inside it—press releases, Senate position papers, Hollywood p.r. crap—you name it. It's what there is of my "legacy" and I'm not sure after I testify tomorrow that I'm going to be living much longer. (And sweetheart, if they make you testify about Tony's drug connections you might consider hiding out too. As for cheap motels to lay low in, I don't recommend the Beachcomber in Santa Monica. Lousy stuff in the vending machines.)

   I know you think it's the crystal meth talking, that I'm being paranoid but Michael and Moe are dead and I don't care what the paper says—that was no suicide. A lot of powerful people don't want me to testify about what really happened with my husband. (I know you hate it, Mimi, when I call him my husband but that's what he was and that should count for something now, even if we all thought it was a big hoot and didn't take any of it seriously before the murder trial.) Actually, the people who want to shut me up aren't even that powerful. They're just rotten, rotten people with rottener friends who do anything for money.

If it's any consolation to you with the bankruptcy and the civil suits, you look great on TV. Poised, slick, sexy—the media loves you almost as much as they hate me. If my senator had been that slick, maybe I'd still be cranking out press releases back in Washington. Maybe I'd be White House chief of staff by now.

As journals go, I admit this isn't worth very much—not even a good TV movie in it, I suppose—some adolescent poems, some fragments of short stories and memory pieces. I've just been reading over I don't know how many years worth and I'm actually sort of impressed. I mean I used to be able to actually write. Still though, not much to leave behind but I want you, Mimi, to have it. Wait a few years before you read all the things I wrote about you. Don't worry! They're all good things. It will embarrass you to see how good!

Speaking of saying nice things—would you look out for me?

I know the tabloids are going to write what they've been writing—some over-the-hill scenester, some druggy strung-out parasitic manager, another piece of Hollywood flotsam. When they write the obituary, Mimi, when they call up for a quote, can you think of something nice to say about your old friend?

You know, I only came out here to Los Angeles because of you. What haven't I done in life thanks to you? I think a lot these days about how we used to be. I don't remember half those girls' names or faces, but I remember how you were, I remember how I was, all the things we were going toward. You always said Smith was the end of the world, but

A WOMAN

OF

PROMISE

NORTHAMPTON

AND

NEW YORK

1978–1983

The approach to Northampton put Samantha Flint in mind of every other American milltown: pool halls and tire yards, laundromats abandoned by day, brown bags disguising empties left on the asphalt, Eagles, Kiwanis, and Lions, a burger-and-shake joint with rusted muscle cars revving in the parking lot, a defunct bowling alley.

Just like the place she'd escaped from.

The shuttle-van driver turned left on Main and began to ascend the small mountain where Smith College rests, past bookstores and cafés and funky used-clothing shops, ever upward past crowded sidewalks of young women hugging books and strolling with purpose, in full possession of the town. The road came to a Y and the shuttle took the right fork, climbing again—higher, thought Samantha, light-headed with the difference of things, up the very slopes of Parnassus!—past a grand columned auditorium and the venerable ivied college buildings. The van slowed to release Samantha (and one other student in transit from the airport) at the tip-top of Northampton on a hill crowned by a high-steepled New England church, white with rectitude.

However doubtful it had seemed her last year of high school, the day of departure had somehow arrived—she awakened to it this morning, already a hundred years ago. The good-byes had been performed, the plane had safely landed, the man with the SMITH COLLEGE SHUTTLE sign was waiting as promised. The UPS boxes with her things (presumably) had arrived, and there was nothing to do now but begin her life, her *real* life. Samantha stepped onto the sidewalk and paused to inhale the crisp decisive northern air of her new home, scented with destinies close at hand.

She unraveled the worn map from her pored-over orientation packet. Serendipitously, she was a hundred yards from her assigned dorm, Haven House. I mustn't, she told herself, say *dorm*. Smith has *houses*, houses with cooks and kitchens and servants—well, not real servants, but people who looked after the house and the girls in it. Smith has Thursday-night formal candelight dinners, just the girls, everyone dressed up and beautiful, and on Fridays in the parlor there will be tea served, a formal tea. Samantha could by now recite the college catalogue, treasuring the cadences of its prose.

Smith and Amherst and Barnard and Wellesley. The schools to which she applied appealed in direct proportion to their distance from Springfield, Missouri, from the state cow-colleges down the road that her friends would attend. Yes, no doubt, there would be snobs and stuck-up little princesses to contend with at a New England liberal arts college, but there would also be elevation, a milieu of educated, progressive women . . . like the pair sitting in the porch swing of Haven House, checking out the new arrivals.

Samantha studied the two-story old-fashioned ochre mansion, now divided into thirty or so rooms, singles and doubles. She wandered around the side to view the sloping hillside behind Haven House and the placid blue pond beckoning beyond. A homemade sign—FALL 1978: WELCOME FRESHWOMEN—was suspended between the upper windows, maples crowding the eaves. Upon reaching the front porch, she offered a tentative hello to the two women who began giggling once she was in the door. Samantha revisited that elementary-school certainty that all laughter was at her expense.

An aggressively friendly student with a Yankee accent new and sharp to Sam's ears escorted her through the kitchen, past the dining room, up the stairs, past showers and sinks, depositing her politely at her assigned room with her own printed name card on the door.

The welcome-woman babbled about house rules and forms to sign, how lucky Sam was to have this light and airy room with such a large window, asking finally, "You're the Missouri girl?"

"Yep, that's me." Samantha pointed to her UPS boxes, which had made the journey. "I see Grandpa sent my still."

Her guide smiled politely before departing.

We're not gonna do that again, Samantha thought, methodically unpacking her clothes and books. We're not gonna work up an Ozark-hillbilly image that will plague and haunt me for four long years. I shall not be a figure of fun or local color. I shall establish a dignified, embarrassment-free persona.

Her fantasy: tweed skirts a little too long, glasses resting down her nose, walking around an autumnal campus with the collected Dickinson in hand, classical music (though she didn't own a record player, let alone any Mozart for it) audible from her room, other bright young ladies stopping in for . . . well, we'll start with super-strong tea, decided Samantha. Then, once her *salon* was established, she might dispense bourbon. If she found that she could negotiate life with the smart and the well-bred, she could then inject a bit of danger and waywardness into her persona, be the wild girl on the floor. Within reason.

Othwerwise, it will just be myself, Samantha Flint, English major, curled up in a chair near the window, reading poetry or laboring on my own novel. I will be quiet and studious and nice. I will be known for being quiet. There's nothing wrong with *nice*. I'm not gonna be the loudmouth smart-ass I was in high school.

Samantha sat on her chosen bed, bouncing lightly on the mattress. She next assessed her view through the coveted window: the Victorian house next door, two wind-stirred sharp-leaved maples already a bit yellow, a glimpse of the main road through town, sidewalks of sweatered and sweatshirted female traffic, snatches of laughing conversations almost audible from the open window, the recounting of summer adventures, shrieks of unexpected reunion . . .

"That window's going to be rather cold in winter, I think," said a girl standing in the doorway with a suitcase.

It was Melanie Rexroth, Samantha's roommate.

Samantha repeated what the welcome-committee girl had said, that their window was the envy of the house—

"Yes, well. We'll have to put up some thick curtains," Melanie considered, looking unhappily at the bed—the better bed—that Samantha had left for her.

"Do you want to switch?" Sam asked.

"No, this will do. I wonder if I'll ever get used to this. You can't imagine how good my bed is at home."

Melanie radiated all the dry elegance and spirited affectation that exclusive finishing schools could provide. "Mother" presently appeared to instigate an unemotional good-bye in which they did not kiss or touch, and subsequently several young men carried up her boxes. Samantha toyed with the notion that they were valets rather than brothers pressed into service.

In the following weeks, Melanie and Samantha rarely ventured beyond small talk. Melanie had a limited interest in topics beyond her clothes or furnishings, though when neither young woman could sleep there were confided tales of wealthy boys she had danced with at the club, shopping in Paris, shopping in London, an "absolutely *mad*" misadventure concerning leaving her shopping in a London taxi, an "absolutely positively *mad*" misadventure in which she was of a party that sneaked out to sea on Chip's father's sailboat last summer at Hyannis, neither of them knowing how to bring it back in—so "utterly deranged," indeed, that particular adventure, that the Coast Guard had to be alerted. Can you imagine?

"Actually," Samantha trifled upon the second time she heard Melanie's nautical tale, "my father had a number of boats."

Samantha vowed not to let this kind of coerced snobbery get out of hand, but after a week with Miss Moneybags, a little truth-stretching could be permitted. The Flints were newly arrived middle class. It seemed to Sam improbable that this could be kept secret all four years at Smith. Or maybe it could. Samantha sensed that Melanie wouldn't exactly be coming home for Christmas in the Ozarks.

"Your family sailed?" Melanie asked.

"Uh, no. Dad has powerboats, motorboats."

"Oh."

Samantha had wasted a half-truth for nothing; no class of motorboat could impress Melanie, for whom sailing was the mark of aquatic aristocracy. Truth was, Mr. Flint *sold* boats. The boat trade had moved Herbert Flint from the world of his father's cornfield to proprietorship—one of five partners—in a small business. Indeed, until the Ozark lakefront boom faded, the Flints could glimpse and nearly grasp the green expanse of upper-middle-class respectability.

"In Missouri?" insisted Melanie.

"Beg your pardon."

"Where exactly do you put a boat in Missouri?"

"We have lakes."

Reservoirs scooped out of the red Ozark clay. The Bull Shoals Reservoir—Samantha had no intention of sharing its ugly name with Melanie—southeast of Springfield. The lakes were near Branson, the rapidly expanding Nashville-themed tourist trap, a sub-Vegas (i.e., the Tony Orlando and Dawn Theater), a place of trashy white tourists on bus trips to outlet malls and fudge shops, thrilling each afternoon to a matinee gratefully given by a country-and-western has-been or never-was. Samantha's mind flashed to the traffic tie-ups and overheated polluting RVs and their seedy cargo: the pale redneck masses, Mawmaw and all her pink jiggling rolls of flesh, splayed on the gloppy gravel beaches of Yogi Bear's Jellystone Park Public Campground—

"Are they very beautiful, these lakes?" Melanie asked.

"In the off-season," Samantha said, not wishing to enter her brown lakes in competition with Melanie's blue Atlantic.

Melanie obligingly nodded off, but Samantha, despite a tiring day of class orientations and errands, was wide awake. Would she ever have the confidence to make a complete public assertion? *My name is Samantha Flint and my father used to work at Boatland.*

She smiled grimly to think of the place. When the reservoirs began filling in the late '50s, local moneymen envisioned acres of lakehouses and mega-powerboats to be moored as status symbols in front of them. An artificial town—Boatland—was created outside of Branson, and in 1963 Herbert Flint entered into a partnership to open the biggest boat dealership in Missouri, with a market extending into nearby Arkansas and Oklahoma. Her daddy gave off light in those heady days, making up business cards, designing artless but effective newspaper ads, predicting nightly that this was their family's "ticket."

Samantha remembered when the boatyard was being constructed, how Mr. Flint loaded his three girls in the old green Rambler Samantha adored—it had a sweet plasticky smell to it its whole life. Their mother had outfitted them in their best 1966 birthday party-wear, taffeta and white pinafores and hair ribbons. The girls met their father's partners in a flurry of introductions and affectionate "what a little lady you are" condescensions, and then followed in their father's footsteps as he traced an imaginary path that defined a future showroom. Stopping at a thornbush, he declared, "And this right here will be your ol' daddy's office."

"Daddy's gonna sit on the thornbush for a chair," Bethie, two years older than Sam, said, giddy with her new clothes.

Mr. Flint lifted Kelly, two years younger than Samantha, high above him, then nuzzled her, suggesting she could get down on her hands and knees and serve as his desk—

"And I'll be your secretary!" Sam squealed, jumping in place.

From the fourth grade, when asked what she wanted to be when she grew up, Samantha would say *secretary*. She liked to play at her vocation in the living room, rehearsing imperiously with a plastic toy phone ("No, I'm sorry, Daddy can definitely *not* speak to you now") and eventually a cheap kiddie typewriter was supplied for her one Christmas. She would type gibberish all afternoon and then sit waiting for her father to arrive, studying the clock, asking every ten minutes when Daddy would get home; then when he did, she would present her day's "work" to him with dotted-crayon lines across the bottom for him to sign. Often he did sign her papers, with a great flourish of fatherly approval. But as things worsened in his business, he became short-tempered. No childhood shame is as acute as when a child discerns she is behaving childishly; Samantha could still recall every detail of the time her father finally, gruffly declined to sign her papers. Samantha never played with the toy phone or typewriter after that.

She turned her mind to happier associations: her father's Vitalised hair, the minty-cool aftershave that glowed aquamarine in a bottle in "Dad's bathroom," a much-forbidden place but known to Samantha from furtive, secret missions into that chamber, to stand on a chair, take down the bottle and smell the intoxicating aftershave. Sam could conjure the sight of her father's three-piece salesman's suit (yes, there was a beige synthetic leisure suit as well, that Samantha favored at the time).

Mr. Flint regularly brought her along on weekend trips down to Boatland to watch the complex take shape—including a voyage or two without her sisters, who were bored with boats and business. Sam recalled a wooden frame redolent with newly cut pine, then a plastered and newly painted hall with giant green-glass windows. Much of the lot was mud and Sam was thrilled to be hoisted to her father's shoulders as he navigated a trail of planks laid between cement blocks through the construction site.

Samantha, proud as her father, would bring to school some of the slick, smooth boat brochures, radiant with the hyper-color of the period, as show-and-tell in sixth grade. The boys passed them around and oohed and ahhed and claimed specific boats as their own. In packing for college, Samantha had unearthed one of the old mid-sixties brochures: how over-streamlined and space-age everything was, monstrous gas-guzzling boats with names like *The Shark*, *The Ancient Mariner*, *The Rocket*, the high-haired models in Catalina swimwear and ruby-red lipstick waving from atop water skis as the boat sped away carrying its laughing family clad in life preservers pointing with pretend interest to some offshore wonder (in Missouri!). Mr. Flint had hoped to use his family for a brochure, but Mrs. Flint put her foot down: it would make the girls vain.

These were the golden years of Flint family life.

And somehow, here in her first foray into the world, Herbert and Hester Flint and sad, boarded-up Boatland, the muddy waters of Taney County, all were rising and threatening to inundate her high ground in Massachusetts, insisting upon a place in her present.

Samantha threw herself into socializing, reciting rehearsed conversation at those dinners and those teas, waylaying carefully chosen schoolmates with pertinent questions after class, walking a half-mile in the wrong direction in order to accompany newfound potential friends. The real gems seemed to be the upperclasswomen who were aloof and happily entrenched in their own social circles.

There were not many keepers otherwise:

There was Tam, a dominating tomboy who liked everyone, who prided herself on her loud softball-cheering-section alto, who would have been rendered speechless if deprived of sexual or scatalogical references (her voice braying at 8:00 A.M.: "Who do you have to SCREW around here to get some new toilet paper in the fuckin' stalls?"). Samantha had never before met anyone so lavishly rich who behaved so delightfully uncouth.

Jane, whose melancholy Samantha mistook for thoughtfulness, was from Long Island. She had been deemed a problem teenager with a "rebellion complex," and she told Samantha how she'd been sent to this $50,000-a-year school for troubled kids where discipline and order were taken very seriously; for any misbehavior, large or small, one could be confined to one's own possession-crammed dorm rooms. Happily, the parents could be "punished" too if they weren't supportive or made a scene at a gathering. Jane's mother once dropped by the school impulsively and brought the dog, only to be informed that no pets were allowed and some fat booklet could have told her so. The mother was banned from seeing her own daughter's performance in the spring musical; her mother was reduced to sitting, sniveling, in the parking lot during the play, not even allowed on the grounds.

"Figures," Jane told Samantha. "My mother *would* mess things up." (If one criticized the school as Dickensian, then Jane would defend it; if one liked anything about it too much, Jane would compare it to the Siberian gulag.)

Sam: "But if she didn't know bringing the dog was wrong—"

"Oh, she *says* she didn't know!"

"But why would she be out weeping in the parking lot if she didn't truly want to see your play—"

"So she could be a martyr, why else?"

Samantha ceased defending all the sympathetic, rational figures in Jane's stories and began retreating imperceptibly from her extended family's three houses with two broken families misallocated between them, from tireless reports of spiteful half-brothers, unhappy stepmothers awash in tranquilizers and therapists, a stray younger half-sister assumed to be happy until a botched suicide attempt suggested differently . . . Samantha didn't want to be near people who couldn't manage the simplest thing on earth: to be happy with lots of money.

Another early selection was Alex, beautiful and quick-witted, who entertained and eventually wearied the floor with considerations about whether she might be a lesbian. The established lesbians felt the matter could be cleared up simply enough, but Alex never consented to sleep with any of the many young women who offered; meanwhile, the straight women regularly feared being the target of Alex's postmidnight touchy-feely conversations. Alex's redemption was her electric popcorn popper; she would hold court in midhallway where all had to perform gymnastics to step over and around.

"But the thing is," Alex said one night, blocking her regular stretch of hall, "I'm not sure if Gayle knows how I feel about her."

"Not if you haven't told her," said the friend of the moment, a never-say-die lesbian who had invested too much time on Alex to give up just yet.

"But she might just freak out—"

Just then an upperclasswoman emerged from her single and swooped down to pick up a piece of popcorn. "Imagine," said the upperclasswoman, deadpan, "imagine if you *did* say something, Alex, and you actually *had* sex. Whatever would you talk about then?"

The upperclasswoman was dressed like a '50s Village bohemian— black beret and red scarf, formfitting black Chanel dress, opaque black hose, and (as Samantha had enviously observed) a way of walking that justified the outfit.

Beret Woman continued: "Your having sex, besides, would destroy the unparalleled record this *loser* freshman floor has acquired for virginity and atrophy."

Samantha was enthralled by this upperclasswoman.

She knew there were parties and teas and—less publicized—evenings of whiskey (and one heard rumors of cigars) with the brighter grad students and young female professors, plus a couple of the good ol' girls on the faculty they'd built the college around that could drink Paris in the 1920s under the table: wonderful unexpurgated female conclaves, nights of Parkeresque wit and McCarthyesque savagery at the nonattendees' expense, sisterly schemes hatched to further the interests of American women. Samantha was determined to ingratiate herself, and she would start with the Beret Woman.

The card on her single room at the end of the hall identified her as Miriam Mohr. Samantha had already heard a number of the girls talking about Miriam—pro and con, mostly con.

"Who does she think she is?" Melanie grumbled, "dressed up like Princess Grace to go brush her teeth."

Miriam's daily display of fashion provided an air of maturity, poise, and purpose; even as a twenty year old, she could be taken as a member of the faculty or a corporate representative come to interview someone for a Wall Street position.

"I don't own, have never owned, never *will* own a pair of blue jeans," Samantha heard Miriam say to the hall at large. By 1985, she predicted, no woman would wear jeans anymore; a new formalism would return to fashion.

"Doesn't anyone," Melanie was known to bleat, "have anything better to do on this floor than talk about Miriam Mohr?"

Samantha was increasingly the woman's lone defender. "When someone's that beautiful—"

"But she's *not* beautiful. She just acts like she is."

"I think she's beautiful."

Miriam had dark brown shoulder-length hair that had traces of auburn when she stood against the sun, an arresting face with high cheekbones that drew one inexorably to the expressive, all-seeing hazel eyes under dark subtle eyebrows. Her faintest emotion registered clearly on her face; you knew when food tasted bad or someone's politics were objectionable. Her gaze met your eyes and held you like a great cat staring down its prey; she dispensed an intimidating energy field, an electricity.

"I think she's larger than life," Samantha suggested.

Melanie: "Yes, and with anyone larger than life, there's not much room left over for anyone *else's* life. I don't know what she thinks she's playing at."

But Miriam wasn't playing—that was just it! In this whiny congregation of neurotic women with their Boston psychiatrists, girls from the coldest New England homes this side of Hawthorne—*here* was a woman who seemed to float free of her class, her family background (everyone was adamant, despite appearances, that Miriam Mohr was *not* rich), her ethnicity (Jewish, as no woman on Samantha's WASP floor failed to mention). Miriam Mohr was her own creation. She had willed herself into fascination, into beauty.

Miriam, Samantha observed, was always in transit, racing back to Haven House (clutching a wine bottle or a shopping bag from somewhere stylish) or scurrying to class, reading the assignment as she traveled, maybe a loose strand of chestnut hair across her face, as close to dishevelment as she ever got. She would primp in the dorm-hallway mirror, twirling stylishly, trailing intoxicating perfume, venturing into the chilly autumn in a long black Parisian coat.

"How do I look, girls?"

And her housemates, pulling their terry-cloth bathrobes a little closer, lifting a hand to check a plastic curler, assured her of her elegance . . . though she was out the door before her chorus had finished their grudging praise.

Late October supplied the much-heralded autumn. Smith's Paradise Pond was a shimmering mirror of volcanic oranges and hot-coal reds, maples and oaks and elms; even the shoddy poplars, so mediocre a performer in most of the country, were coerced by their neighbors into spectacular fire. The maple outside Samantha's window burst from its yellow interior to its branches of sugar-dusted orange, to its outer meretricious reds, which even in windless moments would offer themselves to gravity, twirling and spinning to the splayed leaf pile below.

"Mountain Day" at Smith happens once an autumn, when the president looks out her window and decides the fall colors are sumptuously peaking and that no one should be in class. With a papal wave of the hand, the college's bells are signalled to peal at seven A.M., giving everyone the day off. Students try yearly to out-guess the inscrutable president; some gather outside the poor woman's home and chant "Mountain Day! Mountain Day!" on nights when the weatherman has promised gorgeous blue skies ahead.

The prayed-for bells sounded the next morning, sending screams of riot and relief up and down the halls of Haven House; Samantha snuggled an extra warm hour in her bed, joyous at being awakened by the euphony of bells, sensing in the music something ancient and romantic, a daybreak of earlier centuries.

Later, from the bathroom window, Samantha spied Miriam standing beneath a scarlet maple. Miriam wore a wool sweater and skirt, hair back in a ponytail, and in the crook of her right arm, a picnic basket full of gourmet goodies—did she have such things ready at a moment's notice? Her left hand expertly held two cham-pagne glasses and a bottle of Taittanger. Then, in a scatter of fallen leaves, appeared a speeding sports car driven by a man—thirty years old at least, up from Harvard where he had an appointment in art history (Miriam's major), Sam heard whispered. Samantha watched them zoom away up Highway 9 to the Berkshires, leaving Smith behind in a plume of dead leaves, deserting the convent of dull women ("Don't know about you girls, but *I'm* using this Mountain Day to catch up on all my homework!") and their romance novels and soap operas watched in groups on tiny black-and-whites, diet sodas in hand and Hershey's Kisses in a common bowl, left to their gossip about others and their lifelong yearnings for love elusive and delayed . . .

Fine, thought Sam, dressing, grabbing her journal and a few pens, hoping to claim a solitary tree to write beneath.

Samantha knew what her novel would be called: *A Woman of Promise*. It would be really quite formal, Edith Whartonish; it would be set in the rich private-school set of New England (indeed, what was her time at Smith but a four-year research project?). Her own persona would be that of Nick Carraway in *The Great Gatsby*—on the outside looking in. There would be loveless, arranged marriages and one heroine struggling to break free from her family and society's expectations, culminating in . . . well, she didn't know precisely what, but it would be great, great writing.

Alas, her Creative Writing 101 assignment for next Tuesday had
been to share a happy childhood memory, no more than three
pages. "One would have to have a happy childhood," Samantha
had mumbled to a classmate, "to have a memory to pick from."

Inevitably, Samantha found herself back at Boatland:

> I remember a summer evening, back when I was nine,
> when my father had driven us from my hometown of
> Springfield, Missouri, to his boat dealership on Bull Shoals
> Reservoir.
>
> It was to be a short errand, merely to pick up an in
> voice, but when we got there, one of my daddy's partners
> was having a barbecue with twenty or so members of his
> extended family. My father and I had been expected
> home for dinner but Daddy called and said we'd be stay
> ing at the lake, and I, like any child, was giddy at the
> change of schedule.
>
> There were other children whose names I never
> learned, but my own age, from less citified places in the
> Ozarks, seductive with wicked words in rural accents, hy
> peractive and fun. It was one of the few times I remember
> "playing" as hard as I could, chasing, tagging, hiding in
> the woods, crouched down and dirty and sweaty, tackling,
> being tackled, part of an aching jumble of bodies and tick
> lings and punishments and, for myself, crushes on each of
> the scrawny anonymous Missouri boys who allied with me
> rather than their wild-haired sisters and cousins. I remem
> ber one boy

Jesus, muttered Samantha as she scanned the page, this is right out
of a Walker Evans dirt-smeared-children photo. She was going to
share this with her high-collared, hair-banded, cutthroat writing
workshop? I'll find something more neutral to relive, she decided.
Something with less mud-wallowing. Samantha then thought about

writing a generic Christmas memory from the Flints' first home, the only home she had ever cared for.

Her sisters Bethie and Kelly sided with Mrs. Flint in pronouncing their first house shabby and the people in the neighborhood *no-count milltown trash* (in Mrs. Flint's memorable phrase). Mother's talk of white-trash always spurred Bethie to endless interested questions: were the Gants next door trash? was our funny-looking neighbor Mrs. Beacombe trash? was it all right to tell Dana Lee Swain, who wore patched-up dresses to school, that she was trash? Samantha, who wouldn't care if an earthquake swallowed Missouri whole, nevertheless felt protective of this little house in its factory-workers' neighborhood, downtown, right off of Central Street.

When Samantha got her driver's license and was out doing chores in her mother's station wagon, she used to idle back by this childhood home and imagine it happy inside, warm now with the bustle of a new caring family who put blue electric candles in the windows come Christmastime, who taped a cartoon jack-o'-lantern to their front door on Halloween.

Sam couldn't forgive her parents' betrayal of her childhood province: the squirrel feeder, the oak with the rope swing that broke and hung busted for years, the old-fashioned front-yard hill upon which their cramped two-story, three-bedroom house sat, requiring the visitor to walk up a flight of (occasionally icy) slate stepping stones. How many times Sam had lingered at her father's legs, watching an aunt, uncle, and a bundle of cousins slowly move to their car, the well-wishing, the final forced jollities, ya'll come visit, a final replay of the too-repeated punchline that had convulsed the adults at the dinner table, and Sam laughing too without comprehension, wishing for adulthood. Sam felt protected and proud on their little hill; she had memorized every flagstone of the steps, every uneven joint of the city sidewalk that marked the frontier of her world and the beginning of a street she was forbidden to cross.

But to the spacious suburbs south of town they went. Lake Springfield. And with the new life, a new round of problems.

It soon became clear even to the children that Mr. Flint had over-extended himself, between his capital-hungry boatyard and the payments on the new house. Competition arrived. First another dealership on the far side of the lake, then a national chain with flashy showrooms and enticing television ads, sidling into a building across the street. Then the recession of the mid-1970s.

All the 19 percent bank loans and remortgages weren't discussed in front of the girls, but Sam was aware of tense mumblings from her parents' room, silences at the dinner table, men in suits over at the house attending to "Daddy's business." Sam came to understand that a new investor, Chet Diddle—his name came to be a curse word, source of every evil—wished to buy out Boatland and merge it with the franchise across the road. Her father went from founding partner (his fellow investors and partners had sold out long before; her daddy loyally hung on), to one of many debtors, to, in the end, employee. Mr. Flint declared himself a "glorified errand boy" who drove to every farflung hollow in the state to see about customers' complaints. Sometimes he hooked up the trailer and delivered their brand new boats; sometimes he hauled their malfunctioning boat back to the Boatland garage. If the demotion embarrassed him, it at least allowed him a lot of time away from home, away from Mrs. Flint's nerve-racked insistent reminding him of it.

The marital fights began at "Dad's dinner," when Mr. Flint was tired (the girls were fed earlier at a normal time; Dad had his supper at nine or ten when he came home).

Bethie and Kelly, huddled in their rooms, declared in furious whispers that "Mom should divorce him!" but Sam felt that her mother got the best of the fights, becoming more shrill and caustic, her father all the while more desperate and pleading. To hear that particular crack in her father's voice, the sound of a man about to give up or cry in frustration—that was intolerable.

"Mom ought to get a job to help out," Samantha insisted.

"Women aren't supposed to work," Bethie informed her. "Mrs. Fetzer across the street doesn't work."

Mother, despite her hillbilly antecedents, always thought of herself as having arrived, as being A Lady, and having worked hard in her youth she had set her mind never to work again. If she'd gone out and found a job, maybe Mr. Flint wouldn't have been so financially pressed. Maybe, Sam was sure, Dad's 1976 heart episode could have been avoided.

There was denial foremost in Mom's refusal to help.

If she had to work, then that meant failure and bankruptcy were possibilities. Mrs. Flint couldn't live in a world in which she might be returned to the country farm of her youth in Dent County, her old job in the small-town Woolworth, a pink smock and a plastic name badge. No, if there were financial difficulties, it was Herbert Flint's fault, and if he'd just put his heart into it, "be the man you used to be," then everything would work out.

The girls camped in their bedrooms, monitoring the nightly arguments, waiting for a personal reference to drift down the hall: "... the goddam girls and their dresses ..." or "... if Bethie hadn't scratched the goddam car, we wouldn't be stretched this month," variations of blame and indictment. Each girl's heart would leap in turn as she was mentioned in the roster of intolerable burdens.

With Sam, it was first her asthma and bronchitis that made for lots of doctor visits, then her overbite and braces, then her bad eyes, a rich vein for the town ophthalmologists to mine. Samantha felt most guilty about her eyes, because once at an eye test, with her disgruntled father in the waiting room, she had lied to the eye doctor and said she could read lines she couldn't read, and ended up with an inaccurate pair of glasses. A junior high math teacher noticed Samantha squinting and referred her to the school nurse, who correctly assessed the problem, occasioning a new round of eyeglass procurement, following another dinnertime scene with Samantha loudly berated for her foolishness.

Then followed an unsuccessful trip back to her eye doctor; he refused to give a refund (only because of Mr. Flint's anger and impertinence); sending Sam and her father upon a hot-tempered drive from one doctor to another in search of a cheaper fee. Mr. Flint would linger in a no-parking zone and send her in to ask about prices.

Sam reported back: "The reception lady said, it all depends."

Mr. Flint slammed the wheel. "You tell her we want a quote on how much it'll cost, or they don't get our goddam business!"

Miserably, she rephrased the request but got no clearer an estimate from the unhelpful receptionist. Sam thought about making up a price to tell her father, but then if the glasses were pricier, she would face her father's wrath anew . . . When she returned a second time to the car without completing her mission, Mr. Flint just howled "Get in the goddam car!"

Samantha froze.

"I said get in the goddam car!" he repeated, reaching for her arm to pull her inside.

"You gonna hit me?" Samantha asked without emotion, just wanting to know.

In some dreadful family episodes, this would have been the opening act in an evening of violence, but Mr. Flint was not violent. All he could take from the question was shame.

"No, baby," he said, shaken. "Let's . . . let's just go on home."

The same catch in his voice. That same masculine surrender—a man about to cry. All the way home she refused to look at her father. I will deny to my dying day that I made him cry, she swore to herself.

Nope, Samantha said to the Massachusetts autumn day, closing her journal, no "happy" memories today. She directed her thoughts instead to *A Woman of Promise*, set among the salons of Europe and yacht clubs of Newport, less known and less real but not as sullied and inconvenient as the past.

One chill November morning, as Samantha tottered back from the showers clutching her bathrobe, her wet hair in a towel turban, she turned into her room to see Miriam Mohr standing on Melanie's bed, tape-measuring the wall above it.

"Moving in?" Samantha asked, happy to earn a proper introduction to her idol at last.

"Oh god," Miriam said, briefly startled. "Thought you'd left town."

"Nope, no one invited me anywhere."

"I never go home for Thanksgiving either," Miriam said, continuing her measurements. "Like my fat Jewish calves need seven thousand fucking calories in one lousy meal . . . Hmm, not quite long enough . . . There's this tapestry in a store in Stockbridge that I had my eye on—not that I can afford it. Well, that's that." Miriam stepped down from the bed, and quickly put her brown-suede Capezio pumps back on. "You can report me if you like," she added, then extending her hands to be cuffed.

"Are you moving in?"

"Let's talk about that. Melanie's your roommate?"

"That's right."

"You best of buddies?"

"Well, I wouldn't exactly say—"

"There've been three Rexroth sisters at Smith, and the previous two were real cunts, so I can't imagine little sister is any kind of prize." It was the first time Samantha had heard the forbidden c-word spoken aloud in the hallowed confines of Smith.

"You know who I am, don't you?"

"Miriam Mohr."

"That's right, except my friends now call me Mimi." Mimi sat on the bed, no rush to leave. "Well, my friends *will* call me Mimi, I hope. I'm converting. All new acquaintances are being told I'm Mimi now."

"All right, Mimi," Samantha obliged. "Happy to get in on the ground floor."

"Miriam has got to be oldest dry-cunted name on earth." (No woman was ever more fond, Sam would learn, of the epithet *dry-cunted*.) "So I'm going to be Mimi now. Mimi Mohr. Me-Me-More," she enunciated. "I am the embodiment of the age! It'll help the dimwits in the art world remember who I am when I get to New York." To Sam's delight, Mimi reclined and stretched out, surveying the ceiling, patting the mattress. "Not bad for a dorm bed. This yours?"

"Melanie's."

"Well, unless you want it, this will be my bed after the changeover."

Mimi this morning wore a pressed cream silk blouse, casually open a few buttons, a hunter-green wraparound skirt that matched her hair band—this in Haven House, habitat of the sweatshirt and the bathrobe. "What's with your curtains?" she asked. "They look like carpet samples. You could keep Eastern Europe behind those things."

"Melanie thought there was too much light in here—"

"Yes, a creature of the darkness, our Melanie. We'll put my linen curtains up instead. Macy's Veterans Day sale—just two hundred bucks, and you know what you'd pay at one of those little Madison Avenue places."

Samantha had no idea what you'd pay. She pulled her chair closer to Miriam stretched out on the bed; they resembled psychiatrist and patient. "How do you intend to eliminate the evil Rexroth?"

"First, I ask nicely, to switch rooms, which won't work because I'm at the ass-end of the hall, next to the bathroom door that slams into my far wall. It is a *single*, however. There's a constant muffled flushing noise, not to mention the dykes on this floor who take noisy midnight showers. Someone's gonna slip on that goddam scented oil on the floor of the shower stall—" Mimi turned to Sam suddenly. "It's not you, is it?"

"Oh, no. I'm not—"

"Don't get me wrong, I *love* the lesbians here; the ones that don't breathe fire and want to crucify me for screwing men. They have the best sense of humor, they want something out of life. I'd have made a great lesbian. I think like a man most of the time anyway. All my best friends are men," she said extravagantly.

They passed another half an hour, hatching plans and assassination plots of every sort, a climb on the roof gone horribly wrong, three shots from a sixth-floor book depository window, Northampton's first gangland hit . . . Mimi soon sat up leisurely and straightened her dress. "I say let's go for the Seconal in her tea, followed by a pill bottle-by-the-bed tableau." Mimi stood and took her new friend by the arm to walk herself to the door.

"By the way," Samantha added as an afterthought, "I'm Samantha Flint."

Melanie, unexpectedly, did switch rooms. She repaired to her new single, which meant she could attempt a private life. Mimi had persuaded Melanie, with tales of cold winter mornings, how nice it was to have a short walk to the showers. Samantha sensed that Melanie would miss neither room nor roommate.

"Melanie looks down her nose at you," Mimi confirmed as they carted furniture and rugs and clothes from Mimi's former single. "She doesn't think much of me either. Double whammy, middle-class and Jewish."

As a test, Mimi asked Samantha to notice if Melanie ever said hello to her again of her own volition, without prompting. As the weeks passed and Melanie and Samantha passed in stairwells and lunch lines and hallways, they noted: Melanie never acknowledged Samantha again.

"See?" said Mimi. "She scraped you off her shoe."

Mimi hated the privileged. Bloodsuckers, parasites—every unkind adjective in her vocabulary applied. Mind you, Mimi wanted to be rich—provided she made the fortune herself and didn't marry into it—but the phony aristocracy of America, the fawning before the bog-Irish Kennedys, the Anglophilia of New England that sucked and knelt before and crawled after the slime–trail of every two-bit piece of ever-visiting British royalty, moved her to extremes. Was Prince Charles in Boston this week?

"We had a revolution so we could dispense with these leeches. Elizabeth's worth eight billion—and the people of England still cough up their income to support that shitty family. A bunch of inbred krauts who foisted World War One upon the planet. Morals of a Louisiana trailer park . . ."

Classicial music, contemporary art, the opera, the ballet—there was much, Mimi announced factually, in which Samantha needed to be brought up to speed.

"Don't let her make you into a clone," advised Tam.

"The problem with rooming with her," Alex speculated, "is that everything's always going to have to go *her* way."

Sam nodded, taking in their sisterly advice, but the fact was Mimi's way happened to be irresistible.

"I wasn't planning on going to New York before the holidays," Mimi soon declared—before their second weekend together—"but I'm not sure I can let you persist in your unfortunate state another minute, Sam." Samantha had blithely confessed that she'd never set foot on Manhattan. "You're sure you've never been?"

"I told you, just La Guardia Airport when I flew up—"

"Jesus—La Guardia. No wonder you're happy here, you've never even glimpsed civilization!"

It wasn't until her freshman spring term that Samantha properly understood that the Mohrs weren't native New Yorkers at all. Mimi made no effort to publicize an upbringing in Brookline, Massachusetts, where her father had a jewelry shop. At first Sam assumed that Mimi had adopted Manhattan out of Jewish solidarity, but eventually she decided Mimi's embrace of New York was a form of homage, a veneration of the center of art and fashion and culture and the wisecracking no-nonsense social realpolitik that was Mimi's personal currency.

"They sound . . . eccentric," Samantha said of the Mohr family.

Mimi: "I think *dysfunctional* is the word you're looking for."

On paper, perhaps: father separated from the family, Mimi's mother stuck in a sapping role as companion for her bachelor brother (Mimi's neurasthenic Uncle Eliot). Mimi had an older sister, Connie, an investment analyst, whom she didn't speak to ("Who can talk to that money-grubbing Wall Street human calculator?") and a brother in whom she saw no wrong, Jonathan, an assistant district attorney among the battalions of young résumé-padding lawyers in the New York courts.

Sam once asked, "Is your brother cute?"

Mimi paused as if weighing the consequences of having Sam as a sister-in-law.

"It was just a simple question."

"Yeah, he's cute."

Sam returned to her Wordsworth essay, looking up ten minutes later to see Mimi still mentally at work on whether Sam and Jonathan should be brought together. "Yeah, you know," Mimi admitted presently, "you two would really get along."

That did not turn out to be the case.

Jonathan was cute, all right, an olive-complexioned, dark, curly-headed Jewish boy who had mastered manipulating women with a downward shrug and a flash of big brown eyes. He had two personalities: the public one, a smug, confident, fast-talking young lawyer who wouldn't let anyone get a word in, and then the private personality he had around Mimi, a man-child who reverted to their kiddie language. When Jonathan visited in Northampton, the siblings totally regressed to infancy, poking and tickling, squealing at reprisals, talking of nothing but childhood incidents and absurdities of relatives—no matter that nonfamily members were in the room, with patient strained smiles. It was news for Samantha to learn that Jonathan was four years older than Mimi; she had taken him for a baby brother.

"Of course," Mimi said periodically of Smith, "this dump is nothing. Just a holding pen before the big show begins in Manhattan. New York is fortunately big enough that on most days I can forget my family is mouldering away in some corner of it."

New York, Manhattan, Broadway, the Hudson, the "sides" Upper West and Lower East—these mythological lands now began to breathe enchantment for Samantha who soon became equally sure that she belonged there: Mimi with her art gallery in Soho and Samantha scribbling at her novel at some Village café. Samantha had spent her high school years determined to get out of Missouri for New England; longing-for-elsewhere was becoming a familiar way of life.

By spring, Mimi had whisked Samantha away to New York three times and Samantha could still quantify her journeys:

She had taken exactly five taxis.

She had been on the F train once (for Washington Square and the Village), the 1 train twice (for the Cloisters, and once to eat at a little French place near Lincoln Center), and had taken the 6 to the Upper East Side (for the Metropolitan Museum of Art).

Samantha made a mental collection of bridges as well; she had been taken across the Triborough, the Queensborough (for the incoming view of Manhattan, Mimi announced, since "there's nothing from goddamn Queens all the way to the Hamptons worth a shit"), and she saw the Brooklyn Bridge, finest of the lot, from the passenger seat of the Mohr family car, a stale-smelling Buick that hibernated in its expensive garage near the East River for months at a time.

"Am I scaring you?" Mimi asked, squeezing between a stopped delivery truck and a taxi that rewarded her with a full ten-second horn blast. Mimi's driving was "New York Driving," a Darwinistic form of motoring in which if there were an available space in an intersection and ten cars were competing for it, the prize went to the alpha driver who was first with the least trepidation.

It was possible, Mimi assured her friend, that one could speed the length of Manhattan Island in a single titanic acceleration along the north-south avenues *if and only if* one caught every timed traffic signal, which in practice meant that Mimi would go 70 MPH, yellow and just-red all the way, narrowly missing pedestrians and cutting off taxis going 65 ("I see Ahmed is gaining on us . . .").

For Manhattan locations, Mimi would drive until she found what she was looking for, circling and surveying, cursing and berating the city ("They've changed the street name, I swear to you—this is supposed to be Varick"), doubling back, putting the car in reverse for an entire block to look at a street sign again, never admitting to being lost despite all the earmarks of it. These Manhattan–centered treasure hunts were preferable, thought Sam, to trips to a gallery in Hoboken, New Jersey, or the Tibetan Museum in Staten Island or a trendy restaurant in Brooklyn Heights because, once off Manhattan Island, Mimi required use of the ancient, glove-compartment map (a free Esso map back from the days when service stations gave them away, and Esso was still Esso). Mimi, cruising over the potholes at 65 MPH, talked extravagantly while folding and unfolding the map (unfolded, the map took up most of the front seat). Simultaneously, Mimi would take another opportunity to unstick the cassette wedged in the tape player for the last two years, effecting this repair with a pencil.

Once Mimi arrived at a museum and the ordeal of parallel parking on the street had concluded ("Like I'm gonna pay twenty bucks to park in the museum garage!"), then Samantha was swept along behind Mimi the tour guide. Mimi, like a ship's prow, would part the crowds, her long coat and scarf trailing, surging toward her evening's fixation as if in search of a lost child. Samantha was pulled through the Metropolitan's warm, brown Rembrandt and Vermeer rooms, then a detour to some moody Spanish oils . . .

"If El Greco was alive today he'd be painting Jesus and Elvis on black velvet for sale at road stands in Ohio," Mimi said, the spirit of Savanarola surfacing, capable of pitching her least-favorites onto a bonfire. Then followed an airy loop through the Impressionism galleries, radiant with all of art's sunny, bespattered greatest hits, known from calendars and jigsaw puzzles. "*Pretty* paintings," Mimi grumbled.

The Buick was called into service frequently for the Brooklyn Museum, where Mimi's favorite American art treasures lay unvisited and underappreciated. (This was deep into Samantha's sophomore year, by which time she'd stopped counting taxi rides and bridges.)

"Deborah's from Brooklyn," Mimi sneered as she tried to keep the four wheels on the ground of the impossibly potholed and patched Flatbush Avenue.

"It's official that everyone hates her?"

"*Everybody.*"

Matrimonial tragedy was looming. Over the summer of 1979, Jonathan had affianced himself to Deborah, a whiny girl from Carroll Gardens with a weight problem who utterly ran his life, measured his progress in the law firm against her friends' husbands, bullied and kvetched and made no effort to get along with the other Mohrs.

"I'm sure," Mrs. Mohr would say, "we'll all grow to love Deborah in time. She seems to be a very unhappy person."

Samantha was touched by Mrs. Mohr's stoic acceptance of her son's impossible choice of spouse. Indeed, she was drawn to Mrs. Mohr's manner generally. Her own mother specialized in two equally impotent modes: hysteric worry about things she couldn't control (which manifested itself in incessant nagging), and plodding, clinical depression that in other parts of the country would have qualified her for counseling and lithium, but in Springfield, Missouri, just kept her isolated in her kitchen, bickering with Dad (when he was there), eating too much, never changing out of her bathrobe or attending to any of the few chores the cleaning lady didn't get to.

Mimi's mother always wore a variation of the same outfit. A high-necked dark sweater, and a navy or black blazer with embroidered rhinestone designs on the lapel, black tapered slacks, a colorful scarf spread around her shoulders or her neck, and large earrings sharing a color with the scarf of the moment.

"She's a Bloomingdale's middle-class Jewish lady of leisure," Mimi explained, "and she rarely varies the uniform."

(Mrs. Mohr did actually work, part-time behind a perfume counter at Saks Fifth Avenue, but this was almost never mentioned; when it was, Mrs. Mohr made it sound like a pastime, a kind of gathering with friends who happened to be equally distracted by similar employment.)

Mimi went on, "I'd faint dead away if Mother came out in a tank top. It's been years since I've seen her in a dress. And the makeup!"

"She wears makeup well," Samantha insisted.

"No, I mean, I, her own daughter, haven't seen her without it in two decades. She's one of those women who doesn't show herself, not even for breakfast with her family, until she's made-up."

Mrs. Mohr had made a tactical decision around fifty that she would tough-out middle age as a jet-black brunette, her hair dyed and pulled back neatly. With her regal facial structure, her daughter's high cheekbones, she could carry off that woman-of-indeterminate-age look so many Manhattan ladies strive for. Her voice was soft, her tone hushing, her natural expression serene.

With Mimi's pathological disdain for sentimentality, she had no choice but to see her mother as a comic walk-on, an object of lampoon to threaten with institutionalization, a "character" to be viewed from an artistic distance. "Mother walks through the world in utter denial of life's unpleasantries," Mimi declared. But Samantha chose to see Mrs. Mohr as heroic, projecting a polished, placid surface upon any event, trying to will the world into civility.

Samantha once asked, "Why doesn't your mother date any-more?"

"She likes looking after Uncle Eli," Mimi sighed. "I don't see how she can like it, but it's her choice I suppose."

After the divorce, Mrs. Mohr moved in with her brother, who imagined he was stricken with a variety of illnesses and complexes that he could not possibly have, all the while ignoring the diabetes and the regimen of blood testing and insulin shots he very much needed to attend to. Until Mrs. Mohr arrived, her brother thought nothing of ordering up whole meals from the expensive neighborhood deli, having cheesecakes and pastries delivered at all hours, running up his credit card bills to the thousands. He would forget to pay the electric and the phone, insisting mistakenly that he had sent in the money while threatening to amass a battery of lawyers to fight his unjust persecution—oh, they'd rue the day they tried to tangle with Eliot Gottschalk! Mimi made clear to Samantha that she too had to play into the official family fiction that Eliot was taking his sister in for *her* own good, and not that Mrs. Mohr was watching over him, seeing his bills were paid, that he was eating the right foods, smoothing over his temperamental relations with his boss.

"He catalogues for the New York Public Library," Mimi explained, "which isn't exactly pointless, but the man should be the curator of the Met or on the National Endowment for the Arts or something." Mimi lightly pulled on a lock of Samantha's hair. "He wrote a short story in his twenties that appeared in *The New Yorker*."

Whatever Uncle Eliot's tenuous hold on reality, Samantha nonetheless envied him this milestone.

In April, Samantha and Mimi were summoned for a high tea. Mrs. Mohr and Eliot Gottschalk shared a Park Avenue apartment in the mid-thirties, a dull, prosperous neighborhood of brick apartment buildings, florid doormen, and mostly (it seemed) elderly tenants. When they arrived, no one answered the doorbell, so Mimi (with her own keys to the place) began a minitour, pointing out and extemporizing upon the array of her uncle's imported possessions and first editions left lying amid Mrs. Mohr's paperbacks and newspapers. Samantha marvelled at this cluttered museum of English prints and Shaker antiques, Yemeni rugs and Pueblo pottery, a Picasso lithograph in the oaken hallway, a silk Japanese print in the mint-green foyer, a jumble of Manhattan eclecticism loyal to no decorative style.

Samantha and Mimi, hankering for a smoke, decided to go outside on the tiny balcony (Sam had acquired Mimi's Virginia Slims habit). Momentarily, a panicked Uncle Eliot appeared, his 250 pounds wrapped in a dressing gown, sputtering that

1) the double doors were wired to an alarm system that had alerted the police there was an intruder, and

2) the apartment's air (despite the choking accumulation of dust and book mold) was on a new, expensive filtration system whose work was ruined—*ruined*—for the whole day by this door-opening, which had allowed every allergen and noxious gas of New York to sweep into his apartment.

"Unspeakable," he said, the poisons kicking in, as he teetered to collapse back in his bedroom. Minutes later the police were at the door with the building manager, and Eliot uprooted himself from the deathbed to wave them away with an apology for the false alarm. And that was "unspeakable" too. Mimi found the whole episode another zany anecdote in the ongoing chronicle of Uncle Eliot; Samantha simply thought him a ghastly hypochondriac.

Northampton became the place Samantha and Mimi endured between visits to New York, an impediment to their future world of artistic struggle and fame, fortune, and affairs. When they weren't vicariously planning the next Manhattan outing, Mimi was proselytizing Samantha with the gospel of Europe, where Mimi intended to go after graduation.

"My problem is Venice," Mimi said, staring at her calendar, lighting a cigarette to consider her quandary. "I got budget problems. If I do Germany and Denmark—where there are some galleries I've got to see—this trip, then I'm caught short in Italy without enough money or time. Plus, August is a terrible time for Italy—the whole country's closed down for vacation. Venice will be full of shitty Amercian tourists."

"Save it for another year," Samantha suggested—then erupting with, "save it for me! I mean, when I'm done my senior year, I'll go to Europe too and we can go together."

"A whole Italy trip—nothing but Italy."

"God, that would be great." Quietly the thought warmed Samantha all over. Had she ever dared to think that Europe was a possibility? She imagined the words in her mouth, *Last year when I was in Venice*, and thrilled to their transformative powers. Suddenly, with Mimi in charge, Venice seemed as close and as plausible as New York.

"I won't let you go to Venice without me," Samantha declared.

And though it took several more months for the Venice-in-1982 Plan to take form, over more wine and late nights back at Haven House, it was agreed that Mimi would not darken the merest cobblestone of Venice—even if a handsome viscount promised her Ca' Rezzonico filled with her beloved Tiepolo, even if kidnapped by marauding *gondoliere*—without Samantha Flint by her side, the two of them plying the waters of the Grand Canal, Doge-like, triumphal.

On weekdays, not surprisingly, there was a paucity of males around Smith College. Come the weekend, however, the rivers of testosterone overflowed from the nearby campuses and the streets of Northampton swelled with potential suitors.

There was no shortage of University of Massachusetts guys from eight miles away, frat boys laying down the groundwork for a lifetime of alcoholic loserdom in flailing pursuit of sports, beer, getting laid; boys who had applied to all the prestigious private universities before surrendering gratefully to U. Mass.

Mimi each Saturday would skip to the newsstand and back to buy *Artnews*, having run a gauntlet of whistles and propositions yelled from slowing cars. "It's like Poussin's *The Rape of the Sabine Women* out there," she'd report.

But Smith also trafficked in Amherst College boys, smart liberal arts students who not only got good grades but usually had some visible talent to boot—art, music, theater—and oh god help us all, they were beautiful. Some discerning old queen must have been in charge of admissions over there, because never was there such a collection of adorable boys—sensitive, androgynous, hippieish, sweet, sports-eschewing, guitar-playing, sandal-treading, earring-wearing, longhaired virginal boys, ripe for the mushiest romance, who shared mawkish passages from ragged poetry spiral-notebooks, who asked one on walks in the countryside intending to *hold hands.*

Prime for defilement.

Mimi: "Please, Sam. Half of them are gonna be gay anyway."

"Well, let me at 'em before they convert."

"Sure I can't set you up with a proper date? With a man over thirty?"

Mimi couldn't tolerate "boys" and set her sights on older men; she relished accomplished lovemaking—no sense pretending about that—and furthermore, "an older man can pay for dinner." While the Smithies negotiated their best deals with the local hounds, Mimi was whisked to Boston or New York with regularity by aspiring gallery owners, art purchasers for the Met, a second-chair violin in the BSO she met at Tanglewood and . . . well, the variety was endless, the turnover prodigious. They were not always handsome men, and, despite her pay-for-dinner crack, not always wealthy. Mimi was susceptible to the loft artist who lived from rent check to rent check. But she couldn't abide "student" poseurs, dabblers who at the first fiscal inconvenience would go to law school like Dad always wanted.

Such a dabbler was David, Sam's first college-era boyfriend.

David was from New York too, and Mimi didn't care for a rival tour guide brandishing an alternative New York for Samantha. David radiated delayed adolescence: he was slender, five-nine, with a giant unruly mop of wiry brown hair that he had been talked into dreadlocking a time or two. His usual look was sloganed T-shirts and cutoff jeans, exposing hairy thin legs (he was the last to get out of shorts in autumn, the first to debut them at first signs of warmth). Like Samantha, he was an English major.

Samantha first laid eyes on David Sutton when she, Jane, Alex, and few more of the Haven House regulars went "trawling for boys" in Amherst to an open-mike night where poetry and prose was to alternate with singer-songwriters. It had been Sam's only motive to check out the competition to see whether her own journal ramblings would pass muster by comparison.

When they entered the café, David was playing original melodies on his classical guitar. The Smith contingent made so much noise scuffling and whispering "excuse me" that Samantha wished they had waited until the guitarist had concluded before sidling to their front-and-center table. Then, mortification of all mortifications, her own raincoat swept a fork to the floor with a clang that might have come from a great Mongolian gong. Sam bravely made eye contact with the performer, apologizing telepathically.

During the break, when the café returned to boisterous conversation and raids upon the pastry counter, David plopped down in a chair next to Samantha: "From Smith, right?"

"What gave me away?"

"Moving in a pack of girls."

"I am *so* sorry we made all that noise. We just—"

"It's all right. Maybe I can give you a private recital sometime," he said intently, touching her hand lightly, "long as you don't bring a fork."

"Maybe I could accompany you on the spoons?"

Hometowns were compared, families alluded to, phone numbers exchanged, and it was David who wanted to make it clear first that he didn't merely have friendship in mind: "So, like, Sam. You got a boyfriend?"

"Nope."

"Want one?"

Samantha, as her sophomore year wound down into a rainy, busy, depressing May, told Mimi that "David is sort of the insta-boyfriend. Just add water. It's strange, Meem. I didn't have to club him over the head, didn't have to fix myself up or even suck in my stomach. He can express his feelings, he doesn't play games, none of the typical-male nonsense. David was ready to be a committed boyfriend from the first five minutes we met."

"Yes," purred Mimi, half-attending as she studied for her last round of finals. "Imagine that. He's a walking bundle of under-graduate hormones and along comes this nice girl who says, 'Sure, let's screw all you want providing you love me, of course,' and he says sure. You oughta do your senior thesis on this astounding phenomenon: horny guy saying what he has to say to get laid regularly—''

A pillow sailed across the room and bopped Mimi on the head.

"This is going to be insupportable," Samantha said a moment later, reminded that at academic year's end, Mimi would be graduated and gone. (Uncle Eliot's "unspeakable" or "insupportable" had been coopted by Mimi and Samantha for their private vocabulary.) "Just tell me how," Sam demanded, "I'm supposed to continue here for two more years without you around."

"You oughta be happy you have a single next year. C'mon, you'll get to sleep over with the Boy David all you want without having to hear me retch. You're desperately undersexed, darling."

Samantha's pre-David sex life could be summed up in one young man's name: Paul O'Connor.

Yearbook photos showed that adolescence had conspired with braces and bad teenage fashions to make Samantha grotesque: thick glasses, blue plastic octagons. A '70s white-girl afro of tight brown curls like Barbra Streisand in *A Star Is Born*, like Janis Ian, whose mopey folk songs she adored then. Ruffled synthetic blouses handed down from her sister Bethie, flung into Samantha's wardrobe the day they went out of fashion.

Sam was in band.

Her social life was divided between band nerds from the cliquish woodwind section (thanks to her asthma, which made her performances less dependable, she played second clarinet instead of first), and the high school Debate & Speech Society, where she was allowed to exhibit all her intelligence without persecution. If she'd had the nerve, she'd have cornered one of the stiff, destined-to-be-a-lawyer debaters, all boyish arrogance and fumbling note cards, equal parts dorky and handsome, and coerced one of them into dating, but she had established a dismissive, smart-mouthed "You boys aren't so great" stance that dampened any attempt at a truce. Samantha smiled, thinking of the wide ties and polyester suits, of championship black-and-white photographs of bookish, bad-skinned teenagers clutching trophies, beaming with mouths full of orthodontia.

Now, playing the clarinet wasn't cool, and Samantha was stranded amid a corps of plain girls hurled to the outer darkness of band geekosity. Somehow the brass section (tuba excluded) was fashionable. The trumpets and cornets and trombones seemed to the girls in the woodwind gulag to be rowdy and talented and rhythmatic and cute, always getting the showy solos—particularly the first trumpet, Devon (but he was black and what an event an interracial romance would have been in Springfield in 1976). Also passable was Paul O'Connor, pale, beefy with blond-brown hair, with green eyes which, in combination with a sharpish smirk, laid waste to the woodwind contingent.

Paul briefly did time on the tennis team until he sprained his ankle badly enough to need a tight bandage and crutches. Samantha saw him chasing their school bus one day as the driver prepared to pull away. Valiantly, she flew from her seat to wedge herself in the open doorway while the students booed and the driver threatened her with a limp sanction. Paul hobbled at last to the bus door, giving her a wink, "You're my hero, Samantha."

He knew her name!

Sam sat beside him on the bus a week after that—following a week of NASA-caliber planning and scheming for how she would manufacture an excuse to speak to him again, rehearsing unaffected naturalness in her mirror, holding summit conferences with girlfriends on what to wear, the implications of hair and shoes. Somehow she blurted out something nonidiotic; Paul flirted back.

It was soon official. Boyfriend and girlfriend.

"O'Connor," her mother pried. "You sure he's not Catholic?"

He *was* Catholic, but Sam managed to hide this fact for months. The Baptist Flints (who rarely attended the old foot-stompin' church that Mrs. Flint had come to find an embarrassment in her middle-class climb) would ordinarily have complained but Samantha assiduously avoided offering any information that would lead to *parental commentary* of any duration. When they did find out, the fact that Mr. O'Connor was a rich lawyer who lived with his family on old-monied Walnut Street with the fake gaslights trumped any flimsy Protestant objection to Rome.

"So Paul was, like, your first guy?" David asked, snuggling closer on the dorm-room floor. (Mimi was in Boston for the weekend.)

"Numero uno," confirmed Samantha.

Whether it was Paul's Catholicism or the general bright-kid fear and overanalyzed awe about s-e-x, Samantha and Paul somehow decided they would respect each other's virginity. This pledge, though tempted now and then (she wanted to when he didn't, then vice versa), held through the prom and graduation before giving way on their freshman-year Christmas break, when it seemed pointless to hold out longer, and neither had met anyone else to take care of the chore at their respective colleges.

They did it when Paul's parents and siblings were away in Joplin seeing an ailing grandmother. Paul was tender, nervously offering hilarious patter throughout, which Sam appreciated. Until David had materialized, Paul and Samantha used to coordinate spring holiday and Christmas visits so they could convene and sleep together in Springfield. Paul recently found someone at college he wanted to date (indeed, he may have found Becky, his eventual wife, long before he broke off their little sex-friendship). No matter.

"I've been with two other women," David volunteered, cuddling in bed. "Well, one was a girl, like when I was fifteen."

Samantha listened interestedly for a while, but David's sexual history was as dull as her own. Seduced by a lifeguard at the public pool, she a predatory not-too-pretty eighteen, he fifteen with a permanent erection. The story had the effect of making Sam wish all the more she had committed a one-night stand or two along the way before battening herself down with David Sutton.

". . . and then there was you," David said, snuggling closer again. "I saved the best for last, huh?"

Samantha warily entertained the thought of being David's last, of his being hers.

Yet, David was in love with her (according to him) from the very start. At first sight. And that was, to be honest, the major force of his appeal, that he worshipped at her ill-attended altar, that his thoughts dwelled upon her, that he wrote dopey poems and lovely guitar melodies with her in mind. Samantha was continually impressed that her young man had put his life in her control; he could be consumed and commanded, and this slight feeling of obligation, of power that might be misused, was troubling and thrilling.

"Well," said the Meem, on her final night of packing, end of semester, Haven House quiet and studious with exam miasma in the air, "at least you'll have someone to play with while I'm gone."

"I'll have to get used to going into the city by myself," Samantha said, wondering if New York was even there without Mimi to narrate it. "Simply insupportable."

"Unspeakable."

"Can I ask a question?"

Mimi's back was turned, and she slowed in the folding of her cashmere sweaters. "Is it going to lead to something mushy?"

"Perhaps."

"Let's have it then."

Samantha paused; she wanted her question answered seriously. "Was it just the room with the big window?" Mimi understood the meaning. Had it merely been a flood of bathroom noises and the prospect of a view that drove Mimi to Sam's room two years ago, or something about Sam herself?

"The window," Mimi said, "made me look twice at the room. So then I was secretly spying on you for a week or so, deciding if I could live with you or not."

Samantha sat upright on her bed, delighted to have been as much an object of inquiry for Mimi as Mimi had been for Samantha.

"You know how Sarah Bettinghurst was always so into causes that year, more bleeding-heart than God? She was going on about white slavery and the U.N. doing nothing about it because no one cared about women, and she was screaming at you and some others, 'Don't you care about women being abused in white slavery?' and you, without looking up from your book, said, 'Yeah, that's why I'm not getting married.' "

Samantha smiled, though she couldn't remember saying it.

"This goddam college is Polyanna Central and I was happy to find an exception." Mimi turned away, her voice a little strained. "All these dingbat women thinking some man or some house in Connecticut or having a bunch of babies is going to lead to living happily ever after. There is no happy-ever-after that falls out of the sky."

"No, there's not."

"You have an edge, Sam. Usually you have to hang out with freaks or women in need of ten years of therapy to get that quality. Just a nice, matter-of-fact life-cynicism that agrees with me. You know, our Dark Vision of the World."

Sam nodded.

"And I'm not going to say good-bye to you with any profundity," Mimi said, turning away again. "Because I'll be back in no time and we'll be cavorting in New York, you'll be writing, I'll be managing a gallery. And we'll look over all the postcards I've sent you."

"None from Venice, I hope."

"No sweetheart, none from Venice."

October, 1982. Samantha settled on a bench in New York's Central Park under the broad vault of embracing oaks along the Mall. There was a ferocious wind in the upper branches and Samantha looked up to view the unsparing stripping of leaves; she followed the progress of a layer of yellow and dull orange alighting upon the statue of Robert Burns across from her bench. All along the pedestrian boulevard of the Mall stood and sat bronze statues of writers and great men (probably some great women of the good-doing Florence Nightingale variety too, but Samantha hadn't found them yet). Emerson. Walter Scott. Shakespeare.

I bet Edith Wharton doesn't have a statue, it occurred to her.

One withered oak leaf landed deliberately on the white journal page before her. A project had occurred to her—find a way to get a statue of Wharton into this beautiful old park. She had no clout for such an undertaking, but becoming a famous novelist herself could change that, couldn't it? She looked down at her journal and the early passages of *A Woman of Promise*:

> A woman of promise must face many obstacles,
> many doubters, detractors, and rivals, but no
> foe so deceptive as her own heart . . .

Samantha turned often to this page where the lovingly belabored first line of her novel-in-progress was enshrined. Aiming for Jane Austen, she had yet to feel fully comfortable with the result. My, she thought scanning the page, it's tough to strike a formal tone without sounding like Barbara Cartland—

"Hey Sam!" David was on roller skates, steering unsteadily in her direction, arms flailing.

Samantha pressed her journal to herself. "Can I have a few more minutes?"

David had trouble holding his place on skates. "You said that half an hour ago. I'll make a deal. You come listen to me play tonight and I'll give you 'til three."

Samantha weighed the burdens of sitting in a coffeehouse until late, listening to his way-too-familiar repertoire. "Sure," she said.

"All right," he said, pushing off, "seeya in a half hour."

"Maybe longer!" He had those skates in college, Samantha reflected, and he's still not very good on them.

"Maybe longer!" he called back.

Samantha watched David carom among the other skaters and cyclists and she felt sharply that she was, by some measure, a coward. As she had approached graduation, Samantha had written Mimi that, no, they would *not* move in together, she wanted to be on her own. She had played out a miserable, tearful scene with David (his tears) about how they should see other people and embark upon separate lives.

Nothing had worked out as planned.

Beginning with Mimi in Europe. Rather than the year she was going to last, she ran out of cash in four months. It was, by all reports, a fabulous, adventurous four months, but she came home broke and moved in temporarily to Park Avenue.

"I know *matricide* is when you kill your mother," she told Samantha long distance, "but when you kill your uncle, what's that called?"

Throughout 1982, Mimi went throughout Soho, charming and impeccably dressed, dropping off résumés and letters of recommendation door-to-door at art galleries, bright and early, hoping for any kind of entry-level opening. She then backtracked north through the Village; then to Fifth Avenue and the cluster of exclusive galleries in the East Fifties; then to a host of not-so-exclusive places on the East and West Sides; then to just about anywhere that sold frames with pictures in them.

"I'm going to be selling Leroy Neiman and Nagele prints on Broadway if this keeps up," Mimi reported.

One lecherous gallery owner on Madison Avenue ("He couldn't tell a deKooning from a cereal box," Mimi reported) offered her a job as a receptionist, and Mimi took it, just to be somewhere. She didn't last a month. She could just about survive the Sephardic brand of sexual harrassment and the enslavement to the coffee-maker, but all her ideas for improvement, investments in new artists, and classing the place up were shot down with patronizing smugness, so she quit with agitation and pride intact, thereby forfeiting any kind of severance check from the man.

"I'm a year too late for the gallery boom," she cried to Sam. "The gallery owners are king now. A no-talent like Julian Schnabel can get six figures for gluing a plate on a canvas, and Mary Boone is making money like she's got a branch of the U.S. goddamn Mint in the back alley, and Mimi Mohr is nowhere to be seen—*nowhere!*"

The indomitable Miriam Mohr was being handed a defeat. And though Samantha was sympathetic, the whole spectacle was not . . . well, not without a certain curious interest. Sam for the first time imagined Mimi having a nervous breakdown, or striking a less-than-heroic pose.

Then Mimi announced she was going into *advertising.*

Sam stammered, "But you don't have an advertising degree! You've never even done any kind of office work—"

"Oh, please. After four years of art history, I can damn sure draw and sketch; I know I can write copy. I have friends who will help me put a portfolio together. . . ."

Then Samantha didn't hear from Mimi for a few months.

When next she resurfaced, Mimi had a foot-in-the-door job at J.

Walter Thompson. Six months later she was copywriting and doing sketches and having has-been partners take credit for her niftiest ideas. Then she jumped ten thousand in salary (up to $35,000!) by going to Farrell & Ritch, then six months later to Ogilvy & Mather, for another raise. In an industry where image was paramount, Mimi was Queen of the First Impression.

A trip to Europe for Samantha and Mimi, for the moment, was off. Mimi was swamped with work and responsibilities, and Samantha didn't have enough in her savings. Samantha did, however, have enough to afford a few months living with Mimi in New York without having to get a job. She would write. This would be her inviolate, sacrosanct time.

A permanent job—like being a copywriter at the firm where Mimi worked, and nagged her to apply—would have jeopardized Samantha's creative time in Central Park. She was certain that this novel would demand odd hours and impulsive gestures—checking into the Plaza and living off room service while one wrote the final chapter; accepting the unexpected invitation to someone's beach house on Long Island where an open window and desk with typewriter waited . . . A novel was a very ornery and rambunctious thing (or so she'd surmised) and Samantha was prepared to see to its outrageous requests.

Tonight, however, she was stuck listening to David play guitar at an uptown coffeehouse.

At one A.M., after his last encore (wrenched from a smattering of tepid claps), Samantha trudged back to the West Village. Her and Mimi's Barrow Street brownstone was once some bohemian's very splendid townhouse, but since divided and halved and subdivided until every renter lived in a space the size of a walk-in closet. Having stayed out late, Samantha ended up sourly spending money on a taxi she didn't budget for.

Mimi rarely lingered in the apartment; with her work schedule she was either rushing in or out, but tonight she was home and waiting up—seemingly with the sole purpose of needling her about David:

"What's he doing for money?"

"He's still living with his mom."

Mimi repeated with crisp enunciation: "Living . . . with his mommy. On the Upper East Side. I see."

"It was a new gig tonight and I had to show up. A bistro up on East Eighty-second. His mother knows the manager—"

"His mother knows the manager," repeated Mimi with an un-yielding gaze. "Davey-boy knows maybe—what? Five pieces. He'll have to play at a place where there's pretty fast turnover so people aren't aware they're hearing 'Classical Gas' thirty times during the soup course. Why doesn't he busk somewhere?" Before Sam could answer: "Can't his mother get him a little busker permit?"

"He did that last summer and some gang member stole his thousand-dollar Ramirez." And before Mimi could agitate further, Sam said, "I don't know what you expect me to do. We're both living here in the same city. It's just easier to keep going out. I know you don't like him—"

"Correction. *You* don't like him. You spent your senior year writ-ing me letters how you'd outgrown him. And it's the '80s, for christ's sake. What are you doing with the last hippie on earth? How often does he wash that overgrown Brillo pad on top of his head?"

"He's not . . . unwashed, Mimi."

Her roommate disappeared and returned with a prescription bot-tle of Bactrim tablets from the bathroom, shaking it like a maraca. "You seem to be going through a lot of sulfametho . . . methoxazol trimethoprim lately."

"Please. I had bladder infections before he came along."

"David's got bacteria living in Woodstock-like communes on parts of his body that haven't known a washcloth since his mother bathed him. Mind you, Mommy might well be performing that function still."

"I'll get rid of him in my own sweet time, thank you."

"I'll leave the pills right here," Mimi said, delicately, absurdly balancing it atop the candle at the center of their dining-nook table. "I'm just giving you a hard time, sweetheart. I've slept with bigger losers than David. Anyway. You and David will be happy to learn that I won't be here next weekend. I'm going to Cape Cod."

"Really? Not sure I want to waste a weekend with the apartment to myself on David."

Living in such a small place (Mimi in the one bedroom, Sam on the foldout sofa in the living room, willing a "two-bedroom apartment" into existence by imaginative effort), this had become the official fantasy: no roommate around, lounging in a robe, ordering in a large pizza, long irresponsible baths with the building's entire supply of hot water, paging through half-read magazines, forty-eight hours of bad TV . . .

"Call David," urged Mimi. "Mimi's Rule of Available Sex: Have it for all the months in your life when you won't be getting it."

Samantha agreed. She committed Friday night to herself—*Dallas* and *Falcon Crest* over Häagen-Dazs triple chocolate—and Saturday afternoon, reading and dozing off. Then David.

On some romantic occasions, Samantha's assessment of David, once the sex was over and he was on his way home, was harsher than Mimi's. David never seemed more dispensable than those bleak minutes after sex. Since her junior year, Samantha had been taking the pill for him. David had been willing to use condoms, but he claimed after much experimentation that he simply didn't feel anything during their lovemaking.

"That makes two of us," Sam joked at the time.

Which was sort of true. It was enough for David, apparently, simply to be inside a woman. Within a very few moments he had his orgasm—no moving about, no rhythms or motion, just put it in and wham. Sam would look up at his uninhibited expressions and noises of enthusiasm like he might be watching the Knicks on TV, and she felt oddly irrelevant to the proceedings. He would fall to her side, recover, and then it was her turn to be worked upon, for as long as she wanted, as long as it took—and David was inevitably dutiful. His lovemaking was as eager-to-please and earnest as he was, so he was a good lover.

Samantha nonetheless longed for someone who was a little more mysterious, dangerous, complicated—even to the point of impotence, she reflected. Some damned young man stricken with some past tragedy that haunted him, rendered him vulnerable . . . Or, fail-

ing that, even a moody silent type would do after so much of David's ingenuous yakking, someone who might be harboring some
kind of secret or two for Sam to pry at. David would cuddle afterwards, heat up the bed, hold Sam in a vise grip and mutter endearments many women would kill for: "I love you so much," and
"You're so beautiful," and "I'll never not want to make love to
you."

Sam's reticence at these cues was accepted by David; he never
demanded that she mouth his sentiments back. She sort-of-loved
him—a qualified love with a number of dependent clauses, shad-
owed by the expectation of someone better.

Tonight, in celebration of Mimi's absence, David rolled back on
top of her and repeated their first round of lovemaking. It was like
watching a video of what had preceded. After the encore, it was
huggy-cuddly time again and Sam, for once, said, "I'm too hot, give
me a moment."

"I'm hot too," he said, kicking off a cover.

She turned toward the window. It was raining outside, a slow
gentle rain without noise, making trails down the glass, catching the
odd glint of taillight and streetlamp from the thoroughfare below.

"Hey Sam, do you, like, ever . . ."

Samantha was charmed by David's shyness about sex.

"Have you done anything really kinky? Or, you know, offbeat?"

"Not really."

"I just wondered if sometimes you wanted me to do something . . . different."

"You have something in mind?"

"No. I was just wondering if you did."

Sam lay on her back, looking at the ceiling. "I don't think I'd like
to be tied up. I don't think I could keep a straight face if we, you
know, pretended you were the pizza delivery guy or something."

David laughed. "I could get my super's tool belt and pretend to
be the repairman."

"Maybe a *real* repairman, a real stranger," Samantha considered,
lifting her arms above her idly. "It wouldn't be kinky if I knew it
was you."

"You ever slept with a stranger?" David's voice was intense; he had moved closer but took care not to touch her, as requested. "A one-night stand?"

"No," she said.

But almost. Her senior year at Smith, earlier this year in fact, when David was down in New York. A Northampton town-guy, Johnny.

Samantha wasn't attracted at first but he flirted from behind the Santini Dry Cleaners counter whenever she came in to pick up her clothes, called her "sugar" with a smile that transformed his average face. She imagined he was Italian, like the people who ran the dry cleaners—that was a major selling point, in fact—but he was just dark-haired Irish and ordinary, with a broad mid-Massachusetts accent, ugly and flat to all other American ears, but somehow exotic when coupled with his smile. Indeed, for much of her senior year Samantha grew distracted with her studies and found herself staring out the windows of the Nielsen Library, thinking of what it would be like to cheat on David, to sneak away for a night with Johnny. She didn't exactly wish to be encoupled with some zitty guy who worked in a dry cleaners and flirted with every girl that passed through, and yet . . .

Johnny offered to take her to dinner, then for a drink; when he lowered his demand for "just a coffee," Samantha relented.

He lived in a dump of a row house beyond the Bridge Street tracks with his brother. The house was a house where men lived, with a smell of socks and last night's pizza, worn chairs aimed at the TV, toy basketball hoops atop door frames. Johnny had tried to spiff it up, filled the room with pine-scented fluorocarbons from a cannister while Sam was in the bathroom. Older brother had cleared out conveniently and Samantha let herself be pinned to the sofa.

Johnny kissed her urgently.

Samantha felt no passion for Johnny, and yet she wanted something to happen. She noticed Johnny's hair smelled like the "fresh" scent sprayed on everything at the cleaners. What was moving, what kept her there, was how much he wanted her, what a prize she clearly was to him.

But dark thoughts intruded: the bragging to his other milltown friends, the possibility of hoots and whistles in the street, the chance that a new reputation would follow her into the dorm and its gossip. The ugly thought of trying to explain this encounter to David if it somehow got back to him.

The doorbell rang and Johnny got up to answer it. Just the Chinese delivery guy looking for the place in back, but that gave Samantha enough time to grab her handbag and press to the doorway, quickly excusing herself. . . .

"So you've just slept with me," David was questioning her, "and that guy from high school?"

She remembered Johnny's stunned, desolate, wordless glance. "Yep. I've been a pretty good girl," she sighed, not the least bit happy with her virtue.

Poverty, not unexpected, at last arrived.

"I don't know why you're scared of a full-time job," Mimi lectured her. "Trust me, there's no goofing-off like the subsidized goofing-off a full-time job provides."

Mrs. Mohr of all people, came to her rescue:

"Samantha darling," Mrs. Mohr said, as she and Sam and Mimi walked along Seventh Avenue South, in and out of antique stores, "Miriam tells me you're in need of a little job to tide you over. You must call my friend Sy Gold at Gold and Bracken."

Mimi: "That silly fussbudget, Mother?"

"It's not the sort of job that you would want to keep for long. But it would give you a chance to write, hm? Mimi assures me you are very, very talented."

Samantha smiled. Mimi had never seen a word of Samantha's writings.

Sy Gold's number was found, and Sam dutifully applied, not expecting anything to come of it. A secretary shuttled her to Sy Gold himself. "You say that *darling* Rebecca Gottschalk recommended you—oh, ho ho, you see, I remember her when she was Rebecca Gottschalk, before she married! I should have married her myself— what a dear thing she is!"

Samantha passed these comments along to Mimi.

"That old queen? You sure you want to work for him?"

Adjustable hours, cocktail parties, a little press-release writing, escorting rich people here and there. Sounded good, as slave-wage jobs went.

Sy Gold, the firm's cofounder, was an effete sixty (or so), with a beautifully pomped and continually managed head of silver hair above a chinless face, with a dusty complexion that had the appearance of having been subtly powdered. He had red cheeks more fit for a choirboy (he drank), and strong *eau de toilette* that suggested wilting rose petals, the potpourri of an old lady's parlor. Sam, years after her employment there, could conjure up that particular fetid, invalid smell and how it attacked the nose. For his many social functions, Sy was always splendidly wrapped and draped in custom-tailored suits; for the office, he padded about in a silk dress robe of the sort Cary Grant might sport, lounging in an art-deco hotel suite with Kate Hepburn. Sy was a living museum of gentlemanly toiletries and lost niceties from when the domestic man was king.

Sy Gold was also, as Mimi promised, an old, fussy Jewish queen not true to either tribe. Samantha amused Mimi with the thought of asking straight out, "You're Jewish aren't you, Sy?" or only slightly more unthinkable, "Sy, you're homosexual, aren't you?" His face would have lost its small allotment of color, he would stammer a hasty retreat, panicked as if a Vichy boxcar to Auschwitz was waiting for him. Sy Gold was what Mimi termed "a William Paley Jew," more waspy than the WASPs, making a big deal over Christmas; not even the common-parlance Yiddishisms of every New Yorker passed his lips.

As for his love life, there were only the airiest, most tortured rumors until the arrival of a former assistant, Shay, who preceded Samantha in her job.

Shay (born Jerry Wayne in Paramus, New Jersey), according to Deanna the grandmotherly receptionist, was intensely spoiled, legendarily slack on the job, and supremely manipulative. And apparently he had Sy wound around his finger, accompanying him to operas and charity benefits billed as Sy's "new friend." There were many almost-public scenes in which the office was treated to ig-nominious pleadings muffled from behind Sy's office door, all re-buffed by Shay with a practiced petulance. Eventually Sy came to his senses and banished Shay from his firm, his apartment, his life; Shay's name was not to be mentioned; further, a Soviet-style diktat descended upon the office that no such person ever existed.

Sam was the *fourth* assistant since Shay in this position, and for the first weeks she couldn't imagine in this relaxed, undisciplined office of five workers, all casually cobbling together publicity pro-jects at the last minute, why the turnover had been so high.

But then a dinner-benefit at the Russian Tea Room neared and, quite late in the game, it was discovered some detail was overlooked (namely the matter of reserving the Russian Tea Room) and a hys-terical Sy Gold turned the office into a maelstrom of negative en-ergy. He was harpy, sweeping down unsuspected on people doing their job ("Why the hell would you be working on that when you are needed over here!"); he was Lear raging at the storms, hurling a cardboard cup of pencils to the floor ("They want to drive me out of business, but I won't give them that satisfaction!"); he was Christ at Gesthemane ("What did I ever do, O Lord, that these caterers should do this to *me*, Sy Gold . . .")

Sam would hunker down, dodging the tirades, looking to the of-fice of Joan Michaelson, Sy's press-release person, possessed of the only office besides Sy's with a closeable door. Joan would with a twitch of the head communicate for Sam to come close the door behind her.

"Thanks," Samantha said, relieved.

"Sy's deranged," Joan said evenly. "You can hide in here as long as you don't tell about *this*." Meaning her cigarette. Sy spent half of her hour-long orientation informing Samantha of his intolerance of ciga-rette smoke, claiming the mere hint of it brought upon him paralysis, inflammations, and *episodes*. "He manages to go to these smoke-filled society parties well enough, you'll observe," Joan added.

Sam watched Joan open her office window and blow her smoke out into the chill spring day. Joan was not warm, though she was serviceably nice; as a single woman in her forties who had met thousands of people in twenty years of p.r., she had lost the capacity to generate enthusiasm about making acquaintance. In Sy's office with its turnover, why bother? But that's how Gold & Bracken worked—no, correction, that's how *all* of New York's two-room office p.r. or publicity or advertising or consulting or talent agency or management firms thrived: off the backs of the newly arrived young and poor, the talented with energy to burn at both ends of twelve-hour, minimum-wage, no-time-and-a-half days. The sole reward, a few commending words from a boss possessed of a religious belief in his or her own importance.

Joan retrieved a manila folder on her desk. "Here's the clunker of the week."

Sam read the file: "The Sheboygans."

A representative couple plucked from among that class of people who paid personal publicists to get them on the *Times* society page or crammed into a photo in the back of *Town and Country*. With luck they might rise to the heights, occupying a chair next to some Eurotrash castoff with bad teeth, booze breath, and a dispossessed title next time some American Friends of the Goethe House fundraiser rolls around. . . .

"Not a lot to work with here," Joan said, scowling at the paucity of the Sheboygan résumé. Joan wouldn't be talking about any of this, Sam understood, unless she intended to pass the file to Sam. "Originally from Akron. They weren't even in society *there*. Jake made his fortune off some tire alloy he patented, blah blah blah, married a Cleveland socialite, and you know the story."

Sam didn't know the story.

"Wife gets obsessed with moving in New York society, rubbing up against Nan Kempner and Brooke Astor, right? So husband sells his interest for millions and moves to Long Island. They give a few parties; no one of importance comes; they come to us."

"What do they pay Gold and Bracken?"

"Oh, I shouldn't tell you that." Joan exhaled the last of her Camel Light, morose from its hasty conclusion. "Do you believe $2500 a month? If you don't charge a lot, these people don't think you're doing anything. Sy gets them invited to some benefits, mostly the low-rent diseases.''

Sam looked puzzled.

"What's hot varies from year to year. Any kiddie illness brings out society—Make A Wish, leukemia. When you get around to kidneys and colon benefits, you're lucky to get a TV weatherman to show.''

Joan regaled her young protégée with a selection of further social-climbing strategies, give the Met a zillion, find a poor neighborhood and build a new library. Another idea: hire the hot interior decorator of the moment, and then call *Architectural Digest* and cajole them into doing a feature on the Sheboygans' living room.

"There are people who've spent half a million to get in that magazine." Joan tossed the folder back on her desk. "Sorry for them, really. Pissing all their money away." Joan explained that most clients would drop Gold & Bracken the second they reached the first rung of the ladder and felt they didn't need Sy anymore. But others were doomed to the Sheboygans' future: no matter how much was spent, they would never reach a light lunch with Lee Radziwill and Diana Vreeland at the Giraffe.

"So Sam. How would you like some added responsibility?"

Added responsibility was New York code for *work from my desk I don't want to do.*

"Joan, I just got hired two weeks ago."

Outside the office, Sy was bellowing: "I smell cigarettes! Deanna! My inhaler!''

Joan threw the butt out the window and watched it head to the roof of a building on 49th Street. "Hell, two weeks qualifies you for a goddam senior partnership around here."

The following rainy April weekend, Samantha caught the Long Island Railway to East Hopogue. She watched the train empty at the connections to Jones Beach, Fire Island, the Hamptons, leaving her alone for the final stops. Long Island, for all its reported beauty—Sam expected Fitzgerald's "green breast of the new world"—in early spring was not so beautiful, carpeted with brown grass, fields of weeds, and short still-bare trees, shrouded in watercolor-gray skies. At the station, the driver was waiting in the drizzle to take her to the Sheboygans' mansion.

Jake Sheboygan was a jowly man in his sixties, quite fat from rich meals and retirement, who rocked and limped when he walked due to his accumulation of aches; he would position himself in front of a chair and collapse back into it (winded from even the short expedition from the sofa), where he would sit good-naturedly red-faced, patting his knees.

"I suppose it's how you New Yorkers do things, eh?" he'd ask, never convinced that spending thousands a month to worm their way into charity benefits was justified. "Just like anything, you gotta pay to get in, right?" None of his comments to Sam seemed to require answers. "It's just money, so what the hell," he'd laugh, looking at his wife, Fran, who seated herself at some remove.

Jake told Samantha the story of their fortune.

Then he told her about going to Europe on a high-priced bus tour connecting one Ritz with another.

Then a joke about old women who wouldn't let a bartender put soda in their whiskeys ("You know we old ladies can't hold our water!"). Why, he'd heard that one on the bus goin' around Europe, from some ol' character, what was his name? Frannie, do you remember his name? That retired Jew from New Jersey, that bond trader . . . The irrelevant detail would make for ten minutes of ramble, the longed-for name would never come.

Upon each visit, Jake would welcome Samantha genuinely, wave a hand at the bar ready to struggle from his chair to fix her any ol' drink she might want, and then proceed to tell the very joke or story she had heard the previous visit, word for word, while she sat politely smiling. Although he was a windbag and an old wreck, Sam liked Jake Sheboygan for his lack of pretension; he was harmless and sweet. There was no way he would ever mingle with *tout* New York, but clearly he didn't care a damn—the nights at the opera (where Mrs. Sheboygan swatted him semiregularly to regulate his snoring), the charity balls, the fundraisers, the small private dinners all bored him, and whenever possible he would discover a pain in his gut and stay home.

"So what rat hole's our money gonna go down today?" he asked cheerily. No matter how fine a suit Jake was wearing, he always looked uncomfortable, transforming the custom-tailoring of Bond Street to something synthetic he could have grabbed from a discount rack, always hiking up his pants to reveal his pale leg above the sock, always publicly arranging the material's stresses upon his crotch.

His wife Fran, at first glance, seemed to offer a familiar story, a much younger woman who had married money, her life a social martyrdom of providing her husband some cultural amelioration. Among her many successful deceptions was her surgically enhanced appearance; she was, in fact, the same age as Jake. She couldn't do anything about her age-spotted talons, the Achilles appendage among society's tightly tucked set.

Her surgeons' work was often for naught, though, due to Fran's trademark expression of furtive concern, her eyes darting, squinting as if some prize might elude her. Her eyes shifted right: haven't they seated me at a table of nobodies? Her eyes shifted left: isn't that someone over there I'm supposed to be meeting instead of talking to you? No amount of surgical beautification could compensate for those lupine eyes.

She was further undercut by the impediment of her husband; Jake would natter about something dreadfully personal ("In 1981, Sam, I went in for my gallbladder. . . .") and Fran's face would go into a catatonic blank waiting for her husband to fall silent, as if she were pausing the videotape of life, then she'd continue as if he'd never spoken, back to the subject of guest cottages and their landscaping, the loveliness of a gown glimpsed at the Met, a recitation of praise upon some social superior who had taken the merest notice of her.

"How *is* Joan Michaelson?" Mrs. Sheboygan asked pointedly, wondering why an underling was sent in her stead.

"Joan," Samantha improvised, "is at Saratoga this weekend catching up with some London social editors." For a moment that seemed to satisfy Fran, but then her eyes signalled trouble as she imagined the vast English social scene functioning without her.

"Joan sent me out with these brochures and articles. . . ." Sam opened a Gucci leather satchel, lent to her by Joan for this presentation. On the glass table of their garden patio, Samantha arrayed her prospectuses from various top interior designers, laminated clippings from magazines.

"How lovely," Mrs. Sheboygan murmured, running her hand over the luxe graphics.

"That, Mrs. Sheboygan, is a ski chalet by Akio Fukushita," Sam said. "Joan tells me that the last two clients of his had their rooms featured in *Architectural Digest* and the Style section of the *Times*."

Jake Sheboygan leaned forward to look and grunt. "Ehh, you couldn't exacty *sit* in that chair, Frannie."

"I've heard good things about this man's work," said Fran.

"He only does two or three rooms a year in the United States," Sam said. As she talked, the middle-class girl within balked: who are these charlatans who do *one or two rooms a year* for millions of dollars? How do you get a gig like that at twenty-nine years of age? A glance at Mr. Sheboygan showed his thoughts were identical. "It's sure to mean an article or two," Samantha added, "and Joan didn't believe he has done anything on Long Island yet."

Fran Sheboygan's eyes were dazzling, a talon-hand rested expectantly on her chest. "Yes, perhaps the guest house—"

Jake: "But it's already decorated."

"It can be redecorated."

"Aww, I don't see any sense in spending money twice."

Her husband was invisible. "It must be difficult to book Mr. . . . ."

Samantha: "Fukushita. He's very expensive, of course."

Fran was now anxious that someone might stage this coup before she could. "How soon can Joan contact him?"

Later, back in Manhattan, Sam recounted the whole afternoon for her roommate.

"Fukushita's terrible," Mimi pronounced. "He's the guy who does those trinagular tabletops balanced on twisted coat hangers. Those tables wouldn't support a Kleenex. What a con man."

"God, Meem," Samantha said, closing her eyes, "I feel like *I'm* the one selling medicine off the back of a wagon." She pressed an ice-cold gin and tonic to her forehead. "Publicity, I've decided, is basically lying for a living. Can you imagine what would happen to your soul if you did this job the rest of your whole life?"

That Saturday Samantha was expected for Passover at Uncle Eliot's apartment.

"I've never been to a seder," Sam reminded Mimi, as the day of the invitation approached. "Do I have to . . . study anything beforehand?"

"Yeah, we'll have to get you your very own non-Jewish prayer shawl." Sam wasn't sure if she was kidding. "I mean, traditionally, we ought to shave your head before the blood sacrifice on the dining room table—"

"All right, I just asked a question."

"The way *my* family does it, don't worry, you'll be the kosherest one there." Mimi turned back to her checkbook. "Naturally, Mother is doing this two full weeks after everyone else in New York has had their seder."

As they taxied to Park Avenue South, Mimi promised Samantha a veritable food-orgy: the creamiest, earthiest chopped liver, a chickeny matzo-ball soup, gefilte fish, diabetes-inducing Manischewitz cherry wine, and, despite threats of a new main course every year, Mrs. Mohr's succulent braised beef and vegetable stew, in another much-lauded appearance.

"The traffic is unspeakable tonight," Uncle Eliot said, ushering them inside his apartment. "Particularly happy to see you, Samantha, dear. I'm hoping your presence will improve our usual performance."

Samantha quickly became invisible as Mimi's brother arrived, and Mimi and Jonathan reverted to their childhood personalities.

"Mother," they both yelled through laughter, "isn't it true you love *me* better?"

Samantha sat in her appointed place at the dining table, a refuge from the chaos, while Mrs. Mohr swept in from the kitchen to bestow hugs all around and then spiraled back to the kitchen, where there was greater disarray. Jonathan's wife, the dreaded Deborah, was lodged before a portable TV set that she'd brought (Uncle Eliot didn't have a TV), and each plane passing overhead muddied the reception: "*Everyone* has goddam cable, for christ's sake . . ."

Jonathan's twins, Josh and Chris, almost four, ran wild through the house, disappearing only to give away their location by a crash of something in a distant room. Uncle Eliot lumbered after the boys indulgently, repairing or restacking whatever had been destroyed, always a room behind the current commotion.

Samantha took the opportunity to give Uncle Eliot the once-over. He was a gentle man, an eminence soft and vulnerable that perhaps only Manhattan could sustain. Though he was in his fifties, his face was pale and boyishly plump, with thick dark hair (in need of a trim) that lankly hung in his eyes. His hands were tapered and delicate, unlike the rest of his girth—a perfect rotundity, a flaccid feminine fat never distressed by exercise. Uncle Eliot's tweed sports coats with padded elbows and corduroy trousers were near becoming rags, worn down by breathless evenings among his things.

In the kitchen, Mimi and her brother continued to concoct nonsense that their mother accepted without question:

Mimi: "Since Sam and I are going to move to Denmark and get married, we thought it would be best if she converted."

"That would be very sweet of Samantha. Darling, can you get mother the paprika there . . ."

Mrs. Mohr could be convinced of *anything*, having absolutely no guile or sense of irony—or, it seemed, any sense of humor. Samantha marvelled that someone who never laughed could nonetheless be charming. She wondered whether Mrs. Mohr's serenity came from never believing anything reported by her mischievous children, or because, as Sam suspected, she was that rare mother who genuinely ascribed to the "whatever makes you happy, darling," doctrine where her children were concerned.

Mrs. Mohr: "Miriam darling, have you seen my gourd?"

"Mother, what would I want with your gourd?"

Mrs. Mohr hunted throughout the kitchen. "I think I lent it to Mrs. Finkelmann."

"Mrs. Finkelmann who died this winter?"

"Yes, dear. I don't suppose it would do to go trouble her family about that gourd now."

Jonathan, looking ceilingward, said, "I heard Mrs. Finkelmann was buried with it, Mother. She was clutching it at the end, so they put it in her casket."

"Then I suppose we'll never see it again," Mrs. Mohr said with regret. "Perhaps there's some lamb in the freezer . . ."

Mimi explained to Sam that a gourd could substitute for the shankbone. Each Passover table was to have a shank bone, matzoh bread, and *maror*, the bitter herb.

"I think this is the only meat we have," said Mrs. Mohr, holding up a frost-covered cutlet for Mimi's inspection.

"Mother, this is a pork chop."

Mrs. Mohr replaced it and began rummaging through the frozen wares. "I think there's a lamb chop in one of those Swanson's TV dinners, dear. Salisbury steak . . . Salisbury steak . . . Eliot, look, I found another tortellini after all!"

"Wonderful, Rebecca, I *sensed* there was another back there somewhere in the arctic wastes."

"Tortellini," Mrs. Mohr said to Sam, whose apparent confusion had to do with the gourd and not the tortellini, "is an Italian dish, darling."

Mimi brightened. "Don't worry, I've got a lamb-substitute that would pass the strictest rabbinical supervision. . . ." She grabbed Jonathan and they made their way to the walk-in closet in the hall and started pulling down boxes. Jonathan's boys ran screaming through the hall, tripping on a box and tumbling forward into another. "Chris," said Jonathan inattentively, "don't run in the house." Chris sped after Josh back to the bedrooms, determined to tickle his brother into paralysis.

"I found it!" cried Mimi, retrieving something secretively before she and Jonathan disappeared into a back room.

Sam, left with Mrs. Mohr and Uncle Eliot, offered to help.

"How kind! No, I think I've got everything almost ready here." Mrs. Mohr raised the pot lid to check the simmering roast. Sam's appetite sharpened at the warm meaty aroma. "How are things working out at Sy Gold's?"

"They're giving me a great deal to do. Again, I can't thank you enough for helping me—"

"Mr. T. S. Eliot," Mimi's uncle began, "worked in a bank, Mr. Herman Melville at the custom house. Mr. Wallace Stevens sold insurance." (Uncle Eliot referred to all authors, no matter how far past or contemporary, with *Mr.* and *Miss* or *Mrs.* as if he were reviewing for the *Times* of London.) "We literary types, Samantha dear, must pay for our habit, no less than an opium addict."

Samantha was pleased to be gathered among the "literary types."

They sat down around the table. Mimi's substitute for the shank bone was the puppet Lambchop from the Shari Lewis TV show, rescued from earliest youth. Mimi, never given to silliness except around her brother, put the puppet on her hand and spoke as a sheep: "Please Mr. Rab-baaaaah, I don't wanna be a blood sacrifice."

"I think of all those poor little lambs in ancient times," Mrs. Mohr said, shaking her head.

The Mohrs had five different booklet versions of Haggadah, all out of sync with each other—some Reformed and streamlined, some Orthodox and endless, some with songs and cartoons, some with lengthy passages in Hebrew, and one somehow in Spanish.

"I want the Spanish one!" Jonathan said, before Mimi and he began a tug-of-war over it.

"No, *we* have to have the same Haggadah," Mimi insisted. "Remember our bet? Here you go, Sam." Mimi made sure Samantha got the nearly all-Hebrew booklet; she tossed Deborah the Spanish.

While the roast beckoned from the open oven, ready to be eaten when the religion was out of the way, Uncle Eliot led the ceremony. He read the text with flourish, hoping it would masquerade as gravity. " 'You shall keep the Feast of the Unleavened Bread for on this very day I brought your hosts out of Egypt; you shall observe this day throughout the generations as a practice for all times—' "

Mimi: "Yeah, this family's still practicing."

Deborah snapped, "*Quiet*, this is supposed to be serious. You want your sons to hate God?"

"What's to hate?" Mimi returned, staring her down. "God kills tens of thousands of innocent firstborn Egyptian children and we sit around celebrating."

Chris looked at his grandmother, "Does God kill little children?"

Mimi answered, "Yes, yes he does."

Mrs. Mohr soothed him, "I'm *sure* there were exceptions, Chris darling."

"I gotta admit," Mimi went on, "I sorta pulled for Pharoah; he was such an underdog. Do you remember Yul Brynner in *The Ten Commandments*? Running around in that little pharoah skirt and that big phallic hat? Wouldn't see *me* leavin' the Land of Goshen."

Uncle Eliot was starving. "Shall we move on to the wine?"

Sam whispered, "Are you supposed to drink the whole glass or just take a sip?"

Mrs. Mohr and Uncle Eliot politely sipped, while Jonathan and Mimi knocked back a whole goblet.

"My my," Samantha coughed, wincing at the Manischewitz.

Mimi swallowed and made the same face: "Jonathan, get us some proper stuff—not this cherry *jew* wine."

"Oh, I quite agree," said Uncle Eliot. "This wine is insupportable." (Mimi gleefully winked at Samantha, his trademark word noted.)

"Jonathan, darling," Mrs. Mohr implored, "won't you read the Hebrew line for your mother?"

"I can't read Hebrew."

"Oh, but you used to—"

"I never could. I just made sounds."

"But for your mother—"

"Bring out some food and we'll talk about it."

Mimi, siding with her mother so her brother might be embarrassed, pointed to the English phoneticization at the bottom of the page. "Oh all right," said Jonathan, who without much enthusiasm uttered, " 'Baruch atah adonai Eloheinu melech . . .' "

"No, it's Baruccchhhh," Mimi demonstrated, mustering her most guttural *heth*.

"That is *such* an ugly noise, dear, please," said Mrs. Mohr. "We're

going to eat in a moment. At Jonathan's bar mitzvah he could say
all those big long Hebrew words—"

"Mother, they were different words."

"—he said them just like the rabbi, I was so proud—"

"Motherrrr."

"—a little angel up there with all those unpleasant bearded old
men." Mrs. Mohr hopped up, promising the table she'd be back
with an *angelic* photo of little Jonathan at thirteen—

"Someone stop her!"

"Mother, sit down," Mimi said, rifling the many pages to go.
"We're not gonna eat 'til Hanukkah, if we don't keep going."

"You mean," Jonathan corrected, taking his turn at the throat-
clearing sound, "C*Chhanukkah.*"

"That's what I said, CCC*Chhhhanukkah.*"

Jonathan turned to Samantha. "We joined a synagogue just to get
me a bar mitzvah. We certainly never set foot in one before then."

Mimi: "Or after."

Mrs. Mohr had returned with a faded photo and handed it to
Samantha. Jonathan looked almost exactly as he did now, though
at thirteen his hair had fallen in longer curls. "He *was* a little angel,"
Sam concurred.

"Wasn't he an angel?"

Uncle Eliot implored, "We simply must move this along. 'Each
person takes some greens and dips them in salt water. . . .' "

Mimi stuck her pinky in the bowl and tasted. "It's not even salty,
Mother."

"You know your uncle's on low-sodium."

By increments they arrived at the Questions. "The youngest person is supposed to ask Ma Nishtanah," said Uncle Eliot. Eliot looked
unsurely at his twins, wondering which boy to select.

Jonathan: "Let Josh do it—"

Deborah: "Why not Chris?"

Jonathan: "Josh is paying attention and Chris isn't."

Deborah: "Why do you always favor Josh?"

Jonathan: "I don't, but at least he can—"

Deborah: "Chris, can you repeat the line for Mommy?"

Chris stared at all the grown-ups staring back in expectation, and Uncle Eliot gently enunciated the question so Chris could repeat it. Chris began to cry.

"Now son," said Jonathan, "Can you say these words for Uncle Eli, for grandmother?"

No, he couldn't, squirming and snivelling.

"Don't make him do anything he doesn't want to do," snapped Deborah.

"He virtually knows how to read—"

"You're traumatizing him!" she shrieked, traumatizing the table.

"Well, *I'll* read it then, Chris darling," Mrs. Mohr volunteered, smiling at her grandson and looking right through her daughter-in-law: " 'Why is this night different from all other nights?' "

Mimi: "This family's getting along for five minutes?"

"No, darling. 'On all other nights we eat leavened or unleavened bread, but on this night we eat only unleavened bread.' "

Jonathan: "We're not gonna eat anything at this pace."

Mrs. Mohr read the other distinctions of the seder feast, then Jonathan took over, flying through the next page. "Four times the Torah bids us, yadda-da yadda-da. Here comes the four persons bit."

Mimi's stomach growled. Jonathan grumbled, "Let Samantha be the Wicked Person."

"Samantha is not wicked," said Mrs. Mohr.

Jonathan: "Mother, she's the only gentile in the room. You don't mind being the Wicked Person, do you, Sam?"

"Well, no, but I—"

"There's nothing to it, is there Mimi?"

Mimi, like Jonathan, stared at Samantha trustingly. "You have to read one little question," she prompted.

Samantha was lost in her Hebrew Haggadah, so Jonathan found an equivalent page in his American copy. Sam read: " 'The Wicked Person asks, "What is this observance to you?" ' "

"You know what happens now, don't you?" Jonathan took her hand and stood.

Mimi: "Oh, now you've done it . . ."

Jonathan: "The closet."

Mimi nodded, "In a real seder, the goy who asks the Wicked Person's question gets locked in the closet until—what is it? The second glass of wine or the third dipping of the bitter herbs. . . ."

Jonathan: "No, she's in the closet until the spinning of the dreidel."

Mrs. Mohr, confidentially to Sam: "A dreidel is a Jewish top, dear."

Mimi: "She stays in the closet, I believe the Talmud says, until the first side of *Fiddler on the Roof* has been played—"

Jonathan: "Only, says the Mishnah, the original Broadway cast album, not the latter-day Topol LP."

Mrs. Mohr hopped up excitedly, "Why didn't you children remind me sooner?"

"Mother no!" they yelled, hoping to forestall the almost-annual playing of the show tunes from *Fiddler on the Roof.*

Uncle Eliot: "Sit down, Rebecca! Mimi, Jonathan, you too Samantha, sit down everybody!" Uncle Eliot watched his niece and nephew convulse and punch each other, tipsy beyond the potential of the wine so far consumed. "That's enough nonsense; we will now skip ahead to the end!"

"Yes!" Mimi screamed to Jonathan in triumph. "Pay up! I *told you* page eighteen!"

"Jesus Christ," he muttered, reaching into his pants pocket for a five-dollar bill, slapping it into his sister's hand. Mimi later explained that in twenty remembered Passovers the Mohr family had yet to get through the whole service once—Jonathan had bet they'd make it to page 23 of the Haggadah before surrendering.

So at last it seemed that the food, torturously aromatic and enticing, was seconds away from being brought out . . . when Mrs. Mohr rose in mild panic: "Oh goodness. I nearly forgot about the whatever-it's-called."

Mimi: "Give us something to go on, Mother."

"I hid a gift for the boys earlier today, somewhere in the apartment. . . ."

In some Haggadah there was an instruction to hide a gift for the young princes to find. Somewhere hidden in the house was a gift for Josh and Chris! The two boys escaped their parental restraints and tore off looking under and in and on top of everything.

"We're never gonna eat!" Mimi wailed.

Uncle Eliot suggested the food be brought out; the boys could eat when they felt like it. Mrs. Mohr took her platter of roast and vegetables and served everyone much more than they could expect to ingest.

"Grandma!" cried Chris, running into the dining room, his mouth smeared with chocolate. "Look at Josh's new hair!" Josh, the next moment, walked in fully pleased with himself. His head was covered in green shreds of Easter-basket grass.

"Oh, boys, that was *next* week's treat."

"Deborah," requested Uncle Eliot, "perhaps you better wipe their mouths before they press against something."

Deborah used Mrs. Mohr's linen napkin to spiff up her sons' chocolaty smiles.

Mrs. Mohr asked, "Chris, did you share the chocolate bunny with your brother?"

"No."

"Did you eat it all?"

"No."

"Do you remember where you left it?"

"No."

After dinner, Deborah reinstated herself in front of the portable TV to watch the end of *Love Boat* and the start of *Fantasy Island*. Jonathan transported half the dishes to the sink and then collapsed in stuffed-full exhaustion on the sofa; Mimi lay down on the Persian carpet beside him, moaning, cursing the concept of holiday meals. Sam, uttering, "Gonna die," sank into a soft chair.

"That's the throne," Mimi mumbled, not able to turn her face from the carpet. "Uncle Eliot's chair of chairs."

"I'll surrender it, if he wants it. Of course, they might have to bring in a crane to move me."

Jonathan buried in the sofa: "It's all that chopped liver beforehand—that's what gets you."

It was announced from the back reaches of the apartment that a half-eaten chocolate bunny had been found atop the radiator in Uncle Eliot's room, in liquid form. Then, semiasleep in the soft chair, Samantha heard a soft voice beside her:

"Quite enough excitement for one evening, hm?"

Uncle Eliot had changed from a tweed jacket to a billowing dressing gown. Sam immediately removed herself from Uncle Eliot's seat and scooted to the hard-backed chair nearby.

"I suppose back in—Missouri, is it?—it's all pretty much the same," Uncle Eliot suggested, sinking into his rightful chair. "Family holiday dinners, lots of noise and bother."

Sam nodded simply, then corrected herself: "I dreaded our family occasions, actually. It seemed our worst fights were always at holiday dinners."

"Yes, you see how badly we get along here."

"But you don't *really* get along badly," Samantha smiled. "I think everyone loves everyone else and it's obvious. I would have been happy to grow up in this family." She heard how sentimental she sounded, but Uncle Eliot seemed pleased to hear it, so she went on. "You know, Mimi thinks the world of you."

"My niece will eclipse us all, won't she?" He pointed at her lightly. "And you as well, young lady. Miriam tells me you are hard at work on your novel."

"Yes," she slowed, "such as it is. I have this ludicrous fantasy that I deserve to be published one day—"

"You can be *un*published, of course, and still be a writer," he insisted, stirring in his chair, smoothing out his dressing gown. "I'm sure that the finest writers of this century are unpublished, in fact."

Sam didn't believe this. If you're not published, you can't say you're a writer, she'd always believed—simple as that. She now looked around the room to discover that Jonathan, Deborah, and their boys had left for home; things had settled into a somnolent quiet. Only a snoring Mimi on the sofa was extant.

"I'm published," Uncle Eliot said, enunciating the word *published* in all its uncleanness, "but it was a bit of a fluke. A friend sent the story to a friend who knew Mr. Shawn—I had nothing to do with it, really. And if my story had never been published, I would be no more or less a writer."

Sam nodded politely, suspecting the literary world was smaller and kinder in the 1950s, when Eliot Gottschalk made his mark in *The New Yorker*.

"This is not a republic that values its artists," he continued. "We writers constantly face the specter of poverty, ignorance, obscurity . . ."

Mimi had told Samantha that she couldn't swear whether Uncle Eliot left his apartment anymore. His job, Sam understood, was something he did at home: recataloguing the ancient, handwritten file cards for the New York Public Library, and replacing them with typed ones.

". . . and not every writer is allowed to endure or prevail," he lectured. "Myself, for instance. I never wrote another story."

"Did you want to?"

"Oh yes. It would have been so . . . so perfect had I been able to do it. I was besieged with offers and solicitations from other magazines. . . ." Uncle Eliot lifted his round hand toward a small antique bookcase of burnished hickory beneath a Tiffany lamp, narrow but tall enough for four shelves of ten books apiece. "These are the anthologies and collections that have included my work—what a life that little story has had! If only I had one to match it!"

Samantha felt defensive for Uncle Eliot: his "little story" had touched people, after all, had strode as a living thing into people's thoughts and lives, no matter how briefly.

"I once was marooned in La Guardia wasting time before a flight to Boston, having a glass of wine, and I began a conversation with a businessman. He gave me his card, and I gave him mine, and he read the name . . . 'Eliot Gottschalk, Eliot Gottschalk,' he wondered aloud. 'You know there was an author by that name! One of the finest short stories I ever read was by an author by that name.' "

Mimi was drowsily awake now. Samantha could guess by Mimi's patient stare that she had heard this tale told this way before.

"Ah," Uncle Eliot concluded, losing the incantatory trace, "but my story will be nothing compared to your novel, I suspect!" Sam knew instinctively that he was not patronizing her. "What does it concern, or have you thought that far?"

The phone rang.

"Miriam," called Mrs. Mohr from the kitchen. "It's for you."

Mimi struggled to stand upright. "Why didn't someone stop me after my first bottle of Burgundy?"

With Mimi gone, Samantha felt able to speak freely. "I only recently came to the conclusion," she said, "that my life wasn't terribly interesting, not the stuff of novels."

"Nonsense. There's nothing more interesting in the world than to follow the progress of a bright woman through life's travails. Will she sacrifice nobly for a man? Will she be undone by love?"

"Nah, I'm too independent. Like Mimi," she added, liking the sound of it, feeling it to be true.

"Then there is the peril of not knowing love at all. For such a heroine, an equally tragic fate."

Sam assented, while finding this odd coming from Uncle Eliot, alone in life except for his indulgent sister.

"All great novels," he lectured, "about women have but a single premise, really, whether Miss Eliot or Mr. James or Miss Austen. However many novels are written, there is but a solitary theme: Can a woman do as she pleases and not pay a horrible price?"

"Yes," Samantha said, considering.

"Men, it seems, have the luxury to embody any number of moral dilemmas and grand questions in novels, but women only one question." He repeated it, "Can a woman follow her heart and not come to a dreadful end?" He paused. "What do *you* think?"

"I . . . think times have changed. I think a woman ought to be able to live her own life without paying some horrible nineteenth-century price, like Isabel Archer or Dorothea Brooke."

Uncle Eliot's eyes glowed at the mention of these heroines. "Remember," he said, raising a pudgy finger, "the novel's golden age was in the nineteenth century. A very old-fashioned genre. *The Sorrows of Young Werther* predates Beethoven's Fifth, the Jefferson presidency, and Napoleon at Waterloo. A novel might adapt on rare occasions to modern purposes, but essentially to write a novel is to do that most nineteenth century of activities: to attempt to order the universe."

Sam murmured, "But many contemporary novels mirror chaos and not order—"

"Ah, but I would hesitate to call some of these, uh, works, novels. It is not the job of the novel to mirror real life, to capture it like a photo. We have real life all around us—why should we wish to open a novel to find what we already have? A novel is an alternative world, a world of art! A world of human creation in which moral truth may prevail! As it hardly does in real life."

They talked this way some time longer, until an excited but clearly tired Uncle Eliot excused himself for bed.

Samantha wanted again to visit the balcony, having been assured earlier that all alarms were disconnected because of the boys. Samantha stepped outside surreptitiously, valuing a moment alone with the night and the pulsing city, the obligato of taxi horns, squealing tires, and roaring bus engines that churned along Park Avenue South below.

"You and Uncle Eli hash out the fate of Western Literature?" Mimi asked, appearing. "I apologize for any boredom my relatives may have put you through."

"Oh no, Uncle Eliot's wonderful. God knows, I can't talk literature with you," she added, smiling. Sam wouldn't hear the Mohr family apologized for tonight. If asked, she would have sworn that the better part of civilization and devotion to the arts that America had achieved was due to this Manhattan species: the wholly secular New York Jew.

"Funny," said Mimi. "I saw Uncle Eli through your eyes tonight and he seemed, well, a little pathetic. I hate fragility in people—"

Mrs. Mohr rapped on the balcony door. "Miriam. The phone!"

"Jesus H. What now . . ."

Sam decided after a moment to go to the kitchen, belatedly, and see if anything could be done to further clean up. She passed through the living room, happening to hear Mimi on the phone.

"Lewis," Mimi was saying impatiently, "it's bad enough that you call me here. Did you look up my mother's number in the personnel file? No. No . . . it wasn't . . . Now get a hold of yourself; no one knows we've been together, *no one*." Mimi stepped into the bathroom, stretching the phone cord to reach, and closed the door.

Lewis was Mimi's boss at Farrell & Ritch, account executive for their work on Health-E Vitamin E milkshakes.

Mimi was sleeping with her boss.

It came to Samantha as one of those truths she should have known earlier. That's what all the phone drama has been about, here and on their message machine at home. Come to think of it, when Mimi was at J. Walter Thompson, she had come right out and told Samantha that she was having a fling with an account executive. Was that her project supervisor then too?

Maybe Mimi slept with all her bosses.

Not to get the job or even to hold it—Sam knew Mimi wouldn't have *needed* to stoop to that behavior. But Mimi hated to have a detail left out, any chess piece unguarded. This was her insurance policy. Sam, wandering back to the balcony and the New York City night, stood there wondering if this meant she had to think less of Miriam Mohr, take down the pedestal—

"Look what I've got!" Mimi chanted, returning to the balcony, doing semaphor with the two contraband Cuban Churchills. "Uncle Eliot got a box for his birthday from a college friend, but he's been forbidden to smoke and of course I *hate* waste, don't you?"

Mimi put one in Sam's mouth before she could protest.

"When we get down to the last two cigars," Mimi said, while lighting her own, "we'll save them to smoke, you and I, in Venice."

On the way home in the cab, Mimi nodded off and slumped over to Samantha's shoulder. Her hair—both their hair, probably—smelled of cigar smoke, but Samantha could detect the light floral orchidy scent of Mimi's perfume, a scent that stuck to sofa cushions and bedsheets and lingered in their apartment bathroom. When Mimi wasn't around, Sam could bring her back in spirit by pressing her face to Mimi's bedroom pillow.

Samantha was determined as ever to lose her retread Smith-based social life and she was going to drop David Sutton at her first convenience. But her friend Mimi must never get out of her grasp. She pulled Mimi closer and propped her slumbering head on her shoulder. Nor must Mimi be allowed, Samantha decided, to have another friend as close.

Back in the apartment one afternoon, playing hooky from work, Mimi was spread out on the sofa reading magazines when Sam got home from Midtown. "Your mom just called," Mimi said. "Said it was extremely important. Tell her I like her country accent."

That was the last thing Samantha would pass on. Being called "country"—especially by a New Yorker.

Sam suddenly was reminded of her grandmother on her mother's side. An unpleasant woman, though to be fair, Sam only knew her after she'd become sick. Her skin was raw and red, her worn face impossibly creased, her Dent County accent pure hillbilly. She was undergoing a cancer treatment in Springfield, so she stayed with the Flints one summer, but wouldn't stay put in her bedroom; fought Sam's mother to do chores and be useful. She made lunch for the girls and Samantha remembered her bony, red fingers, her cracked yellowed nails. There was one finger Sam had tortured herself with—would she look at it or would she not? Claws from a lifetime of farmwork and hard living. Sam could barely force down the sandwiches Grandma made, imagining her hands having touched the food, those small dry bites swallowed dutifully.

"Do you mind if . . ." Samantha motioned to Mimi's bedroom and her deluxe bed; Mimi understood that Sam wanted to lie down for awhile.

"Aspirin by the bedside."

Samantha figured Mom was calling to announce her parents' divorce. It had been brewing for years, and both sisters had called over the past months to hint that the longed-for divergence was at hand. Sam was of two minds about it: I want Mom to have to go to work, she thought, support herself, see what life was like for the rest of us, let reality knock years of watching afternoon TV in her housecoat right out of her. And Dad could damn well learn to wash his own clothes and fix his own meals. Let them be lonely, she thought—like we were, hunched down in our rooms waiting for the fights to be over.

But she also knew that divorce meant her parents' deficiencies in life-skills would somehow careen oh so surely back to her. Samantha the "responsible" daughter, who would have to involve herself more than she cared to.

"My parents don't have fights," Sam once explained to a high school guidance counselor. "They just have one fight—over and over again."

"Why don't you tell them how the fights make you feel?"

Sam had no intention of doing the dirty work back then—couldn't some kind of social services agency be called in? There were *no* moments of heroism for the Flint girls. No running down the hall to say "Stop picking on Mom!" or "Mom, leave Dad alone," no noble attempts to unify the family. "Nope, not this Movie of the Week," said the sturdy fifteen-year-old Sam, when the counselor suggested she ought to perhaps call a minister.

"I'll go with Daddy," Sam thought night after night, plagued with teenage insomnia, her clock just having clicked to four A.M. "If they split up, Mom can have Bethie and Kelly, and I'll go down to the lake with Daddy."

Odd how that worked: Sam, the middle daughter, sympathized with her father, had been told her whole life she resembled him, dark-haired and brown-eyed. Bethie and Kelly had made common cause with Mom, the blondes against the brunettes.

"We can't let the blondes win, can we, Daddy?" Samantha often said growing up, the refrain of her childhood.

"No, Sammie, we can't!"

Same with politics. Sam's family on all sides (the Flints, the Mabes, the Kriteses, the Burnleys) were all yellow-dog Missouri Democrats, but when Mr. Flint became a businessman he felt he'd been upgraded to a Republican. When Walter Cronkite announced on TV that Nixon beat McGovern, Sam sat at her father's feet, saying, "We won, didn't we, Daddy?"

"Yes, Sammie girl, we beat the blondes this time."

When Mr. Flint announced a trip to the store, Samantha as a little kid always ran ahead of him to the car to install herself in the backseat, presenting her father with a fait accompli and a fellow passenger for even the smallest voyage. Mr. Flint cruised the Chestnut Expressway, U.S. 66, in the Rambler, singing "Get Your Kicks On Route 66," which in those days ran through downtown Springfield. Sam sang along uncomprehendingly:

"Kingling, Boston, Sunburnarino . . ."

"Naw Sammie, it's *Kingman, Barstow, San Bernadino.* All out in California."

But Sam always knew the real names. She flubbed the line because it always made her father laugh. She was his favorite daughter though that never was specifically said. Being his favorite meant something, continued to mean something through college and into adult life.

Until Dad's disappearing act, Sam's senior year.

"He's probably in the Happy Acres Trailer Park with Shirley what's-her-name," sneered Bethie, during one long weekend without a sign of him.

"That's pretty low," Sam shot back. "Making up rumors about your own father."

But Bethie was right about this, actually.

Long after everyone had gotten used to Shirley-in-the-trailer-park as a fixture in family mythology, Samantha insisted that it was merely a no-sex friendship, or that the rumor was just a figment of her mother's pettiness, or just another example of Bethie's vindictive mind . . . but it was true, except for the trailer park. Shirley lived in a small millworker's cottage, nicely fixed-up, outside of Branson.

Samantha, last time she was home from Smith, drove by Shirley's place just to see. Who could blame the man for wanting some comfort after life with Mom? And yet at some level, this adultery mattered to Samantha, beyond any question of what the neighbors might think. It was that Sam worried there might be an alternative family out there, some other little girl who got her daddy the way he used to be, since Shirley had kids from a former marriage. Did her kids know the happy Herbert Flint, of the cigars and the sharp suits and the aftershave? The Dad who lifted me above his head and whirled me weightless with delight into the spring sun—

The phone rang.

Mimi called from the living room, "Want me to get it?"

Samantha rose from the bed, blearily taking the receiver. "Mom, hi. I just got in. I hear you've been calling . . ." Samantha stammered, "I must say, that's a little unexpected, Mom."

Mimi mouthed, *"What?"*

It was not a divorce. It was a reconciliation.

Dad had decided to take an early retirement his bosses were offering, and sell his now-miniscule stake in Boatland, and reward himself and Sam's mother with a move to sunny Florida. Wasn't it wonderful! Florida, Sammie!

"You and Dad are gonna . . . sell the house?"

Dad took the phone. Did Mother tell you about Florida? (Sam rolled her eyes; she knew he was standing an inch away when her mother told her.) They could send her some money for a flight, so she could come home "one last time." Samantha had no love for that second house or much nostalgia for the years in it. But this was still a displacement, the tearing down of a personal monument without warning or consultation.

"Well, you know I ain't been much on church for a long time," her father was saying, "but your mother and I decided we'd better talk to someone so we, uh, went to talk to—oh, you got to hear this guy, Sammie—Reverend Coombs. Young fellow, 'bout thirty or so."

Samantha could hear her mother prompting her father.

"He just cut right through all our problems—*right on through*. We'd been having a lack of communication. Well, he just put it all in a different light for us, and uh, we just got very far from knowing Jesus, and we weren't letting him guide our lives . . ."

Boy, she didn't like the direction this was going.

"Now Sammie, I haven't been the father I shoulda been to you, you and the girls. We should have seen more to your going to church, for one thing. And I'm not accusing anyone of anything, but you girls haven't lived up to your potentials as daughters either—which was our fault! Totally our fault."

Samantha drifted away. She'd spent so much time perfecting her resilience to her family; now she was being expected to plunge back into the morass.

"Now Reverend Coombs wants to meet with all of us some time over Christmas," her father was saying, "and we can bring these things to Jesus."

She did not want to pray and hold hands with her family while Reverend Coombs laid on hands and thanked Jesus. She did not want to see her father cry or share "a special moment" or even be asked to hug and touch anyone; no public recitals of "I love you" to her folks. This Jesus-mongering was yet more weakness and squalor, and there'd already been too much of that.

Samantha glanced at Mimi in her business suit: even rumpled and sprawled on the sofa, absently chewing on the end of a Bic ballpoint, her friend seemed an emissary from a world of grace and light. . . .

"Forget about the money!" her mother was saying, having commandeered the phone again. "Don't you worry, Sam-Sam, we're going to send you a ticket!"

So her Christmas plans were settled, after all.

Her sister Bethie, separated from her husband of three years, was dispatched to the airport. After a hug, the sisters gave each other the once-over. "You look like a real New Yorker," Bethie declared.

"You like the hair?" Samantha had taken the advice of a salon hairdresser and had it cut into a bob with bangs. In her long black raincoat, she resembled a Bond-movie Russian secret agent. Bethie, on the other hand, had gone hardcore country and western: tight jeans, big hair, and heavy eyeliner. It suited her, though; Samantha in high school had once disloyally remarked that Bethie's personality "took its cue from her hair."

"So you and Buddy are completely through?" Samantha asked, putting her one suitcase in the backseat and hopping in the front. She heard her Missouri twang return on the word *through*.

"Yep. He's screwing somebody new. Not the same somebody he was screwing during our marriage, naturally."

Samantha listened to the litany of Buddy's adulteries and outrages. In the cold front seat, unsuccessfully warmed by the station-wagon heater, Samantha could see Bethie's breath, and smell it.

She'd had a beer or two before picking her up. Probably this airport excursion interrupted her night at the bar rather than preceded it.

As Bethie shared every tangible detail of her failed marriage (". . . Buddy may have been hung, but these big ol' guys take forever to get fully locked-and-loaded, if you know what I mean . . ."), Samantha made a concerned assessment of what Bethie spent her money on: those two-inch long fingernails one has affixed at nail parlors, enameled blood-red, jeans with a designer's name on it, junky looking bracelets that were no doubt 24K gold and expensive. And baby-sitters, apparently. Her three year old, Jennifer, must have been parked with somebody.

". . . so I've got both guys chasing me—and Dwayne's brother who's six–five for chrissakes—and it's my own damn fault! Neither looks like marriage material, you know? But I've *done* marriage. Honey, I'm just looking for love in allllll the wrong places."

"How's Jennifer?"

"Just a little doll. Askin' about her Auntie Samantha. You come out to my place once the bullshit starts getting too deep at the Flint Compound."

"You met this Reverend Coombs?"

"Hoo boy," she sighed. "He looks like one of them child-molester TV preachers. I about burst a blood vessel when I heard he'd talked Herbert and Hester back into marital bliss—not that it's gonna last. I wonder how much money he's sucked outta them. Not to mention Herbert and Hester movin' to Florida—that'll cost 'em. Although the thought of getting H and H outta Springfield and my line of sight works for me." Bethie studiously, throughout the visit, resisted calling her parents *Mom* and *Dad*. "Whaddya bet they use up all their savings and me'n you have to take 'em in, wipe their chins, and change their diapers!"

Bethie said this horrible thing so lightly that Samantha could only laugh. Bethie continued to rant while Samantha turned toward the passing streets of her hometown, the same drab boulevards of faded and failed commerce, same ugly, squat stoplights hanging above the intersections, billboards featuring the nightly-news crew on Channel 2, the anchorlady's red blazer the only color on the scene. Samantha remembered there used to be a Route 66 placard on this corner. U.S. 66 passing through Springfield was the town's one interesting feature, so naturally they've taken that down.

"... and *I* ain't gonna do it. After *our* childhood? Herbert and Hester can just go live in a home with Nurse Ratched—you see that movie?"

That's funny, Samantha thought. Bethie mourning her deprived childhood. Mrs. Flint had made Bethie the conventionally prettiest daughter, into a princess. She got to accompany Mom to the beauty shop at fourteen, was given the nicest clothes ("Because Samantha, you and Kelly can't take care of the nice clothes you have!"), got dance lessons—Sam put up such a fit about having to go, that she was allowed to opt out of Miss Hortensia Bumgardner's Springfield Academy of Dance.

Bethie exceeded all princess expectations as a head cheerleader; she was one of four elected beauties in the high school homecoming court, not to mention winning the ingenue role in the school production of *Oklahoma!* even though she sang flat and without inflection. Bethie dependably brought a staggering parade of handsome jock-boys into the den to meet Mom and, when he was home, Dad.

Bethie, depriving Samantha of the succession, had skipped over Sam for Kelly, whom she tried to make into an homage to herself. Kelly submitted without resistance to endless hair and nails and makeup sessions; Samantha would cock an ear to Kelly's room and eavesdrop on their conversation, incessant and giggly, never ensnaring anything that qualified as a topic.

The day Bethie left home to live with Buddy, Kelly, unexpectedly, began to evolve into a more independent creature. Kelly didn't go out for cheerleading. Maybe it was simply the fear of not succeeding and having it etched in stone: you'll never be as good as Bethie!

"How's Kelly?" Sam wondered.

"Who knows? All right, I guess. Their little girl looks like Chuck, poor thing. I've seen their baby twice—once at the hospital, and once when she brought her over to Hester's—and that's *it*. She's too busy gettin' that fat-ass husband of hers a beer to go in for much sisterly quality time."

Kelly was the quietest Flint girl, unexpressive about her preferences from childhood on, and her passivity led to her marriage to Chuck McConnell, the first boyfriend she ever had. Marrying Chuck had saved her the trouble of rearranging things.

"So what about David?" Bethie was asking.

"What about him?"

"What I was just talking about: is he endowed or not?"

"Bethie!"

"Oh, like you don't notice these things."

Sam hoped a quick answer would keep her curiosity from metastasizing into other personal areas. "Average, I guess. I don't have a lot to compare him to."

"Sam, just how many guys have you been with?"

Samantha made a laugh of protest.

"C'mon, we're sisters! We're supposed to share these things."

"Four or five," Sam said, enlarging the stable. "And you?"

"Since Buddy and I separated? Hard to say. I guess each weekend I . . . Some of these ol' farmboys get all sweet on you and start clinging, but I tell 'em all, this girl ain't lookin' for a husband." She continued with a touch of sarcasm. "I'm twenty-five for chrissakes. All these cherished *priceless* years of my youth stretching in front of me. Ten whole years *before* my sexual peak, if you believe *Cosmo*."

Bethie lapsed into her familiar side-of-the-mouth smirk and tone of voice that could be seen as premature bitterness. No, adjusted Sam, that's too strong. What is the emotion right before bitter? In her pinched expression and joyless squint, there was an expectation of disappointment before the fact, a hotly tended pessimism.

Samantha was home all of two nights, but that was enough time to walk into the middle of a family fight.

"I've done made the phone call," Mr. Flint protested. "Now Reverend Coombs is expecting us."

Mr. Flint had hinted all day about going down to the church that night to an informal gathering, a small Bible lesson, where the concerns of the congregation were prayed over, and Sam would get to meet Reverend Coombs.

"And it wouldn't hurt you," Mr. Flint added to Bethie, "to see the inside of a church once in a while."

Bethie folded a towel. "Leave me out of your *cult*, thank you. I'm only over here to do my laundry."

Samantha begged off a bit more diplomatically.

Mr. Flint insisted.

Bethie sarcastically suggested that her dad call Kelly and see if Kelly could be suckered into it.

Kelly was called. Kelly said she was going to some family event—her husband's family.

That set Mr. Flint off: Kelly went to church with Chuck, only let Chuck's family baby-sit their newborn, took their entire vacation with Chuck's family in Brunswick, Georgia, every single year. "I'd just like someone to tell me," Mr. Flint said, setting Bethie up, "what's wrong with *our* family?"

Bethie supplied him with the top five items on her list, finishing by asking, "What do you expect? You two fight every night of our childhood and warp us for life, and then you're shocked when we run for the hills!"

Mother protested, Father protested.

"Kelly doesn't even want her kid *near* you guys," Bethie added, lumping all her laundry into the basket for a quick escape. Mother reminded everyone that there wouldn't have been fights if not for Father, Father reminded Mother of her contribution to their collective misery . . . but before the squabble escalated, Mr. Flint calmed everyone down—he was the only one who needed calming—and pointed out that this was the very reason that they needed to see Reverend Coombs.

Still no takers, Mother included.

The next morning, Samantha's last full day, she awoke to learn that Mr. Flint had escaped. He had moved a sales trip to Fayetteville up by a day.

"And he was looking so forward to being with you," Mrs. Flint told Samantha, shaking her head in dismay as she made Sam's breakfast. "It was all he talked about for weeks. And now he's out the door again."

"Just like old times," Sam said, sipping orange juice.

"We don't fight anymore, Sam-Sam. It's different now."

Guess not, Sam thought, if Dad just takes off on sales trips every time it gets rough. A nasty little apprehension crossed her mind: did Dad get kicked out by Shirley? Is that what was behind this sorry reconciliation attempt?

"It'll all be better in Florida," Mrs. Flint was saying.

It was always grim, Sam thought, to eat in this kitchen. Mother's rubbery scrambled eggs, toast made from old bread, that table the site of hundreds of silent mediocre meals. "Are you sad to leave the house?" Samantha asked, changing subjects.

"You know what? I never liked it in Lake Springfield as much as I thought I would, honey."

Samantha was surprised. "I thought you were just dying to get out of our old neighborhood."

"It's good we did." Her mother settled into a kitchen-table chair across from her daughter. "That old neighborhood is really in bad shape now."

"Boatland," Samantha said, glad to be openly disloyal to their suburban split-level, "started going bad when we moved here. Chet Diddle and all that—"

"Lord, save me from hearin' that man's name again, Chet Diddle, Chet Diddle. Your father can be a broken record. You remember, Sam-Sam, when we first moved in here, how the moving van took our stuff to the storage warehouse instead of coming here?"

Yes, for their first weekend in the house they didn't have luggage or furniture; they had to stay in a motel until Monday.

"Maybe that was a sign," sighed Mrs. Flint, sipping coffee.

Now they were performing once again the same set of moving rituals. That afternoon, Mrs. Flint and Samantha began the task of assembling cardboard boxes to pack and ship to Florida. Samantha's adolescent room had been turned into a guest room two years before, so her nostalgia for that corner of the house was dim to begin with. Still. That evening, she stretched out on her childhood bed and remembered the smell of the central heating, the creaks and whirs of the furnace downstairs—and how, in their first years there, she was terrified of all the noises. Later, those noises would be her companions for those insomniac nights. A blue-white suburban streetlight made a pattern of squares on her far wall; every once in awhile a passing car would blur and rearrange the grid of shadows with its headlights.

"Keep what you want," said her mother, "and we'll drive the rest of this to Goodwill." Mrs. Flint heaved a box of clothes onto the end of the bed.

There's something sad about a girl's rejected wardrobe; she held a lacy dress blouse against her chest, flouncy and synthetic. How did she ever think this flapping, tent-sized doily made her look thinner? She wore it with a black blazer to speech and debate tournaments. There was no shortage of T-shirts and sweatshirts advertising her high school and the University of Missouri, those courtesy of Paul. She pressed them to her face to see if she could smell Paul, but there was only the moldy smell of the closet. Samantha came upon a cache of hip-hugging bell-bottomed jeans.

"It can all go," she said.

Samantha walked through each room and tried to whip up a bit of good-bye-forever sentimentality. Basement play areas—once where they huddled during a tornado warning—and Bethie's room (still full of her things); a cold undervisited living room full of overstuffed furniture, now dated and unloved. At the end of the main hall glowed the light of the kitchen, where Mrs. Flint continued her regimen of coffee drinking and paging through magazines, the sporadic glance at the microwave clock: 9:40 P.M. Past her bedtime. Samantha joined her again in the bare nook, staring at the yellowed emptied shelves and cabinets. "The neighbors must be sad to see you guys go," Sam suggested. "Mrs. Chapel."

"Oh, the Chapels moved a year ago. Did Kelly tell you that she and Chuck might move to Brunswick?"

Chuck and Kelly, five months pregnant with her second child, wanted to be near Chuck's folks, who had retired to the southern Georgia coast, so they could be rooked into baby-sitting duties. Kelly had run to Chuck's family as an orphan might, happy to trade in the Flints for the ever-game McConnell clan.

"The Blakes across the street," Mrs. Flint recited. "She's got cancer. Not a hair on her head now—she has this wig. All Jack Blake does all day long is mow his yard, clip his weeds, prune this, sweep that. . . . Anything but go inside his house now."

"You told me she was on death's doorstep my senior year in high school, five years ago."

"Well, now it's true."

Mrs. Flint reviewed the news up and down the street. The Hendersons' oldest boy is on drugs. The Wakefields' oldest of five killed himself. Kevin Wakefield smashed up his father's car in a drunk driving incident, lost his license, drives anyway. Old friendly Hank Marvin on the corner has been in the paper about financial irregularities at his bank and everyone's starting to think he's in trouble— and what a shame for Margaret Marvin whose whole world is Hank. And had Bethie told Samantha about the Fetzers?

"What about the Fetzers?"

Mrs. Flint sighed. "Bev—did you ever play with her?—the oldest moves out and Sam and Doris Fetzer are all by themselves, and Sam retires in . . ." Mrs. Flint devoted a minute trying to remember whether it was '79 or '80. "Anyway. Sam Fetzer, Sam Fetzer who can't swat a fly, has a drink at his retirement party at JCPenney's and he goes home and hits Doris."

"Mr. Fetzer?"

"Sweetest man on earth and he goes home and almost puts Doris in the hospital. He apologizes a thousand times over. But—I guess it was a few months later—he brings home a six-pack of beer and starts hitting her again."

"I can't imagine."

"Well, Doris did eventually leave him for her sister's place, and Fetzer is in A.A. now, but it looks like the marriage is over."

Later, after Mrs. Flint went to bed, Samantha put on her coat and sat on the brick steps of their ranch house, out in the cold. Samantha surveyed the surrounding houses, all dark except for the bathroom lights left on all night. She counted the neighborhood's catastrophes, the financial woes, the kids that didn't work out, the life failures, some hushed up, some public, but all of them *borne*, all manner of unhappiness waded through, endured by people who got up and left for work and the church potluck, who went on with things, aging all the while with the knowledge that their lives hadn't been a great success, methodically shelving hopes, letting the dreams fade and lose their colors. Then, like Mrs. Blake with her cancer, it comes to an end; in inescapable pain and ever-increasing doses of morphine you look out the window you have sat beside for half a century and watch your husband pick a scrap of blown trash off his freshly mown lawn. . . .

And poor Mrs. Fetzer. The golden years stretch before her and her loving husband. But—surprise—he becomes an alcoholic at sixty-six and knocks her to the floor she's waxed and mopped for decades. Can any happy memories survive attached to this kind of ending? No, decided Samantha, there's no salvaging wreckage like that. So off goes Doris Fetzer (does she take that bridal portrait down from above the piano?), sixty-four, alone and without income; she would never trust a man again (and never be troubled by one either); a gray-haired unattractive woman, stooped with the beginnings of osteoporosis.

Samantha returned to New York on a Sunday night and took a taxi in from La Guardia. She was never so happy to see the apartment, this Promised Land from which she'd traversed the deserts of Missouri! After the roommates broke into a bottle of Mimi's Haut Brions, they got silly and put on their college-era music.

"If you ever, *ever* hear me," Sam screeched, "threatening to marry a nice boy and go back to Springfield—kill me! We can buy the gun tomorrow—"

The neighbor upstairs pounded on the floor three times.

"Oops," they said together, guilty for only a second.

Samantha was too tipsy and tired to undress or brush her teeth; she flopped down on her sofa bed. Mimi turned off the lights and, unexpectedly, flopped down right beside her. "This crappy sofa bed," Mimi remarked, "is better than my real bed, whaddya know?" Then out of nowhere: "You're never gonna have kids, are you?"

"No."

"Me neither." Mimi turned to Sam on the creaky bed. "That's another thing we have in common." Mimi gently touched Sam's arm. "No diapers, no spittle, no three A.M. feedings—"

"I *really* don't want to go through labor."

"I guess that makes us . . ." Mimi fumbled for words sarcastic enough.

"Barren, loveless, cold, incomplete. Monsters of selfishness."

"Sounds about right." Mimi tittered and they both started giggling, escalating to suppressed cackles.

"*Sssssh*," Sam hissed presently, "the old guy upstairs."

They were silent a moment, listening for another stomping.

Mimi continued, "I don't want to have a kid because I know what would happen, with my luck. A boy who grows up to be violent and disturbed. A girl who's a heroin addict or—god, imagine having a kid with autism. I couldn't deal with autism."

"Or a Down's syndrome kid. Of course, you'd love it—I'd love it—but then *that* becomes your whole life and you don't get to have any other kind of life."

Mimi sighed. "And what if your kids just didn't *like* you. Spent their teenage years rebelling and hating you."

"Or wind up in endless therapy. Where everything's *your* fault."

"It's creeping back whether we like it or not, huh?" Mimi briefly snuggled into Samantha, before doing a bad Bela Lugosi accent: "The Dark Vision of the World."

Samantha put a hand on her shoulder. "I just want to be happy."

Mimi said, "I've been thinking about that. Happiness. Centuries of humans have lived with no expectation of being happy—it's an unworthy goal for an adult life. *Content*, yes. I want not to be actively miserable."

"It's still tricky just knowing what would make you content."

"I can tell you what'd be perfect for you." Mimi turned on her side, making the bed squeak. "Okay, I see you in Vermont, maybe. I see you teaching at a small liberal arts place, a Bennington, a Williams. Teaching English."

That was not the vision Samantha had. "How blah."

"What's blah? You get to teach, read all the time—and Vermont! Vermont's progressive and gorgeous . . ."

But Mimi's prediction didn't include being a famous novelist.

"Sam, you could learn to ski. You could invite me up and we could go be ski bunnies in Stowe." Mimi poked Sam. "Turtlenecks, capri pants, wraparound sunglasses."

"Vermont and teaching English wouldn't make me happy."

Mimi was quiet a moment. "But you could be content."

Joan exhaled her smoke, frowning. "Sy will have a hissy fit if he finds out you substituted for me at the Met Egyptian Wing gala. And yet . . ."

That was Sam's cue to talk her into this improvidential switch.

"There'll be free food," Joan prompted.

Sam saw she was drafted whether she liked it or not. Actually, she was sort of in the mood to see crotchety old Mr. Sheboygan; Randall, the *Times* society page photographer, was cute and he flirted with her at the last benefit.

"Name your price," Joan needled.

That evening, Samantha arrived at the Metropolitan Museum of Art at seven—a full hour early—to stake out the scene. She escorted herself through the dimly lit Egyptian Wing, following a trail of candles to the hangarlike chamber that housed the Temple of Dendur, a reassembled Egyptian sanctuary once alongside the Nile. Tonight, illumined by torchlight, the temple loomed; its shadows and recesses, its hewn hieroglyphics and crumbling stone, sensuous and oriental.

Sam did what any slave-wager would do: made a filling dinner off the refreshments and downed two free cocktails, while making world-weary conversation with the bartender.

"My people," Sam confided, "should be here by now."

"Taxi driver's probably taking them by way of Connecticut," he suggested, cutting several limes into segments.

"They can afford it, trust me."

Jake Sheboygan appeared amid the mob, already red-faced from drink and the near-fatal exertion of the stairs. Samantha saw Fran talking with one woman, a rich, garrulous widow she had been seated next to at the last function; Fran, all the while, peered around the room at her social betters, longing to make contact. Joan would have at least been able to introduce Mrs. Sheboygan to someone prestigious, but Samantha didn't know anyone. Sam had a brief—maybe her only—pang of pity for Fran Sheboygan, who stood under a palm, gnawing desolately on a pretzel, looking lonely and old.

"If it's not my favorite publicist."

It was Randall from the *Times*.

Unlike the rest of the spiffed-up gathering, he was dressed shab-bily, a baseball cap on his bald head, a late-day stubble. No matter, since he brandished the society-page camera, the grail before which all would bow down. He was living dangerously, unprofessionally flirting with flaks like Sam, who only wanted one thing from him: a society-page photo featuring their clients.

"I'm only your favorite," Sam teased, "because I'm the only woman here under twenty-five."

"Nyeh, I like you because you're not shmoozy and slick and thor-oughly insincere yet, like all the other handlers." With a wink, he added, "You're such a beginner."

"All right, then," she said, raising her eyebrows, "I will just have to commence some serious flakkery here. See those guys . . ." She pointed out the Sheboygans. "If they get anywhere near royalty or aristocracy, snap away."

Randall popped an hors d'oeuvre meatball on the end of a tooth-pick into his mouth. "What's in it for me?"

"My undying affection."

"And your phone number?"

"Let's start with my undying affection and work back, hm?"

Samantha surveyed the society mob, smiled at a familiar face or two, shmoozed with some of the older men (dragged here by wives) who charmed and impressed her. It occurred to Samantha in a mer-cenary moment that despite her disapproval of women who married for money, she might actually make a nice "trophy wife," as they say. If one could stand the conjugal relations, imagine the *ease* of being one of these men's spouses. Think of the time to write. Of course, few of her heroes had made that devil's bargain. Jane Austen had eschewed the marriage marketplace so she could stand at her hall table and write in spare moments between family obligations and chores—a dutiful nun of letters.

"Not a bad piece of real estate," said a dapper man in his sixties, self-exiled to the palms and ferns away from the main currents of the party. Sam was greeted by a familiar smile, but she couldn't decide whether she'd met this man or if he was archetypically avuncular. "The temple, I mean."

Sam turned to stare at the Temple of Dendur.

"By Egyptian standards," the gentleman continued, "this is pretty puny. The Aswan Dam flooded so much valuable property, Anwar Sadat hastily scooped up a temple or two and mailed them to his friends. Then they got a bunch of senators and State Department hacks to go say thank you." He sipped scotch from his plastic cocktail cup. "I went along on that junket."

His demeanor suggested that he was a man in public life. "I take it, sir, you're on the board of the Met?"

"Ah, nothing so vital to the health of the nation. I was one of the senators. Am one still, sorry to say. Senator Warren Proctor."

He waited until Sam put out her hand to offer his. Old school.

"Samantha Flint," she smiled, covering the fact that she didn't know which Western state he represented. She played at being more abashed than she was. "Forgive me. I've seen you on *David Brinkley* a hundred times."

"Shouldn't have revealed myself," he laughed. "Now you'll probably lobby me for something. What brings someone of your young age to an old-fogy tea party like this?"

"I hesitate to confess that I am a public relations shill for hire."

"And for what or whom do you, so creditably, shill?"

"Well, I've lost sight of my charges at the moment." Samantha scanned the room, hoping to find them. "A Mr. and Mrs. Sheboygan, newly arrived to Manhattan society from East Hopogue, Long Island. Newly arrived to Long Island from Akron, Ohio, before that."

"With a fortune perhaps newly arrived as well?"

Sam risked, "One can almost discern the scent of the plastic alloy in the tires that brought them to this. . . ."

"This zenith, where they might mingle with senators well into their third term and . . ." He raised his plastic cup. "Fourth cocktail."

Samantha admired Warren Proctor's tone of invitation. He was unmistakably a man of power, yet he wore his mantle imperially, in the most ideal sense, august and confident. He was also a study in refinement—his solidly fashionable Brooks Brothers suit, the hint of handkerchief in the pocket, the way he crossed his legs, his subtle cologne that suggested spice and a snifter of brandy.

Sam was fearful of letting the conversation flag, lest he leave her side; fortunately, she was babbling intelligently: "Perhaps I'll lobby you, after all. Virtually all of our great men of letters have a statue in Central Park. But New York's own Edith Wharton—I can't find one of her anywhere. So I am scheming to put together a committee to raise funds."

"I would be happy to contribute to such a cause, Miss Flint." He reached into his breast pocket and produced a card, and set the elegant item into her open hand. "I've only read *The Age of Innocence* myself. I intend to read the rest of Wharton in my dotage . . . which may begin sooner than I think, if the voters turn me out of office because I miss tomorrow's farm-bill vote!" He made a polite bow. "I have to race to Newark for the midnight shuttle. But do write my office about the statue." Then he slowed, not ready to rush away yet. "It strikes me as remarkable, Miss Flint, that anyone your age should be attracted to the world of Wharton anymore."

"But I love the formality. The manners of that time."

He lightly challenged her. "But it was often a mask, wasn't it? For so much hypocrisy and snobbery."

"Yes, Senator, but the same hypocrisies and snobberies exist today without the benefit of manners to make such behavior tolerable." Samantha felt she could proceed, having his full attention. "Manners were . . . were in those days like a veil that society projected itself upon. A veil not to be lifted often—"

"*Lift not the painted veil called life!*" the senator interrupted agreeably. "Or so Shelley warned us."

"What lay beneath the beautiful manners of Victorian society may have been intimate, scandalous, shameful—but manners allowed those things to stay private. We have no such concept of privacy now. Everything is known, talked about."

"I could talk with you all night, Miss Flint," he said at last, checking his watch again. Samantha couldn't remember ever having an older man listen so intently to what she said. "But before I go—of course, I surely must meet the . . ."

"The Sheboygans?" Sam cried, thrilled at the offer. "But I couldn't ask it—"

"Tonight, and always, I am *your* public servant."

Jake and Fran were by the temple, Jake filling his face methodically with stuffed mushrooms while Fran was regaling some woman with her shopping adventures. Senator Proctor and Samantha meandered through the crowd, dodging the glad-handing men, their flocks of wives, through the eddies of tipsy celebrants until the Sheboygans came into range. Sam, to her relief, saw Randall and frantically flagged him over.

The senator, center of all attention, called out, "You must be the Sheboygans!"

No one was more surprised than Jake and Fran as they stumbled forward to shake hands, openmouthed.

"From Canton, I believe?"

"Akron," they said in unison.

"Lovely countryside around the Cuyahoga," said the senator automatically. "John Glenn is always trying to get me to go fishing with him . . ." Sam surmised there wasn't a corner of the country that he couldn't generate something pleasant to say about. Senator Proctor leaned close and mumbled to the couple, "Now let's get ourselves in the funny papers, shall we? Follow my lead."

The senator stood before the Temple of Dendur and struck an Egyptian pose: head in profile, both arms cocked at right angles, one behind him, one in front of him, like the procession of two-dimensional relief-figures on the temple walls. The Sheboygans stood on either side of him, doing the same, while the gathered crowd laughed approvingly—that society-bred public laugh, breathy and performed, even when sincere. Randall snapped away, the flash gun eerily illuminating the upper reaches of the temple.

"Well, you know that one's going in," Randall said, when the senator stepped down from the platform, readjusting his suit.

"You think?" said Sam, not believing her luck. "You may get my phone number yet."

———

Back to the temping pool.

Having completed the typing and alphabetical tests on her last visit, now Samantha was ready for her FasTempsNow!!! interview, which had brought her to Midtown this evening.

She looked around the lobby at her fellow desperados. A swankly attired, handsome dark-skinned man with neatly arranged Jamaican-style braids. Probably no matter how spiffy his suit or neat his braids, this white-bread temp agency and its conservative clients probably wouldn't welcome this man. Beside him sat a heavyset woman with strong perfume and a splendid suit that flattered her bulk. It was almost 8:00 P.M. and there were only two counselors working this shift; Sam had spied them yakking near the coffee machine, leisurely delaying the process and the moment she could go home.

"Samantha Flint?" called the receptionist. "A placement counselor will see you now."

Sam broke out her best smile for the woman, knowing from the past six months of temping that it was the receptionist who communicated to the placement people who had called in at dawn ready to work. This weary woman, however, was not to be won over.

"Samantha," said Rick, her assigned counselor, skimming her paperwork. "Smith College," he murmured. Rick was thin, in his mid-thirties, balding with dark hair and a mustache; he wore a lemony cologne that reminded Sam of chalkboard cleaner. "All girls' school, right? Heh-heh." Sam waited. "Sounds like I'd be right at home there, heh-heh. What'd you girls do up there on those cold winter nights without any guys around?"

"We got by somehow."

"We have a problem, Samantha," said Rick, leaning back in his swivel chair, arms behind his head. "I called your references, a Deanna at Gold and Bracken, your former employer."

And now Samantha braced for the inevitable.

"I couldn't get this Deanna, but I did talk to a Joan Michaelson. She said you were *fired* from Gold and Bracken."

That's right.

After the picture of Senator Proctor and the Sheboygans ran on the front of the Sunday B section and everyone in town knew who Jake and Fran were, Joan became apoplectic. Samantha had naively expected to share credit with Joan for the coup, but the incident served to make Joan look expendable (not to mention a liar, for telling Sy that she herself had gone to the function herself), so Joan took credit for everything, and then convinced Sy that Samantha had been dishonest about her hours on the time cards. Deanna, in a shaky, humiliated voice, told Samantha by phone not to bother coming in that Monday.

But Samantha did go in, determined to threaten a lawsuit, make some kind of protest. Sy knew Joan was lying, but Joan and he had a history and of course he wasn't going to contradict her. Deanna swore she had defended Sam to Sy, and Sam imagined the scene: Sy suffering, Sy concerned, wringing his hands, yes it's an injustice, yes Samantha's a sweet girl, but what can I do?

The only scrap thrown Samantha was that Deanna promised, if contacted, to give her a good reference. And it wasn't entirely surprising the way Sam's luck was running that this grimy temp agent, this $21,000 a year uneducated paper-pusher from Queens who sat on his ass while skimming fifty percent off his temps' backbreaking labors, had phoned his way past Deanna to Joan.

"Fired," Samantha began, barely finding breath for the exhausting explanation, "is too strong a word. I was hired for a project and that project was terminated . . . Rick?"

Rick wasn't listening. He was following the progress of the heavy woman as she was escorted through the office to a counselor. "I see I'm lucky I got you," he said to Sam, smiling, "instead of Moby Dick over there."

"I beg your pardon."

"Did you see her?" He puffed out his cheeks in an impression of obesity.

Sam needed work very badly. She had been with four other agencies—still with them, in fact. Nobody in 1983 was getting her work. She'd thrown away two days on tests and paperwork at Fas-TempsNow!!! and she couldn't afford to mouth off.

"It's a shame when people don't respect themselves, let themselves become like that. It's a matter of respecting your *self*."

"I think, Rick, that sometimes family history has something to do with why some heavy people—"

"No no no, that's just fat-people propaganda. You see, and this is going to surprise you, *I* used to be fat. Really fat. Want to see a picture?" Rick opened the bottom desk drawer and took out a binder. "See? This was me? Unbelievable, huh?"

Samantha smiled patiently.

"Most people think you have to starve yourself or exercise round the clock—and granted, you do have to change your diet and do some aerobic movementization. . . ." He demonstrated by flexing his hand this way and that. "Movementization. Not quite exercise, but more than simple moving around. It was created by Dr. Wayne Potts, at his Selfing Institute." Sam bobbed her head, pretending to have heard of the great man. "But to lose weight it's most important to conceive of yourself as thin, and this moving toward your conception of your ideal Self—that's called Selfing."

"Selfing."

Next up from the lower desk drawer was a box of Powder Positive! which featured Dr. Potts's beaming face on the label. Rick explained at length how he had lived for three months on special herbal teas, fiber bars (made by the Potts Institute), and Powder Positive! milkshakes made from water and this mix. These milkshakes weren't like anybody else's diet milkshakes—with Dr. Potts, you got a tape that accompanied the making of the shake and the drinking of the shake, during which Dr. Potts encouraged you in your Selfing evolution.

"Of course," Rick glowed, "I don't think I would have made it through, if it hadn't been for the retreats where we got to hear Dr. Potts himself talk. There's a Self Center here in Manhattan."

"Really."

"Here's a brochure . . ." A prepared packet of materials was slid across the desk to her. "And, if you don't mind, I may make a call at your home number when there's a special introductory party going on. Almost everyone at FasTemps has attended and gotten a lot of good from it. Don't worry! At first, it's free. When you start the tapes—that costs a little but it's worth every penny!"

Sam nodded mechanically.

"So you think you might be interested?"

"It . . . it sounds great, Rick. I might need you, um, to get me a choice assignment or two so I can think about the tapes and the—"

"Powder Positive!"

So maybe Rick would call with assignments, maybe not.

For this she'd had her business suit dry-cleaned. She had five short blocks to walk for the subway, but Samantha was tired physically (FasTempsNow!!! was the third temp service of the day she'd been to) and she was tired mentally. She had ten dollars for dinner and she decided to blow it on a taxi to her front door. She saw the friendly-faced Caribbean man a few yards down the sidewalk.

"You headed downtown?" Samantha asked.

"You be doin' yourself no favors trying to get a taxicab with me," he said pointedly, but still pleasant.

However, a taxi soon stopped, driven by a black immigrant.

"You in the Village?" the dreadlocked man asked Sam.

"Far west—virtually on the river."

"Some good clubs down there," he explained, naming a bunch of reggae-music palaces nowhere really near the Village. Had Samantha ever been to a Caribbean dance club? Did she think she might want to go sometime? He could teach a fine mama such as herself some moves, yes indeed.

"Here's is de stop," said the driver, pulling over to the curb at Union Square and 14th Street to let the man out.

"See you around," he smiled at Samantha, winking.

She might have gone to a club with Mr. Dreadlocks but she and Mimi had arranged to have a drink at the White Horse Tavern a few blocks from their house, famous for the Guinness, the rowdy crowd, and the curbside death of Dylan Thomas—oh, wait a minute. That's right. Mimi had told her this morning that she had to stay very late at work, after all.

"He wanted to sleep with you, I think," said the cabdriver.

Samantha didn't respond. Then she attributed the comment to third-world directness rather than insolence. "You think?"

The driver nodded seriously. "Black men in the United States of America, miss, dey all want de white women."

"Is that so."

"Yays, miss. Your family would be very much angry, yays? If you was to be with a black man."

"It is not my family's business."

He shook his head. "No no no, eet is *always* a family's business who their girls take to de bed."

"Well, maybe in . . ." He had that rarest of taxi possessions, a medallion photo that flattered him. He had simple African features, a perfectly oval face, plum-black, with large guileless eyes. She read his nameplate: Ahmadou Diop.

"Ahmadou. Are you from West Africa?"

"Senegal, miss."

This was a cab without a partition between backseat passenger and driver. Samantha looked at his thin forearms, hairless and shiny black. His hands gripping the wheel were skeletal and long-fingered. Sam wondered what it would be like to press her smaller white hand against his, palm to palm. "Well, maybe in Senegal things are more strict. In America, a woman can be with whom she pleases."

"That is why de United States of America is in no good shape, miss. All de babies having for themselves babies. No girl in Africa would do what de girls do in the United States of America, no no."

Sam was entertained by his innocent impertinence. "I've gone out with black men, for your information." She hadn't, but having no objection to doing so, she claimed it for discussion purposes.

She saw Ahmadou's face in the rearview mirror, his eyebrows raised. "What did your family say, miss?"

"I did not tell them. I suppose my parents would not be too happy, but they're from another generation." This was definitely the kind of conversation one had in taxis after an exhausting day. "And your family?" Sam pursued. "They expect you to marry a Senegalese woman?"

"My mother and father are dead, and I have only a sister back in

Senegal. I send her de money every month, yays? I drive two shifts most days—it is good money."

"Yes." Samantha leaned back, imparting a small distance from his immigrant life full of relentless toil. "It sounds lonely."

"I have no time for a wife. I drive two shifts, de morningtime and de nighttime. Sometime I sleep in de taxi. It is good money."

"You want to go back to Senegal a rich man?"

"No no no. I bring my sister to the United States of America very very soon." Samantha smiled at his saying the full name of their country each time.

"You have a girlfriend back in Senegal?"

"No, miss."

"You have a girlfriend here in New York?"

"No, miss."

"That's sad, Ahmadou," she said, watching the West Village crawl by as the cab snaked its way crosstown. "Because you're a very attractive man."

What on earth was she doing? Yet, now that she'd started, she needed encouragement to consider any further overture. Ahmadou, for his part, didn't say anything. After a few blocks downtown on Seventh Avenue South, Barrow Street approached in a tangle of triangular blocks and five-street intersections.

"Right here," she directed. "This is the one."

He pulled up outside her house and stopped, still silent. Samantha decided not to say anything either. She glanced at the mirror and connected with Ahmadou's eyes, who looked away the next second. Suddenly, he pulled a little further down the block to an open parking space, where he hovered. If he goes into the space to park, then I will ask him up, Samantha thought, her heart racing. If he tells me how much the fare is, I'm hopping right out. It's all up to him.

"You have a man?" he said at last.

"Yes, but he's not around. He lives in a different city," she pretended. "It gets sort of lonely . . . left alone by myself night after night." God, this was *Peyton Place* dialogue—she called herself a writer?

Ahmadou turned completely around in the seat, his open face expressing curiosity and trepidation. Samantha slid forward on the seat and kissed him lightly on the lips. "Come on up for a minute," she whispered.

"I cannot leave de cab. . . ."

"Just for a minute." Sam touched his face. She was not even that attracted to him, not really. Why couldn't she put on the brakes? Because, she thought, letting herself out of the car, *my dull, drab, unspectacular life craves incident*, happenings, impulses, follies—something!

Ahmadou meticulously locked all his doors and double-checked them, he arranged his fare-clipboard and other papers in a neat pile; Samantha wondered if he was dawdling. Was he a virgin? She had no idea how old he was—at least twenty-five, surely. Finally he put on his emergency flashers and got out. He was shorter than she was.

Samantha looked up to make sure no lights were on. This wasn't, perhaps, the best guy to take home to Mimi.

Once inside the dark apartment, she locked the door's two locks. She threw her coat to the sofa, her handbag. Ahmadou was just a silhouette in the streetlight glow that filtered in the box window. She could hear him breathing rapidly, nervously. She took his hand and pressed her palm against his; even in the shadows the contrast between her pale white and his purple-black skin was obvious.

"So," he whispered, "you like a negro man all the time? Your man is a black man?"

Samantha didn't answer. She undid the buttons of her blouse, and placed his long hand on her breast, above her brassiere. She looked below to observe, again, the difference. "You have never had a white girlfriend?"

"No, miss."

"Have you been with a woman?"

"Back in Senegal."

Maybe she knew when she first saw him that he was timid, that unlike Dreadlock Man he would be tentative and let her control the situation. Romance or physical beauty did not lead her here, though his eyes were very beautiful. He was very thin underneath his stale-smelling patterned shirt; she felt his ribs and his sharp hipbone. He remained motionless as she kissed him; she could taste the spearmint chewing gum he had discarded on the street. She reached lower to massage him through his thin, worn khakis. To escalate matters, Samantha took his hand again and placed it on her abdomen and pressed herself against him. Ahmadou was too respectful, patting her inconsequentially instead of letting his hand wander further down—

The phone rang.

Ahmadou jumped, his head darting, as if someone else had entered.

Samantha calmed him, "The machine will get it."

BEEP. *Hey Sam, this is David. Whatcha up to? Haven't seen you in awhile, huh? I'm gonna be playing at the Bean 'n Brew—you know—on 93rd and Lex this Tuesday and it'd be, like, really great and supportive if you'd come and pretend, like, you're a stranger and just crazy about my songs which you've heard one zillion times. . . .*

Samantha had unzipped Ahmadou's khakis; he wasn't wearing underwear. The answering machine was impossible—she broke away, whispering, "Lemme get that," racing to the coffee table to turn down the machine's volume.

Call me, Sam, when you get in. And David hung up before Samantha could feel for the controls. She turned back to vaguely make out Ahmadou fumbling with the door locks.

"Wait . . ."

Dimly, she saw that he had fastened his pants again and tucked his shirttail back in his trousers.

"Ahmadou, don't leave. What's wrong?"

"I must go now."

She ran back to him, held him firmly, and kissed him again; this time, unexpectedly, he kissed her back passionately, sighing with emotion, suppressing what seemed like a sob. Sam reached back to his waist, to continue from where . . . but she felt through the cloth that he had ejaculated.

"I must go now." He fumbled with the door locks, closing one only to open another, trapped and frustrated. She undid both locks for him and he escaped, a quick-moving blur into the hall.

So. That was that.

Samantha didn't know how she felt about what had just transpired. She sauntered exhausted to the bathroom and decided to fill the tub and take a languorous bubble bath, maybe fall asleep in the water. She decided that in a muted, factual way she was proud of herself. She had gone where people usually didn't go, willfully off the established road, touching a foot tonight upon the shore of West Africa, and the writer within had been rewarded—however ineptly—with visions, aromas, sensations she had not been fated to know. Her life agreeably resembled someone else's for a moment.

She sank down into the bathwater—careful, however, not to wash the hand that held the scent of her Senegalese friend.

CONSTITUENT MAILING,
FEBRUARY 1, 1993

My Fellow Americans! Greetings from your senator. My visit home over the holiday recess was especially rewarding. Not only did I get to see so many of my wonderful constituents but I got to sit down and hear what's on your mind!

I ran for this office four years ago as your strongest proponent of family values and I hope that, with this despicable tabloid–driven scandal staged by our liberal enemies fading from the left-wing media's short attention span, we can get to the serious business of doing something about the evil that is pornography.

I am introducing into this very session a bill in memory of Ronnie, whose national tragedy was made partisan use of by those in Congress who would stop the march of conservative ideology any way they can. Our family has endured much—and Lillian and I continue to thank each and every one who has written with your kind thoughts and prayers by personal note—but for Ronnie's sake, we must stamp out this sickness of smut. I assure you my able staff, with my legislative director leading the way, will bring just such an urgent reform measure to the floor of the Senate before another Christmas passes!

What a Christmas present a filthless world for our children will be!

"*Family*" *Frank*

The Hon. Frank A. Shanker
U.S. Senator

THE

BETTER

PART

Not that she had one spare second this day—or any day during this busy September legislative session—but Samantha Flint tarried at the Library of Congress catalogues to look up her own name.

Senator Proctor would announce for reelection any day now, which would mean the hacks and political operatives would sweep in and take center stage through 1990, her legislative chores would dwindle, and stretches of luxuriantly free time would present themselves. She'd get back to the novel. Well, more accurately, *begin* the novel, afresh with ironclad rituals, a page-count expected each week, a sacrosanct set-aside time to write each morning.

FLE . . . FLI . . . FLIG . . . here we are: Flint.

It wouldn't do to discover there was another "Samantha Flint" or some guy named Sam Flint messing up her posterity. Ah, there was a Sam Flint. He had written a book on microorganisms in 1956, *Our Tiny World*. Beyond him, though, the field was clear.

Samantha caught sight of a small herd of librarians, chattering, pointing to her . . . avoiding her eyes, it seemed. Sadly for her admirers in the library crew, "Samantha's Bill" (as they dubbed it) was probably years away from happening, due to the slow peristalsis of committees. Yet one of the young librarians had sent her the *sweetest* little fan letter of appreciation, writing that her faith in the government was somewhat restored by the work of staffers like Samantha Flint. So because Samantha hadn't had *quite* enough adulation today, she decided to make an appearance at Hazel's office.

"Samantha," said Hazel, behind the paper piles on her desk. The plate on Hazel's door announced that she was Assistant Librarian (one of a hundred such women, apparently). "I've been thinking of you all day," she said gently.

Odd. That tone of concern.

Hazel added, "It must be a madhouse over there."

No, why should Proctor's office be a madhouse? Into Sam's mind crept that most-feared intimation for a Beltway insider: *I'm not working with all the information.*

"Let me thank you again for all your efforts," Hazel said, putting aside one stack of papers among scores of such stacks, obeying a system she alone could fathom. "You'll call me if our bill goes to committee before the recess?"

"Yes," Samantha said slowly.

Samantha's Bill. Writer residencies in all fifty states, administered by the Library of Congress. Often at night, too caffeinated to get to sleep, giddy that her four-years-in-the-making piece of legislation was about to become reality, Samantha would repitch it to herself:

Think of all the federal property not in full-time use. Cabins in the national forests, closed officers' quarters on bases, discontinued Coast Guard lighthouses, boarded-up farm bureau offices on midwestern Main Streets. Her bill would provide funds sufficient for a writer—novelist or poet or historian—to live and work for free on federal properties for a fixed but renewable time. And the Library of Congress would be arbiter, picking from among each of the fifty states' native scholars and writers.

Who could object? The underused housing units would depreciate less with people caring for them, and the cost of fifty writers' living expenses would barely cause a ripple on the vast trillion-dollar budget sea.

When Samantha began working for Warren Proctor in 1984, at the bottom rung, constituent correspondence, she had taken the senator at his word. He said he wanted to hear legislative ideas from everyone in his office including the receptionist and cleaning lady— and Warren Proctor, extraordinarily a man of the people, actually meant it. So Samantha had told him about her plan, maybe somewhere imagining herself ensconced in one of those cabins, filling recycled Forest Service stationery pads with prose, contacting the local ranger whenever she needed more—

"I'll keep my fingers crossed for the bill," Hazel was saying. "I mean, who knows what will happen in '91 with the changing of the guard. Have you got something lined up, dear?"

Okay, something was definitely amiss.

It was all she could do not to *run* back to the Hart Building, two monumental blocks away from the Library, with the Supreme Court and its protesters reliably slowing her journey with fliers and petitions. Did Proctor have a stroke—was he languishing in a Bethesda emergency room?

And yet, something haunted at the periphery . . .

Warren had wordlessly escaped the office after the nine o'clock staff meeting, toddling down the hall clutching a legal pad with his floor speech. But retirement! For god's sakes, he's healthy and lively, a certified Capitol character, 65–70 percent favorables in his home state! Why would he retire from one of the safest Republican seats in America? And yet . . . that floor speech, the speech he didn't run by anybody, his refusal to talk about the '90 election for weeks now.

Samantha Flint considered herself Warren Proctor's *friend*, in addition to being his legislative director. He talked with her about history and philosophy without condescension; he joked about his senatorial colleagues with the highest trust for her discretion, telling tales intended to be off-the-record for eternity. Despite whatever Capitol Hill's furtive gossips might have imagined, she and the senator were not in love; no May-December romance for Sam and Warren. He was faithful to his wife and his principles. Theirs was an apprentice-master relationship, with a touch of father-daughter.

Back at the office, it was like a wake.

Wanda the receptionist, a pillar of indifference most days, was dabbing her eyes. From the usually boisterous staff cubicles came only the sound of sniffles amid a grim silence.

"You know this was coming, Sam?" asked Wanda.

Samantha's authority was tied up in knowing things first, so she saved face. "There'd been a rumor but I didn't think it could possibly be . . ." She glanced at the senator's oaken office door, the state seal centered in its polished wood.

Wanda: "Said he was not to be disturbed. Except for you."

The enormity of what had happened hadn't registered yet. First, she was sad; this was a death of sorts, a loss for her personally—and for the nation, though the country would never know half of what they were losing. Second, some nasty little facts started creeping into her consciousness: her $65,000 salary, gone. Her prestige, her reputation as one of the up-and-coming senate staffers, gone—hell, her parking-place-others-would-kill-for was gone. The ability to pay her $1800 Capitol Hill townhouse rent, gone. Her sense of her own power which fueled everything from her basic self-esteem to her sexual confidence, gone. It figures, she told herself, just when I pull even with Mimi in the career sweepstakes . . .

She opened the door.

"Samantha," he said, confirming the worst by his expression. Senator Proctor's eyes were weak; she was melted by the thought of his crying alone.

"Not much warning, Warren." She tried to sound feisty, game for what came next, tough ol' Sam Flint.

"Shameful, really," he said dropping ice cubes into the glass of whiskey he was preparing for her to match his own. "But if I'd told you in advance, you might well have talked me out of it."

"I certainly wish I'd had the chance to try."

"I know I'm putting a lot of you out on the street in a year. And if I'd had to face the staff I would have lost my nerve. I knew I had to make this announcement quickly. And I saw the morning was reserved for floor speeches, so . . ."

"Has Jack, um, prepared the press release?" she asked automatically, as if this were some workaday statement.

Undoubtedly, his press officer had typed up a brief statement, which the media would already be holding up to the light for any signs or secret meanings. Did anyone have dirt on Proctor? Was he sick? Why would anyone so popular and beloved walk away from power? Proctor didn't answer her question, which she had asked, after all, only to fill the silence.

"We'll try to get your thing through," he said after a moment.

"My thing . . ."

"Your writer-in-residence authorization. We'll try to get it on a rider before Christmas recess."

"Senator," she had to say, "it breaks my heart—"

He raised his hand. "No! Let's not have any folderol about how the Capitol dome will collapse without my being here."

Samantha in a flash saw the removal of his name from the door, the packing of files and mementos, the death of a thousand knick-nacks and constituent-presented gewgaws, genuine honors as well as inside jokes (like Proctor's Bovine Association Man of the Year brass hereford), all to be packed or put out in the street, just like Samantha herself . . .

Senator Proctor quietly handed her his silk handkerchief.

Samantha slid across the resistant vinyl seat of an overheated cab outside of Tortilla Coast on Massachusetts Avenue, letting herself out in the unseasonably chilly night.

"Have a nice evening," the driver said without feeling.

Sam studied herself in the large glass pane of a closed real estate office. Her bob had become more severe in recent years—Louise Brooks, an angular Cleopatra. When the dark brown had started to turn mousy, she began dyeing it, gradually darkening it to a silky black. She darkened her eyebrows too and applied a more theatric eyeliner, pleased with the intimidating effect. "Why, ah was plumb scayred to talk to you, Miss Flint," Senator Thurmond said to her during a Judiciary hearing, winking, surprised that a woman who looked like a soap opera vixen could be running a legislative office.

The staff had gathered for a further session of mourning, wailing, gnashing teeth, and getting drunk. Julie Bingham, Sam's closest of-fice friend, asked: "Whaddya think we'll all be doing a year from now?"

"Starving," Sam said, joining the table with a new round of mar-garitas. There were six staffers from Proctor's office, an array of boyfriends and girlfriends whose names Sam had never learned, and

Cameron Platt, formerly of Senator Dale Bumpers' office, now a bigwig Senate staffer on Environment & Public Works. A job for life, since the powerful committee staff positions didn't depend on some senator being continually elected.

Cameron tried to rally them. "C'mon, every single one of y'all's gonna be snapped right up by other senators."

Fran said, "It took me six months to get *this* gig."

Fran and Julie supervised constituent correspondence and actually enjoyed the tedium. They'd be rehired within a month, thought Sam objectively. Gene, sitting beside her, had given his life to "special projects," dealing with stalled entitlement checks and constituent gripes—a month, max, and he'd be back at work. Samantha finished off her margarita too quickly, giving herself neuralgia.

The only office bigshot not in attendance was Jack, Proctor's chief of staff, equal to her in power. He handled political and public affairs, came most alive at elections; Sam handled the legislative business, bills, votes, riders, and amendments. Jack, who with his contacts could get Warren on national TV in under an hour, would find work again in no time.

In fact, Sam figured everyone would bounce quickly to new employment with the likely exception of *herself*. There were 100 senators and 100 legislative directors, 43 of whom were Republican in the 101st Congress, and you can damn well bet no other l.d. was planning to retire out of deference to her.

"Truth is," Cameron was saying, mouth full of nacho chips, "the other Senate staffers hate y'all's guts, 'cause you've spent the last ten years making 'em look so bad."

True. It would make for some schadenfreude, some unreturned phone calls. Proctor, with his populous home state and seniority, was entitled to scores of aides and assistants, and yet he ran his crack personal office with a scant staff of *twenty*.

"Samantha," Cameron chided, "now's the time for you to come out of the closet for the *Democrat* you are. Send some résumés across the aisle. Walk toward the light!"

"Change of party, Mr. Platt, is a last resort."

Cameron Platt, not quite forty, was born in Fayetteville, Arkansas, and raised in Charlotte, North Carolina; this produced a smooth how-ya'll-doin' demeanor that belied his Ivy League education and years of political gamesmanship. He was six-one and broad, never thought of as tall, though when you stood next to him you were surprised. He had the beginnings of laugh lines around the eyes, sandy hair beginning to thin, which he did nothing to impede (a rarity in the toupee, plug, and dye-obsessed Senate—"the combover capital of the world," as Samantha dubbed it). It was precisely the unashamed aging, the twenty extra pounds he never bothered to lose, the big appetite, and hearty cocktail party behavior that drew Samantha to him. His love of food and drink (and she imagined his gusto for sex) was part of his general exuberance to be working in these halls.

"I'll ask around," Cameron offered, "and see if any moderate Republican's l.d. is fixin' to leave. I've heard rumors about that woman in Cooper's office."

Cameron's desirability had snuck up on Samantha. Her attraction had started with his green eyes, then the hands, manicured and large, and then Sam's eye moved up the sleeve to the hint of blond hair on his arms. What she had found off-putting, she now began to fetishize.

"Why be so stubborn, Samantha?" he was asking while attacking the deep-fried mozarella sticks. "Why be such an ol' snob about going to K Street?"

To leave the Senate to shill for a lobbyist. Temptingly, there might be no shortage of offers, opportunities to double and triple her salary, provided she used her Senate entrée to favor American-made fertilizer or cheap Japanese exports. "That day may come," she answered, "but I'll let Packwood chase me around his hideaway first. I'm not leaving Capitol Hill."

"Well I'm gonna be chased around my house, if I don't get my butt back there," Cameron said, standing, tossing a twenty to the table. "S'posed to be home an hour ago. You guys take care." He departed without a farewell glance to Samantha.

Married, of course.

Samantha wondered just how happily, though. Margaret Platt was a brittle, pale product of charm schools and a two-year junior woman's college, steeped in Southern-debutante rich-girl twaddle: "I consider it my vocation to make a nice Christmas for Cameron," Samantha overheard her say at a party last year. "I'm gonna bring out Nanna's porcelain nativity scene, and these candlesticks which have been in the Beauvoir family for *hunderds* of years . . ." How on earth could he of all people married a nonpolitico? Margaret offered a femininity of interminable house-redecorations and pricey catalogues. What Cameron needed was a woman who could channel the stress of Washington into good old-fashioned sex—

"Hey Sam," Fran interrupted her thoughts. "I hear over in the House they're hard up for talent—"

"No way!" cried several longer-term Senate staffers, Samantha included.

The walk across the Capitol lawn to the Cannon Building, was a spiritual demotion not seriously entertained by anyone who worked in the high-profile Senate, where you could see yourself on CNN during newsmaking committee hearings confiding importantly to your senator ("Mimi, I'm on TV today"), and where the six-year election cycle of its members gave one a hint of job security instead of the every-two-year crapshoot of the House.

And there was the *real* reason to cling to the Senate: despite the rogues you had to deal with, it was nonetheless possible for a staffer to shape legislation, organize the passage of a bill, see your pet project become the law of the land. Nowhere was anonymous power more accessible, more addictive and intoxicating.

While the other staffers moaned and planned their futures out loud, Julie leaned into Sam confidentially, whispering, "Let's get out of this romper room, I've had enough of the kiddies."

All around were the newest wave of D.C. professionals, 21-year-old Senate interns doing shots of mezcal, 25-year-old lobbyists-in-training picking clean their plates of nachos. Too rowdy and hormonal for seasoned old pros like Samantha and Julie, on the verge of thirty. They announced a departure for home but instead adjourned to the Monocle, a darker drinking establishment quiet at this hour where one could glimpse the more mature Senate staffer and the occasional spectacle of Ted Kennedy, Al D'Amato, Christopher Dodd, those rare senators who would drink in public.

"So, Sam," Julie said as they settled into a booth. "Where'd Cameron go? Home to his *wife?*"

"That would seem to be the case." Sam tried to extinguish this subject. "He's not flirting back. Another dry hole for Samantha Flint Explorations, Incorporated."

"Hell, months ago he was flirting with you bigtime. Whyn't you go after someone who isn't getting fat?"

"He's not fat, he's cuddly."

"You know, I'd like to marry Paul one day without worrying about you stealing him," she added unseriously.

No worries there. Hunky soloflexed Paul, the squarest ESPN-watching hulk in the world. Julie selected all her boyfriends from the gym. They could have the IQs of paramecia, as long as they were buff. Julie once had a fling with this Ecuadorian mailman, all of five feet tall, who had bulked up his little frame until he resembled a thick-necked fire hydrant. "I've never had an affair with a married man who didn't initiate it, Jool. And I always fight it off too."

"Before relenting."

"Before relenting," Sam confirmed.

"How many has it been? There was Ben . . ."

Ben was an accident. Samantha met him at Moynihan's St. Patrick's Day party, where everyone drank too much, and a one-night stand ensued. In the morning he mentioned he was married-but-separated, his wife didn't understand him, marital sex life was dead, divorce pending—

"And Lawrence," Julie went on.

Lawrence told Sam up front he was married. Married-but-separated, his wife didn't understand him, marital sex life was dead, divorce pending. Well, hell, it would have been hypocritical to act pious post-Ben, so Samantha met Lawrence at the Holiday Inn in Crystal City a time or two. But neither man was living with his wife at the time—

"And don't forget Bob," Julie said, humming approval. "Someone ought to make a plaster cast of that man for my private home use."

Bob was newly married *and* looking to cheat. A Democratic pollster. Probably banged the hotel maid on his honeymoon. His way of sidling up to a woman, placing his hands over yours for a simple hello, his naughty little-boy voice, the incandescent twinkle in his eye—he might as well have hung a sign around his neck: looking for hot meaningless crazy thrills, willing to provide same. Not only did he and Samantha dishevel a few hotel rooms on a few afternoons, but that lying dog probably went home and went a few rounds with his wife those very evenings.

Julie retreated. "Oh, now don't go and get all defensive on me. Lord knows, I've tried to date in this town."

Social-policy wonks, political hacks welded to their beepers, creepy Pentagon nerds, lobbyists whose slick insincerity poisoned all subsequent human contact, economist bores, know-it-all lawyers—not to mention the vast ranks of the "bitter," the disenfranchised whose man got voted out of office, whose project got cut from the budget, whose policies were yesterday's back-page item. Of the available single, straight men out of that spindly pile, you had varieties of unattractiveness, sexual stuntedness, and social retardation no other major American city's women had to endure.

But Julie *did* manage to turn up single unattached men, and it was hard for Samantha not to feel improper.

Samantha had not abandoned her Smith-forged female solidarity—she knew women at large would despise her for not finding a "man of her own," nor had she wholly expunged her thou-shalt-not Baptist upbringing. It expiated things a little bit, she figured, that she never wanted to *steal* men away from their wives or get involved in "waiting for him to get his divorce" melodramas. It was precisely the expected discretion of the quick affair that made married men so appealing.

1. They would not slow her career trajectory, longing for home-making and kids.

2. They would not take up all of her exceedingly precious free time—just a few nights a month.

3. They would not make for social difficulties, i.e., boyfriends who didn't get on with Samantha's female friends (like David vs. Mimi), boyfriends who had to have their softball matches or

guitar recitals attended. None of the just-going-along-to-make-the-relationship-work bullshit.

4. They would not make her miserable, because no matter what these men's natural bent for mind games and sadism, there was a limit: Samantha could always pick up the phone and call the little woman. There was power and control in that, and Sam valued both.

5. They would not have any problems with the sex. When it was fresh and furtive—a little guilty, a little angry, driven by the delicious lure of the forbidden—then it was great; when it got stale, the affair was over. And yet for all this worldly courtesan talk, unspoken in Samantha was a stir of misgiving. Adultery, she hoped to persuade herself, like yeast infections or spermicidal jelly, was yet another imperfect part of a modern woman's sex life . . .

"I bet we'll hate each other," Julie was saying of Mimi, whose long-threatened visit neared. "The Clash of Samantha's Best Friends. Only one can walk away!"

Julie was Samantha's best Washington friend. And, though she was a dear, Julie was no Mimi.

Sam and "Jool" had lunch almost daily, often watched TV shows together over the phone from their separate apartments, and shamed each other into joint gym visits. There was something of a '50s housewives-gathering-at-the-clothesline quality to their friendship. Food, men, shopping, weight, clothes, family. Samantha longed for a good old Mimi Mohr dissection of Western philosophy, a tractate on the decline of liberalism after Vietnam, on how Mimi "could paint a goddam Jackson Pollock in five minutes," on the disintegration of the New York Phil under Zubin Mehta. There wasn't a single life-crisis of Julie's that Sam couldn't rectify in one sentence.

". . . but Sam, if my mother comes this weekend, then everything will be messed up and I'll be all moody, and she'll get critical—"

Samantha: Jool, tell your mom to come another time.

". . . but Sam, the thing about Perry is when he's really angry he gets quiet, and I'm afraid he might have a drinking problem like he did back in high school—"

Samantha: Jool, break up with him.

In New York, Mimi's advertising ascent had plateaued at McCann-Erickson and the Coke account (1983). She upped her salary by taking a marketing job with Coca-Cola itself (in 1984), which at that time owned Columbia Pictures. Then she worked for Columbia in marketing (1985, with a move to California). Then, the Motion Picture Association, who rate movies R, PG-13, G, with whimsical inconsistency, had hired her as a p.r. flak (that was in— Sam had trouble keeping the dates straight—early 1986). Then Mimi gambled by taking a *huge* salary cut to start at the bottom at the Creative Artists Agency, which, Mimi saw, would run Hollywood single-handedly one day. The jury was out on whether Mimi, who never watched TV or went to movies, would be well-cast as a Hollywood mogul.

It was surprising, considering how Mimi and Sam professed to miss each other, how little they visited or even talked. They would play phone tag for a month. When they'd at last find each other at home, they would run up sixty bucks in long–distance between them, planned evenings out would be cancelled, alarm clocks turned to the wall so neither would know how disastrously late she was staying up.

And then another two months would go by.

Since Sam's move to Washington and Mimi's to California, Samantha had only laid eyes on her friend twice in nearly five years, both times in New York. Ah, but now Mimi was coming to D.C. Sam would have the Meem on her own home turf! Samantha had envisioned elaborate dinners and cast the principals; she had planned visits to the smaller art collections that—she prayed—even Mimi hadn't heard of, with Samantha leading the charge and Mimi racing behind. Then, tea at the Willard Hotel, or cocktails and the killer view at the Hotel Washington . . .

"Think you'll sleep tonight?" Julie asked as they left.

"Not planning on it," said Samantha.

Riding home in the taxi, Sam's thoughts moved from job-anxiety to money-anxiety: Sam had a debt of $2500 plus on her VISA, a relatively innocuous $850 on her MasterCard. She had spent twenty-five bucks earlier tonight, and she and Julie had just racked up another twenty apiece. Starting tomorrow, she was going to stop pissing her money away.

Drunk, dispirited, cried-out for the moment, anxious for her future, not especially proud of her present, Samantha returned home and flopped on her sofa, grabbing the remote. It was a reflex gesture to turn on her TV, permanently set on *Headline News*. The cycle of headlines, she knew, would eventually lead her back to the fact that Warren Proctor had announced his retirement . . . and so she turned it off. Guess, starting tomorrow, she'd have to start confirming the news to friends and acquaintances.

She noticed she had only one phone message on her machine. Figures. Headline goes out that my senator is retiring and none of my Washington friends calls to console. She wondered if any of her non-Washington friends, Mimi, her sisters, Dad or Mom, ever watched five minutes of the news in their lives.

"Good," her mother will say when she hears. "Now you can find something down here in Florida so we can all be close together again. You know, my health isn't what it was . . ."

Mother was never a great source of career encouragement. Every time Samantha asked what Mrs. Flint thought of her daughter's job she would say something like, "Darling, your world is so far beyond anything I can understand that you might as well not listen to your old mother . . ." or "I hear those politican friends of yours on the TV, Sam-Sam, and I just wonder how anything gets done in this country at all." Last family visit, Samantha had asked directly if her mother was even proud of her. "Sam-Sam, of course I'm proud, but I'd be proud of you, honey, if you worked in the Kroger's checkout line, you know that!"

None of these was *quite* the yearned-for response. Something was shaded or withheld or exquisitely dismissed—and her mother didn't do this consciously. Even that, though, constituted more of a loving effort than her father made. Her father, now divorced and in permanent retreat to Shirley's trailer in Orlando.

Samantha checked the phone message.

BEEP. *This is the prodigal Mimi, Sam. Something . . . oh god, something has sort of come up on our planned weekend*

Samantha glared at the machine.

Hong Kong. When am I gonna get a chance to go to Hong Kong, for chrissakes? I'm supposed to go on this junket that's going to open up the Hong Kong film distribution market to

Samantha pressed the erase button, not wanting to hear the rest of Mimi's perfectly splendid alternative to visiting Samantha in Washington, D.C. Mimi was going to Hong Kong, Samantha was going to a cardboard box in Anacostia . . .

Just as well. Sam was not in a hostessing mood.

"No offense," Julie said to Sam, during their declared last round, "but I always wondered how you got such a good job out of Proctor. And I guess now we know."

Samantha and Julie had begun making nightly trips to the Monocle, and as for the money being thrown away—screw it.

"Yeah," said Sam, "I guess a lot of stuff makes sense now."

However did Samantha Flint, without a political science degree or J.D. or any experience at policy, become legislative director for a U.S. senator? Samantha had been content to chalk it up to Proctor's faith in her, his own inscrutable hiring practices. But now she understood.

After she had worked two years for the senator as a junior member of the staff, there was a giant brouhaha when Proctor's l.d., Carla, took a job with another senator in midsession 1986. What disloyalty, people thought. Proctor and his l.d. had been together since he was a state senator! Was there a falling-out?

Julie finished the last of her vodka. "Remember the gossip? Everyone thought Carla left because she and Proctor were having an affair?"

"He must have known," Samantha sighed, "that he wasn't going to run again, even back in '86."

Sam saw now that Proctor confided his eventual retirement to Carla, allowing her to hunt quietly for another job. That done, Warren couldn't very well hire another experienced Senate aide knowing he'd be disemploying that aide in four years. So Warren did the decent thing—he gave a young, well-meaning, politically astute person a big break. Samantha Flint. It had felt nice to assume her own excellence had brought her so far so fast, but finally discerning Warren's wisdom and kindness in the whole thing didn't erase the accomplishment or negate the first-rate job she had done for him. It only confirmed how good he was, how rightly he did things.

Despite a shot of Nyquil, Samantha couldn't get to sleep. She hadn't been sleeping well all week—this was like high school all over again.

She heard the newspaper hit the front stoop.

The sunrise was a gray hour away. A foggy, bluish chill misted Samantha's street, obscuring the streetlights; the few cars at this hour made an occasional *slish* along the wet roadways, a garbage truck rumbled away. Samantha bent down to retrieve the *Washington Post*, pulling her bathrobe to herself. Today's retrospective quoted from the now-famous retirement speech:

> "If I could will this chamber to reform in only one measure, that measure would be *age*," Proctor intoned to the amusement of his fellow senators one term ago. "All of us should retire at seventy, gentlemen. . . ." With a nod to Sens. Barbara Mikulski (D-Md.) and Nancy Kassebaum (R-Kan.), the senator added, "I don't propose this rule should apply to the ladies since they are in grievously short supply as it is. But gentlemen, we have a gerontocracy here to rival the People's Republic, the Politburo, if not the waning days of the Ottoman Empire!"

Samantha wistfully appreciated his rhetoric. All week long, in *Time*, in *Newsweek*, in the columns and on the talking-head shows, the senator's high principles were praised. George Will, this Thursday morning, liked Proctor too:

> . . . By the late '80s, the national mood coincided perfectly with his windmill-chasing and what had once seemed curmudgeonly now beckoned to the nation heroically.

Warren Proctor, with his gaunt face, his mane of white

hair, his owlish eyebrows permanently raised in expectation of good news, had become, to his own surprise, a "Washington character." And there was not a colleague who wouldn't postpone present business to chat and be lightly chided by the elder senator when he padded into their offices brandishing his familiar rust-red clipboard. The clipboard (to be enshrined in a case in the lobby of the Hart Senate Building) crackled with his yellow legal pad, bearing lists of bureaucratic atrocities that the senator he was petitioning might alleviate.

Alas, Proctor sensibly said that no politican should serve past his seventieth birthday or make the Capitol his permanent home, so consequently he is not seeking re-election. A man of his word.

As if we needed fewer of them.

The phone rang three times.

"Okay, I'm in the shower already," mumbled Samantha. Sometimes he sent the signal twice, in case she'd rolled back over and went to bed.

Liaisons, when done right, took a lot of trouble. Scented, soft sheets on the bed, a clean apartment and liquor on premises, low and flattering lighting, easy-to-reach (yet subtly positioned) birth control devices and upscale lubricants. Not to mention the endless self-preparation, worse as she got older: the douche, the hot shower with perfumed after-bath oil, the trim of the pubic area, the shaved legs and armpits, the hair, makeup lightly applied. Sam would like to have kept the old sheets on the bed, but this affair wasn't at the sixpack-and-let's-order-Domino's stage yet. Truth be admitted, she needed this particular affair worse than he did, as a balm for life and career insecurity.

She had hidden the affair from Julie, since this was a more delicate situation than the previous flings. Besides, Samantha reasoned as she perfumed herself, splashing *eaux* strategically, Julie thought he wasn't anything to look at. They never could agree on who was sexy; i.e., Mitch.

Samantha once nudged Julie to notice the maintenance guy who came around to adjust the office thermostat nightly at seven P.M.

"Mitch?" Julie made a face.

Mitch was sort of seedy, a working-class white guy in his early twenties with a broad Baltimore—"Bah'more"—accent that made him sound dumb—which, well, he was. Bad skin, Jesus-length brown hair parted down the middle, a faint uneven mustache that hadn't filled in completely, an attempt at a Seattle goatee. He would have been perfect for a Civil War re-enactment, playing the dirt-poor Confederate soldier, itchin' to kill some Yanks. The congressional maintenance staff had tight little uniforms that never failed to elicit Sam's attention whenever these workers came or went. She had once asked Mitch about his tattoos and he had flirted back, and now every time they passed in the hall, he nodded a "Hey there."

Mitch was a fixture in Samantha's fantasy life. She wondered what he thought about her. Maybe he fantasized about finding her alone in the office and, with a little encouragement, taking her, there on the senator's desk. What if she were to visit him in his supply closet and workshop by the elevator? What if it was midnight and everyone had gone home? Samantha had glimpsed inside the janitor's closet and seen the lockers, the girlie pinups. What if in the dead of night, between floor waxings, he aroused himself looking at those siliconed centerfolds and then what if, after checking up the hall and down, he stepped out of his uniform—

Doorbell.

"I thought I'd bring you breakfast." Cameron stepped inside and set down a box of Krispy Kreme doughtnuts.

"Hey, what happened to croissants?" she lightly complained. Last week it had been still-hot pastries from Bread & Chocolate.

"Not open this early for some reason," he said, taking off his winter coat and tossing it to the sofa. "I brought you a North Carolina delicacy, the Krispy Kreme doughnut. They have a 24-hour place out on Jeff Davis." He opened a box of lighter-than-air doughnuts and the aroma of sugarglaze filled the room. "Open wide. They're still warm."

Sam did as instructed. Gorgeous, caloric, supreme creations . . . She held his hand at her mouth and began licking the glaze off his fingers, hoping to hurry along the small talk and proceed to the main purpose of his morning visits. (A great time to cheat. "Going in first thing to get some work off my desk, honey," hadn't made for a ripple of suspicion.)

The sex was good. The conversational aftermath, the groping self-justifications between her fulfillment in the bed and his departure out the door, less so. "After the two miscarriages," Cameron was saying, "Margaret's uninterested in sex. She goes to bed hours before me or hours after me—she thinks after months of this behavior that I can't figure out what she's trying to avoid."

"Why don't you adopt?" Sam asked.

"Aren't adopted kids all screwed up?"

"Aren't all kids nowadays screwed up?" Samantha, like any single person exposed to her married friends' offspring, felt no one was currently raising their kids correctly. "Seems to me America's chief glory in world history is the liberation of the woman from baby-making against her will—the death of the multigenerational family, great-grandfather living in the same hovel as the babies."

"Now, now." Cameron pulled her near. "They're not gonna let you lead the prayer at the next Republican convention."

"Get to work," she nudged him away, nodding toward the digital alarm which read 8:10. "You're sure," she added, wondering if his former job was available, "there are no openings down at Bumpers?"

Dale Bumpers of Arkansas, generally conceded to be one of the finer men to work for. No screaming tantrums like Mikulski or Moynihan, no get-the-faggot witchhunts like Sam Nunn, no fear the old geezer was going to keel over and die and leave you unemployed as might Thurmond or Pell or Burdick . . . Oh, for a job in Bumper's office.

"Nope," said Cameron, dressing, a little distant.

"Sorry things aren't going well at home," she offered.

"I guess *we* wouldn't be together if they were."

Samantha truly *was* sorry to hear the Platts had troubles. These affairs with married men were enacted under the contractual understanding that the guys would remain married.

"Gee, Sam, I dunno about next Thursday."

They'd played out this scene before. Samantha knew not to say anything.

". . . and Margaret's mother's gonna be in town. And that'll be a nightmare. She's offered to pay for Margaret and me to go to a fertility clinic. That old biddy probably wants to conduct the sperm count herself."

"Well, you come over here with your plastic cup when it's time to give a sample, hm?"

He turned for another fond, emotional look at her before heading out into the drizzle. Samantha wished these transitions were more quickly ended, these performed lighthearted departures. This particular morning she even wondered if she had chosen wrong: stripped from the trappings of his professional allure, Cameron appeared older than he was, dishevelled and saggy, a preview of a bureaucratic, dull-married Washington middle age.

"Doughnuts," she said to the empty room upon his departure. And she got up and helped herself to the spoils.

A cold 1990 arrived and the capital prepared for the off-year elections. Robert Byrd and George Mitchell fought in public over coal miners and in private over who was really going to run the Senate; President Bush conceded to a budget deal with Congress which raised the taxes he swore he'd never raise, occasioning the predictable political fallout and backstabbings. The parade of eulogy and honorific for Warren Proctor began to fade. Long-treasured constituents and beseeching lobbyists receded through the spring with the sprouting of the cherry blossoms along the Tidal Basin.

Samantha would turn from the elevator and see Proctor's office dead ahead as she'd done for five years . . . and yet the aura had dimmed, the frisson of power and importance that once accompanied her through the door was no longer there, replaced by an air of inconsequence.

Her résumés, connections, owed favors had come to nothing, and

Warren Proctor's round of calls and arm-twistings couldn't help her either. There were no l.d. openings. At this point, she would take a lesser Senate staff position—a mere legislative aide—but the salary cut would be extreme, maybe $20,000 less.

That means good-bye to the townhouse, the nightlife, the gourmet markets and bakeries, the chichi Sumatran coffee beans and her fancy Italian bean grinder and her fancy French espresso maker and her Secla bowl-sized multicolored cups from Portugal . . . What's the point of staying in D.C., she mourned, if my lifestyle goes back to square one?

Maybe the novel.

In that irrational play of mind that visits the condemned, Samantha toyed with the idea she could finish up her novel, sell it, and sling her VISA and MasterCard as in days of old.

That evening Samantha knelt before a bottom desk drawer, the crypt of old floppy disks and notebooks that lingered in a large brown accordion folder she had emblazoned THE COLLECTED WORKS OF SAMANTHA FLINT with a semiconscious mix of irony and hope. She had been scrupulous to keep every fragment of every story, every journal sketch and false start, not to mention press releases, constituent mailings, white papers—anything she had ever written.

You never know, she figured.

I remember a summer evening, back when I was nine, when my father had driven us out of my hometown of Springfield, Missouri, to his boat dealership on Bull Shoals Reservoir.

It was to be a short errand, merely to pick up an invoice, but when we got there, one of my daddy's partners was having a barbecue

The memory she had hidden from her college workshop—replaced, she recalled, by a more sophisticated, urban, fictitious memory for display to that Smith circle.

There were other children whose names I never learned,
but my own age, from less citified places in the Ozarks,
seductive with wicked words in rural accents

No. Not colorful enough, really. A very ordinary childhood, whatever its bad points. If she'd been born in a dirt-floored cabin in the
Ozarks, then perhaps. To Sam it seemed the only thing that had
ever been interesting about her life was that she worked for Warren
Proctor—and now she would have to give that up.

One September evening, Samantha, Jack the chief of staff, Fran,
and some others from constituent correspondence, sat back to watch
TV with the senator. C-SPAN was televising the debate between
the leading Democrat and Republican for Proctor's Senate seat.

The senator, tie loosened and shoes kicked off, had broken out
the scotch; informality was, for once, the rule. He had insisted on
his being called "Warren" in his final months in office, though no
one could manage it—his adoring staff realized the day would come
soon enough for "Warren" and "Mr. Proctor."

"If I'd known this horse's ass was going to win the primary,"
Senator Proctor was grumbling, "I wouldn't have stepped down!"

Governor Arnie Bascomb, a moderate Democrat, was having
health problems, campaign problems, focus problems. His Republican opponent was a right-wing talk show radio host with the post-
Rush Limbaugh drive-time hour in the capital city. Frank Shanker.
Very handsome, happily married with three boys, all in military
academics back east. His nickname, and campaign slogan, was
"Family Frank."

He ended each radio hour with a salute to one of the veterans
living in the state; he had honored every living World War I soldier
and was schmaltzing his way through the World War II vets. He'd
call the "Veteran of the Day" and they'd chat about the Battle of
the Bulge or Omaha Beach or—every so often—Korea or Vietnam,
and then end his show on an uplifting thank-you and a bit of pa-
triotic music. Like Vice President Dan Quayle, Pat Buchanan, Senator Phil Gramm, Defense Secretary Dick Cheney, House Minority
Whip Newt Gingrich, the Republican platoon of gung ho pro-

Vietnam warhawks, he himself had never served a day in the military.

Shanker, his black hair a molded wave above his photogenically empty face, was being asked about the federal deficit.

"For forty years the Democrats in Congress . . ." Boilerplate. When pressed about the fact that it was ten years of Republican administrations that racked up those trillions, he reiterated that the Congress was Democratic and it was their fault.

"I've balanced eight state budgets," Governor Bascomb claimed. The governor was distressed that Shanker had run an ad claiming that the state was in debt. Its only debts were issued bonds, all approved by voters. Did Mr. Shanker not understand that bonds were a form of debt used to finance everything from schools to dams to highways? How dare he take that figure and twist it to convince the good people of the state that we are verging on bankruptcy?

Senator Proctor laughed. "Go after him, Arnie!"

Shanker soon took to waving around a large xeroxed copy of a check—a check, he claimed, that was made out to Arnie Bascomb. ". . . money was raised in a *gay bar*. I understand this is a bar in which boys dress up as girls and dance around, and bodybuilder types dance around in their jockstraps. Ever been there, governor?"

Bascomb answered a muted no, eager to defend himself—

"Is this," Shanker asked, waving the graphic of the check, "the grass-root support you talk about? Perverts and 'drag-queens,' as they're called. Supporters of the hoe-moe-sexual agenda . . ."

Same tactic, Sam thought, that Phil Gramm—one of the least-liked senators ever to come to Washington—used on Lloyd Doggett weeks ago in Texas, to great success, naturally. Shanker spoke of the nationwide conspiracy of gay people with their putative anti-family, pro-pedophilia agenda and then segued into a set piece about how the state had been destroyed by one tax-and-spend liberal after another.

". . . it's time for a Republican who's a *real* Republican. Warren Proctor is a veteran of World War Two, and I honor his service, but he's *pro-abortion*. He voted for affirmative action. He has voted to increase taxes twelve times . . ."

"You pathetic man," Proctor barked at the set, "I've spent the last ten years trying to balance the budget!"

". . . and we need someone up there who won't stay forever, become part of the Washington elite, cutting deals with Democrats!"

Sam closed her eyes.

". . . and siding nine times out of ten with *environmentalists*."

"What is happening to our party?" mumbled Senator Proctor.

"Governor Bascomb and his tax-and-spend friends aren't the answer, any more than Proctor was. I'll vote how *you* think. I'm Frank Shanker." There was raucous applause; whoops from the gallery carried over the moderator's protests. "I can't help it," Shanker said, when asked to heel his imported mob, "if the people support my politics. Hey, Arnie, maybe you can get your hoe-moe-sexual supporters to come and cheer for you in debate number two!" More whoops and forced laughter.

"Samantha," an intern called out, "it's the Hot Line."

Every senator had one line in his phone bank used solely as a summons to floor votes. Sam picked up to hear the Republicans' automated voice announce that the senators had five minutes to get downstairs, ride the Senators' Subway to the Capitol, and vote on a resolution bill. Typical. When the recess neared, unfinished business backed up and votes were scheduled late into the night. The leadership was not above scheduling these bills at impossible times with full knowledge that some key no-votes were out of town or too old to be awake in the wee hours.

Warren Proctor was a very senior senator, and therefore was provided with a "hideaway," a high-ceilinged personal chamber in the Capitol itself.

"Well, that was a waste of time," Proctor groused as his keys opened the heavy door to his hideaway. The senators had convened in their chamber only to learn that the vote would be delayed for another hour of speeches concerning irrelevant riders and amendments. "Might as well have a drink," he further suggested.

Proctor didn't turn on the lights in his hideaway, preferring not to upstage the view. He poured Samantha a glass of the good stuff and sat behind his desk, facing the window. From this location in

the west porch, the senator and his guest looked out the tall un-
curtained window to see an unequaled view of the Mall, the Washington Monument, the Lincoln beyond that, and then Robert E.
Lee's neoclassical mansion in Virginia, seized during the Civil War
to bury the Union dead in his front yard—the start of Arlington
National Cemetery.

Samantha flopped into a sturdy, high–backed leather chair, probably contemporary with Henry Clay. Only a select few among the
staff ever saw this room, and even then not very often. She peered
into the shadows: a room of dark wood, lined from floor to ceiling
with books of history, first editions of Toynbee and Gibbon, beautifully bound texts of Xenophon and Tacitus, an eighteenth-century
globe once owned (the story went) by Benjamin Franklin.

"I'm gonna miss the office," he said.

"It'll be difficult not being a senator."

"Not my elected office, this physical office," he said, knocking
on his cleaned-out desk. "This view." They were momentarily rev-
erent, both realizing this corner of the American Capitol, of American history, would soon be lost to them forever; a mutual awe
overcame them that they had been allowed to tread this ground in
the first place.

"The Washington Monument," Senator Proctor remarked, lifting
his glass toward it, "was begun in 1833 and finished in 1888. A
perfect monument for this city: fifty years of delay and argument to
build something so architecturally simpleminded."

Sam sank into her chair, warmly lost in her scarf and raincoat.

"Henry James passed through town in—what was it?—1905, got
wined and dined by the White House. Teddy Roosevelt hated him
for being a Europeanized, sissified American who talked with a British accent; Henry Adams fawned on him for the same reason. James
looked down the Mall and called the monument a giant exclamation
mark with nothing preceding it." He chuckled. "I've never been
able to get that description out of my head." Then the senator
turned tentative. "Samantha, I don't know how you will feel about
something I did . . ."

Samantha didn't say anything.

He paused. "It's alas quite likely, says one of my pollsters back home, that Shanker's going to win the seat. His people have called me to put feelers out for a legislative director, since that moron has no political background whatsoever. . . ." He took a strategic sip from his whiskey. "I forwarded your résumé and gave you a glowing report."

"I'm not sure he'd want me any more than I'd want him, Senator."

"You'd be doing your duty. To yourself and your career. Maybe to your country."

She waited for an explanation.

"Samantha, I have an inkling Frank Shanker and his demagogues may be the inevitable future of this apathetic country. Republican party's being taken over by that sort. He'll surely do a lot of damage, but perhaps if you are here to bring out the best in his ideas, to stop the worst of them . . ."

Samantha marvelled: Warren was torn, imagining her more idealistic than she was, believing he had to convince her to take such a job! Her heart raced at news of this possible reprieve! Samantha had just that afternoon been mulling over her old, default ideas: grad school, maybe an M.F.A. program where she could work on her creative writing, or a Ph.D. on Wharton. She had bravely turned her face to the storm and was prepared to walk into it—but here, at the very last, was a way to cling to the life that she loved more than anything!

"There was a small part of me," the senator said, still somber, "that thought, somehow, even if I offered myself up for retirement that it wouldn't happen. That the folks back home wouldn't allow it, or the party would talk me out of it." The senator swivelled in his chair to face her in the dark. "That's what this job will do to you if you stay long enough, Samantha. It'll swell you up, make you forget that your real life is *not* in these halls."

Samantha tried out the title: Samantha Flint, l.d. for Senator Frank Shanker. Imagine, living that down. Imagine, actually having to pull for him to win on election night—

"Not only," said Proctor, "has the world kept turning since my announcement, but I'm already as irrelevant as these hallway portraits that no one ever looks at. I nod to my colleagues in the Marble Room and they look right through me."

Imagine telling Mimi who her new boss was. No, the last was unimaginable—she would keep it a secret until the grave!

"Ever been out to Wyoming? Sam?"

"Hm? I'm sorry?"

"Have you ever been out to Wyoming?"

"No, Senator, I'm terribly ill-traveled."

"Work for Frank Shanker, if you will, if he's got the sense to hire you," he advised. "But don't let this place become your life. Don't let yourself believe that getting a bill to the floor, or getting your way once it goes to committee, can substitute for . . . for life, the stuff of life. Marriage, children—or if that doesn't do it for a modern woman like you, an affair in a small hotel on the Left Bank, sailing through the Bosporus, moving to Australia and finishing that novel."

Sam took a moment. "I'm surprised you—"

"Oh yes, I remember. In your job interview, I asked what your real goal in life was and you said you were going to write the Great American Career Girl Novel, you told me. I wrote down the title . . ."

"*The Better Part*," she supplied.

"A marvelous title, from the Bible. A wonder that no other woman novelist has got to it."

Actually, Sam had in mind *The better part of valor is discretion*. Her heroine in Austenian fashion would be forced to suffer for such discretion, before her inevitable triumph. "The Bible . . ."

"Mary and Martha. Martha is in the kitchen fixing up a meal for Jesus and his flock, and Mary sits at Jesus' feet like the male disciples. When Martha criticizes Mary for not sharing in the housekeeping, the Lord says, 'She has taken the better part and it shall not be taken from her.' Proving our Lord was for equal opportunity. *The Better Part*. That's why I hired you."

"So I could have been pecking away at my novel during office hours when I was supposed to be working for you?"

"My dear, I kept hope that you *were*! I'd hate to think your gift with English has been limited to position papers for some footnote named Warren Proctor."

She found tears swelling in her eyes. "You're at least a whole page, Senator."

"Put me in the only page that counts. Put me in one of your novels. If you need an old geezer, that is. Come out to Wyoming with your typewriter, Samantha. Maude will put you in the guest house and I can write my memoirs in the ranch house—two great works of *fiction*," he chuckled. "We can meet for dinnertime, compare creative ordeals and sore wrists."

In the months that followed, Samantha would think back on this evening with fondness, sadness . . . and a regretful wonder that, this once, she hadn't taken his advice.

"You're gonna be proud of me now!" Senator Shanker boomed.

Mort, the chief of staff, followed two steps behind with his notebook. "The senator kicked some butt down there," Mort prompted as if the office were posed to hip-hip-hooray.

Samantha sat in her cubicle eating from a tub of butterscotch pudding and a bag of Fritos. Couldn't the man go unattended for one lousy hour while she had her lunch? "What'd you do now, Senator?"

What he had done was show up for a photo opportunity on the Capitol steps with some House Republicans protesting all the pork in the Budget Resolution Bill.

"You didn't . . . you—"

"The press was all over him," said Mort. "I think it was a real coup—since he was the only senator there!"

"Of course, he was the only senator there. The House is full of *weenies*, Frank. Every other day they're doing some silly stunt on the steps of the Capitol. Was this the ethanol protest?"

Yes it was. To raise a stink about all the corporate giveaways and subsidies for ethanol producers in the current budget, some House members (bought and paid for by Big Oil interests) had rigged up a cartoonish fiberglass pigmobile that ran on ethanol. While the pig, chugging and sputtering, wheezed round and round in front of the Capitol, the Republicans matched it with their own blasts of rhetoric.

"For heaven's sake," Sam cried, "at least tell me you didn't actually get on and *ride* the motorized pig."

He looked momentarily panicked. "Well, I, you know, stood sort of near it . . ."

Mort: "People hate government waste! We want Frank way out in front of this."

Samantha followed the senator into his suite. "Am I wrong, or did you tell leadership you were backing the Ethanol Provision?"

"Well, that was before I found out what was in it."

"What is in it is what was always in it, Frank." Samantha used his first name when she tried to get through the wall of his radio-show personality. "You can't just tell leadership you're going to vote one way and then vote another. This is ethanol, Senator, Bob Dole's lifeblood—he's *preserved* in it. Ever heard of Archers Daniels Midland?"

"Sam," Wanda interrupted, "it's Sheila from Dole's office. She says call her back immediately."

Samantha winced at Frank coldly and said with whisper-quiet intensity, "Are you happy now? The minority leader wants to know why you dicked him over."

Mort: "It's your job, Sam, to keep the senator from this kind of tit-for-tat stuff."

The senator faltered, "I don't want Bob Dole mad at me—"

"That's what you've got." Then Samantha explained in as level a tone as she could manage: "As a veteran staffer, I have to ask you to please listen to this: a senator frozen out at staff level is *dead* in the Senate. If they can't depend on you to do what you say you'll do, then they won't deal with you. That means no airports, no highways, no bills with your name on it—*nothing*. This building is full of senators who crossed Byrd or Dole or Mitchell and have been powerless for *years*."

The next day, Samantha got another angry call from a l.d. from the office of Senator Kassebaum. "Yes," said Samantha, frowning as she listened. "That's right . . . I'll have a word with him. Yes, he's new and . . . Okay, I'll get right on it."

Samantha went to Frank's office and knocked lightly, entering in the midst of a meeting: Mort with his notebook and Young Republicans 1 and 2—confusingly, one was Don, one was Dan. "Senator," Samantha began, "I got a call from Kassebaum's office. Did you make some kind of statement about health insurance reform?"

"Well, yes, as a matter of fact. I called in and talked to Rush."

Shanker's newest venture was making regular calls to the Limbaugh show, during which he insulted his fellow senators, affirmed to the country that Washington was inimical and incompetent and had no legitimate function—not to mention joining with Rush in his usual potshots at women and blacks. Shanker's incoming staff beatified Limbaugh, blaring his broadcast daily.

". . . and I just told the country," Shanker explained, "that I was fixing to introduce a bill that helped people keep their insurance when they changed jobs, and that I couldn't get my fellow Republicans interested."

Young Republican 2: "Our polling shows health care is a big issue in the state. We want it to work for the senator."

Samantha crossed her arms. "There's *already* a bill like that, sponsored by Nancy Kassebaum, in *your own* party. It's called 'portability.' You can't steal the idea of a senator who's been working on this for years, then turn around and insult them too."

Frank picked up a nerf basketball and flung it toward a plastic net attached to a bookshelf. "Well, damn it, I can say what I want! What I think is best for the people back home."

"Frank, you're not a *player* on health care. You don't sit on Finance, on Appropriations, on Health, you're not on *any* committee to do with health care. Now you can keep making public statements all you want, but you can also get shut down for your six years—"

Young Republican 2: "Six years? Frank's gonna be around eighteen, twenty-four years! Least, uh, that's what I think."

Shanker speculated giddily: "Can you imagine me, still here when I'm an old crank like Proctor?"

"I thought," Samantha said, "you were for term limits."

Mort solved this dilemma by predicting Frank would be president one day. "Sam, all this is *process*. You're killing us with process."

"Why in god's name did you hire me if you don't want my expertise?"

"Any other complaints, Sammie dear?" The senator threw up his hands in mock despair, 1 and 2 chortled condescendingly. Samantha looked around the office: Frank Shanker, throwing a Nerf basketball through the little play hoop, unconcerned. Young Republican 1 rereading his notes, waiting for the girl to have her say and get out; Young Republican 2 waiting for Frank to say something to agree with fulsomely. Mort, Shanker's crude campaign manager turned nincompoop chief of staff, impatient with the ways of Washington, preferring that his senator become a showboating jerk marginalized to the dank corners of the Dirksen Building.

For the third night that week, Samantha couldn't sleep, tossing and trying to get comfortable in the bed, reliving tirades she should have delivered to her boss's face. She cursed, hopped up, and started a town house–wide search for some prescribed painkillers she had saved after a root canal last year. She wasn't in pain, but she knew the Tylenol IV with codeine would knock her out and allow her to rest more than the three or four hours she was getting each night. As she tore through an overnight bag where the pills might have been, she swore to herself: no more ten cups of coffee all day, no cigarettes after 11:00 P.M., no drinking with Julie until 1:00 A.M. and then getting home and being adrenalinized by watching CNN until dawn.

She found the pills, hesitated a moment, then took two.

"This is a bad thing," she said aloud to her apartment.

She then sat at her word processor and started a new file. *I hereby resign my position as legislative director immediately*, she typed. *You are the asshole of the Western World, Frank Shanker*, she added before deleting the line. She polished the simple paragraph until she felt a wave of drowsiness surge through her body, and at last fell into bed ready to sleep.

A month and many Shanker missteps later, Samantha had the resignation in her top desk drawer, ready for use when she'd reached her breaking point. But when the senator committed the most prominent of his public idiocies Samantha was surprised to learn her breaking point wasn't *quite* yet.

Shanker phoned in to a local Utah right-wing radio show and tossed the mob some insulting scrap about PBS being the "network for nerds and fags"—words he swore he didn't use, until Nina Totenberg on NPR produced a tape. Press releases and clarifications proliferated until finally Senator Shanker appeared before a network news camera and apologized for any offense taken.

"So Sammie." The senator began their Monday meeting with Mort in attendance. "This PBS thing is killing me. Little kids are sending me drawings of Big Bird, begging me not to kill him off."

"Frank," Sam began tersely. "Your going on these kooky radio shows has got to to end. You're here to be a senator, not a radio act."

"We understand that, Sam," Mort said, patting the sitting senator's shoulder. "We've cut way back on our future commitments on radio. The correspondence people tell me this is our number one letters-against issue, this PBS thing. We need something going for us, something to make us look human to the moderates." He grinned. "What we need from you is some kind of arts-friendly, touchy-feely p.r. thing. Something that doesn't cost anything."

Sam just sat there a moment. Was this a setup? Were they that clever? "Um, well . . ."

They were all ears.

"Senator Proctor had this plan that never made it to the floor," she said, arranging her thoughts unsurely, "through the Library of Congress, which is funded out of D.C., so it's a committee Frank is on." Yeah, with every other loser and outcast of the Senate; the District of Columbia Committee is a dumping ground for legislators with time on their hands. "The Library choses writers, historians, and poets to be writers-in-residence, to live on government property that's not being used. . . ."

Mort: "But does it cost—"

"It doesn't cost anything. The government already pays for upkeep on these properties, that's the trick of it."

And she pitched her plan. The Samantha Bill.

And they liked it. That would teach 'em to say ol' Frank Shanker is anti-art, wouldn't it?

Samantha gathered up her things, still dazed from her plan's sudden resurrection in Shanker's office. She'd have to revisit the Library of Congress, reinitiate contact with Hazel, whom she'd been afraid to talk to since she took up with Shanker. Meanwhile, various male staffers, ties loosened, were watching basketball on little TVs in their office cubicles:

"Fuckin' A!"

"Bullshit, man!"

"That is fucked!"

This family-values crowd sure can cuss; Proctor would have fired them in no time. Proctor had had a personal staff of twenty competent people. Shanker had a staff of forty–five incompetent people, many working for free, many just hanging out and getting in the way, playing at being Ehrlichman and Haldeman, spying liberal conspiracies behind moderate compromise bills that should have received their boss's automatic support, giving Frank bunker-mentality advice from the trenches.

"Hey, um, I'm sorry . . ."

The young male staffer had forgotten her name. "Samantha."

"Yeah, Samantha, do you have change for a five, for the drink machine?"

"Ask Wanda," Sam said, perfectly able to make the change but preferring to cast him into the lair of the black receptionist.

Wanda was a fearsome fixture in the office, a holdover from Proctor days. The outgoing staff, amid many spontaneous tearful episodes and hugs, hesitated to propose that Wanda refuse to work for Senator-elect Shanker, who had won the election by exploiting every racially divisive issue.

"*You're* staying on," Wanda said, not looking up from her morning bear claw, "why shouldn't I?"

Sam despaired of ever having a substantive conversation with the woman.

Samantha sickened to notice, soon after the swearing-in of 1991,

Shanker's staff began to accrete with rich volunteer envelope-stuffers, snotty white kids of contributors, fratboys who guffawed and high-fived and celebrated every Democratic setback.

"They're fucking *screwed*, man!"

"Did you see that fuckin' old fart Metzenbaum?"

Shanker's troops were overgrown boys in their early twenties with little experience of life, but very many opinions, savage and heartless ones if you happened to be nonwhite, nonmale, nonstraight or non-wealthy. Taking their cue from Rush, they knew the main fact about feminists ("femi-nazis") was that they were ugly. Gays wanted the right not to be fired because of their private life which constituted "shoving their lifestyle down our throats." Black children in D.C. with crack mothers and absent fathers, growing up surrounded by hopelessness and gangs, attending violent inferior schools should just, by golly, get up off their keysters and pitch in (at the McDonald's, say for $4.25 an hour) and walk away from the thousands that could be made by selling drugs to white people (you know, the people who have good lawyers and never do time), and, durn it, stop going on about racism which doesn't exist hardly at all anymore anyway.

The baby-faced intern in a light-blue Sunday suit (favored in the rural districts of the home state) approached Wanda. "Could you, uh, you, change this five?"

Wanda: "It's after four."

"After four."

"That's when the banks close in the District. Four o'clock. And you obviously think I'm a bank."

"Well, no, it's just—"

"Do I look like a bank to you?"

"No, but—"

"Is there a sign on me *saying* that I am a bank?"

And so began the hail of unanswerable questions. ("Is this a blinkin' sign or one of those bank signs that goes round and round, stickin' out of my head?") If she were really exercised she would raise her bulk to her feet, leaning forward on her sturdy arms to create a titanic visage.

After the kid retreated, Wanda turned to Samantha. "Call for you," Wanda said calmly handing Sam a message.

Mimi had phoned. She was flying to Europe and her flight had been rerouted through Dulles, where she had a layover. Any chance in the middle of a workday, in the middle of a crowded Senate session, that Samantha could just drop everything and drive forty miles out to Dulles in the snow to glimpse Mimi for a few minutes?

The traffic did not cooperate. Just getting to the Potomac from east of Capitol Hill was impossible. Goddamn L'Enfant. Who thought it was a good idea to let some eighteenth-century Frenchman design this town like an overgrown lace doily, monumental circles and diagonals colliding in nightmare twelve-point intersections? Well, George Washington, but that's no excuse. She remembered somewhere reading that the father of our country fired L'Enfant eventually, for being too baroque. Not before the damage was done, George.

After crossing the river, she hit an impossible tangle trying to get north on the George Washington Parkway to connect to I-66—a four-lane maintained by the National Park Service with discreet, miniature park signs rather than the huge informative green highway signs that Sam needed in order to prevent a wrong turn at the Memorial Bridge Circle . . . which she indeed made, sending her *back* across the Potomac to the Lincoln Memorial for another D.C. escape attempt.

Samantha hit the wheel in anger, thoroughly out of sorts, soon to be late for their airport get-together.

The intermittent snow flurries grew into a squall of wind-driven white, slowing all the Southerners who, despite years of practice, couldn't manage more than five MPH in winter conditions. The more Samantha had time to think, the more she wanted to get off the freeway and abandon this command performance.

Samantha was at her all-time fat weight. The past few months of nightly drinks with the old gang (who all had found better jobs with decent senators), the junk-food lunches, the stress of working for Shanker, the skipping the gym (Julie had secured a job in Senator

Cooper's office and their exercise schedule was kaput)—all contributed to the recent ballooning. Mimi looks more like a movie star every passing year, Sam reflected, while I revert to Missouri peasant stock.

And then there was the political rub.

Samantha had mentioned lightly to Mimi that she was "helping in the transition," from Proctor to Shanker. Just the mention of Frank Shanker—whose national notoriety had mushroomed with every new offense—occasioned a twenty-minute blast from Mimi. Mimi was an East Coast Democrat who could tolerate the thought of Proctor, one of a small list of Republicans who carried on the Rockefeller tradition of progressive, pro-business policies with religious and moral issues left at the country club door. Mimi was now a certified "Hollywood liberal," who helped plan Dukakis fundraisers for her CAA bosses, who gave money to women's political action committees. Imagine Mimi's wrath, Sam contemplated, when she discovers the full extent of my involvement with Shanker.

Well, the job with Frank was just temporary, of course.

Any day now another l.d. position would open up and, bang, she'd be out of there. Any day now.

Sam had proposed to Mimi that they meet at the Rumor Mill, the bar by the international check-in. Front and center at a high cocktail table was Mimi. Sam took a moment to study her friend the fashion plate, slim, stylish, her slender fingers wrapped around a martini glass, eating the olive on the end of the swivel stick. Sam observed that the businessmen nearby were eyeing Mimi, appraising her backside, ignoring the hockey game on ESPN. She was poured into a simple black Armani dress; her hair was a reddish-brown now, shoulder-length and upturned. Samantha felt a chasm open between herself and Mimi's glamour, Mimi's ever-improving beauty.

"Mimi," she announced herself.

"Samantha!" Mimi hugged her lightly, kissed her cheek airily, then stepped back to survey Sam, and praise her unchanging youth—all sincerely meant, though Samantha wasn't inclined to believe it.

Two more martinis were ordered and the small talk commenced: Mimi's travails as a CAA executive assistant, Mimi's Madonna and Michael Jackson sightings, Mimi's purchase of her new handbag, Mimi's boredom due to her first-class companion . . . Not unaware that Mimi hadn't quite managed to ask about *her* life, Sam nevertheless played along, listlessly asking about celebrities—

"Yeah yeah," Mimi waved it aside, "they're all shorter or not as good looking—all the guys have big heads on little bodies—or they're gayer-acting than you thought they'd be."

"Really."

"Yeah. Anyway, speaking of big-time clients, the pressure's on now that I'm working for Brillstein. Remember, how I told you a few weeks ago—"

"The last time we really talked was Christmas."

"Oh jeez. Then you're not up to speed on me and the boss from hell. Neuroses up the yin-yang—no wonder nothing ever gets done without someone holding his hand . . ." From Sam's expression, Mimi knew something was wrong. "What?"

Sam couldn't speak.

"What . . . Did I say something that . . ."

Mimi trailed off and Sam contemplated speaking further, or perhaps, turning for the exit. A tense half-minute passed.

"I work in this fabulous city for six years."

Mimi waited.

"I worked for one of the most powerful men up here, Warren Proctor, who with a phone call could get us any reservation in town. Drinks with Ted Kennedy, a White House reception with George and Barbara, a private tour with the head of the fucking National Art Gallery. I could take you to the Palm and introduce you to any of your Democratic heroes as they came in. I'm actually a player, Mimi—no, wait, *was* a player. It's all gone now. Proctor is in private life and I'm in Outer Mongolia. My power and influence gone, all gone.

"And you decide, *now*, at my lowest ebb, when I'm twenty pounds overweight and taking pills to get to sleep and drinking too much and generally hating this phase of my life, now, *now*—not the fucking glory years, not when Samantha Flint was Somebody—*now* you decide, 'Let's visit my ol' pal Samantha.' And not even a real visit, mind you. Not a full stop—just a goddam drink at an airport. Sam's a sport, right? Let her drive two hours in Beltway traffic in a blizzard so I can bestow—whatcha got for us today?—twenty minutes? Long enough for Miz Showbiz to tell a few Hollywood stories, flash a few bills, and breeze on to Europe. I mean, screw you and the 747 first-class sky lounge you rode in on."

Mimi, shaken, set her drink down and played a moment with the cocktail stirrer. Then Mimi's face almost seemed to break, her eyes blinked back emotion. The sight of the unflappable Mimi in distress got to Samantha as well.

"I'm sorry," Mimi said. "I didn't know Proctor's retirement was such a setback. But you never told me about any of this—"

"Who can get you on the phone? I leave a thousand messages."

"Sweetheart, I always intend to call you, but I'm in this West Coast time warp—by the time I come back from dinner it's eleven, which is two in the morning here." Mimi eyed the waiter desolately, and tapped their glasses for another drink. Then she put a hand on Samantha's arm. "Not that I've misrepresented myself, but you've got to surely know I'm just . . . a glorified gofer. Michael Eisner gives me a smile, but I'm nowhere careerwise. Sam, you're my role model."

"Oh please—"

"*You've* made it in the world," Mimi insisted. "All my big talk and I'm still cranking out marketing proposals and p.r. copy like I did in New York. Not to mention: 'Would you like your coffee with two Sweet 'N Lows, Mr. Brillstein?' That's *my* fucking life." Mimi grasped at the sleeve of Samantha's wool coat. "The thought that you were knocking 'em dead in Washington, rubbing shoulders with the big boys—that's what keeps me going."

The drinks arrived and Sam clutched hers.

"If, Sam, I took your success for granted, it was because I was comforted by it. If Sam can stick to her game plan, I'd tell myself, then so can I."

Sam sipped the martini and felt it burn her mouth. She had

waited her whole friendship with Mimi to hear words like that. "I'm sorry I flew off the handle."

"I'm such a selfish pig, you have to put a stopper in my goddamn mouth or I'd talk about myself for years—"

"I just miss your tirades and your . . ."

"I miss you too."

". . . all that excitement, Mimi. Your conspiracy theories, what you're thinking and reading. Washington is wonderful but it is a self-obsessed city—"

"Oh, sweetheart, try Hollywood!"

Mimi put her drink down and gave Samantha an ardent hug, burying her face in the damp wool coat. Samantha closed her eyes and allowed herself to be held tight. Mimi's perfume, by the way, was fabulous. Carolina Herrera, $85 an ounce. Samantha, through the clothes, could also tell that her friend was remarkably in shape. "You've been working out," Sam said.

"Discount gym membership comes with the agency," said Mimi, recovering her equanimity, weakly smiling.

"Is that Armani?"

"Yeah, well I—"

"Comes with the agency?"

Mimi laughed. "I got this in 1988, Saks after-Christmas sale, eight hundred dollars—best buy I ever made. Oh Sam, you can't believe the Hollywood overhead, keeping up appearances, trying to act like I belong in the power-lunch set."

"Meem," Sam said, putting a hand on her shoulder, "if anyone in this world can shmooze her way into the upper echelons, it's you. But I've always wondered . . ." She wasn't sure how to put it. "I just never thought you cared about all that stuff. I mean, have you ever watched TV in your life?"

Mimi beamed. "The entertainment industry is front-loaded. If we record it and promote it, they will buy. If we film it and the marketing and distribution is right, they will come. It has next to nothing to do with what people *need*, nothing to do with my personal likes and dislikes. Or high quality. It's a giant Pavlov experiment," she averred. "We ring the bell, they salivate."

They retreated to an inner, darker table in the confines of the airport bar. By their third drink, the women had become animated and voluble and close to slurring with the momentum of familiarity. Things came up that had gone unaddressed for years.

Samantha wondered openly, "I might be an alcoholic."

"When you can drink gallons," Mimi postulated, "and you *don't* gain weight anymore, then you're metabolizing differently and you're an alcoholic. That's my rule. I drink at a cocktail party and it all goes to my thighs and calves. The curse of the Jewish calves . . ."

"I just wonder sometimes."

"Sam, can you go a day and *not* drink?"

"Yeah, often. But then the weekend comes and it's just party following dinner following boozy brunch. I have this little secret cache of tranquilizers to help me sleep, which I don't take every night, but when the stress gets too much, I'll use them. And every once in awhile when I'm facing a seventy-two-hour day—like when a bill's coming up? I'll do what I did at Smith and take a tablet of speed, or swallow a few No-Doz with coffee."

"Poo, I've done all that, sort of," Mimi shrugged.

"But I can never come down after a big project goes through. In order to get all that adrenaline out of my system, I *have* to drink."

Mimi: "Ever drink by yourself, alone in your apartment?"

"Never."

"You're not an alcoholic," Mimi said, wiping the topic away with a head toss. "I've been doing some self-examination too. I'm beginning to think I'll never be in love."

"I thought you'd been in love. That Gregory guy, the artist."

"Nyeh. I'm always still detached, like I'm watching the relationship unfold in a movie."

"You think too much," Sam nodded, sophisticated with drink. "Guy A is a good match, he likes art and goes to galleries. Guy B is rich and emotionally stable, and goes to Christie's auctions. Meem, all your men are planned out and logical. You need to fall heels—head over hells about a . . . about the, you know, like a maintenance man in your office building."

"You know that gene other women have that allow them to fall in love with maintenance men and janitors and utter deadbeats? I don't have it."

"Not even driven by lust?"

"I'm immune to a guy whose only credential is good looks. Gorgeous eyes, great hair, tight abs, developed arms, flawless tan, big dick—they still gotta get by that sign over the Meem's bedroom door: WHAT ELSE YOU GOT?"

Samantha threw her head back and laughed.

"Good looks gets you through the front door, but not through the bedroom door. A man's got to have something going on in his life—that's why I ended up sleeping with so many of my bosses. God, that was bad news! But they had authority. They had plans and ideas, dreams, Sam—I wanted to hear everything they had to say, and I thought the bedroom was the place to do it." She sipped from her martini. "Shit, this is like water now. Anyway, I thought, just recently, I'd found True Love. This man had so much going for him—the perfect guy, on paper."

"So?" Samantha encouraged.

"So I went and did . . ."

"What?"

Mimi peered at Sam with some anxiety.

"What'd you do?"

"I'm just . . ."

"What?"

"I can only tell *you* this," Mimi said, turning away, sort of smiling, then becoming weak in the eyes. Mimi was too direct and undramatic to play out a revelation for mere suspense; she was honestly weighing the effect of her secret.

"You don't *have* to tell me." Sam tried reverse psychology.

"I . . ." Then Mimi started drunkenly giggling. "I can't tell you."

"If I guess it, you'll tell me?" Samantha tried her own vice: "You were a homewrecker."

"Like I'd get upset over doing a married man!"

"You . . . you got arrested?" Nope. "You killed someone, or took out a contract on someone—"

"Nothing like that." Mimi took a deep breath. "I got married."

Samantha was suitably stunned. "You . . ."

"And divorced. All within a month. Started regretting it five minutes after the 'I do' in Las Vegas."

Sam, smiling with her eyes, remained open-mouthed.

"Get that look off your face!" Mimi buried her own in the crook of her arm.

"You?" Sam stammered. "Of all people? Why you were the one who—wait, what'd your family think?"

"You kidding? I knew it was a mistake so soon that I decided never to tell them, and sure enough, Jeffrey was gone before it became an issue."

Before Sam could repeat the ex's name—

"Jeffrey Speier. Head of marketing and publicity for Spartan Pictures, a tiny independent but it makes money. CAA client."

"What was wrong?"

"Not a thing. Soap-star looks, thirty-six, drop-dead hunk-gorgeous, self-made wealthy, up-and-coming. He adored me."

Samantha waited.

"Hard to say why I folded and said I'd marry him . . . You know what it was? He was perfect, and I figured, hell, Meem, you'll never get this combo of goods together in one man ever again. He didn't want children, neither did I. We liked sex, particularly with each other. He had ambitions to run a major studio, and I wanted to run a major agency—I mean, we were set to be the Hollywood Power Couple of the 2010s . . . or whatever that decade will be called. I let that fantasy totally suck me in."

"Maybe you should have given it a chance."

"No ma'am. I knew as soon as we got back from Vegas. We had let a few dirty weekends get out of hand. We got back to his house in Pacific Pallisades and he said, 'Well Mimi, I suppose we ought to see about moving you in . . .' and then my blood ran cold. You mean I can't have my own house? Continue to run my own life? Have affairs as it suits me? Hold it!"

Sam shrugged. "Maybe you could have worked out a deal along those lines—"

"You might want to talk having an open marriage after years together when the passion dies, but not," she began to cackle hysterically, "but not the first week of your marriage!"

"The first day, it sounds like!"

Samantha and Mimi doubled over shrieking, turning heads in the airport lounge.

"I wasn't going to even tell you, I was so embarrassed. How humiliating. You hear about Hollywood showpeople-antics like that. Well, Jeffrey and I split in a month. It lasted until the first weekend we could both fly off to Vegas for the divorce. Very civilized. No lawyers, no trying to take each other's VCRs."

"What about the children?" Samantha joked.

"Despite your Republican friends," Mimi said, gazing at a far wall, "there's still the right to an abortion in this country."

That wasn't funny.

"Yeah, I got pregnant," Mimi elaborated slowly, not intending perhaps to share this either, "just to make the whole experience even more joyous. I found out three weeks after the divorce, and . . ."

Samantha read her mind. "You didn't tell Jeffrey about it."

"Right," she concurred quietly. "It would have been a gorgeous kid, I'll tell you that much." Mimi stirred her drink pointlessly. "I did it for the same reason I canned the marriage. It's not *time*. I'm incredibly behind schedule as it is. I gave myself until thirty to be established at whatever I was doing, and I'm still screwing around."

Samantha considered all the drama that must have played out in the last few months: Mimi's indomitable will to retain her sovereignty, the crushed romantic hopes, and somewhere a guy named Jeffrey who didn't know what hit him.

"Besides," said Mimi, "it occurred to me if I got famous it would only be 'because she was Jeffrey Speier's wife.' People would be whispering that he gave me my career to play with like a toy. I figured, no way."

"Well," Sam commenced, "speaking of marriage—while we're confessing—I'm going out with a married man."

"Is it serious?"

"Nothing I do is serious," she said dramatically. She began to list her flings before the four married men, trying to paint a bleak picture: ". . . and there was an intern in William Roth's office, a young Republican type you'd have hated. And there was a thing with a nongovernment guy I met in a bar last June, who cleaned pools. And then a few affairs with married men—"

"A very profound question, Samantha." Mimi wagged her finger tipsily. "Have you *ever*, in all your adventures, ever had a lover who was your intellectual equal?"

"Yeah, sure. David—"

"*Ppppfflllbst.* He was *not* your equal."

"I guess not."

"Why do you think that is? Why the dumber, lower-class men? Or the married men who can only get so close?"

Now Samanatha looked in her empty glass, stirring the melted ice. "Who wants to be rejected by . . . by someone good?"

Mimi lowered her voice, snuggling in female solidarity. "Sam? Can you believe I've never had a one-night stand?"

"Yeah, I can believe that." There was nothing Mimi could gain from a one-night stand; she wouldn't find the elements of danger or novelty worth the effort. She was a deliberate woman who belonged in a war room, a boardroom, not in a motel room throwing control to the wind.

"Hell," Mimi said, their good spirits returning, "aren't we at least *interesting*? We might belong on a therapist's couch for the rest of our screwed-up lives, but aren't we interesting?"

Sam: "Can you imagine one of us having to visit the other one of us in, like, the suburbs and put up with each other's shitty husbands and crummy kids—"

"Oh god. Don't ever make me be an *Aunt Mimi*. 'Children,' " Mimi did an imitation of the married Samantha, " 'this is your Aunt Mimi and she's got a present for you—' "

"Never happen! No kids! I don't want to bring kids up in a world where men like my boss can be elected . . ."

Oops.

"Oh Sammie . . . don't, don't cry—what?"

Samantha suppressed a sob deep in her throat, which the next second drunkenly veered into a laugh. "It would almost be funny . . ."

Mimi prompted, dejectedly, "I told you about the marriage."

"You know how I was going to work during the transition of Proctor to Frank Shanker?"

"One of the great assholes of the Republican party."

"Yes well, I said . . ." She made meaningless hand gestures. "I said, okay, I don't wanna, but—"

"You're working full-time for Shanker?"

Now Samantha was weepy again and her lip trembled, and she raised her hands to pull at her hair. "There was not one other goddam job in the whole fucking Senate that paid me . . . I mean, it wasn't really the money—but the power that I had, I had to . . ."

Mimi had put a hand on Sam's face and raised her head so they could look in each other's eyes. "Sweetheart, it's all right."

"It's all right?"

"You do what you have to do. When a space opens up in John Chaffee's office one day, you'll take it. Until then you do what you have to do. You think I don't have to work for some shits out in Hollywood? Don Simpson told me to go get him some coke or he'd fire me. Joel Silver, Barry Josephson? I can tellya some stories. You have to eat a lot of crap until you get some real power. I know that better'n anybody in the whole world."

Samantha unsurely walked Mimi to the ticket check-in, bracing herself along the handrail with one hand, carrying her last martini with the other. Mimi, still grasping hers, said, "See? You're not an alcoholic. Otherwise those six drinks wouldn't have hit us like . . ."

"Like six drinks." Samantha took her friend's arm. "You're so lucky, Mimi, getting to go to, like, Germany."

"Oh please, I picked the short straw back in L.A. We're entering Wolfgang Wurzberger's art house film in the Berlin festival, then Venice—"

"*Venice?* You're going to Venice?"

Mimi slowed. "I'm only gonna deal with Venice by . . . by phone."

"Now you're just saying that."

"*No*," Mimi thrust a fist in no particular direction. "I won't go to Venice until you're with me, sweetheart—that's a promise." Sam was scooped up in Mimi's arms, and hugged crushingly, which sloshed the martini to the floor. "Let's start doing a daily phone call," Mimi pleaded. "I need this . . ." She made a drunken back-and-forth gesture between them. "I need this every day."

"Ma'am," said the stewardess gently, "you can't board with that glass."

Mimi nodded and toasted her martini toward Sam. "To," she suddenly remembered, "our Dark Vision of the World."

Clink. "To our Dark Vision of the World."

Samantha's buzzer sounded. It was Julie, calling from Cooper's office. She could barely contain herself: "I think I've got a way out of Frank's cesspool! Amelia, our l.d.? Well, she's going on maternity leave for six months. And Coop needs someone to take her place."

"But in six months, Julie, I'd be out of a job again—"

"No. You're so good, you could draw up a few bills with Cooper's name all over them, and end up being a full-time replacement. He's desperate to look like he's doing something."

But Samantha didn't jump at it.

"Besides," Julie assured her, "Amelia's having twins and I don't think she's coming back, no matter what she says. It's not like she's any good."

Samantha had to say something. "Julie, that's great. I don't know what to tell you—"

"Say I can march right into Coop's office and tell him you're interested."

"Let me get back to you Monday with an official answer."

Samantha knew Julie expected her to seize the opportunity, despite an inevitable salary cut. It would mean they would be working together again. It would mean escaping the madhouse with Mort and the Young Republicans and Angeline, the newest terror of the Shanker crew. Angeline, just now rounding the corner to linger in front of Sam's desk. "Lemme call you back."

Angeline Bunche made her way into Samantha's cubicle with a pad of expensive bond stationery. "I know you're going on vacation, Sam, but I wondered if we could schedule a time to talk?"

"No," Sam said, turning back to her computer screen.

Angeline was twenty–four, shapely in a turtleneck and tight black slacks, with a head of long ink-black hair that she tossed and shimmied and twirled with her scarily manicured fingers with four-inch painted fingernails. Put a flower in her hand and she could pass for Cher circa 1969 without further costuming.

"I want to discuss a bill that's real important to the senator."

"If the senator wants me," Samantha began crisply, never taking her eyes off the computer screen (which unknown to Angeline, displayed the game of solitaire Sam had been wasting the morning with), "then the senator can come talk to me, I'm very busy."

"Samantha," she tsk-tsked, "I wish we could be friends."

"I wish you could go back where you came from and leave the running of Frank's agenda to me."

"You know, I'm hearing . . . I'm hearing hostility here, am I wrong? I think you have an *issue* with my being here, and you're not letting me play my part in Frank's mission."

"Oh you're playing a part, all right. It's called Bimbo Attached to the Philandering Senator. I wish it wasn't a speaking part."

Angeline, hurt and frustrated, stormed away. Samantha immediately reached for her phone. "Mort, can I see you a minute?"

Momentarily, Mort appeared and took a chair beside her.

"I know we don't work together as a rule," Sam began.

"We both do what's best for Frank, Samantha—"

"You intrigue against me, you pour poison into Frank's ear—"

"Samantha, I assure you—"

She held up her hand for him to stop. "I don't care if you don't like me. I have worked with lots of people I haven't liked. But we have a common enemy."

"Angeline."

"Tell me what you know."

Mort took off his thick glasses and wiped them with a tissue. Mort could look downright hobo-like: the almost bald head with uncontrollable patches of side hair, the tie that always went crooked, the five o'clock shadow that arrived by noon, the sharply pressed suit that by lunchtime was a mass of wrinkles, most of all, his expression of constipation and ongoing worry. "She showed up during the campaign. She got in the way of all the operatives. Somehow she got to be in charge for a few weeks, approving press releases and TV ads. We'd send something to Frank for his approval, her handwriting was on what came back. Only when I threatened to quit as campaign manager did she disappear."

"And now she's returned. Frank's screwing her, right?"

"I'm not comfortable talking about the senator . . ."

"Is he screwing her?"

"She went to Yale," he added, as if that meant anything.

"Do I have to tell you how it would look if 'Family Frank' Shanker got caught in a Gary Hart? Wayne Hays had an office down the hall—heard of him? Wilbur Mills?"

"I've already had a word with Frank. It probably won't do any good for me to keep needling him. Maybe if you have a word—"

"No way. I'm off for the Memorial Day recess next week and I'll be in the sun in Florida. This is *your* baby, Mort. And when I get back, Angeline better not be on staff. Mistress on the payroll? Do I have to write the tabloid headline for you?"

All Samantha wished to do on the weeklong recess between May and June was to get her Florida visit to her father and mother out of the way for the year. She had that morning purchased a pint of Jack Daniel's for the flight (since flying made her nervous), and if it didn't get consumed at 35,000 it would no doubt come in handy once she started dealing with her mother at sea level. The secret cache of tranquilizers was coming to Florida too.

Friday, her last afternoon in the office, Sam sneaked out early with Julie to go to a bookstore for the first time in ages, allowing herself a slow browse in the fiction aisles, imagining that as dull as her family was, there would be time to escape into a worthy novel.

"I hear this is good," Julie announced, brandishing some romance twaddle Samantha had no intention of reading. Future novelist Samantha Flint's own comedy of manners, *The Better Part*, wasn't so conceptually dead that it couldn't use a little inspiration from Edith Wharton or Anita Brookner—

Her beeper went off.

Sam looked at it: 911 ASAP, the standard SOS in beeper-speak. "Figures," she told Julie, abandoning the search, "Frank's probably shit his pants again. Gotta go change the baby."

When Samantha got back to the Dirksen Building office, Frank was nowhere to be seen. On Friday afternoons, the Senate not in session, things tended to be low-key anyway, but the office was desolate. Wanda's lunch was half-finished at her abandoned desk. Samantha stepped back outside the door and saw a notice saying that Senator Shanker would be unavailable for comment, and would not have office hours until next week—and that donations could be made to a charitable memorial fund.

Who died?

Samantha spotted Wanda in the hallway, returning from the ladies' lounge, dabbing at her face. "I thought you were gone on your vacation, Samantha."

"I fly out tomorrow morning. What happened?"

"The senator's second-oldest boy, Ronnie. Died up at his school."

Samantha registered the news. An equal marvel was the untouchable Wanda so extravagantly moved.

"How did he . . ."

"Some kinda accident, I'm not sure."

How do teenage boys die? A car accident, drug overdose? A sensitive boy packed off to a third-rate military school in Virginia (all of Shanker's children were shipped somewhere out of the way)— maybe a suicide? Samantha went back to her cubicle and checked her messages. A few staffers from other senators' offices had called to console, offering to reschedule meetings . . . Sam kept fast-forwarding. Cameron had called and pointedly asked to be called back.

Sam heard it in his voice: he knew something.

Cameron's voice dropped to a whisper. "Downright tragic, poor li'l kid. Ronnie Shanker goes to the same school where Dale's former chief of staff has got his boy. . . ." He paused.

"You know how he died?"

Cameron paused as if looking both ways before gossiping. "What I heard was he hanged himself."

"Oh, no."

"He was found in . . ." Someone passed by and he waited until he was gone. "Found in the shower. Now darlin', nobody commits suicide by hanging in the shower. I think it was . . ." Another passerby. "One of those autoerotic deaths. You know? Every year so-many hundred guys die because of this sexual asphyxiation thing."

"That's . . . that's terrible," Samantha brought out. Oh please please please god, she thought, don't make me have to go out there to Virginia. My plane to Florida leaves first thing tomorrow.

Cameron: "I bet Mort and the gang are having a monster session with Shanker figuring how to play this for the press."

That was wicked even for Cameron. The man's son had just died and to think he was plotting a press strategy . . . Well, come to think of it, that's probably what *was* happening. "The press might not find out the gory details," Samantha offered.

Wanda interrupted them: "Sam, line two. *It's the senator.*"

It was actually Mort. She was wanted at the senator's house in Falls Church.

"Mort, I've got tickets for Florida and my folks . . ."

The senator would gladly pay to rearrange her trip.

". . . but Mort, I don't see how I could be of any—"

Samanatha was assured she could go the week after.

"But the Senate's in session that week, and Frank—"

Mort declared it settled; Sam was to come out to Virginia right away. And could she bring her red notebook?

The one with all the press contacts?

An hour later, taking the long way to Falls Church—putting off the inevitable—she had arrived at 3913 Belmont Hills Lane, a beautiful two-story, ivy-covered brick Federal house, in a nicely wooded and landscaped yard. She recognized Mort's car in the driveway; five or six others on the street connected with events inside, all festooned with the last election's bumper stickers, FAMILY FRANK SHANKER, and ABORTION STOPS A BEATING HEART and the like.

She took a slow step forward along the slate paving stones to the front door.

"Come in, Sam," said Mort somberly. He turned and called over his shoulder, "Sam's here!" He turned to her. "We were worried it was the press already. We have just a little time, I figure, to decide what to tell the papers."

It was just as Cameron had reported. Seventeen-year-old Ronnie Shanker, surrounded by a pile of graphic porn mags, was masturbating in the shower with a noose around his neck. Having tied the knot wrong, he ended up strangling himself. The family lawyer had gone up to the school and taken care of the details, the transfer of the body to the funeral home.

"My god," Samantha stammered. "How . . ."

"How goddamn embarrassing," Mort finished.

Lillian, the senator's wife, was glimpsed briefly, being steadied by a doctor and another woman Samantha assumed to be a sister or family friend. Lillian rarely came out and met the world, suffering from depression and, since having her last child fourteen years ago, agoraphobia. Samantha remembered Mort suggesting to Frank that his wife could be a national chairwoman on an agoraphobia aware-ness campaign ("We could make this thing work for us, Frank. She could do benefits, talk shows, public appearances . . ."). When Frank approached Lillian about this proposed national tour, she ran in terror and now rarely left her room. Mrs. Shanker and her doctor departed, leaving Senator Shanker with Samantha in the silent foyer.

"I'm so sorry, Frank," said Samantha, taking his hands, feeling here she could risk the intimacy. "If you'd like, I'll get with Mort and prepare a statement about what happened, so you don't have to deal with the media at a time like this."

"I appreciate that, Sammie, but we've got to hash some things out in the study."

Samantha felt the senator's hand on her waist escorting her to his library. Wandering hands, even now, she noted. And, fittingly, no sign of Angeline. In the library, the senator's grand antique desk was free of papers; the books on the library shelves were standard-issue Great Books that looked never to have been opened. A large Bible was displayed with great show on a lamp table that no visitor could miss, though it was offset by the presence of *People* magazine, an *American Spectator* and, bizarrely, a *Playboy* no one had thought to remove.

The study held Young Republicans 1 and 2 in black suits, and a new person, a graying saggy-faced man who was soon introduced: "Sammie, this is Abe Hackett, my personal lawyer." The conversation picked up, Samantha assumed, from where it left off:

"What we need, Senator," Mort said, "is a sympathetic reporter to do the story, someone in our camp."

Young Republican 2: "Hank at the *Washington Times*."

"Damn Moonie," the senator muttered.

"But Hank does good puffwork. This needs to be sensitively handled, as we agreed. I don't want it to be a field day."

"But this isn't that type of situation," Samantha voiced inaudibly.

"Frank," intoned the lawyer, "maybe the best thing is to go with the suicide angle. No one needs to know how Ronnie . . . you know."

"No can do, Abe—I'm Family Frank here. What's it gonna look like?" Senator Shanker pinched the bridge of his nose; Samantha wanted to believe this was grief.

Young Republican 1: "From now on he won't be able to get the word 'family' out of his mouth without voters thinking about all this. The Democrats will be all over this."

Samantha found herself speaking. "Honestly, Senator, I don't believe . . ." She stalled, not knowing which unbelievable thing to express. "No opponent will use something that personal."

Mort said, "Sam's right, no one will use it, but it still prevents us from playing the family card like before."

The senator: "If we go with the suicide, could we make it the media's fault somehow? They were harrassing him, they were trying to get at me through him—something like that?"

Young Republican 1 liked it. "Maybe his girlfriend was pregnant and had an abortion without telling him and with his heart broken for the unborn child, he got depressed, he hanged himself. We could say, 'See how abortion has taken two lives here?' "

That was painfully overreaching and everyone looked at the floor. But the senator consoled, "Well, Don, I liked the abortion bit, but we'd have to produce a girl at some point."

Mort interrupted. "Was there a girl?"

Abe seemed to wave this away with distaste. "Best not to get into the boy's private life."

Young Republican 2: "We could do an antipornography thing. See what tragedy pornography has led to."

Mort chided, "Whaddya wanna do? Outlaw *Penthouse*?"

"No way," said Young Republican 1.

Abe sighed. "I don't want to tell you this, Frank, but you better know. There was this club of guys at the school—the guidance counselor told me all about it. The Society of Onan. They try to banish it, it keeps coming back." He sighed again. "Sort of a jerk-off club. You have this several-step initiation. You gotta beat your . . . you know, play with yourself in chapel, gotta do it in the dining hall, do it in class—"

"How do they prove that you did each step?" asked Young Republican 2, genuinely interested.

Hackett's right hand kept waving away distasteful topics. "Someone watches and the tissue is brought out at the next secret meeting—this kind of nonsense." He sighed again. "Then the last initiation is to do the noose thing."

The senator shook his head, disgusted. "I don't get the noose business, Abe. So help me god I don't."

"The lack of oxygen initially heightens the orgasm, Frank," Hackett said dispassionately. "You can get geishas in Japan to watch over you as you do it—safer that way." Samantha wondered whether the lawyer spoke from experience. "Anyway, the school confiscated the materials, porn videos, magazines—not all of it is heterosexual, Frank. Lots of unusual toys, vacuum pumps, the like." Hackett sighed again, hoping he could withdraw now.

Mort mused, "We could go with the homosexual teacher thing, seducing the young boys into evil. A whole national campaign against gay teachers in positions of power over kids. Save our children."

"What's this vacuum-pump thing, Abe?" asked the senator.

"It's a thing that . . . just forget it, Frank."

"What? The boys put their dicks in a vacuum cleaner?"

"It's a vacuum *chamber*, Frank. You enlarge yourself. Nothing to even speak of here."

No one said anything.

"You enlarge yourself?" Shanker asked.

"You put your . . . self into the vacuum tube, you evacuate the air, you blow up, what? Twelve, fourteen inches, you release the vacuum, you take a polaroid. It's not pretty."

"You can just buy these in stores?"

"Yes, in a sex shop. I dunno how these boys were able to get these things. Let's not worry about it."

"Can't say I've ever seen them in a sex shop." Frank muttered, mystified.

Young Republican 1: "What about the gay teacher idea? Going after gay teachers who lead our kids astray?"

Samantha cleared her throat. "But no teachers were involved, were they, Mr. Hackett?"

He shook his head.

Mort: "But we got ammunition on this gay teacher thing—"

"I don't understand," Frank went on, "that you put your cock in some tube and they let the air out . . . I mean, do you blow up all at once, like a balloon?"

"No, Frank," said Abe, "bit by bit."

"Doesn't it hurt?"

"I'm sure it hurts."

"Seems like you'd bust a blood vessel at least."

"I'm sure that happens, Frank."

There was another paper-shuffling, awkward silence before the senator burst out, "We can't let on about this kinky school club, Abe—what will people think of a family that has a . . . a kid like that?"

Samantha: "He was a teenage boy, Senator. All teenagers are full of hormones and do foolish stuff."

Senator Shanker had become theatrical in his misery: "Why?

Why did he have to do this to us? Why now?'' He slammed a fist down on the desk and then looked away from his aides.

The *why* and *why did he do this to us* were selfish but understandable sentiments, but the *why now* sent a chill through Samantha. She rambled, trying to fill the moment: "Look, you can't be the only grieving parent, Frank,'' she said, as if reminding him to grieve. "There's bound to be other parents who've gone through this.''

"There are around a thousand autoerotic deaths each year, Senator.'' Mort, always with the facts and figures.

"I mean,'' Samantha continued, "tell the media the truth.''

The senator looked up sharply.

"The truth?'' Abe mumbled.

"Just say, this is a terrible thing . . . and that it happens to thousands of parents a year. Families are torn apart.''

The yes-men were quiet, waiting to see which way the senator was going to lean.

Samantha: "You have a press conference and say it's time the silence was lifted from these incidents—to prevent future tragedies, right? You'll get tens of thousands of condolence cards, the media will applaud you for your concern for children, your sensitivity—''

Mort could not contain himself. "You know we have problems, sir, in your sensitivity-perception numbers.''

"—you've shared a family tragedy with the nation, which will bring forth other parents who've suffered as you're suffering . . .'' Samantha could detect little suffering, but she pressed on. ". . . who at the time claimed their sons were suicides and have lived with the false story for years. I see *Ladies Home Journal*, a positive profile in *The New Yorker*, a somber appearance on Oprah.''

Young Republican 2: "You do Donahue surrounded by crying mothers whose sons died this way too. You reach over and take their hand, offering a handkerchief, et cetera, et cetera.''

The senator nodded, envisioning himself in that role.

Young Republican 1, overreaching as usual: "I like Samantha's plan. It could be the cover of *Time*. 'Ronnie Shanker: An American Tragedy.' ''

Abe: "The girl's right, Frank. You accuse the school or a teacher of condoning this club, they sue, it gets messy."

The senator was on board. "Yeah, it'll show I have a . . . a human side. The great man in grief, that sort of thing."

All the way back in her car to Capitol Hill, Samantha tried to keep one word dancing in her mind: vacation. I am going on vacation. I am getting out of this insane asylum to see my family—which is a madhouse of a kind, but at least a vacation from *this* madhouse—

HONK! She had drifted into the adjoining lane on the freeway bridge across the Potomac, not paying attention. She pulled the car over, distracted, upset, teary, amazed, and unable to shake the nervous laugh that accompanied each breath. Sitting there in the emergency lane, she bowed her head against the steering wheel and reviewed her circumstances:

I don't want to take a salary cut. Nor, with my debts, can I afford to.

I don't want to work for Chauncey Cooper, who was no more a player than the coat-hangers in the Cloakroom. With Frank's bloated staff I have five legislative aides—we could become a legislation *machine*, for god's sake.

Furthermore Samantha, think of the future: with Frank's good looks, a few productive issue-driven Senate terms, he might very well be what this country votes for for president. Then we were talking White House Chief of Staff Samantha Flint.

She closed her eyes.

Not an ounce of nobility or virtue in the entire account, she realized—but hey, I admit it. I'm not evil, right? I'm still "decent." I don't want to use power to crush anybody, and I'm not driven to have more and more money. I just feel I deserve to be in this stratum, to be a player.

Mimi's going to be a player and I have to stay one too.

Flying out of National Airport the next weekend, Samantha could see the monuments of her world miniaturize and disappear beneath the cumulus. Outside the Beltway; she noted the stagnant crawl of commuters on Interstate 495 below. Now, sighing, cocktail in hand, she was beyond the reach of punditry and lobbyists, astray in the heathen continent below her, populated by the teeming uninformed who, from time to time, happened to wreak some mild effect upon the city that had become her life.

She was doing the unthinkable: leaving town, on an abbreviated family visit, during the first week of the June session. Actually, she was happy to let Mort and the gang deal with Ronnie's death. Sam helped write up a simple, poignant statement for Frank to read at his press conference on Thursday (allowing for a few tasteful days of apparent grieving). The *Washington Post* noted Ronnie's death on the back page, mentioning a rumor of suicide from "an unnamed source at the school;" come Thursday, Frank would tell the nation the rest of the story. Friday, an appearance on *20/20*.

"I'm a legislative director," she had told Mort when he started pressuring her to postpone her vacation another week. "You're the guy who handles the politics, and Bernie handles the press releases. It's *allll* yours, kiddo."

But she should have been there. She should have been there to hold his leash.

Samantha had gone back out to Virginia another time or two, and she had seen Frank in his backyard garden walking, moping, probably not blessed with enough soul or self-awareness to make full sense of what had befallen his family. Passing through the first-floor hallway, she had paused to look at the framed childhood photos of Ronnie, a dreamy, airbrushed portrait from his military academy. He was handsome like his father, but more vulnerable to the world, with something helpless in his eyes. Poor boy.

It was tropical in Jacksonville, Florida, and Sam stepped out of the terminal, only to step right back into the air-conditioning. Kelly was late to pick her up, so Samantha sat on the edge of the luggage carousel. At last, an automatic glass door at the far end of the terminal opened and Sam spotted her sister with two of her three children in tow. Kelly had really gained weight; all of the Flint women plagued by Scots-Irish matronliness . . .

Oh. On closer inspection, Kelly was pregnant again.

"Hey Aunt Samanfa!" yelled Chuck Jr., six, cute as a button.

Samantha rose and hugged her sister and then the eight-year-old niece, Elizabeth, and then the squirming nephew. It suddenly struck Samantha that she had brought no gifts for the kids—it had never even occurred to her.

"So . . ." Sam stared in the direction of Kelly's stomach.

"Yeah," she shrugged, "it wasn't my idea, but . . . you know. I'm waiting until month five to start making announcements, given my . . ." She whispered the word as the children played and squealed around her legs: "*Miscarriage* track record. And Chuck is determined to have a hundred kids, I think."

The drive north to Brunswick was a change of scenery for Samantha. Interstate 95 was enlivened by the frequent bridges over wetlands of squat hardwoods wide at their base, glimpses of lily pads and cattails, wading long-legged birds in dark slow waters en route to the Atlantic.

"Aunt Samantha," Elizabeth said, tapping Sam's shoulder. "See? See there? That's an American egret."

"Ooooh-eee," said the little boy, thrusting his face deep into his mother's purse.

"Chuck Jr.," said Kelly, "you have no business in there."

"Somethin' smells *vomitty* in this purse," he announced, before returning for another deep inhale. "*Uullllch.*"

His big sister: "Why don't you stop doing that, dodo-brain?"

"*You* smell it then." He tried to force his sister's face into the vomitty purse.

"I don't wanna smell it!"

"Chuck Jr., pass the purse up to the front, please."

They exited onto a two-lane country road that led to an old-fashioned bridge, a cage of silver steel high above an inlet, a relic of the 1930s, a setting for a fat-sheriff movie. Kelly drove Samantha circuitously through downtown Brunswick. Chuck Jr. made further noises as commentary on the smell of the paper mill.

"Do you ever get used to that?" Sam asked.

"Never," said Kelly. "It gets in your clothes, in your pores."

They passed an old church, a number of grand pre–Civil War

homes, then turned on Bay Street. Kelly's children delighted in the mayhem of seagulls and shore birds swooping and seizing upon the fish wastes beside a crabmeat-processing plant. "A beautiful little town," Sam contributed, feeling called upon to approve.

Elizabeth recited that Brunswick was founded in 1771 under George III. Chuck Jr. asked, "Mom, why'd they call him George the Third?"

Elizabeth: "I know why!"

"I said *Mom*, not *you*."

"But I know why, poopwad. It's because . . ."

"Nyah nyah nyah," Chuck said over and over, hands to his ears, refusing to listen to any explanation but his mother's.

"Cupcake, I'm trying to talk to your Aunt Samantha."

Elizabeth: "Shut up, pea-brain."

Chuck Jr.: "Mama, 'Lizbeth said *pee*!"

"No, I said *pea* like black-eyed peas."

Sam scanned the passing houses with their sagging front porches, low-slanting roofs, lazy dogs in yards, country elderly whitefolk sitting uneventfully on their porches next to an unworking refrigerator, watching their cars rust, up on cement blocks. Most properties on the fringe of the town were ramshackle, occupying a small clearing against an oppressive crush of vegetation, vines, kudzu, ivies, weeds, Spanish moss in the trees, green-scummed swamp inlets lapping at the side of the yard. . . . U.S. 17, lead out from the main outdated business strips, past brickfront stores from the '60s, then past the modest homes of rural black people; a farmer's pickup truck with a crude sign advertised the sale of boiled peanuts, beside a historical marker and sign for Hofwyl-Broadfield Plantation.

"About this plantation," Sam asked.

"Oh, I've never been," Kelly said. "Idn't that something? How you never see what's in your backyard? I bet there's stuff in Washington you've never seen!"

Elizabeth: "General Sherman burned it down in the War."

Chuck Jr.: "Who's General Sherman?"

Kelly said to Sam, "We'll get Chuck to take us all out in his truck, like over to St. Simon's Island—"

Elizabeth: "Mama, can Daddy take Aunt Samantha and me out in the boat?"

"We'll have to ask Daddy."

The kids started begging please please please, could they all go waterskiing this weekend? They could do tricks for Aunt Samantha. Aunt Samantha never got to see them do tricks, please please please—

"We'll have to ask Daddy."

Sam contemplated if every spontaneous or happy activity had been delegated to Chuck's sanction. Samantha privately warned herself not to be talked into waterskiing in this alligator swamp. "So," Samantha began, "I'm off Wednesday to see Mom and Bethie—"

Elizabeth: "Mama, he's being a nasty mouth."

Chuck: "*Am not!*"

Elizabeth: "Mama, he's saying 'potty-poots' over and over, under his breath."

Chuck: "I *am not*."

"Ya'll cut it out," Kelly said with no authority.

Under the road noise, Sam could barely discern the faintest whisper of "potty-poots."

Elizabeth: "*Maaaaahm*, you can't hear him but I can."

"Ignore him, princess."

Chuck was like a little machine: "Potty-poots potty-poots potty-poots potty-poots . . ." Elizabeth verging on tears: "*Maaaaaahm*, make him stop or I'm gonna have to hit him!"

"No hitting," said Kelly emotionlessly.

With the kids swatting each other, they were sufficiently occupied for Kelly to say to Samantha discreetly: "Chuck and I have been going to counseling. At our church."

Samantha was just as discreet. "There a problem?"

"Well, it's my problem."

Sam waited but Kelly didn't continue. "Here's the driveway," she said by way of explanation. "When Chuck goes to the gym, we'll have a talk."

They pulled into the crunchy gravel of a small one-story house with a lovely Carpenter Gothic front porch, clearly a recently painted addition to a very unremarkable house. How on earth do three kids—make that four soon—fit in this box, Samantha wondered? Aside from the showcase front porch, the house was distressingly shabby: the white paint of the siding was cracking, the red paint of the shutters was peeling; a separate barnwood garage, slightly leaning, was home to Chuck's Dodge Ram and his workbench. Beyond the backyard with its birdbath, rusted swingset, a plastic deer and an askew plastic flamingo, there flowed a narrow dark-watered inlet, a rickety pier, and a large powerboat moored there. Sam glimpsed Chuck at the end of the pier, waving in energetic welcome.

Samantha waved back. She allowed herself a rare moment of vicarious maternal longing, watching Elizabeth run beside her mother, bouncing and laughing while holding tight to Kelly's hand, melting into her, walking in and around her without getting underfoot . . . this mother-daughter dance of security and total love. Chuck Jr. appeared at Samantha's side: "Aunt Samanfa, Aunt Samanfa!"

"What, honey?"

"Potty-poots."

"Well, if it idn't my good-lookin' sister-in-law!" called Chuck, making his way down the pier, wiping his hands on an oily rag. Chuck hadn't merely discovered the gym, he was the poster child for steroid manufacturers worldwide.

"Good lord, Chuck! What have you turned into?"

Chuck, when Kelly met him in high school, had been a broad-shouldered, stocky guy, handsome in the face, with very dark eyebrows and mustache despite having light brown hair. Except for his 5'7" height, he was the early 1980s vision of Marlboro Man macho. Samantha remembered him being soft and teddy-bearish, chunky around the middle his senior year. But no more. Those broad shoulders now were rounded; his upper arms were bulbously pumped and smooth; his head now sat upon a veined and defined stalk of a neck. His relation to the earth had changed: he bounded, cantered, swaggered, using his body at every opportunity, tossing his kids in the air, picking up his wife in a swirling hug, chinning himself on the swingset, picking up Samantha's suitcases, demonstrating his ease.

"How's my favorite in-law?" Chuck gave her a grizzly's hug.

Samantha begged for mercy while Kelly and all the children laughed at her predicament. Chuck released her and Samantha recovered, realizing that she had never put her hands on such a well-developed male body in her life.

"We'll go out on the boat later if it doesn't storm," Chuck assured her, as if this was why she had come.

Chuck's not pumping himself up just to strut around the home-place, Sam decided. He's cheating on her.

Samantha watched her sister waddle into the house, lifting the crying baby (Minnie, nine months, named after Chuck's mother) who had been sitting in a stroller being "watched," supposedly, by Chuck.

Kelly and Chuck's house reeked.

Samantha never got used to the little airless house which smelled of sweet baby urine and pungent baby excrement—that and their mangy border collie no one had time to bathe. On the sofa bed that night, in between baby-feedings and ear-splitting bawling, Samantha calmly considered the consequences of asking to be moved to a Brunswick motel for the two nights.

Samantha tried to conceal an actual terror of the baby, Minnie, an infantile fountain of spewed, upchucked, thrown, and excreted food. Sam struggled to find patience with the chatterbox six year old, and the pubescent know-it-all eight year old, who was well on the way to becoming a spoiled princess, like her Aunt Bethie. In the daily chaos of the house, Samantha would fix upon Kelly and wonder what kind of natural lobotomy occurs in one's head at the time of maternity that allows a woman to put up with such ceaseless trauma alternating with drudgery. It's a wonder, Sam concluded, that women aren't found killing or abusing their children more frequently.

Samantha's last evening coincided with Chuck at the gym and Kelly home from work, vegetating in the La-Z-Boy before the VCR watching her prerecorded *All My Children*.

"Why don't we have that talk now?" Sam prodded, when the soap was over.

Kelly shifted, clicking off the TV. But there was a long silence as she organized her presentation. Sam recognized her reticence: discussing the failures of one's life out loud makes them official, leaving words of disappointment and disillusion hanging in the air where they might never be relieved.

"Like I said," Kelly began, "it's mostly my fault. I just feel my life is slipping away from me, and I really . . ." She shrugged. "I just wasn't ready to have another kid so soon."

"You don't use birth control?"

"We do, but it slipped up somehow." Samantha had a hunch that Kelly wasn't being entirely honest about that. "It's the money thing. My working checkout at Kmart is a few hundred a week but it keeps me on my feet all day, which is killing me."

"Well, Kel, you gotta take some time off."

"Chuck says the same thing, but we just won't have enough money." Even though they were alone, Kelly whispered their secret: "We are in so much debt, Sam. We owe on the house, the boat, our store credit cards are full-up and we're even in hock to Kmart."

"I've got a ton of debt myself," Sam said, just to fill the silence, although surely Kelly knew Samantha made a salary greater than hers and Chuck's combined. "Can you cut back?"

"Our only luxury's the boat, and I can't ask Chuck to give it up."

Samantha said gently that Chuck's boat wasn't essential to life.

"But the kids love it," Kelly mumbled, unable to envision a world in which she deprived her husband of his boat.

Samantha imagined Chuck's streamlined, jacked-up sport model Dodge Ram was worth $15,000 on a trade. But when Sam suggested as much, it was clear Kelly couldn't see her husband deprived of that toy either. How about Chuck's gym membership? "Those things are always hundreds a year, Kel. Couldn't he just work out in the garage?"

"Yes, but his few hours at the gym every day are his—"

"*Every day?* He goes for hours every day?"

"He couldn't look like that if he didn't," she said indifferently. "His goin' to the gym in Brunswick is his time away from the house."

"When's *your* time away from the house?"

She huffed, "The kids barely see me as it is, with me at Kmart and them in school or daycare."

"Can I be honest?"

Kelly nodded warily.

"Chuck can't have all his toys and put you guys into years' worth of debt. He's not eighteen anymore, and it's not important in the least that he pump himself up like a balloon for hours every day. You ought to lay down the law."

"Well, that's what we went to counseling about."

"How'd that go?"

"Well, Reverend Gandy said we weren't communicating and I had to be more understanding. 'Cause, well, it's in the Bible, he's the husband and I'm the wife and I have to give him support in Christ. There's this prayer circle for young wives each Wednesday and, really, I wanna go, but that's my one time-and-a-half night shift at Kmart and I can't drop that."

"That's what . . ." Sam repeated his name, hating him without laying eyes on him. ". . . Reverend Gandy said, when you told him your husband was bankrupting your family?"

"Oh, we didn't talk about money. Chuck and I agreed not to . . ."

"Agreed that you wouldn't talk about Chuck being a bad provider in front of the minister. Great." Samantha heard an internal voice coaxing her to cool the gathering firestorm, but she was too stirred up. "Have you ever stood up to Chuck about anything?"

"Lots of things," Kelly said slowly. "But it's like . . ."

The baby was bawling again and Kelly went to deal with it. In the meantime, Samantha studied the threadbare chair she was sitting upon, the recliner, the 35-inch screen TV (another Chuck indulgence), the modest furnishings of their house. They managed, Sam thought sadly, to get into debt over these things.

"What I'm saying," Kelly returned, with the baby nestled against her shoulder, "is that it's really difficult with Chuck's family. I mean, he's their golden boy and I think Mrs. McConnell doesn't think I'm good enough for Chuck—"

"She said that to you?"

"No, she wouldn't, she's really sweet," Kelly insisted. "It's just a feeling I get. And Chuck's two brothers when they visit are always commenting on everything, the housekeeping, the food, how I look—"

"I remember those assholes in high school," Sam snapped. "You tell Chuck you don't want his freeloading brothers over here until they learn some manners. This is as much your house as it Chuck's."

Samantha's advice continued, spilling out the moment she thought of it, all bromides, "You have to tell him how you feel," and "You can't be walked on," and "It takes two people, not just you, to make a marriage work."

How much of our existence, Sam wondered that night on the sofa bed, was spent having these sorts of talks where women took each other's hands and offered up the glaringly obvious, recited the most exhausted of clichés, wallowed in some man-created trough of deprivation or abuse, investing all their hopes and wishes, every prayer to God, in the improvement or altering of some *man*. Somewhere, in some sunny place of charity, women turned to other women to talk of poetry and painting, philosophical systems and the explorer's horizon, somewhere far from the baby factory, far from spittle and soiled diapers, dishes waiting in the sink for a female hand . . .

"This sucker can really go, can't it?" said Chuck Sr. of his Dodge Ram, as Chuck drove Samantha to the airport in Jacksonville for her short flight to Tampa. Chuck was blasting Lynyrd Skynyrd in his octophonic car stereo. The sun was low and the estuarine landscape was breezy and pleasing, the reeds and marshgrass in soft yellow light, above a blue sky with cumulus clouds white as the frenzied gulls that darted and soared, the summer scene of a thousand retirement brochures that led northerners southward.

Kelly had wanted to take Samantha to the airport, but that might impinge on her Kmart night shift, so Chuck volunteered. Chuck wore a tank top to show off his bulbous arms and his even tan, and khaki shorts that rode up his powerful thighs. From some corner of her memory, Samantha swore she remembered Chuck at a barbecue in their backyard in Springfield with prodigiously hairy legs. They were lightly dusted with hair now, and smooth as if shaven and polished. Maybe that's what bodybuilders did nowadays.

Sam knew—as a woman, as much as she knew anything—that if she put out the slightest encouragement, Chuck would make a pass at her. The strutting, the showing off, the posing, the lingering touches as they passed plates at dinner, as he slowly untied her mildewy life jacket when they all went for a boat ride.

"Did Kel talk to you about . . . ," Chuck began. "Did she tell you we were having some problems?"

"She mentioned you had talked a time or two to your minister." Sam tried to draw out her brother-in-law. "It sounds mercenary but in my experience it's true: there are few problems that married people have that wouldn't blow away like smoke if sufficient piles of capital were injected into the situation."

"Amen, sister." He shook his head. "I just was not ready for another kid so soon. We said we were going to stop at two, then an accident happened with Minnie—not that I'm complaining. Now here we go again."

"You didn't push for this child?"

"Hell no," he said, immediately rushing to soften the impression that left: "I mean, I love it already—don't get me wrong. But it's gonna bankrupt us, I swear."

Oddly, Samantha knew it was Chuck who wasn't lying.

It was Kelly.

Samantha pressed a finger to her temple, already fighting off the headache that a night of sofa-bed sleep had planted smack in the front of her forehead. Hold it together, she sighed. With Bethie and her mother looming ahead this evening, she couldn't afford a collapse at this stage.

Her flight to Tampa, less than an hour long, was a hell of Gulf-front turbulence and landing delay and obnoxious second-class travelers, and the two miniscule airplane gins and a can of tonic did nothing to relax her. Samantha put aside her worries about Kelly and Chuck's life—but only long enough for old worries about her mother and Bethie to flood in and take their place:

Mrs. Flint had divorced Mr. Flint in 1985, at sixty years of age, thereby doing herself out her husband's life-insurance policy, and anything Herbert Flint might leave her in the will—all of which would now redound to his *second* wife, Shirley of long-running affair fame. Bethie, who was divorced herself, sensed that her own life might become more sympathetic if Mom and she shared "a divorce experience," Samantha figured; Bethie had goaded and counseled Mom into the proceeding, stoked by watching too many *Donahues* on breaking free, being your own woman. Mom should have separated and taken a lover if she had to have one—well, there was an impossible thought—but she should have in any event hung on to the loot that was due her from thirty years of marriage!

Samantha plodded from airport gate to baggage claim to rental-car desk, surprised to find it was dark outside. She picked up her car and began the drive across Tampa Bay.

What little income Mrs. Flint got from her doubled-up Social Security *evaporated* thanks to Bethie and her two kids: Jennifer, ten, from the failed marriage to Buddy the dumb-jock white guy with a college-football gambling problem (if I have to hear from Bethie how "he sure was hung" one more time, Sam decided, I'm going to puke) and Dejohnn, five, courtesy of Jermaine, the black live-in she never married but whom she helped through technical school for two years, before he decided a relationship with Bethie wasn't what he wanted. Who could blame him, shrugged Sam. If my sister has ever made a correct life decision, then—

Oh, enough.

Samantha pulled into her mother's driveway and paused before getting out of the car. It was the Florida retirement suburbs; no traffic or lights, just the high obligato of crickets and chirping bugs.

"Is that my little Sam-Sam?" Mrs. Flint appeared, bathrobe pulled around her, towel on her head. Samantha was struck by how old her 66-year-old mother looked in the ghastly yellow porch light.

"Mom," she said, getting out of the car to hug her mother. "You'll catch cold, out here like that."

"You were just sitting there in the car, so I had to come out to *you*," she laughed. "My little Samantha . . ." She clutched her daughter's arm, not as sure of foot as the last visit.

"Your morals have loosened. Letting the neighbors see you in your bathrobe."

"Oh," Mrs. Flint waved this away, a decades-perfected gesture of dismissal with a guttural sound. "I could come out here buck naked—no one would see. They're all *dead*!"

"Mother, *sssh.*"

"Oh, no one's awake—they're all in their coffins by eight P.M. Dead as a doornail. I can't *stand* old people. Your generation will make better old people than my generation!"

Samantha smiled and fetched her suitcase while her mother made her familiar rant: "My generation just poisoned ourselves, that's why! Red meat, cocktail hour, smoked like chimneys—wouldn't allow the smoking in my house, you'll recall—they're all on death's doorstep now, thanks to that. Know what they call Clearwater, Samantha?"

Mother had told this joke. *Clearwater: God's Waiting Room.*

"They call it 'God's Waiting Room,' " said Mrs. Flint as she and her daughter went inside and padded toward the kitchen. "Everybody on their last legs, talking about their digestion and their *bowel obstructions.* God, that's why I left Phoenix."

That six-month detour to Phoenix in 1987 was a folly Mrs. Flint (who blew her cash settlement) and Samantha had paid dearly for. After the divorce, convinced that Florida wasn't big enough for her and Mr. Flint, Mrs. Flint had the fantasy that she'd be happy in Phoenix. Samantha commuted between D.C., Florida, and Phoenix for four weekends and took an inconvenient week's leave while Congress was in session to transport Mom, put up the Clearwater house for sale, move her mother into a retirement condo . . . only to discover that Mrs. Flint hated it. Completely hated it. Fell into depression, made no friends, couldn't find card partners. "Golf, golf, golf," she said on each desperate, nightly long-distance call, "all anyone wants to do is play golf in hundred-and-seventeen-degree heat. Some of these old men have been hit by lightning, recover, and then go back to the golf course where they left off. I hate it here!"

So Samantha took some more leave, combined with the Easter recess and moved her mother *back* to Clearwater—where the house hadn't sold, thank god. Bethie, throughout, managed to make herself scarce.

"Kelly called," Mrs. Flint reported. "Said y'all had a good time."

"Yes, we did," Sam said, before reciting the blandest possible rendition of her visit.

"Chuck's a good man," her mother said automatically. "I wish," she added, putting decaf in the coffeemaker, "that I was in a position to do more for them."

Sam watched her mother pour the requisite amount of water in the coffeemaker with a shaky hand. "*Your* health's all right, isn't it?"

"You know I'm indestructible. If your father hadn't finished me off by now, and Bethie and those kids of hers, nothing will get me."

"Speaking of that, when is Bethie gonna clear out and stop freeloading?"

"Oh it's not like that. . . ."

"It is too."

"Bethie keeps me company, you know. Nothing to do all day in this tomb but sit and watch soaps and . . . it's just the kids are getting so rambunctious these days—and when their friends from daycare are over here it's just a loony bin!"

"Why are Bethie's kids in daycare? She's actually working?"

Mrs. Flint became strained. "Oh Samantha, we go through this every time and you only get mad. She's at Baskets 'n Balloons over in Dunedin, working part-time."

A strip-mall craft shop. The woman has two kids to support and she goes and *volunteers* her time at this kountry kitsch shop that hawks silk flowers and baskets and old-lady old-timey crafts—with cornhusk men and holly-hobbies and gingham rag dolls. In addition to their full selection of balloons. You know how important it is that people have unlimited opportunities to purchase balloons. Samantha had ventured inside the shop once; the place so strongly stank of potpourri and aromatic wood chips, it was amazing its geriatric clientele could draw a breath. Bethie sits in the store all day, gossiping with the other women who actually own the store and keep all the money. "Mom," Samantha said, "they don't pay her anything there. She's—"

"Now Samantha." Mrs. Flint's tone was firm, though her face remained kind: "I'm tired of you two tangling, do you hear me? For my birthday tomorrow, I want you to let her alone. She's had a difficult life—and growing up in Springfield with your father who didn't lift a finger to help me. It's a wonder she's in one piece!"

Samantha sipped her coffee, thinking: *I* grew up in our house and *I'm* a functional, responsible adult. Let it go. Not only let this go, but let the next five things go—*get used* to letting things go, she told herself.

"Are they still working you to death?" Mrs. Flint asked, transparently changing topics.

"Nearly."

"You won't have time for a social life if you don't watch out, Sam-Sam. They'll suck all the life right out of you, then you'll end up forty years old alone without a husband, if you don't watch it."

Sam just sipped her coffee.

"It's a shame what's happening up there in Washington. I hope your new man Shanker isn't a crook."

"I don't think he's a crook." Just an idiot.

"I read something on him, Sam-Sam, in the *Parade* I think it was . . . no, maybe it was those *Reader's Digests*—you know, Mrs. Dellafini, when she's done with her *Reader's Digests* lets us have them, which I like for the health articles. She must keep them in her bathroom, because they smell just like deodorizer . . ."

Mrs. Flint got up to find a *Reader's Digest*. Samantha stared in her coffee cup, knowing in a moment she would be asked to sniff the *Reader's Digest* for signs of the spice-scented Airwick beside Mrs. Dellafini's toilet. But Mrs. Flint came back empty-handed.

"Anyway," she continued, "that Frank Shanker is *so* right-wing."

"Yeah, I know. But he'd be a lot worse if I wasn't up there."

"Why don't you get with some senator who's not so mean?"

"I've applied everywhere, Mother. Those jobs don't come open very often."

"Hmm."

Great. Sam lay awake in the guest room that night replaying her mother's look of bemusement (why do you live the life you live?), her look of concern (where's your husband?), her look of mild disapproval about whom she worked for ("Hmm"). Mom earlier: "Maybe you should get a teaching certificate and teach school down here in Clearwater—you know, Sam-Sam, that English degree we paid all that money for didn't do you one bit of good, now did it?"

Samantha Flint may be respected up and down the corridors of the Capitol, yet it meant absolutely nothing, Sam decided, to her mother, who once said, "You've proved your point, little missy." Like Sam's career was some . . . some exercise in teenage rebellion and she could stop now and come home.

Where were those tranquilizers?

"Let's eat Italian," Mom suggested the next afternoon, especially giddy with two of her daughters in the house to make things happen. Mrs. Flint suggested the Olive Garden, where you could get a plate of overcooked pasta (restaurant cost: ten cents) with some runny saline glop on it for $6.95. Ask for a dish with garlic and they present you with a shaker of garlic salt.

"Sam-Sam, in Tarpon Springs there's the best Greek food outside of Greece!" Last year, they went to a feeding-mill called Pappas' and got an "authentic Greek salad": *white lettuce on a bed of potato salad*. Would you like that with thousand-island dressing, miss?

Nothing "ethnic" in Florida was allowed to stand un-Americanized, unprefabricated for easy microwaving, made bland and chock-full of the familiar fat and salt for the hordes of white- and blue- and gray- and violet-tinged heads feeding their faces in silence, chewing mechanically, jowls and chins moving up and down, their eyes fixed on their plates as if at any moment someone might take their food from them. . . . Sam was always depressed by dining out in seniorland. These poor things condemned to the Florida food-treadmill—prisoners!—nevertheless, often the high point of their day.

Mrs. Flint, who ate regularly at Countrytyme Buffet, lunch and dinner (seniors eat cheap, $3.95!), wanted to go there at 4:30.

"But Mom, for your birthday, let me take you somewhere nice—"

"Now that's why my girls don't have any money, always eating at those fancy-schmancy places, never cooking for themselves."

"Mom, c'mon, it's going to be my treat."

Bethie appeared out of nowhere and said it would take ten minutes to get her kids ready. Sam tried to muster the strength to inform Bethie that it was Mom she was taking out, Bethie would have to pay for herself and her kids . . . Oh, for heaven's sake, how *petty*. The check would be $30 tops, even with the kids. Sam threw that away in Washington on a round of drinks.

"Don't worry," snapped Bethie, reading her sister's mind, "I'll pay my own way, and my kids'."

"I said I was treating!"

"It's no problem, I've got money."

"Look, you're not working so I'm happy to—"

"Well, I'm not happy, and I'm paying for my own kids and that's that, okay?"

Samantha was unmotivated for battle. "Whatever."

Bethie was aging around the eyes, Samantha noticed, and it was still a bit of a shock to watch her sister getting older, her beauty fading—wait, there had been no fade, no slow easing into her thirties, but rather some process without any grace at all, just a parody of her teenage buxomness settling into drawn haggardness on top, while she filled out pearlike on the bottom. Cigarette lines, crow's-feet beside eyes that crinkled her foundation, skin ravaged by tanning beds and heredity, the same raw reddish skin that Grandmother ended up with. Her pastel aerobic wear—just thrown on for the casual afternoon, Sam realized, but there was a time when she could have stopped traffic in jeans and a T-shirt. Samantha had grown up considering Bethie the most beautiful thing on earth.

Mom's birthday extravaganza at Countrytyme Buffet.

A sullen Jennifer and a hyperactive Dejohnn were corralled and herded to the car, both permitted to bring toys. Bethie drove Mom's car and smoked, which nauseated Sam, imprisoned in the back with the two hellions hurling their toys at each another. Bethie circled the parking lot twice looking for a spot which would save her walking a few extra yards. Mrs. Flint, in delirium to be going somewhere, talked excitedly of the soft ice cream machine which extruded a white frozen chemical paste and an off-white frozen chemical paste, a.k.a. vanilla and chocolate, next to the tubs of mass-produced banana pudding.

There was a wait of twenty minutes.

Jennifer and Dejohnn were allowed to cut up, squeal, pinch and push, bump into elderly strangers, get down on the filthy floor and interpose themselves in the paths of waitresses and the hostess; despite a hundred hostile disapproving stares, not a word was said to contain their menace by Bethie or Mrs. Flint for whom, apparently, this chaos was invisible. In Sam's own childhood, the merest divergence from polite behavior would have occasioned intense correction. *This is your niece* and *this is your nephew*, Sam reminded herself, and when they grow older, I will be their Auntie Samantha and they will come visit.

At Countrytyme one paid a flat fee of $4.99 and then served oneself from the steam tables full of vegetables imbued in a soup of salt or fatty sidemeat (the nutritive value leeched into mush under the hot lights), and vats of various meats in suspensions of grease.

Sam decided that the roast beef was least repulsive, and was asked by an attendant, "Would you like some *aw juice* with that?"

Sam, to no purpose, said, "It's pronounced *o zhoo* and it *means* 'with juice.' You're asking me if I'd like it with *with* juice."

"So do you want the *aw juice* or not?"

Once at the table, a waitress approached to take one's drink orders and condiment orders, ensuring the need for a tip even at this self-service establishment.

Since Bethie's declaration that she'd be paying her own way, she had spent most of the afternoon reminding her children that they better not order this or that (like two dollars extra for chopped steak, cooked to order) because Mommy had to be economic. But Grandma is having a steak, Dejohnn whined.

"If he gets steak then I get steak!" cried Jennifer.

"Grandma can have a steak," Bethie said, "because Aunt Samantha is paying for her."

Samantha crossed her arms, but then smiled broadly at the kids. "But Auntie Samantha will take you both for ice cream later if you save room!"

"But Samantha," said her mother, pointing with her fork to her beloved do-it-yourself ice cream machine, "we've got ice cream here!"

"Don't worry," Bethie said coolly to her sister, "it's not extra."

"Bethie," Sam said, matching her tone, "did you ever get that child-support business straightened out?'' Her ex-husband, Buddy, wasn't exactly timely with his checks. Since Jermaine never married Bethie, it would take legal wrangling to produce a court order to make him pay something, and that had always been avoided. It was my choice, Bethie perenially announced, and I accept the responsibility for my son—a gesture of nobility quietly underwritten by her near-destitute mother.

"I got a check last week," said Bethie.

"Really?" said Mrs. Flint. "Why didn't you say something?"

"It may have been two weeks ago, actually. And anyway, I had a hundred million bills to pay and it just disappeared."

That was a lie, Samantha thought, yawning. Everybody in this family lies to everybody else. Between this family and working in Washington, I am an all-American expert on lying. She tapped her coffee cup, hoping to get the Yankee waitress to fill it.

"Your generation," Mrs. Flint lectured, "has to have everything right away. Purse full of credit cards!"

This morning, Samantha had taken her mother to an upscale mall in St. Petersburg, shopping for a birthday dress. Samantha tried to be generous, tried to get the woman something she looked good in, putting up with her crotchets and declarations; "Oh Sam-Sam, that makes me look like an old lady!" and "That's just wasting your money—I'm not worth it!" Her mother's rejection of fine clothes was countered by an ardent attraction to the polyester stretchwear at Added Dimensions at the outlet mall an hour later. Some mothers would have been pleased to have their daughter buy them a present, she thought, but not mine. No, my taking out my billfold was Exhibit A for the failures of my generation.

"Your father and I spent twenty years paying off that first house, and we didn't have a washing machine. And my own mother—"

"Why," Sam interrupted, her voice with an edge that only surfaced in family disputes, "don't we stop this speech right now, because I'm not sure I can stand another celebration of the Great Depression and the moral superiority it conferred on your generation. You weren't providing for a family, you were a *child* then," Samanatha added, muttering, "what did you care?"

"Now Sam—"

"I hate this constant, patented generational comparison." She imitated her mother: " 'When we were your age we were married and had a family on the way! When we were your age we were nearly done making house payments!' Well, good for you Mom, you got to enjoy the post–World War Two mannalike rain of American prosperity. Can you walk, talk, write your name? Here's a job, fella, for the next forty years with a nice fat pension and stock options! And here's a GI Bill and a fixed mortgage of four percent for a house that only cost sixteen thousand dollars in Springfield, Missouri!"

"I'm just saying we weren't always thinking of ourselves—"

"Bullshit. *Your* generation, Mother, taught us everything we needed to know about selfishness. You are socialized from home ownership to savings insurance to retirement to the grave, all paid for by *my* generation who'll never see a dime of it. Claude Pepper down here tried to get you people catastrophic health insurance, that goddamn AARP put out propaganda telling seniors they'd have to pay *six* more dollars a month, and Washington rescinded the law! Knelt down in front of the all-powerful senior lobby, the richest generation ever to come out of the richest country in the richest time in history! Health-costs? No prob, just pass it on along to my generation—those kids'll figure it out!"

Bethie and her children were quiet; Mrs. Flint stared lifelessly at her plate waiting for Samantha to wind down, which she didn't feel like doing.

"These old women in Florida, outliving their husbands by thirty years, sucking up Social Security, never having worked one goddam day in their lives, taking out *eight* times what they put in, bellyaching for more so they can have some 'fun money' at canasta—and I mean, christ, seniors don't pay a cent for anything! Discount fares, discount rooms, you don't ever have to eat a meal more expensive than *five bucks*. The richest segment of society are seniors and our government ships back to them *half* of everything it takes in! And you should read the letters we get from seniors, hear the calls we get: racist, stupid, ill-educated, raging against the EPA because it's keeping another goddamn golf course from being built, all the while shoving that ol' time Christian Nazi gun-nut religion down the American people's throats. Your generation squeezed this country like a grapefruit and it's all gone now, Mom."

Samantha didn't know what else to say or do, so she reached for her fork, as if she could simply return to eating. Her appetite drained away, the lettuce in her mouth was impossible to swallow.

All was quiet.

"Mother, am I gonna have to take you to play cards in St. Pete this Thursday?" It was Bethie.

"No honey, I think Mrs. Landros is driving."

Did they not have a clue? Did they not see the big picture on all fronts? My father worked his whole life and nobody has a dime to show for it. I make more than my father ever made in his whole life, and yet—college loans, car payments, rent, overhead—where has all the money gone? Why wasn't there anything left—

"Who wants ice cream?" Mrs. Flint asked her grandchildren.

Jennifer and Dejohnn took their grandmother's hands and went to the dessert area.

"Shall I get you something, Sam?"

"No thanks, Mom."

Samantha rearranged her salad with her fork while Bethie sat across the table glowering at her.

Bethie said, "Some kids sing 'Happy Birthday' to their mothers."

"She makes me crazy." Samantha risked eye contact with her older sister, wondering if they could agree on the difficulty of dealing with Mom and her tape-loop litany of dissatisfactions. What Samantha discovered was no connection, no bond at all.

"You've become a real snob, sis. Nothing we do is ever gonna be good enough for you. You sit in judgment of us all, like your life's anything special."

"My life *is* special—"

"You work for a bunch of shits. Proctor was some ol' talk-show windbag, and Shanker ought to be ashamed of himself. I can't believe you work for that ignorant bigot—*you* ought to be ashamed of *yourself*. You may think we've messed up our lives, but maybe we don't think you've done so well with your life either—but hey, I guess the money is nice.''

"It *is* nice. You ought to try working for some, one of these days, instead of mooching off of Mom—''

"Oh fuck you!''

"Go to hell, Bethie. Sitting in a silk-flower store running your mouth all day. Don't you want to do better by your kids?''

"I do just fine by my . . . Mom's coming back.''

Samantha furiously concluded, "I make eighty-five thousand dollars a year. And all along the way I've made sacrifices to get there. I'm not gonna end up like Mom and you, living hand-to-mouth.''

Mrs. Flint, all smiles, returned with the children; Dejohnn's mouth was already smeared with vanilla.

Mrs. Flint sang, "My, my. What were my precious little girls talking about?''

"Samantha was just saying,'' Bethie reported, "that she makes eighty-five thousand dollars a year, Mom.''

Her mother looked pained and then she smiled broadly, "How . . . that's—how wonderful for you, Sam-Sam. So much! Isn't that a lot, Bethie?''

Samantha glared hatefully at her sister. *God knows*, she had not meant to throw that figure out to her family—they who got by on so little, for whom the Countrytyme Buffet was an extravagance. Nothing good could come of her salary—which she'd pridefully inflated by twenty thou—being public information.

"Here, Sam-Sam,'' said her mother, setting a bowl of banana pudding down in front of her. "This is so tasty, I wanted you to have some. And you can go back all you want for seconds.''

That evening Samantha retired to her room to read, to hide, waiting to emerge until her mother padded off to bed at ten P.M. Bethie was out on the town.

Samantha couldn't sleep. Instead she crept out to the living room to turn on the TV, the volume next to zero, and lie down in front of it like a kid. Today was Wednesday, the day before the press conference where the country would learn about poor Ronnie Shanker. She watched *Headline News* for an entire half hour, wondering if any mention would be made, but it wasn't. It would be all over the air tomorrow. Perhaps it would simply be a short item, Frank in a clip, a sound bite. Maybe he'll shed a tear or two for the cameras. Maybe for his own good.

The front door opened and closed. Bethie was back from her honky-tonking.

Sam decided not to look up or turn around, just pretend that she was engrossed with the TV. Bethie passed the living room and moved on to her bedroom. Good, thought Samantha, relieved. Then Bethie's footsteps came back. Sam waited breathlessly for Bethie to announce herself.

"Whatcha watching?" her sister said softly.

"Boring old news," Sam said, turning back to see Bethie. All the anger had evaporated in an instant from both of them. "Seeing if they were going to mention Frank Shanker's kid."

"I saw that in the paper last week." Bethie sat on the edge of the sofa. "Suicide?"

"Looks like it," Samantha said, reluctant to sidetrack their reconciliation with the story of Ronnie's autoerotic finale. "I was such a bitch tonight. I'm sorry."

"I started it, gettin' all testy about you paying four-ninety-nine for that pig slop at Countrytyme . . ."

Both sisters started giggling, shushing each other for their mother's sake.

Samantha managed to whisper, "We always eat garbage when I come down here."

"Hell, when did we ever eat good?"

"Never. Mom wouldn't know food if it wrestled her to the ground."

"You know Hester ain't gonna rest until you have a big-ass bowl of that soft-serve ice cream . . ." They snickered together until Bethie turned to go, smiling. "I'm drunk and danced-out and nobody looked twice at me tonight."

"You're looking good," Samantha insisted.

Bethie waved this away.

Sam heard herself speak before she processed the offer's implications: "Look, I'm doing pretty well, as I blurted out at dinner like the bitch I am, and one of the reasons I . . . well I mean, if you . . . I can give you some money for the kids if this is a thin time for you."

Bethie opened her mouth but didn't speak for a moment. "Oh, Sam, I couldn't."

"A loan? We could—"

"You know how it is when siblings start lending money—"

"Well, let me *give* it to you. I'm thinking of my niece and nephew. . . ." *My niece and nephew.* Sam's sudden ownership seemed, for a moment, to transfix them both. Sam went to her room to fetch her checkbook.

"Well"—Bethie didn't look directly at her sister—"their friends all have computers and I know someone who's got an old model he's looking to get rid of—"

"Good. Let that be Auntie Samantha's birthday present this year." This was the right thing to do for everyone and Sam felt spirited about it, but damn, how bad would this be setting her back? Samantha immediately short-circuited any thoughts of money and opened the checkbook and clicked her pen.

"I think . . . let's say, a thousand," Bethie said, again not meeting Samantha's eyes when the checkbook was dug out of her purse.

"Yeah, okay," Samantha said, light-headed at putting herself another thousand in debt in a matter of seconds.

Bethie took the check quickly, patting Samantha on her shoulder, neither of them up to a sisterly hug. "Again, I'm sorry for gettin' all testy."

"Mom makes us both crazy, that's all it is."

Bethie rolled her eyes before departing. "You think this end of the family is dysfunctional, wait 'til you go see Daddy tomorrow."

"Shall I give him your love?"

Bethie produced a beer belch which, crude as it was, was the right note to end upon, sharing a mild conspiracy and a laugh as they never had in childhood.

The whole point of her vacation was to see her ailing father. She had shirked her office duties for it, done without Cameron for it, and walked across the coals of dealing with the rest of her family along the way. Yet at the city limits for Orlando, all her desire for a father-daughter reunion disappeared. The last visit, over a year ago, hadn't gone well. Samantha bolstered herself for how bad he might look, having been shocked at his gauntness and age in her last visit.

Whatever his decrepitude and ill temper, she lectured herself, I will finish out my role as daughter as well as I know how, so I can hold and cherish the past without regret. These visits, these dilapidations, are not for the permanent memory; this is transition, a last little bit of housecleaning.

She left the interstate for the Orange Blossom Trail, following the scribbled directions Shirley had given her on the phone. Samantha had never been to Paradise Acres, where her father and Shirley had moved last year. The previous trailer city, Sunniside, was pretty grim; Shirley swore Paradise Acres was a move up.

It was noon, a full hour before she said she'd arrive.

At four this afternoon, Frank Shanker would be having his press conference, which CNN might or might not cover. Maybe she'd call Washington and see if they knew yet whether—

No, stop. This is vacation.

Samantha stopped at a 7-Eleven to kill some time, look at magazine headlines, buy cigarettes. Back at the house, she had bummed a few of Bethie's cigarettes which had brought her addiciton roaring back in full; she'd take another stab at quitting again when she got back to D.C. She looked into her purse to see that the air-travel pint of Jack Daniel's was in its place. She opened the bottle and took a swig. As usual, she had drunk five cups of strong coffee in her mother's kitchen and the whiskey made a small dent against the overexcitement of the caffeine. She went inside, browsed the magazines (Ronnie Shanker's death was mentioned briefly in the *Newsweek* obituary column), looked at the bodybuilding women, then the women in the fashion mags—to whose perfections she had abandoned any pretense.

Samantha, ten minutes later, found the overly grand corrugated-metal baroque entrance to the Paradise Acres trailer community and parked in a spot with a trailer-shaped VISITORS sign posted before it.

Sam made her way down a gravelled walkway. Other retired couples sat in the shade of awnings at plastic tables, underdressed grandparents with a proportionately aged dog asleep beneath their masters' lawn chairs. "You must be Herb's little girl," said one snaggletoothed woman, suggesting to Samantha that everyone here knew everybody's business.

Sam knocked on the flimsy sun-dulled aluminum door and Shirley answered, on the way out with a shopping pullcart. "Why good to see you, Sam! You're still in Washington, D.C.?"

Either her father relayed next to nothing about what his daughter was up to, or hardly remembered himself. Shirley, Sam noted, had passed through her high-hennaed hair and too-much-makeup phase and was now the archetypical swingin' silver-haired lady on the go so favored in TV ads.

"Herbert!"

There were rumblings from within their trailer, and the high-pitched yapping of the dog. "Aw, shut up, you mutt!" Sam heard her father say.

Samantha leaned in the door, encountering the stale smoke of the trailer's interior. "We do need to air the place out a bit, don't we?" Shirley said, noticing. "I'm going shopping, so I'll leave you two to have some time without me in your way!"

Shirley was convincing in her performed gaiety, though Sam suspected she probably hated it when his former family made contact.

"Sammie-girl!" said Mr. Flint, pacing into the light, a U-necked undershirt hanging on his tan skeletal frame, a short cigar in his mouth, a day's beard stubble, gleaming white.

Sam had lovingly fixed her father's appearance by his after-the-army photo, taped to her dresser mirror. Mr. Flint's 1948 snapshot showed a handsome, high-cheekboned country boy with a full head of oiled dark hair hanging in his face, more timelessly hip than he could have realized—a photo that invariably got a "Whoa, that's your *dad?*" from her hallmates back at Smith. Now the black hair was gone, his skin had an olive tint from its exposure to the Florida sun and ever-present smokes; his mouth was brown as the wet end of his cheap stogie. Shirley smoked too, so now Dad had free reign with his tobacco.

"So where you draggin' your old man?"

"Well, Dad," she considered as they walked to her car, "I don't know what's good around here. . . . On the way in I saw this chicken place. You still like fried chicken, don't you?"

Mr. Flint with some effort hunched down to scoot into the passenger seat of the Taurus. Sam focused on a vague middle distance, a buffer against her father's decline. There had been a prostate operation last year—the family was informed after the fact. Sam never knew if that was a kindness so she wouldn't worry or pure indifference. "This your car?" he asked.

"Rental."

"Write it off as an expense?"

"Not really. This is vacation." Sam drove out of the trailer park. "Paradise Acres looks like a nice place."

"Some of the neighbors," he shook his head, not explaining.

Samantha wondered out loud where she'd glimpsed this fried-chicken place; conversation was hard to come by. She asked questions to fill the void: How was Shirley? Did he ever see her kids? Didn't one of the girls live nearby? What were their names again? Did he go out this year to see the Cardinals in spring training? No, since he left St. Pete it was too far to go. Orlando had the Astros and who cared about them? Baseball was no good anymore anyway. Oh, I thought you still liked the Cardinals. Yes, those—you shouldn't say the word *nigger*, Daddy—do make too much money. Well, I don't know if I'd say the game is ruined because . . . Yes, you have a point. Yes, they should let St. Pete have its own team. Didn't you tell me you and Shirley were going to go over to the Cape to watch a space-shuttle launch? Oh well, shame about the car giving out, but wouldn't that be something to see, Dad? Wouldn't it?

"Wouldn't what?"

"The space shuttle," she said, "wouldn't it be something to see?"

"I smell whiskey. You haven't been drinking, have you?"

It was as if she were a little girl being scolded again.

"Gotta have a drink to see your ol' dad, eh?" he laughed.

"No, it's—I stopped off to see a friend from college for brunch who also lives in Orlando and we had a drink—"

"Not gonna be an alcoholic, are you? I know they turn up the bottles in Washington. Bunch of drunks up there."

"Daddy, why no—"

"Well, you probably wouldn't tell me if you were. It's your life. That's what I told Bethie when she had that little . . . colored boy. 'It's your goddam life,' I said. Do what you girls want."

With relief, she finally spotted the place she had seen on the drive in: Kenny Rogers Roasters. "See, I remembered you liked country music, right Dad?"

No response.

This wasn't a fried-chicken place, though. They did slow-roasted oven chicken, which Mr. Flint didn't care for. He liked the crunchy chicken, like Kentucky Fried or Popeye's. There was a Kentucky Fried Chicken within walking distance of Paradise Acres. We could have walked there and saved all this gas. Sam, are these rent-a-car folks ripping you off, making you pay by the mile?

"I'm not sure," she said, tentatively reaching for a tray.

"You signed a contract didn't you? You gotta watch what you sign your name to, Sammie-girl."

"Do you wanna eat somewhere else? We can—"

"Naw, let's just do it here. I hate getting in and out of that car. Gets my lower back. I remember when they bought me out at Boatland and I started working for that SOB Chet Diddle. I had to travel to boat shows. Had to rent cars. They always try to get you to take insurance, those bastards. You take the insurance, Sammie?"

She didn't know what the right answer was. "Yes, I took it, figuring if some old man hits me . . ." Oops. ". . . that I'm not liable."

"But you're insured in D.C.?"

"Yes, but—"

"Then they ripped you off! Your local insurance oughta be good down here in a rental car . . ." A line was forming behind them, so Samantha reached over and prepared a tray for her father, who she herded down the aisle. ". . . and these goddam people skin you alive. What's that?" he asked the server. Kenny Rogers's chain was aiming at an upmarket chicken-lover, offering new potatoes with dill, creamed spinach, macaroni salads, fat-free side orders. "You don't have any mashed potatoes and gravy?"

Not today, sir.

"Kentucky Fried Chicken always has it."

This isn't Kentucky Fried Chicken, sir. The new potatoes are very nice.

"No thank you, I'll just have the chicken by itself and a roll. You do have rolls, don't you?"

Yessir. But a plate comes with two vegetables—

"Don't want to pay for any extra, just give it to me like that."

But sir it's included in—

Samantha: "Please, just give it to him like that."

She and her father sat by the window. Kenny Rogers's own songs were playing on the piped-in muzak. Hits from the '70s and '80s. Samantha with her healthy salad plate ate silently, listening to "The Coward of the County," a jaunty pop-country song involving a woman's gang rape and how her husband went and beat up the guys.

"Kenny Rogers isn't country music."

Sam had her mouth full. "What?"

"He ruined country. All that California stuff. He did that album with those, oh what's their name . . ." After many inaccurate and inconceivable descriptions it became apparent that her father was talking about the Bee Gees. "That shit wasn't country music. He and that Dolly Parton, who went all Hollywood, and what was that terrible woman with her dingbat sisters?" Barbara Mandrell was who he meant. "It's all a long goddamn way from Hank Williams and Merle Haggard, I'll tell you that. Now I see he's built himself a restaurant and put pictures of himself up everywhere."

"Dad, if you don't like it, let's just get in the car and go to Kentucky Fried Chicken."

"Oh, don't bother about your ol' dad. Not much hungry anyway. Maybe I can take this home for Bowser." Bowser was the yippy, barking spaniel back at the trailer. "I had something just a few hours ago anyway."

"You ate before I came to take you out to lunch?"

"When you're my age, you eat when you eat."

Samantha threw most of her food away and escorted her father back to the car. She watched her frail father struggle to lower his body into the car seat again.

On the way back to Paradise Acres, Mr. Flint lit up another cigar and the blue smoke blended with her half-eaten dinner to nauseate Samantha, who soon rolled down the window.

"Just like old times, huh Dad? You and me driving through downtown Springfield, on old Route 66? Remember that?"

He didn't respond, preoccupied with trying to get keep his cigar lit, cursing his lighter.

"Saw your pal Proctor on the TV the other day," Mr. Flint said.

"Yeah, he was on *Larry King*."

"Was he Republican or Democrat, Sammie?"

How could her father not know something so fundamental to her life, let alone what most people knew off the top of their head? "Republican, Dad. Like you and me."

"Hell, I'm no Republican. That B-movie man, Ronald Reagan"— her father pronounced his name *Ree-gan*—"bankrupted the whole damn country. Tried to get at my Social Security too."

Sam was adrift. "You used to be Republican—"

"Yeah, and I'm goddamn sorry I voted that way a time or two. They don't care about nothin' but the rich."

Samantha barely knew where to take her mind. But Dad, *I'm* a working Republican. *You and I* were the Republicans—

"Let's stop here," Mr. Flint said, pointing to one of Orlando's innumerable, identical pink-and-ochre pastel strip malls. "Need a few things, if you don't mind."

Samantha let him out in front of the drugstore, went to park, and then joined him inside. She carried the basket as her father selected a shaving cream, some razor cartridges that fit his model of razor, shoe polish, paper towels for the trailer, bathroom cleanser, soap . . . Sam began to question if they had anything at all inside that trailer. Then Mr. Flint stopped at the prescription window and uncrinkled a prescription that was a week away from needing to be refilled—could it be done now? Mr. Flint, Sam observed, took something called Proscar.

"What's that stuff do, Dad?"

He shrugged as if he didn't know.

"I figure I've got your genes, so you might as well tell me what's in store for me."

"It's for prostatitis, Sammie-girl. I think you're in the clear." And then with absurd delay he began to chuckle; Sam laughed along with him. See? This isn't so bad, here we are, Daddy and his little Sammie, laughing, having a good time . . .

The cashier pushed the total button. It came to $78.65.

Sam turned to her father but didn't see him make a move for his wallet. She was to pay for it. "Uh, you . . . you take a credit card?"

It was a silent drive back to Paradise Acres.

"You wanna come in?" Mr. Flint asked.

"Oh, that's all right." Suddenly she wanted to drive right out of Florida, ditch her return flight and just drive her rental car all the way to Washington, a nightdrive with the truckers and the loners, hand in the keys in D.C., pay the drop-off fee—

"Naw, come on in for a minute. It's time for Sally."

The trailer was cramped and smoke-ridden as if there had been a four-alarm blaze. Out came Bowser: *arf-arf-arf-arf-arf-arf-arf* . . .

"Shut up, you mutt, 'fore I take you to the pound!"

Mr. Flint settled in a recliner in front of the TV and turned it on with his remote. Sam was reminded of her last visit to see her father: Mr. Flint lodged before the set, letting it play through their entire visit; through every intricacy of conversation paraded a succession of shows he wasn't even watching . . . and yet he infallibly muted the commercials, out of habit. He flipped through the forty channels, past CNN—

"Hold it," Sam said, as her father backed up.

"My senator, Frank Shanker, has a press conference at four today." But CNN was featuring an update on some Libyan atrocity.

Mr. Flint zapped ahead to Sally Jesse Raphael. "Almost missed Sally," he hummed contentedly. "I'm sure these people aren't for real. I'm sure they pay people to come out and act like this."

Then why on earth would you watch it, Sam thought. Sally's exhibits of the day were husbands and boyfriends who didn't want their girlfriends to have their genitals pierced. Some fat blonde with missing teeth was telling her skinny black boyfriend, "No two-timing [beep] is gonna tell me [beep] about what I can do with my [beep]-ing [beep]!" while the audience hooted and rolled in delight.

"Shall I put this stuff away?" Sam offered when it was clear that her father was watching Sally and CNN wasn't going to prevail.

"Just put it all in the bathroom. Shirley'll mess with it," he waved toward the other end of the trailer, as if the bathroom could be anywhere else. Samantha passed the kitchen nook, peeking in the bedroom, spying the dog basket inches from the unmade double bed. Shirley must love him, Sam thought clinically, because she could do better than Dad. She wondered if Shirley had a lover on the side.

In their bathroom, Samantha unwrapped the new bar of soap and stared at herself in the mirror, judging her appearance harshly. Same dark features, same eyes as Dad. Was her own future forecast in her father's face? She stooped to open the cabinet doors under the sink, to put away the Comet cleanser, and found herself staring at a box of Depends. A moment to register: Dad is incontinent now. He wears a diaper.

"Hey Sammie-girl, come see this!"

On Channel 9, Geraldo Rivera had women who were telling their husbands and boyfriends for the first time that they had a secret profession of stripping. How Geraldo decided to break the news to the husbands was to have them sit on a stage while their wives came out in stripper's attire and disrobed to the howls and cheers of the mob. Coming up next segment: a wife tells her husband she's a prostitute during the day while he's at work!

Sam came around behind her father's recliner and placed a hand over his hand, muting the TV, then bent down and kissed the top of his head tenderly, placing all the pity and unrequited love that overwhelmed her into this simple gesture. "I gotta get back to Clearwater, Daddy."

No protests, no can't-you-stay-awhile. She hadn't hoped for much.

"Give everyone my best," he said.

"I saw Kelly earlier this week. She sends her love." Wasn't true—

but Samantha didn't want to let him go quite yet. "She and Chuck are hoping to bring the kids to Disney World and bring 'em all by to see Grandpa," she manufactured.

"Aww, we couldn't have all those young'uns around here."

"And Bethie says hi . . ." She let him go and he instantly pushed the mute button to reactivate the sound. He nodded, but his silence showed he knew she was lying about Bethie for sure.

"You drive careful," he said, resolutely fixated on a chunky redhead unbuttoning her shirt. Wide electronically produced black boxes appeared to cover her distended breasts.

"You call me in Washington if you need anything, okay?"

"All right . . ." Dad trailed off, mesmerized by the TV.

Sam made her way to the gravel parking lot.

She sat in her car a moment. It wasn't as if she told him how much she loved him either. Maybe because she didn't love what he'd grown into, this relic of a once-hopeful man, this castoff left behind. Did he ever really care? Was that in her imagination too?

She started the car and turned back onto Orange Blossom, an avenue just like U.S. 19 back in Clearwater, or main roads all over Florida, eight lanes of untimed stoplights, bad elderly drivers, an infinity of commerce, mega-malls, mini-malls, strip malls, stucco and pastels, ochres and pinks, K-Marts next to Wal-Marts next to Targets and snarls of traffic leading to, fro, and between—how do they all stay in business? Eyesore follows eyesore, the Shell-O-Rama with conchs on special, two for five bucks, House of Carpet, Tire City, Shoe Town, Lawn Mower World. Imagine that, a world of nothing but lawn mowers. Harry's Sports Bar & Grill—

"Hold it," Samantha said to Harry's, the neon OPEN sign in the window. She swerved the car into the parking lot.

There were a few Orlandans in the corner, a guy in a baseball cap playing the one video game in the back hallway. Harry (or whoever) served her beer from the tap.

"If no one cares," she asked, trying to be flirtatious but seeing only a tired squint in the bar mirror, "can I watch CNN on this set?"

"Whatever you say," said Harry, obliging with the remote. "You oughtta stay for the Braves game. Don't get enough ladies in this place as it is, heh?'' Harry named an athlete—Sam supposed he was an athlete—that often appeared in Harry's Sports Bar & Grill. Why, it was practically the athlete's second home; he called Harry by name. You wanna meet him sometime? Well, ol' Harry could arrange it. There's his autograph right up there, the framed photo above Chompers—Chompers, the shellacked alligator head with a miniature Orlando Magic basketball in its jaws—you want me to take it down so you can look at it up close?

Four P.M. and CNN suddenly flashed up a picture of Senator Frank Shanker behind the newcaster.

"I'm sorry," Sam interrupted as politely as she could, "but this is what I wanted to see."

Harry, unoffendable, turned the volume way up, as the news station presented its montage for *A CNN Live Event*. There was the lectern in the Senate radio–TV gallery on the third floor of the Capitol, and a moment later Frank Shanker, somber and subdued, adjusting the microphone.

"It's a sad thing when a young man loses his life, particularly sad for his family and those that loved him . . ."

So far, so good. Samantha allowed Harry to slide a full shotglass of whiskey beside her beer, on the house. Sam studied the washed-out portly figures beside Shanker: Mort, Dan and Don, Bernie the press officer, everyone in black suits, trying to appear mournful.

". . . but as his father, I cannot stand idly by and allow the killer to get away scot-free."

What?

"The killer I refer to is pornography."

"Oh, Frank, no," Samantha said.

"My son, Ronnie, and a group of his friends at the Fairfax Academy where he was enrolled were part of a club, of sorts—for all I know this had the sanction of the officers in charge, maybe even some of these perverts were involved . . ."

Samantha, as in a cartoon, slapped her forehead, lecturing the TV: "What are you *doing*?" The slander, the defamation suits . . .

"It would appear this club catered to the worst in adolescent boys, exciting prurient urges, and this led to a series of dares culminating, sadly, in . . . I think they call it, an autoerotic asphyxiation. None of which was possible without the pernicious influence of pornography on a young impressionable mind."

"I'll need another." Samantha tapped her shotglass.

"Now, let's not pretend that young people can't get pornography. They're not supposed to get cigarettes or six-packs of beer or drugs either, but they do—and yet the pornography is worse . . ."

"Looking at pictures of women's boobs," Sam said intently to the TV, "is NOT worse than drugs, Frank."

"He's upset about his son," Harry said, absorbed.

Jesus, Sam thought, this go-after-porn is actually gonna play in the Heartland. If Shanker thinks I'm going to have ONE thing to do with this crackpot legislation—

"I have instructed my legislative director to finalize a bill that goes straight to the heart of crippling the pornography industry in this country. I call it the Ronnie Shanker Defense of Decency Bill."

"Your legislative director is doing *what?*"

"In the past, our liberal left-wing Democratic appointed Supreme Court has been protecting the scum who fill our children's minds with this garbage, who wreck the women's lives who participate in this miserable business. Therefore, my office is preparing to submit a constitutional amendment . . ."

"You have got to be kidding!" Samantha snapped back a second shot and tried to calm her shaking hands. She turned for sympathy to Harry. "A constitutional amendment has no chance in hell of getting out of Congress, do you realize that? Do you know what a laughingstock he has made himself on the Hill?"

Harry stared at her unsurely. No, it occurred to Samantha, Harry would never believe she worked for the man on the TV—that would sound too crazy even for a woman at a bar knocking back whiskey at 4:15 in the afternoon.

"The plan was . . . ," Samantha mumbled nonetheless, ". . . the plan was to say something simple and dignified, so the whole mess would go away—is there a pay phone here?"

Harry nervously pointed to the one by the bathrooms.

Her fingers were unsure. She misdialed the office twice.

Wanda picked up. "You watchin' CNN?"

Samantha: "You bet I'm watching it. Who's around?"

"Everyone's at the press conference."

Sam hung up and tried Senator Cooper's office, hoping for Julie, getting her voice mail: *You have reached the office of Julie Bingham* . . . Samantha tore through her address book for Cameron's office number. He was there:

"Sam, I can't believe what I'm seeing on TV. I guess you saw him on *Today* this morning—"

"What did he say there?"

"I have a committee meeting—I've *got* to get outta here. When do you get back to Washington?" Cam's voice got a little ragged and sexy on the last question, hoping by telepathy to communicate his urgent needs. Ha! Samantha could no more think about their little sordid sex sessions than she could her own *name* right now. Now Cameron was laughing. "I can hardly wait to see what kind of bill you draw up to do away with smut! What—yes, Senator, be right there!"

Samantha was speechless, babbling syllables of disbelief as Cameron begged her pardon, hung up the phone, and ran to his meeting.

Mort. Mort that worm, that nincompoop, who probably goaded Shanker into turning a tragedy that could have given even Family Frank a moment of dignity into a right-wing kook vendetta against Bob Guccione and Hugh Hefner! Where is that little shit? She flipped through her book and found his beeper number, his pager number, his home number, his office private line, leaving crazed rants on each voice mail. Finally, he showed up in his office—

"Now, Samantha," Mort said, "I know you won't be happy about how Frank's chosen to deal with this issue—"

"Chosen? I don't know the half of it, but it sounds like he totally trashed the game plan. What happened to playing it sensitive, being a human being, crying with Barbara Walters on *20/20*?"

"Okay, so he went off-message. But I think we can still work with this antipornography thing—"

"Mort, half of the ministers in our home state subscribe to *Penthouse*! Do you really think you're going to win male votes in our state by getting their *Playboys* out of the barber shop?"

Mort lost his familiar composure and exploded: "Like I have any control over Frank! Like I can stop him from getting up there and saying any goddamn thing that comes into his head!" She could hear him panting. "We had a prepared statement like we agreed and then he went haywire, doing his family-values shtick, from his radio show, and the next thing I know he's going on about shutting down pornography in America—and where the hell were *you*?"

"On my vacation, which you told me I could take!"

"He might have listened to you—"

"Like *I* have any sway over him! God, how is Bernie working the media on this?" Not waiting for an answer, she went on, "Of course, the media won't be thrilled by the idea of an amendment to do away with a First Amendment freedom—"

"Screw the legitimate press," Mort said. "This thing is gonna go over gangbusters with the church crowd, the middle class, all the smut haters. Everybody in the country will be talking about it, so we have no choice but to go forward with it, Sam. Now Angeline drew up some reform measures—"

"*ANGELINE?*" Samantha shrieked, turning the few heads in the bar.

She heard Frank's voice in the office, and Mort muffling the phone. Mort said, "Frank wants to speak to you."

The next moment Frank picked up in his office and Mort hung up. "Now Samantha—"

"What happened up there, Frank?" It was one thing to scream at Mort—that always felt good, and Samantha did it as much as she could work it into her schedule—but screaming went nowhere with Frank. Samantha willed herself to be calm. "Did you hear yourself land smack in the middle of a defamation suit from the school?"

"Yes, yes, whatever. I wanted to be the one to tell you the good news about your little writing-initiative thing."

"*What?*" He wanted to patronize her and pat her on the head with her little bill getting to committee in the middle of all this?

"Frank, we have to talk about . . ." But she was curious. "What about my bill? It moved through committee?"

"Better than that, Sammie. Grassley took it over to Agriculture. He put it on the agriculture spending bill. So it's a done deal."

Samantha Flint, her only meaningful mission accomplished, had a strange impulse to quit her job. She'd made the only mark she was likely to make, after all. She closed her eyes and the vision came to her, as it used to, pure and ideal: a struggling writer, making his way to some underused government building to write, to write as she once had dreamed of doing. At the moment it seemed unlikely, but somehow, someway, she dreamed of claiming one of these Samantha Flint fellowships for herself. *She has taken the better part and it shall not be taken from her!*

"Of course, Sammie, we had to make some . . . changes."

"Changes?"

"One thing, it's all set in Iowa now, not the fifty states—"

"Iowa? There's already a famous workshop in Iowa. What do they need—"

"Well, now, that's what I needed to get Grassley on our side. But Sammie, think what we got in exchange for it, though! Grassley's on board for my Fetus Protection Act, which is more important than any old farm-writing project thing—"

"What did you just say?"

"I wrote it down here, just a minute . . ." She heard him rummaging around on his desk. "The Charles Grassley Center for Agro-Journalism. Now before you get mad—"

"The *what*?"

"It's a beachhead, Sammie. You have your little writing center in Iowa—"

"Not for agro-journalism, Frank! This was supposed to be about serious writers! Poems and novels . . . and . . ."

"Aw hell, Sammie, the government has no part to play in that kind of stuff. Grassley wouldn't sign on to Fetus Protection unless we gave him something. And just think, it's a *start*. Maybe next year they'll just be doing, you know, farm report stuff, but in the years to come it could expand into anything you want. In fact, Grassley felt, since you'd been in on his center from the beginning, that you might want to help select a site for it.''

Her hands started to shake. She wanted off the phone worse than she wanted to curse her boss and the town he worked in. ''It's not what I . . .''

''I know you wanted something a little more artsy-fartsy, Sam, but you gotta take time out here to be proud of yourself. This is your first project that's gone all the way to a vote, right? First of many! Now when you get back Monday, we'll start up our anti-pornography drive.''

''Monday . . .''

''We're a team, Sammie, and we're going to change this country! Just you watch!''

She hung up the phone, felt her way to the nearest dark booth and dropped down into it. I'll destroy the man, she decided then and there. She briefly glimpsed her old vision—novelists in spare Coast Guard lighthouse stations and poets in cabins in the national forests—now dispersing, darkening . . . For that she would destroy him.

Courage for this new role of public service came in the form of the Wild Turkey, shot following shot.

Here's to you, males of the species.

Here's to you, Dad. Thanks for nothing.

Here's to you, Warren Proctor. For retiring and throwing your staff to the winds.

Here's to you, Cameron. Can't wait to get back into my bed where your nagging, sexless wife can't get at you. Well, we'll just see how much longer I spend my nights relieving you—you lying, cheating, good-for-nothing adulterous weasel.

Here's to you, Frank Shanker. Proof that there is no cretin so base and clownlike that he won't be lifted to great electoral heights by the American people. God, imagine the office Monday morning. Full-frontal assaults by *Playboy* and the ACLU and constitutional scholars. The obnoxious support of the most dour, juiceless kind of angry feminists, tight-assed church bitches, greasy Religious Right luminaries who don't use pornography because their hobbies run more to child molesting and visiting prostitutes. Oh, wouldn't the antiporn crowd love to know that when I was in Virginia . . .

A thought occurred.

A thought so potent that she froze and didn't move for a full minute. Then she ordered another shot; Harry was starting to look concerned. She talked quietly to herself: "It would mean his complete humiliation" and "No, it'll be obvious that I was responsible."

She walked back to the pay phone. After a number of directory-information inquiries, she then dialed a Washington number . . . but hung up before the call could connect.

Then she redialed, reconnected . . . then hung up again.

Then she committed herself: "Hi, is this Joyce Garrison?"

"You the hanger-upper?"

"Uh, yeah. Joyce, we've met. I'm Samantha Flint, used to be l.d. for Warren Proctor. I'm with Frank Shanker now."

Joyce made a joke.

"Yes, that Frank Shanker. You wrote a pretty sharp article in the *Post* about the senator last year, made him look like a putz."

"Hey. I'm sorry if you didn't like the piece—"

"I loved the piece. I have something . . ."

Joyce waited patiently, recognizing the conflicted pre-leak tone of voice.

"You're going to have to do a little homework," Samantha said, "and check out what I'm going to tell you thoroughly, but how would you like, providing my anonymity is absolutely fucking up-one-side-and-down-the-other-guaranteed, a scoop that will keep you on the front page for a week?"

Samantha arrived back in the capital earlier than intended, Saturday afternoon. She called every friend and acquaintance to reaffirm the fact that she had been in Florida, yes Florida, 1500 miles away, far from the capital and the *Washington Post*. She got especially drunk with Julie and the gang on Saturday night, knowing that Sunday might be D day.

Samantha hadn't slept easily since the phone call.

She awoke at 4:00 A.M. She grabbed a coat and went scouring

the rainy streets for a Sunday *Washington Post*. Nyeh, she told herself, if there's an article on Shanker it won't be in today because
they put the Sunday edition together in advance, right? Yet, having
fed the succession of quarters in the slot with a shaky hand, then
standing at the news rack with her heart beating fast, she turned
each A-section page of the Sunday *Post* . . . until the last page, with,
praise god, no sign of Shanker and her leak. Joyce probably jetti-
soned the story, or an editor thought it was unnewsworthy.

Monday it hit.

Monday morning, Frank Shanker made the front page, bottom
half of the fold. It had a box around it, the way "cute" articles are
set off, a new panda at the zoo, a twelve-year-old writes the president, et cetera. Senator Frank Shanker stared stupidly from the
photo, openmouthed.

SHANKER'S ANTIPORN CRUSADE COULD START WITH HIS
PLAYBOY SUBSCRIPTION

If I don't go into the office, she figured, they'll know I'm somehow
the source. She poured some bourbon in her morning coffee, lifted
it to her lips, pausing for a second, the second that gave her time
to think: alcohol *before* going to work, a new first for Samantha Flint.

Then she drank.

"Did you see this?" Mort screamed, slamming the newspaper
against his palm, tossing it to the floor, only to retrieve it and read
from the article again.

Moments after Samantha arrived, she was herded with the other
top aides into Frank's office. Hold all calls, Wanda!

Samantha: "This will blow over, Senator. It's nothing criminal,
really no big deal—"

"No big deal! Someone on *my* staff, who has been in *my* house
has been ratting me out to the *Post*! And it's a slander. I don't subscribe to *Playboy*, for crying out loud. . . ."

He did, however. And the *Post* had proof, quoting from *Playboy*
subscription services itself. Samantha had read it, oh, ten or eleven

times already, but with their eyes upon her, she read it as if for the first time with great seriousness.

> If Sen. Frank Shanker thinks there's
> too much pornographic garbage and
> America should be protected from it,
> then he could start by taking out the
> trash in his own living room.

"Actually, I uh didn't have time to read the paper this morning," Sam mumbled. "Still unpacking. You know, from my trip to Florida—"

Mort: "Someone in our office must have called the *Post*."

Young Republican 1: "I think we call for mandatory lie-detector tests throughout the office, Senator. Maybe bring in an investigator to question everyone."

"No," said Samantha quickly. She hurried to think of a reason. "Looks vindictive and you'll have the ACLU stopping you with a court order," she fantasized.

Frank stirred in his chair. "I'd have cancelled the damn rag years ago, but, you know, I gotta keep up with what's current."

Young Republican 1: "The interviews are great, Senator."

Young Republican 2: "Yeah, great sports articles. It's not like you got the magazine just to . . ."

They all finished that sentence in their heads.

Samantha asked, "Do you hear yourself, Senator? You denied a few minutes ago that you had a subscription and now you're saying you subscribed for the articles. Whatever story we come up with you have *got* to stick fast to it—"

Mort: "Of course he'll stick to it. What we need to know now is who called the *Post*."

"Maybe *Playboy* called the *Post*."

"No way," Mort said, eyeing her. God, he knew it was her. "Magazines," he declared, "don't know who their subscribers are. They hire out to subscription services who handle all the paperwork and billings. Someone who'd been in Frank's home, or who had gone through his cancelled checks at the bank, maybe."

"But how," she pretended to be as curious as they were, "would anyone in this office know you had a subscription to *Playboy?*"

"The party last Christmas," said Shanker sourly. "One of the staffers saw it in my study, I guess."

Samantha: "And so could any of your guests." She named some of the Democratic senators Shanker had invited, just to be social. "How do you know one of *them* didn't call the *Post?* If you polygraph the whole of the office you're going to make people feel threatened—"

"Fine," said Young Republican 2. "If the staff's afraid of being fired, you can bet there'll be no more leaks."

Young Republican 1: "It's just good leadership, Senator. The kind of leadership we've come to expect from Frank Shanker."

"You know," laughed Frank, doodling on his pad absently, "we all thought *you* were the source, Samantha." Senator Shanker balled up his doodle-page and threw it toward a far waste can like a basketball shot. "You have such personal opposition to so much of what we do."

"Frank, I'm a team player. Why would I sabotage my own—"

"Don't worry." Senator Shanker raised his hand. "We don't think you planted the story anymore. But we did for a little while. You were the first one we thought of."

The story was everywhere.

Time, Newsweek, USA Today, all the late-night talk-show monologues, the *New York Times* op-ed page. Anna Quindlen wondered gently in her column how Family Frank Shanker could claim the title when he sent his sons off to a loveless military boarding school, avoiding the hard work of parenting. Half of the articles (piling up thanks to the senator's clipping service) were scathing attacks on hypocrisy, some suggesting that the senator was in part to blame for his son's death, since Ronnie was no doubt exposed to his father's pornography; the other half (Russell Baker, Donald Kaul) contenting themselves with dark ridicule and disdain.

"Well," counseled an amused Julie, slicing into a runny fried egg, "it sounds like you guys have hit bottom on this thing."

Julie and Samantha had gone from being exercise buddies at their gym, to meeting regularly at 7:30 A.M. for a greasy breakfast at

Sherrill's Diner on Capitol Hill. Just what Samantha needed, another meal to add to her daily schedule of four or five feedings, not counting between-meal snacks, plus a habitual five, six rounds of high-calorie mixed drinks with the gang.

"Are we going to split a cinnamon roll?" Julie asked, having laid waste to the jelly basket and the buttered toast.

"Why do you even ask?"

Sam was distracted. Food all day long and booze all night long and a shot of NyQuil to get to sleep—and if getting up from drowsy drugged sleep proved too arduous, she broke into her small stash of 20/20 speed pills, set aside for special all-night senatorial voting sprees and end-of-session legislative marathons.

"Do you know?" Julie was asking, between gooey bites of cinnamon bun.

"Know what?"

"Who tipped off the *Post*."

Samantha tried out a number of alternative theories; i.e., maybe his fed-up wife? Depressingly, Julie didn't buy any of them. "You know," Julie said ingenuously, "they're gonna think it's you. You better get some ass-covering ready to wear."

Fran, formerly Senator Proctor's constituent correspondent—now deliriously employed at Senator Chafee's, damn her to hell—waved at Samantha from the cash register where she was picking up a coffee to go.

"I don't mean to laugh," Fran said to Samantha, sidling over, "but it just keeps getting worse for Frank. I guess you saw the *Boston Globe*."

Samantha and Julie raced to the Capitol Metro stop newsstand and tore through the *Globe*, letting the commuters flow around them.

FAMILY FRANK GETS AN XXX-RATING

It turns out Senator Shanker also, some years ago before his stint as radio host and senator, had subscriptions to, or placed back orders for, *Swank, Oui, Mondo Ta-Ta's, Big Mama, Hustler*, and half a dozen others Samantha had never heard of. The industry, checking its files, was striking back.

That Friday night Samantha was glued to *Washington Week in Review*, like everyone else in town. Cameron told his wife he was watching the show with colleagues at a wine bar, but in reality he was emerging from Sam's kitchen with a bowl of microwaved popcorn. They had their priorities: first, the inside-the-Beltway media assessment of the week, and second, sex.

Most of the show concerned preelection mayhem, the sinking of the Bush campaign with video clips of the Republican standard-bearer, once the proud owner of a 91 percent approval rating (and a modicum of electoral integrity), now flailing, calling his opponents "bozos," and making McCarthyite insinuations about what Bill Clinton was up to on his student trips to Moscow—wading out ever deeper into public scorn. A man eleven years older than Samantha and four years older than Cameron was about to be elected president, the pundits were confidently predicting.

"Well, at least the Bush follies keep Frank's follies off the front burner," Sam said, lying across Cameron's lap, happy, in fact, to imagine staffers with worse problems than hers.

Steve Roberts of *U.S. News & World Report* spoke of how low-minded the Bush campaign was, trying to drag smut about Clinton's concupiscent past into the public.

"Speaking of smut," said moderator Paul Duke—

"Here we go," Samantha said, burying her face in Cam's lap, while he began to laugh.

Gloria Borger of the *Washington Post*: "I spoke to an aide in Senator Shanker's office and there is talk that this is a big smear by the porn industry, following his comments."

"There's not much, as they say, 'credible deniability' to that argument," added Mara Liasson of NPR. "Though, it's hard to believe a sanctimonious public official like Frank Shanker would be so idiotic as to have a subscription in his name to *Big Mama* and then attack the industry so viciously."

"Well, alas," concluded the moderator, "we come to the end of another 'big mama' of our own. We'll see you next week."

Samantha sighed. "We deserve a kickback from *Big Mama* after all this publicity." She slipped a loose hand within the belt loop of Cameron's trousers, ready for the TV to go off.

Samantha and Cameron were getting sloppy. Margaret took a lengthy family-crisis vacation to North Carolina, and during that time Samantha and Cameron moved around town as they pleased, restaurants and movies and coffeehouses. Now that Margaret was back in town, Cameron persisted in coming over whenever he felt like it. Sam cautioned him, but even she lost heart in taking much effort to disguise things. Hiding their affair would mean seeing him less. And her earlier plans to be rid of him, and the moral queasiness that came in the door with him, had given way to ferocious need.

The sex had changed too. Samantha was no longer the courtesan with the perfumed sheets, conducting sex out of a romance novel, tender and forbidden; she ripped his clothes off, commanded Cameron to take her in the shower, on the sofa, standing against the kitchen counter, with a running patter of shameless dirty talk while he performed—the kind of "naughty" sex Cameron never had, or hoped to have, with Margaret.

"Our relationship is changing," he said once, putting on his pants, having to race back to Virginia this late afternoon for some function with his wife. "Do you want to talk about it?"

"Maybe after the Shanker mess blows over."

Cameron leaned over the bed, his eyes full with emotion. She had seen this open, heartfelt gaze before, but whatever his accompanying thoughts, he had kept them to himself. But not tonight:

"I feel just terrible sayin' it, can't believe the words are comin' out of my mouth, Sam. But I want you to know that I'd leave Margaret for you. I love you, Sam. I realize that I loved Margaret in a kind of immature, simple way that wasn't really passionate love—it's never been, even at its best, what you and I have."

Samantha returned a charitable glance. "Don't make any decisions now, baby."

"Just think about what I said."

Nope, no way. No can do.

She wouldn't think about it. Too much on her plate to add home-wrecking into the mix.

SENATOR FOUND TO FREQUENT
VIDEO PORN RENTAL STORE

The *New York Post* ran a front-page story with a grainy surveillance-camera image of a man who might be Frank Shanker in a northern Virginia place called the Alexandria Art Cinema, where one could— and the senator apparently did—rent hardcore porn videos.

Young Republican 1: "That doesn't even look like Frank!"

Mort and Samantha checked the fine print, calling the proprietor who sold the story to the tabloids. Frank never paid with credit cards—thank god—and so all the press really had was 1) the clerk who swore Frank rented XXX videos there and 2) the grainy image. Bernie put out a categorical denial; Frank did a phone-interview with Gordon Liddy's show about how this was an orchestrated conspiracy by the left to smear him. Liddy and the rabble that listened to his show had no trouble believing that, but the phone calls were consistent: "Are you crazy, man? You're gonna get rid of *Penthouse*? Take away my god-given right to look at beautiful, naked women? If they wanna show it, I wanna see it!"

Mort peeked around Samantha's cubicle, and set down a schedule of crisis meetings—

"Mort," Sam interrupted, "we ought to go home and pull the covers over our head until all the dirt gets out. We're in freefall."

Freefall. Not even the slippery slope to grab on to—just the abyss, no controlling the slant of coverage, no controlling the speed of descent or what they would land upon. Nothing to do but wait, hit bottom, and see what was left.

All phone calls to the senator's office heard the taped message.

Mail went unanswered.

Mort and Bernie fabricated anemic press releases and statements without ever running them by Frank, who dwelled in some doped-up, whiskeyed-up limbo, staring out his office window or holed up in Virginia.

Samantha passed the file room to see an open bottle of vodka set out the way one used to see cans of soda. People took leaves of absence, left in the middle of the day, didn't come back from lunch as planned—one staffer left "to get some fresh air" and never showed up again. Staffers greeted each other glassy-eyed, downcast, booze on the breath; someone left a bottle of Adovan out on the mail-sorting table and, reportedly, it was passed around and everyone present popped a pill. Samantha twice went to use the copying machine to discover an original résumé left under the flap. People were bailing.

BEEP. *Samantha, this is Mimi. I can't believe what I'm reading—mind you, it couldn't happen to a nicer fascist Nazi, but I'll spare you that speech. How're you doing, sweetheart? Why won't you call the Meem? By the way, if all else fails, I can get you a job at CAA. Not what you're used to salarywise or powerwise, but . . .*

Thanks, but no thanks. She didn't need Mimi Mohr's charity just yet. This was her world, the Capitol Hill world; she had marked it off for herself, and she wasn't ready to give it up. She found the resignation letter in her top drawer and tore it in half.

"Look," said Cameron, snuggling her underneath the covers, "if you resign now—"

"If I get out now, I look like I jumped a sinking ship. The fact that I'll stick with the guy and hope for a comeback speaks well of me."

Cameron, who was growing tired of seeing their love life take second place to the distractions of Frank's imbecilities, sighed and stared at the ceiling. "But even if they don't fire you, what have you got left? What kind of legislation can Shanker ever get up to again? C'mon, life means more than being an l.d. in the Senate."

Not mine, thought Samantha.

Why didn't she bail? Because—she would answer her mirror, her reflection in the Metro car, the bathroom mirror in the Monocle—Sam's round of drinks are on the way!—she was a goddamn legislative director; even hanging by a thread, even surgically attached to a nincompoop like Frank, she was *in*. And if she quit then she'd be, once and for all, *out*.

"I don't like *out*," she once drunkenly explained to a listener in one of her regular bar stops. "I like *in*."

"Sounds like you're scared," the person said.

"You're right. I fear *out*."

People who left their jobs—hell, people who went on vacation too long during key sessions!—found themselves *out*. And no one ever came back from that undiscovered country. Samantha had no life or friends or hobbies or passions that didn't depend on her being *in*, a part of Washington's power game.

"I'm not sure outside of this job I even exist," she added to the . . . who was it she was talking to?

Mort was still obsessed with the origins of their misfortunes.

There was an investigator brought in, Richard Mack, an alcoholic-nosed ex-cop whose smoke-ravaged baritone made him seem perfect for the role of private eye. "A lot of fingers are pointing at you, miss," he said to Samantha, waiting for her one morning in her cubicle. He was such a good imitation of a film-noir detective, down to his seedy raincoat, Sam felt obliged to play the Jane Greer role:

"Lot of people want my job," she said, half-flirting. "That happens," she added breathily, "when you're good at what you do."

Dick Mack skulked around the office leaving a trail of stale smoke from his last barroom visit, cubicle to cubicle, brandishing a blank notepad. "Got it all right up here," he said, pointing to his head with the pen. His method consisted of looking a staffperson in the eye and asking, "Why'd you do it? You can tell me. . . ." He met his match in Wanda, who tossed him out into the hall after too many impertinent questions.

Mort let him go after a most entertaining week; Sam mourned his departure, since there was no danger of her being fingered as long as Dick Mack, Private Eye, was on the case.

The Fairfax Military Academy sued Shanker for libel, slander, defamation, asking three million in damages. They had such a strong case that it was difficult turning up counsel for Senator Shanker, who was now hiding out in Crystal City, the Soviet-style cluster of gray soulless hotels and office buildings across the Potomac in Arlington. He now held his crisis meetings in a high-security, rented businessman's suite at the Marriott Inn.

"Have you seen Ellen Goodman's column today?" Mort asked Sam pointedly. Samantha read:

> It's been delightful to listen to Pat Buchanan's "buy American" rhetoric in his run for the Republican nomi-

nation in 1992—particularly as he had to explain away his Mercedes-Benz to auto workers in Detroit.

But in the 1992 hypocrite sweepstakes, another Republican may just have retired the prize.

Samantha laid it on the line for the senator, "You gotta get rid of the lawsuit from the school, Frank. Get out your checkbook and make it go away or this will drag on and on—"

"But I could win that suit!" Shanker mused. "You know, we could take the millions I'd get and set up a memorial fund for Ronnie." Shanker contemplated this noble gesture. "But the rest could go to the '96 campaign, couldn't it, Mort?"

Mort delegated this curious idea to Don, who said he'd present a confidential report later in the week.

The senator: "Damn it, people, now let's move on to something *positive*! I wanna hear positive now—from all of you."

Silence.

"I know," Samantha began slowly, "that it doesn't look this way now. But . . . this whole mess has its advantages."

No one dared concur.

"You have publicity," Samantha continued, "you have name recognition like never before, even though at the moment it's more like notoriety. If you went on *60 Minutes* or, wait, better yet, appeared with Jay Leno on the Carson show—"

"Leno's been crucifying me in the monologue!"

"If you went on a show like that, it would go through the roof ratings-wise. Everyone wants to see what you have to say for yourself. Bill Clinton got booed off the stage for the most boring speech ever during the '88 Democratic Convention; he went on *The Tonight Show* to laugh at himself, and now he's about to be president." Samantha waited for dramatic effect. "You go on with Leno and explain to the nation that these porn subscriptions were your *son's* subscriptions, your dead son's. Paid for, without your knowledge, with your credit card."

That was good.

That was good and everyone knew it.

Frank bore a stupid, canine expression of happiness. "The dead son I love, yadda-da yadda-da. Then what?"

"You talk solemnly about poor Ronnie, whose lack of knowledge led to his death by auto-asphyxiation. You do the shtick you should have done months ago, that it's time for this sort of death to come out of the closet to educate others—"

Young Republican 1: "Don't like the reference to the closet, Senator. It's got the homo taint to it."

Samantha glared at him. "It's time that this type of death not be a secret anymore. And if your being the butt of monologue jokes is what it takes, then you are prepared to endure that embarrassment because this is *your son's life* we're talking about—then you look to the camera and say, 'And maybe your kid's too.' "

Frank got choked up.

Creeping up from behind her chair, Mort put a hand on her shoulder. He too was moved. Sam waited uneasily for Mort to take his hand off her, which he took his time doing.

Sam went on steadily, "No one can criticize you or make fun of you anymore—it's too sensitive. It'll be powerful television. You'll be able to hear a pin drop as you tell about . . . about your pain."

She left Arlington, somewhat relieved for the first time in weeks. They nearly fell upon her as in a rugby scrum: Sam you're a wonder, Sam you're a genius, Sam you're god!

What I am, she thought calmly, is not who I was a month ago. It was a calm realization, worn lightly as one might model a new blouse for the first time, a new hairstyle. Yes, someone is talking, someone is saving their butts, someone is serving the minions of evil, but not Samantha Flint. We've fallen out of touch lately. An emotion almost pushed its way through: Ronnie, poor Ronnie, humiliated by death and now defamed by Samantha Flint, former future novelist now using her ample talents to twist press copy and cover ass. No, she whisked that specter away. This is desperate times for the living, and the living get to use the dead anyway they want.

A thought came to her as she drove across the Potomac: *I am no longer a decent person.*

Do you remember when Mimi and you, back at Smith College,

gleefully talked about the "nice" girls and how many Smithies thought that Mimi and you weren't "nice"? And how Mimi said she didn't put any stock in being "nice." How that quality was nowhere on her radar screen? And you, Samantha Flint, then and there said to yourself that you would strive not to be "nice," not to be friendly with every silly girl in Haven House, but rather, selective, discriminating, self-interested. Well, Samantha old girl, you got your way. You are now officially "not nice." And it wasn't a very long step to "not decent."

BEEP. *Samantha, this is Mimi, pick up if you're screening calls. Are you curled up in fetal position, not leaving the house? I can't find you at the office either . . .*

The office! Not only had the office become wholly surreal—Mort snooping in everyone's files hunting for "the mole," Frank doing his radio-show spiels alone in his office for an audience of himself—but the staff's personal life caught the contagion as well. Bernie's wife left him in the midst of the crisis; Angeline told everyone within earshot that she was in some kind of massage therapy because she couldn't achieve an orgasm since the scandal—yes, in front of five staffers, Wanda, and a delegation of farmers from the home state. Furthermore, the staff nodded sympathetically, failing to find it a strange topic for discussion. Bizarre suspensions of physical laws applied; what qualified as weird psychotic behavior yesterday became today's . . .

"I'm worried about Frank," Samantha told Cameron by phone, late one afternoon.

"You said he was acting crazy."

"Crazy we can cover. Careless, I'm concerned about. I need your help with something."

Cameron, as requested, popped over to Shanker's office, saying his habitual hello to Wanda. Wanda grunted back, barely. She knew about their affair.

"See these?" Samantha laid out a series of receipts with Angeline's signature on them. The Red Roof Inn in Alexandria, Virginia. "Angeline and Frank, I take it, are going here for their little rendezvous. She's such an idiot, she's claiming the receipts as travel expenses—imagine what the GAO would do with this, let alone the *Post*. I'm going over there."

"Where? The motel?"

"Yes. Angeline left early today, so I think they're on. I got her tag number out of the parking–permit file, written down here—"

"What do you want me for?"

"Keep me company. I'm going to stake out the motel parking lot until they show. See? Look at the receipts—they never miss a Thursday."

"Samantha honey, what do you intend to do?"

"Knock on their door, say hello, tell them if I can figure out where their love nest is, then so can the tabloids and the TV stations and the *Washington Post*. We can't afford another scandal at this point. Adultery would sink us. People already think he's an idiot and a hypocrite, but what kind of scumbag on top of everything else cheats on his grieving wife . . ." Suddenly, she realized she was speaking to a man cheating on his wife. She quickly went on, "God, I wonder if the tabloids don't already have someone tailing him—"

"So only a scumbag cheats on his wife?"

"That's what people think, yes."

"Is that what you think?"

"I think you should separate or divorce, if you're not happy."

"Maybe it would be easier to stop seeing you."

"Maybe it would. By all means do what's easy. Don't stand up to the wife you don't love, for god's sake—"

They were talking loudly. Mort passed by her cubicle and smiled peculiarly and moved on. Cameron excused himself and walked out of the office; Samantha, swallowing heavily, just as wordlessly gathered up her Angeline-and-Frank evidence and headed downstairs for her car.

It was dark by five on this cloudy, late November night. Samantha watched 6:00 P.M., 7:00 P.M. pass on the dashboard clock, listened to NPR's *All Things Considered* about the coming Clinton era, until the reports began to repeat themselves. She sat in the parking lot of the Red Roof Inn, heater turned up, waiting for Angeline's Camry to show. There was a nondescript blue sedan that arrived shortly after she had, idling on the other side of the parking lot, the cigarette coal of its driver flaring from time to time. He would get out and pace occasionally, look around, get back in to get warm. A reporter, she figured.

So, was she going to really insist Cameron leave his wife? Then she'd be stuck with him.

But she loved him. No, she didn't.

But she did need him—not so much the sex anymore, but the intimacy, her having a companion through this madness, a confidant.

Of course she hadn't told him she was responsible for the original press leak, so at some level she didn't trust him. It was that secret that was eating her alive, occasioning the bottles of Mylanta, the Nyquil to get to sleep, the speed tabs to provide artificial energy and optimism to get through each goddam day—

A knock at her window caused her to jump.

"Jesus!" she cried. The window was fogged up and she rubbed it to reveal Cameron. She opened the door. "What are you doing here?"

He had coffee and, again, Krispy Kreme doughnuts. "Here for the stakeout." He walked around and got in the passenger side. She had never been more happy to see him! And, understanding as she did the complexity of their predicament, he didn't attempt to return to the afternoon's argument. They would just exist like this, not changing anything, not defining terms or making future plans.

Eight P.M. Cameron was rubbing her leg affectionately. "They're not showing. We could get a room."

Samantha protested, saying they had to wait it out.

Fifteen chilly minutes later: "Okay. Let's get a room."

He stopped her in the doorway as she unlocked the motel room door, his eyes having that mischievious sex glint. "You wanna pretend I'm Frank and you're Angeline?"

She kissed him and loosened his tie; he pried a hand through the front of her long wool coat. "Maybe they lie around," Samantha suggested, "pretending they're *us*."

So a night of exhausting, athletic, reconciling sex knocked them both out. They slept past when Cameron was supposed to be home with his wife. They slept past Samantha's 9:00 A.M. D.C. Committee meeting and Cameron's Environment & Public Works Committee staff meeting that he was supposed to chair.

"What a disaster!" he yelled, checking his watch at 10:30.

Samantha, with the best dignity she could manage, walked in to the office in the same clothes she was in the previous day. A memo was on her desk: Mort had secured the help of a government agency that rented out time on polygraph machines for a fee. He tried to schedule everyone on staff to submit to the indignity—Dan and Don were only too eager, with nothing to hide.

"Wanda," Samantha asked, "you're not really gonna let Mort hook you up to a lie detector, are you?"

Wanda's expression answered that question, as she patched a phone call back to Sam's cubicle.

"Samantha . . ." It was Cameron, sounding like the breath had been knocked out of him. "She knows."

"She knows?"

"Margaret."

Oh, no. Not that they tried very hard to hide it.

"She hired a detective to follow you," Cameron haltingly explained. "He followed you out to the Red Roof Inn and photographed us—"

"What? Are you telling me, that while we were spying on Frank, your wife was spying on us?"

"That's what I'm telling you."

One of those infared videos that worked in low light. Margaret's p.i. had them kissing, fondling in the door at the Red Roof Inn. Cameron demanded a reckoning from Samantha: was it love, and should he leave his wife, or was it not love, and should he beg forgiveness from Margaret?

Mort leaned into her cubicle, mouthing *I need to see you*.

"Got to get over to Ag," she whispered to Mort.

"Samantha?" Cameron was still on the phone, demanding that she resolve and justify the next years of both their lives on the spot.

"I'll get back to you," said Sam, hanging up and fleeing the office, evading Mort.

She would hide out at the Agriculture Committee meeting, taking notes for Frank who had attended maybe, oh, three of these meetings in two years. She wondered if Cameron would come looking for her here—damn that Mort, he made her give away her location. Indeed here was Mort again, slipping into the committee chamber. Samantha raised her pad as if she cared about the proceedings.

A dull event with a dull crowd, farm lobbyists, agricultural-supply people, fertilizer interests. Fertilizer. Mixed-up shit and chemicals. People paid six figures to look out for the interests of shit in Washington—there's a job for you. Now what is Mort doing? Mort was shifting through the aisles, crossing the chairman's view to sneak a note to her.

See me in the vestibule. NOW.

Once in the vestibule:

"Samantha. I know it was you who called the *Post*."

Now nonchalance was called for.

"We know you did it, Sam. The senator's given me authority to fire whoever did it, and that's you."

"He's so gone on tranquilizers lately he'd say yes to anything—"

"Sam, it's over."

Samantha maintained a bothered air. "Mort, you cannot be serious. The only way Frank will pull his career together is with an aggressive agenda in 1993, and you can't do that without me to—"

"Samantha, no one doubts your importance. I wish I didn't have to do this, but you screwed Frank over."

Now the best defense was an offense. "Goddamn it, Mort, *anyone* at that Christmas party could have told the *Post* the senator subscribed to *Playboy*! I . . . I was in Florida—"

"There are telephones in Florida. Besides. We all noticed the magazine at Frank's house, in his study, the day Ronnie died. It wasn't me or Don or Dan—it had to be you. There was never a moment's doubt in my mind that you did this."

Mort was unmoved. He might actually have bounded down here thinking he was going to like this, but it was clear he wasn't enjoying himself. It was as if, in this moment, he had suddenly recognized that Samantha was sane and dependable, where nothing else in the office was.

"If I could see Frank . . ."

Mort took his hanky and wiped his brow; his dirty chore was almost at an end. "The senator won't see you."

Samantha felt her head becoming light. This was really happening. "Mort," she said, barely audibly. "You won't tell anyone why . . . why you're letting me go?" She looked around at familiar faces in the hallway. Were they all observing her, watching for her reaction?

"I'm telling everyone that will listen, Samantha," Mort said. "You betrayed Frank, you stabbed him in the back."

It was the one thing the world of the Senate could not forgive: the self-serving press leak. *If she'd do it to Frank, she'll do it to me*, every senator would think. Her résumé wouldn't get past the secretary.

"You see, Sam," Mort added, raised to full height, "you're very good at what you do and we have no interest in you taking those skills and working for another senator—maybe an opposing senator. If we can't have you, we want no one else to have you."

"So you're ruining me," she said simply.

"You ruined yourself."

All Washington maneuvers have a price, Samantha thought coldly, and she was now willing to pay it, whatever it was. "Name what you want, Mort. I'll clean out my bank account if you'll go and tell Frank it wasn't me. Do you want . . ."

She met his eyes.

He met her eyes. He was considering it . . . but no. Bedding Samantha was nothing he could fit into his life that minute. With her nasty remarks and recoil at his presence, she had always in effect rejected him, made him feel oily and unattractive—balling her would have been cheery *then*. But not now.

"You can't do anything to stop this, Samantha. I'm sorry."

Samantha stared after Mort until he was gone. Moments later she was tapped on the shoulder by a committee intern, smiling, good-natured Noah in his brown polyester suit. "Uh, Ms. Flint? I copied those minutes from the House committee meeting."

Samantha thoughtlessly took the papers from him, still unable to speak or take her eyes off the distant door. The door to C Street, the back exit, through which she would pass, never to return . . .

"Ms. Flint? You all right?"

Samantha smiled faintly. "Thanks, Noah."

"You were going to tell me about which staff member on Senator Pressler's committee I had to liase with."

Noah the intern. A sophomore at Kansas State University, just here for a fall term as part of a degree program—and yet he is more a player than Samantha Flint who is *out*, while he, lowly and insignificant as he is, is *in*.

"Noah, I'm not going to be working for Senator Shanker any more, starting this week."

He was disappointed. "Oh."

"Well, I've got this offer from a lobbying firm on K Street, and I'm going there." But surely, Sam reasoned, all over the building tomorrow they'll be talking about how and why she was fired. "Also, as you may hear tomorrow, the senator and I didn't agree on some important things and . . . and since I was going, they're going to say I tipped off the embarrassing story to the *Post* . . ."

Spin control! She almost fainted: listen to me spinning my crash-and-burn to an unimportant intern!

Samantha, in her office for the last time, opened her bottom desk drawer and spotted the dregs of one of Warren Proctor's good bottles of single-barrel bourbon, bequeathed to her for a special occasion. Nothing in her now-complete political career had so far warranted finishing it off, so getting fired would have to do. She poured some into her FAMILY FRANK SHANKER coffee mug.

These guys are such amateurs.

They don't even know how to *fire* anyone correctly, thought Samantha. Here I am alone in the office. Nobody fires Samantha Flint without an unethical fucking mess of a fight!

She went around to Don and Dan's joined cubicles. They had been playing a computer video game all afternoon and had left their terminals on so they could pick up where they left off tomorrow—and so Sam could get into their files without knowing their passwords. She grabbed a fresh disk and began copying Don's files. She scoured the index . . . There was a document called *RONNIE.*

A few hours later she had drunk-driven to Frank's Virginia residence. She rang the doorbell repeatedly.

"Now, Samantha," Frank Shanker said, shielded by the front door of his home. Samantha noticed Angeline's Camry in the driveway (now that Lillian Shanker was checked into Charter for another round of lithium treatments and electric shock, the home front was available for whoopie). "I know you're upset and I'd . . . I'd hate, Sammie, to have to call the police to escort you off the property."

"Do I look mad, Frank?"

Such a handsome man, Senator Frank Shanker. Even at three in the morning in his bathrobe and just out of bed, his hair, his movie-star profile; yet all of that failed to overcome the utter vapidity of his face, the thorough lack of intelligence of his eyes.

"Mort will *not* pin this whole fiasco on me! Tomorrow there will be papers for two lawsuits served; you tell me where you'll be—"

"Now Sam—"

"One, will be against you for wrongful dismissal. I'm sure the columnists will be interested to see that you fired the most powerful female on your staff without proof. The second suit will be for Mort, for sexual harrassment, and that won't reflect on your office well—"

"Now Sammie, Mort didn't harrass you—"

"Really? *You* should consider the atmosphere of charged sexuality that you allowed to reign throughout the office, Frank. Having your mistress in an office-manager position, well, I didn't want to bring that up before the Ethics Committee, but I don't see how I can help but do that."

Frank's blankness began to sharpen into the simple, animal focus on survival.

"You see this memo?" Samantha handed him Don's assessment of the chances for using the not-for-profit Ronnie Shanker Memorial Fund money for the upcoming election—

"Now Sammie!"

"You want to count the infractions here, Frank? Fundraising out of a Senate office? Using your son's memorial fund to"—she stared at the memo, reading it aloud—" 'be funneled to state and local clubs, which in turn will prompt key contributors to directly write checks to the Shanker Reelect Committee—' "

"I didn't now about any of that, Sammie—"

"That's right, you don't know *any* goddamn thing!" screamed Samantha as a next-door neighbor turned on an upstairs light. "It's women like *me* who run this Senate, Frank. Look up and down Dirksen, for chrissakes—the most powerful senators, all with female staffs, women l.d.s who give up home, family, social life—"

"Maybe you better come in and sit down—"

"We write the bills, we answer the mail, we pick your issues, we save your butts. We think we're going to be appreciated or that our lives are going to lead somewhere, but in reality . . ." She lifted a finger to make a point, swaying. "We're like those pathetic executive secretaries who fall in love with their bosses they slave for for forty years, with no real life to show for it when they retire. Next time you step in shit—and Frank," she sobbed and laughed at the same time, "you friggin' tap-dance in it! What's gonna happen when I'm not there to wipe off your shoe? So next time you send Mort to fire me, you better think about that!"

"I didn't intend for Mort to actually fire you."

Samantha took a step back in the wet grass and her heel went in too far. She fell over. She quickly stumbled back to her feet unsurely, covered in streaks of green fescue. "You didn't?"

"I wouldn't fire you, Samantha. You're my best chance of pulling outta my nosedive."

"That asshole was faking me out? Freelancing?"

She turned to her car, throwing to the ground all her blackmail materials. She stepped in another soft spot and fell forward.

"Come back before you hurt yourself!" the senator called.

She popped up again, this time a bit queasier. She knew where Mort lived too. Five miles from Shanker in Annandale, down the Gallows Road—oh ho ho, he's gonna *wish* there were still some gallows standing by the time I wring his neck, too!

What's happening?

Flashing lights, police behind me. Oh shit.

Samantha, sobering quickly, but not completely, could not even remember getting into the car after her visit to Frank. But here she was. In the car, all right. A policeman's flashlight shining through her window into her face. Oops, no seat belt—she tried to sneak it across her body to buckle it, when the policeman opened her car door.

"Step outside the car, please."

No matter how gloomy the winter, spring in Washington is restorative. The cherry trees bloom a tender pink, fresh leaves return to the deciduous forest at the city's edges, and the ornamental lawns glow green in the sunlight before the statues and monuments. One is reminded that this city of cramped offices, hypnotizing computer screens, and dank oversized neoclassical architecture was once a bend and a mill on the Potomac River, a lovely temperate vale within sight of the Appalachians and the Piedmont foothills, fertile and rich, a promised land where wise men hoped a New Jerusalem would rise.

It was a condition of her probation that Samantha attend Alcoholics Anonymous meetings and live for six months without driving privileges (she had assured the judge she could walk to work). The twelve steps of A.A. seemed to her to be more applicable to the others in her program; she didn't think she was an alcoholic, rather a woman who had drunk her way through a nervous breakdown. But to what degree alcohol had derailed her, what classification applied to her, that was a small detail. The arrest and conviction of DUI was a turning point for Samantha Flint. For some, a DUI would be the beginning of a spectacular spiral of repeat offenses, denials, broken relationships, and more wretched alcoholic antics, but she would not be in that category. And if the present price to pay was attending meetings, sitting in folding chairs in high school gyms, and reciting the recovery mantra *one day at a time*, then so be it.

Besides, *one day at a time* was one of those lowest-common-denominator truths that had something to it.

And things might have ended up a whole lot worse.

Sobriety, rest, and time off from work brought Samantha to the point where she could enjoy this springtime as she never had. She could walk along the Tidal Basin, beside the Potomac, in the National Park Service trails on lush Teddy Roosevelt Island or bike along George Washington's Chesapeake and Ohio Canal, designed when the frontier was simply beyond the eastern mountains, or climb out on the rocks overlooking the Great Falls of the Potomac and watch the foolhardy kayakers take the death-dealing rapids.

Sometimes Samantha brought along Cameron (separated from his wife, moved out of their house, living near Dupont Circle), whom she didn't see very much, although they were still technically "together." Sometimes she took one of the women from the A.A. meeting.

"You must miss working in the Senate, huh?" they would ask, when she'd allude to her former life.

And Samantha was enough of a sport to glamorize her former life a little bit for her friends, but in truth she couldn't remember why it had been so important to her, how her career had been allowed to become her life itself.

The official end came one February day in 1993 when Samantha had sat down to write Shanker's constituent newsletter to the home state—always an exercise in pap. As she followed Frank's notes and envisioned a year of wasted effort trying to outlaw erotica, as she typed his exclamation points and sorry rhetoric, shaped and polished his bigotries and inanities, she froze. She sat at the word-processing terminal for a full hour staring into nowhere.

So this was what her dream of serious writing had become.

"Well," one of her hiking buddies said, mentioning this incident, which she had recounted for A.A., "chalk it up to another growth experience."

But with growth, something surely is *added*. And Samantha felt, on the contrary, that something had been subtracted, amputated. Something positive and youthful, some way she liked to think of herself, a hopeful feeling in the heart, an eagerness in the eyes—small things to lose perhaps, but these things were gone, fallen from her.

Senator Shanker, thanks to Samantha's plan, began his rehabilitation, although she didn't watch him on *The Tonight Show* from her court-arranged substance abuse clinic in McLean.

"I wish my son had been able . . ." he had said, working the audience lugubriously, "had been able to find a nice girl and not live in that world of pornographic images. He loved the military academy—you know, I begged for him not to follow his brothers there. Perhaps it was my fault for not bringing him home and being more of a father. Perhaps it was my fault for not telling him pornography was *wrong* . . ."

Not a dry eye in the house.

If Samantha didn't feel anything for the Capitol world anymore, she could at least pretend like she did, and when Warren Proctor came back to town that spring, appearing before a Senate committee on campaign reform, Samantha Flint—some four months after resigning from Shanker's office and taking a job in a Pennsylvania Avenue bookstore on Capitol Hill—was his favored lunch date. Warren had no doubt heard about the DUI, the resignation, and he no doubt charitably attributed her brief decline and fall to the nonsense attendant with the scandals. And indeed, he never mentioned her Senate ordeals, except to clasp her hand and say, "Samantha, you look better than when you walked in my office trying to get a job eight years ago. Happier."

"You never lied when you were in office, Warren," she smiled.

Samantha sat with Senator Proctor in the private Senators' Dining Room in the Capitol, content in the reflected glory as the grand old men and young turks came up to shake his hand and ask after his health. It was a warm and jolly senatorial welcome-back, but also a shade perfunctory. Because Senator Warren Proctor was, after all, no longer a senator, no longer a man they needed to wrest a vote from, work with on committee.

And as for Samantha Flint? Well, they who were *in*, sad to say, understood that she was *out*.

Proctor sipped his bean soup as if it were ambrosia. "Can you believe I've missed this gruel? Like you couldn't get something better in a can!"

Proctor was back at the capital to tilt at windmills. He was lobbying unofficially for his "Anti-Hassle" Bill, which had wide sympathetic word-of-mouth support but no real votes, no real chance of being legislation.

"You sure were a hit last night on *Larry King*, Senator," Samantha assured him. "Everyone who called in loved your ideas."

"It's not like it used to be, Samantha," he sighed, putting down his spoon, waving for the white-coated waiter to take his bowl away. "My anti–speedtrap initiative. I had a provision about speeding fines and it's been assaulted from all sides. I got a call from the Radar Detectors for America lobby at my hotel room this morning. Can you believe it? The radar detectors have their own lobby."

Samantha set him up. "Is there anyone left who doesn't?"

"The average American taxpayer, I think."

Proctor's dream bill, in addition to ten other nuisances he had singled out, called for puny $10 speeding fines where the driver was within ten MPH of the speed limit on the interstate, ending the widespread issuing of Mickey Mouse tickets for going 65 in 55, back east. Proctor's bill also earmarked speeding-ticket fines solely for education funds, to remove the profit incentive for speedtraps. Cities like Syracuse, Proctor raged, were setting up automatic traps that photographed your car going over 55 MPH and issued you a ticket by computer! Orwell wasn't whistling Dixie!

"And what about the courts deciding that the state can confiscate your car if your child or ex-husband uses it in a crime, and you're completely innocent! It's a wonder the people don't rise up and tear this place apart, stone from stone! And you can get a ticket now for having the wrong tint in your windshield—"

Senator Dole patted his back on the way out the door. "Liked the bit about the plates in our head last night. You keep giving 'em hell, Warren. We miss you here."

Last night on CNN, Proctor had speculated, "I suppose they'll be putting metal plates in our head. Whenever we *think* about speeding, a computer will issue us a ticket. What must the Europeans think of all our hypocritical talk of liberty? We must be the only country, along with Canada, that spends *millions* to set up a gestapo to harrass ourselves—and is there a decrease in interstate crime? Fewer rapes and abductions along the highway? Less drug smuggling on the road, less reckless driving, more civility? Of course not!''

"Senator, the people love you," fawned Larry.

But Warren Proctor's *Larry King* segment was a lounge act. Proctor didn't see it that way, of course, but the folks inside the Beltway knew it was good, populist entertainment. Nothing would come of Proctor's campaign for drivers' rights, or his bill forbidding companies to share your personal credit information, or his provision to let artists and self-employed people return to income averaging, or his plan to ban oversize RVs from the national parks.

"I'm about to drive Maude crazy," Proctor said of his wife, who longed for him to sit still in Elk Meadow, his Wyoming ranch. "I putter around the house all day, waiting for someone to call and get something going . . . eh, I'm a bad retiree, Samantha. Elk Meadow is like a sepulcher." He ran his hand along a fold in the tablecloth, not looking at Samantha. "I'm thinking of involving myself with something. Hell. My grandson loves Tinkertoys. Maybe I'll go join the Tinkertoy lobby on K Street."

And as he talked, something gave way inside Samantha. Oh, they'd pay him six figures all right. Lunches, galas, parties, a box at the Kennedy Center—all he had to do was shill for somebody. And he'd be ornery at first, hard to match with suitable projects. But soon it would be the old carny routine. Beloved ol' Warren Proctor and this year's snake oil . . .

Not you, thought Samantha.

Anyone else in this town can go whore themselves, but please, sir, not you too. Go back to Elk Meadow and bounce grandchildren on your knee and write the memoirs you promised, swing through the capital and raise some hell, do Letterman and *Nightline*, whatever you like, oh but please don't feed at the money trough. I'm corrupt, thought Samantha sadly, wholly and thoroughly. And as soon as I pay off my debts, I'll be leaving town. But let me keep you in my mind's eye as the man of the people, Senator. Please.

PRESS RELEASE,
MARCH 13, 1995

The Los Angeles Mercy Children's Hospital is proud to announce that preparations have begun for the 11th Annual *Run for the Kidz* minimarathon sponsored by Sugarbowl Breakfast Cereal to be held May 12 1995. In the past, the celebrities have always turned out to help little children afflicted by terrible diseases, lending their time, money, and their athletic talents!

This year is no exception! Amber Wentworth, known to millions of young people as Flowerface on the Saturday morning kids' show *Fisher-Price Fun Fest*, and to millions of adults as the oldest daughter on ABC's *Twelve to a Trailer*, is back this year because of a ''special'' devotion to children and children's causes.

''I love children so much,'' says Wentworth, ''that I wish I could run this marathon every weekend. Children are so very, very special. And after the race, when I go to visit the special children in the sick ward, some of their specialness rubs off on me. I get as much out of being a part of the Sugarbowl Breakfast Cereal 11th Annual *Run for the Kidz* as they do, I'm sure.''

Amber Wentworth will be running in the celebrity half-mile, and will have the sponsorship of many corporations. She will be on hand for press before the event (Media Tent, 10 a.m.–11 a.m.), and can be accompanied on her hospital tour (approx. time 1 p.m.). Contact Mimi Mohr & Associates for further details, (310) 555-MOHR.

RUIN

Samantha Flint came to consciousness in her bedroom.

It was her bedroom, wasn't it?

She raised her head off the pillow to confirm. She groped along the bedside table . . . Prozac bottle . . . Lotensin for blood pressure . . . vitamins, ginseng, garlic tablets, bee pollen at fifty bucks a bottle. Her right hand found last night's glass of unfinished diet 7UP in a martini glass. Wasn't she a good girl: she could do without the real martini but found she couldn't do without the props of her once-daily cocktail hour.

By touch she found her portable phone in the darkened room. Speed dial *one*.

"Mimi Mohr's line," said Mimi's ever-chipper assistant, Blakely.

"This is Samantha. What time is it?"

"One-fifteen, Sam."

"Am I supposed to be doing something?"

He checked. "Mimi has you at the Palms-Carlton A.A. meeting at three. She says she'll call you there."

"It's really awkward when she does that. Can I speak to her now?"

His wanna-be actor's voice modulated to convey utter desolation. "Oooh Sam, I'm sorry, she's not *in* right now."

Yeah, right. Sam may have oldest-bestest friend status, but no one got by this creep. Blakely was on call for Mimi twenty-four hours a day, living entirely through her day's schedule.

"Sam, darling, why not check in with your own assistant?"

"Because I hate her and I like you," she lied, hating Blakely as well. "Thank you, dear."

Now she speed-dialed her own office.

"Samantha Flint's line," said her assistant, Tiffani.

"Could I speak to Samantha?"

"She's tied up in a meeting in Culver City, but can I take a message . . ." Tiffani faltered, suspecting. "Sam?"

"I like the bit about Culver City. I could be either at Sony or Tri-Star—keeps 'em guessing."

"What can I do for you?"

Sam asked what time it was again, having forgotten.

"One-sixteen," said Tiffani.

Sam fumbled for a cigarette from her crowded nightstand. Announcing her virtue to anyone listening, she now limited her smoking to after the hour of high noon. Of course, she generally woke up after the hour of noon. "Anyone call for me?"

Despite her new California health consciousness, Sam managed to put on thirty pounds when she first moved to L.A. in spring of 1995, two years ago. She checked into the Pritikin Center at Mimi's recommendation; then when she proved fallible, she briefly tried a personal trainer (another name from Mimi's rolodex) but her perkiness was intolerable—one of the mob of blond California beach babes who, if truth be told, never suffered a goddamn day in their lives to be beautiful and thin. "I got Missouri white-trash genes to work with," Samantha joked to Troy. "I'm doing good not to look like Ma Kettle."

". . . and then Alex Rostov about an audition time-change," Tiffani was saying, having spent some time reciting phone messages to her unlistening boss. "Your mom, hourly from nine A.M."

Oh god. Mom threatening with her annual visit.

"She wanted to know if March sixteenth through the twenty-third would be all right."

"I can't make this decision now," Sam said, putting this off for the fifth time in 1997. "What else?"

"Lots of calls concerning Tomorro Gs."

The bane of her existence.

"You and Troy have an after-show club appearance with Michael from Silver and Gold. You're going to meet T-Jack Cole."

Michael Gold was the reigning king of dance mixes with a gay club appeal. "Club appearance" would mean going down to West Hollywood and trying to park, which was impossible; she'd never driven through without getting a ticket for something. Jaywalking, tires not turned to the curb, too much space between your car and the curb—if they could find something to ticket you for, they would. You'd think that in a town run by gay people there'd be a different tone to law enforcement, but nope, the *fascisti* march as always, with an extra little Gower Champion spring in their step—

"Today's staff meeting at six. If you get out of A.A. in time."

Samantha *really* didn't like her A.A. meeting being such public information. As if the other managers at Mimi Mohr & Associates— all lean, fit, gym-toned L.A. health Nazis who lived on sparkling Evian—didn't look down their noses at her enough already.

Sam stumbled to life, walking as in a trance to her kitchen where the coffeemaker had automatically provided her with a pot, now lukewarm. "Good morning, madam," said the chief housekeeper.

"*Buenos dias*, Gabriela. Is Troy around?"

"Went out on his motorcycle, zoom zoom, this morning. He no wearing the helmet, madam—you must talk to that boy, yes? *USA Today* said seventy-two percent of motorcycle death because the man no wear the helmet."

"Yes, I'll be sure to speak to him about it."

"Don't forget. The helmet . . ." She pantomimed putting it on, fastening the strap, and revving the motorcycle. Samantha decided to talk to Mimi about securing a less dramatic cleaning lady.

Some tree-clearing work on Barranca Canyon forced Sam to drive up the mountain in her leased Acura (Mimi forbade Samantha to buy the used Taurus she was considering; "Image, sweetheart! *Toujours, l'image!*"). She climbed the hill in search of Mulholland Drive and an alternate route down from the Hollywood Hills into Hollywood itself. Providentially, the mountaintop views from Mulholland presented Los Angeles as clear as she'd ever seen it: Samantha could count the skyscrapers in Long Beach, detect the ocean horizon beyond Santa Monica. The sky today was Colorado blue, reminiscent of her brief residence in Aspen, rather than the usual milky haze of Southern California. As a bonus, Mt. Baldy, snow-covered and looming, showed itself against the green, gardened, leisured megalopolis below.

As Samantha pulled into the Hollywood parking deck at the hotel, her cellular phone beeped.

"Hello, Mimi," Sam said before her caller spoke.

"That meeting starts in five minutes, sweetheart, what are you doing in your car? Check in with HQ if you make a visual," she whispered before hanging up. Sam couldn't be sure whether Mimi was serious about the spy lingo.

This wasn't just any A.A. meeting. This was a movie-icon, rock-star and film-exec A.A. meeting, held in a private suite at the Palms-Carlton. A discreet congregation of the famous who didn't want to be gawked at or find their revelations in the tabloids the next day. You could join only if a long-time member brought you to a meeting. Sometimes there was Chris Farley, sometimes Patrick Fox, Mimi Mohr & Associates' hottest client, the next Brad Pitt/Tom Cruise (that is, if you believe the press releases that Samantha churned out). It was Patrick who'd invited Samantha.

Sam thought Patrick looked like a pompadoured Ken doll with his eyes set too close together on his oversized head. Patrick had bounced from ignored sitcoms on ABC to cult status on Aaron Spelling's *Monterey Beach* to a movie for summer of '98—barring pullouts or turnarounds—where twenty-five-year-old Patrick was going to be Arnold Schwarzenegger's teenage son in some blow-everything-up movie.

William and Wolfgang were turned in their seats with faces of expectation. They always saved a seat between for Samantha, even when they knew she wasn't coming. An interesting emblem of their relationship, that invariable, deliberate space between them.

"I was nearly to think that you would not show," Wolfgang said, his cadence more German than his accent. "You newlyweds can't get out of bed, hmm?"

"Yes," said William, "how is your husband today? I take it you got up early and made him a nice working-man's breakfast—"

"Shut up both of you," she said, before kissing each of them on their neighboring cheeks.

They really had a perfect little triangle here: William was infatuated with Samantha, Samantha was drawn to Wolfgang. If Wolfie wanted he could have completed the triangle and been in love with William, but his inclinations were not nearly so refined.

William Butler passed as a young-professor-type, a learned grad student perhaps in his early thirties, but actually he was closer to forty-five ("You," Sam told him, "are a melanin infomercial"). He had perfected a black intellectual's demeanor: he had a shaved head, round wire-rim glasses that he used as a rhetorical prop, for staring down his nose presciently, or to be taken off and used as a pointer if the argument called for it. His voice was resonant, every syllable crisply articulated like a Shakespearean actor. William's anal-retentive housekeeping of apartment and car, his thorough self-education (he had never been to college beyond a two-year CPA course), his fashionable selection of ties and jackets (and an earring in his left ear), had prompted Sam to assume he was gay. But he was merely cultivated. Samantha wouldn't have been so flirty and open with him if she thought he might want a romance instead of a friendship, but that was how they currently found themselves.

William let it be known that there had been many recklessly intense, highly destructive relationships with women before he met Sam. It had been the designated source of his drinking. He had never tried seriously to go cold turkey; his fine-wine habit was too much part of his life. He would abstain for months and then binge for a night, a weekend, confess it at a meeting, and life would stumble back to normal. Each binge was occasioned by an encounter, a rediscovered letter, an upturned relic from one of the tormenting goddesses from his carefully tended pantheon of romantic failures.

Samantha allowed William his delusions, never pressed when he said things like, "Chrissie and I decided after two years that we couldn't go on like that anymore . . ." In fact, Samantha was sure that he and Chrissie had never gone through such a collapse—that they had never gone through such a relationship. He was not a good liar. "It all went sour with Violet," he recounted, "because her folks couldn't endure seeing their little girl with a black man.'' No, Violet was a thirty-four-year-old dancer who worked a stripper's runway and had a daughter herself; it hardly seemed likely that she'd broken it off with William because of Mommy and Daddy.

Samantha had been to his house on Third Street near Wilshire, that select area of numbered streets (L.A. generally avoided numbers in its nice neighborhoods) with lovely 1920s high-ceilinged homes of wood, tile, and Spanish archways. Once, while William was tied up with a tax client on the kitchen phone, she had opened his desk drawer looking for a pencil and found a cache of faded photos; she put names to all the faces: Chrissie, Violet, Susan, Alison . . . all attractive, white, usually blondes. She could have engaged in unwelcome psychoanalysis, but instead she allowed him his fantasies, let him sit across from her in diners railing self-pityingly about his love life. Because Samantha wanted equal consideration and indulgence.

William was tragic: an exemplary man but for his relation to women. He had money and charm and taste, he was handsome and well-groomed, but in this one consideration he was hopelessly immature-for-life. And women quickly gauged his cavernous neediness and withdrew, only to leave him obsessed, capable of even a little casual stalking or harrassment, of demanding an explanation in a public place and making a scene, but always (to her knowledge) stopping short of restraining-orders or police intervention or violence. He had no violence in him, except what he might turn on himself.

"Once you go black," he sang.

"Been there. I had a little fling with a Senegalese man who's blacker than you with the lights turned off."

William Butler would let the topic disappear for months at a time, but he was unhealthily in love with Samantha. Even without Sam's participation, she knew that he considered them, somehow, "a couple." And Sam, with diminishing guilt, knew she could take advantage. She could call at four in the morning and wake him for a trifle, she could borrow money, she could ask him to do her taxes for free (he heroically helped her clear the mountain of debts after Washington and Aspen). It would have been easy to mistreat him; she sometimes speculated if it would please him for her to do so.

To complete their perfect soap-opera triangle: Samantha had an unserious crush on Wolfgang Wurzburger, the once-great German director, aging *enfant terrible* turned TV-hackmeister, American sellout. Something in his misfortunes—his blithe accession to his life's failures, his acid wit and unsparing honesty ("Since I quit drinking, I can have a full erection again, although it returns at a time in my life when it takes so much more *squalor* to arouse me . . .") appealed to Sam immensely. His acne-scarred face, once Teutonic and sharp-featured, sagged and showed evidence of dissipation. His eyes were often rheumy and sad; his long dark-blond hair was often unkempt. It was when he talked, when he said something impossibly frank and met your gaze with his animated face that he was irresistible. In a world of health fanatics and sixty-year-old studio execs face-lifted and liposuctioned into false youthfulness, Wolfie was a delightful, provocative exception. His uniform was jeans and a sweatshirt, with a ratty corduroy sports coat for formal occasions.

Wolfgang Wurzburger had the most exotic bio of anyone Sam had run across. Darling of the art houses, maker of a handful of incomprehensible but visually daring films in the early '80s, renowned in Berlin for wild drug use and his flagrant bisexuality, not to mention the calculated public outrages of his performance-artist wife. His *Schwuchtl*, a film about male prostitutes in Munich, won the Silver Palm at Cannes; his *Die Besiegten*, about Turkish slum life in Hamburg made top-ten lists in 1986. And like Halstrom and Verhoeven and Peterson, Wolfgang followed the money to Hollywood in 1988 and promptly had a smash with *Spill*, a cult hit in the *Death Wish–Dirty Harry* school where a vigilante cop blows away a parade of human scum—very stylish, American high-tech with Euro sensibility. It grossed $70 million or so, was made for nothing, and worked its way into the vernacular: "Someone oughta *spill* that guy . . ." or the concept of the Spill List, a list of people who ought to be blown away; i.e., "You just made my Spill List, sucker!"

Then Columbia invested $30 million to make a big-budget sequel and everything began going wrong. Columbia found the early *Spill*-sequel footage (*Roadkill*, in which Jake Spill takes to the highways) unwatchable, and declared Wolfgang too drunk and drug-ridden to direct competently. Lawsuits, slander, his wife suing for an American-style big-bucks divorce, telling tales in the tabloids . . .

You'd have thought there was no coming back from all that, but this is the town of *Heaven's Gate* ($50 million down the tubes) where Michael Cimino worked again and *Cutthroat Island* ($90 million down the tubes) where Renny Harlin worked again. God knows, there was no destroying the studio men that green-lighted these things; like zombies they stalked the corridors of power, unkillable, never paying for their errors with anything more punitive than a change of offices or a platinum parachute. Wolfgang then took a five-episode directing deal with *MacGyver*, after that a *Star Trek: The Next Generation* here, a *Sisters* there, a *Matlock Mystery Movie*.

"Do you feel like a drive?" was Wolfgang's code, an innocent-sounding invitation.

The Hollywood section of Santa Monica Boulevard was a disreputable strip of wholesale shops, small merchants of rarely-sought items, buildings abandoned and boarded up; those still functional were protected by rusted wire cages and metal gates. Men drove through here for the hustlers. Some boys (usually black and Latino) were in drag, some smoothly masculine and shirtless, bored and greasy from standing in the three P.M. sun, jeans worn low to reveal a strip of underwear.

"They're not genuinely homosexual, really," Wolfgang explained, "even the ones that prefer men. It is a different entire orientation, the hustler. He is a fetishist, of sorts; he wants the danger, the presentation of money—like you always say about drinking, it is the *ceremony* that is addictive. They believe hustling gives them power."

"But they have no power."

"Oh but they do—over any of the men who love them. But sadly they rarely understand how to use it . . . isn't that right, my little cupcake?" This last question was to a blond teenager pouting by a bus stop, glimpsed as they rolled by. "Look at your friends in . . ."

"Tomorro Gs," she supplied, mentioning the pop group that dominated her every waking hour of late.

"Those boys have done time down here—I recognize the faces. Female prostitutes finding careers in show-business, getting a millionaire like in—what was it?—the *Pretty Woman* movie does not ever happen. But with boys, it does happen. You have heard which stars began their careers down here on Santa Monica—I don't have to repeat the gossip everyone knows. Ah, an African specimen . . ." Wolfgang nearly turned around backwards in the driver's seat to get a better look.

Something in Wolfgang's faint German accent, his still-foreign mannerisms, his tossing his head of hair out of his face, his lighting of cigarettes (indeed, his smoking at all) combined to make Wolfgang an emissary from some worldly un-American place where there was no need for pretense or reticence, no fear of judgment.

"Would you let me watch you and one of your purchases?" Samantha asked for the shamelessness of it, to see his reaction.

He laughed quietly. "Ah, you pretend to be more wicked than you are. You're not really serious—besides, I do not think you like sex very much."

"Do too," she answered blandly, now noticing a teenage boy with a hollow chest wearing a worn leather vest, hands in his pocket, face down. Poor-white stock, undernourished, an insufficient mustache. Sam could imagine the Missouri accent.

"I'm not sure if I've had him," Wolfgang said. "He is very loveable, hm? One gets sickened by the perfection of the men in this city, the gymnasium automatons. One develops a taste for . . ." He considered his adjective. "Ugly."

Sam glanced at the boy as they passed; he quickly acquired his working stare of hunger mingled with availability.

"Though I disapproved of your marriage," Wolfgang told her, "you shall find me magnanimous in defeat. I have a lovely late, late wedding present for you."

"If you would have married me," Sam said, reclining to put her face in the sun, "I wouldn't have married Troy."

"Ah but think, when he overdoses on drugs, or whatever rock stars do, you will get all his money. But back to my present—are you curious?" Samantha nodded slightly, eyes still closed in pursuit of her tan. "I am going to buy you a gigolo, a professional. You should experience once in your life what is possible."

Samantha smiled. "I'm not sure I could ever . . . I might burst out laughing. I'd have to be mentally prepared."

"But making psychological preparations for a prostitute is a little like cleaning before your maid arrives," said Wolfgang. "And I will give you the money with which to pay. To put the money into his hands when he is done—that is the most delicious thing of all."

Samantha reflected on her and Wolfie's pleasure cruises while she sat in her A.A. meetings listening to someone rich drone on about the follies and tragedies of drink—oh to be outside on the sunny, ever–fascinating avenues of Los Angeles where something was always entertaining, mystifying, unforgettably visual.

Her cellphone beeped, shocking her from her reverie.

"Ah ah ah," said the A.A. leader with polite firmness. "You know the rules. No cellphones, Samantha. We're here for recovery and *that's* the most important deal any of us have to make today."

"Uh, sorry Bob, but it won't turn off properly. Let me go leave it at the front desk." She departed with her ringing phone.

Out in the lobby:

"*What?*" she hissed, snapping the phone open.

"Is Patrick at the meeting?"

"We're not supposed to talk about—"

"If Patrick goes to CAA, where they hate my guts, the first thing they'll do is recommend that he drop *me* as his manager. I don't have to tell you how we're down the drain if that happens. I heard Jack Rapke had my picture on a dartboard on his closet door."

Samantha had no intention of sharing anything anyone said in an A.A. meeting, least of all with Mimi, who couldn't fathom the recovery movement anyway. All was silent in the rented hall when she returned to her seat, as if they were waiting for her.

They *were* waiting for her. It was her day.

"Hello, everyone."

The group said *hello* in unison.

"My name is Samantha and I am an alcoholic."

Yes, she noticed in the front row, Mimi Mohr & Associates' biggest client was there after all; Patrick Fox gave her an encouraging thumbs-up. Other almost-celebrities were here too, '80s heavy-metal rock stars, sitcom next-door neighbors, studio execs' wives . . .

"Where to begin?"

An awkward silence, but A.A. attendees are used to long pauses. Actually, in her heart Samantha still didn't believe she was an alcoholic. Yes, at one time she drank too much; she drank instead of felt, as a life-lubricant when she was upset, sad, reflective, drinking in order to dull uninvited realities, but she didn't feel chemically dependent. No shakes, no throwing up blood. She may have screwed up back in Washington and Aspen, but booze accompanied her decline, it wasn't the cause of it. After all, she hadn't had a drink in two years, since 1995 when she moved to California—she reminded herself to work that fact into her spiel.

"I began drinking in earnest in Washington, D.C. What I loved most was not the alcohol, I think, or its effect. What I really really loved was the . . . the *ceremony* of booze. Backroom boys, Senate wheelers and dealers, smoking, drinking. That's all I wanted, the life I moved up there for. When I left D.C. for Aspen, I figured I'd left that bad habit behind."

Cameron called a long-standing contact with the Great Divide Wilderness Society, an environmental organization chartered for preserving remaining tracts of Rocky Mountain wilderness. A job with them would mean a salary cut for Cameron, but it came with an apartment on the edge of Aspen, the "Red Bricks," a neighborhood of condos and apartments that feigned affordability for mere mortals who would live amid the superrich—$1200 a month. The GDW personnel people sent a photo of the view out the north window, the famous ski mountain bathed in golden Sierra-Club-calendar light.

"Yeah, let's do it," Sam urged Cameron, wanting out of Washington. "I'm not sure what I'll find to do—"

"The Great American Working Woman's Novel, right?"

There was that damn book again, Samantha realized, digging its way back to the surface, crawling out of the shallow grave she'd put it in. Mimi, of course, had other plans for Samantha:

"You belong in L.A. with me," Mimi demanded throughout

1994. "I'll get you a job with CAA. Hell, Eisner and Ovitz love me—they'd do a fucking threeway with me . . ."

But Mimi's broken-record advice could be ignored for now.

Cameron donned jeans and a Wilderness Society T-shirt and grew a goatee like any number of lead singers from Pacific Northwest bands. Once out of the suit-and-tie with his hair a little shaggy, he looked twenty-five rather than thirty-nine; and Sam, free of Washington stress, faithfully attending her recovery meetings, began to turn back the clock too.

"I'll never go back!" Samantha screamed into the stuffy air of the Ryder cab as they sped across the Great Plains on Interstate 70, the truck packed to its roof (mostly with her things, since Cameron ceded his material life to Margaret in the divorce). Passing Russell, Kansas, there was a proud billboard announcing it was the hometown of Bob Dole, with a cadaverous portrait grimacing at the interstate.

Cameron remarked, "I can't believe how deep we were into all that Beltway bullshit."

"Embarrassing," Sam concurred.

This was their daily ritual, to smash the old idols—they competed to see who could revile their former life more utterly.

"Simple phrases," Cameron rambled as wheat fields rolled by, as sunsets enflamed the cirrus-strewn sky from horizon to stratosphere. "All these simple things Westerners take for granted—the pines. The timberline. Alpine meadows, the summer pass, the early snows. Know what phrase I love? *The high country*. Got off the phone with Shari in Aspen and she said it wouldn't take us any time at all to get used to *the high country*."

"Yes," Samantha repeated, "the high country."

She could hear John Wayne say it, directing his posse to the next ridge; she could also recall its homage in the clean, lucid prose of Willa Cather. A country for spare living without modern clutter, a place of dramatic seasons where one might catch the flow of time, rather than fighting against rush hours and deadlines . . . I'll find the better part of myself, Samantha promised. I'll return to my world of reading and writing. Mimi has abandoned the life of the mind we used to share, but I, Samantha Flint, will retrieve the dipper from the well and drink! In the high country.

Aspen, Colorado, perched 8000 feet above sea level, was not exactly frontier living. Little intelligent bookstores, a newspaper too liberal for the West, a butcher where one could get Beluga caviar and a haunch of elk, French bakeries, hole-in-the-wall antique emporia, all crowded in Aspen's nineteenth-century boomtown setting. But yuppified or not, the essential promise of the West had not faded here, Samantha wrote to Mimi in letters; life could still be renewed in such a place.

Cameron frequently left for overnight trips with the staff, led by nature-girl Shari, a shaggy blond airhead and knee-jerk environmentalist. When it leaked out somehow that Samantha had worked for the antienvironmental Frank Shanker, it was clear that she'd never be accepted by the Great Divide Wilderness Society, no matter what latter-day conversion she claimed.

"Makes me feel bad not to be invited," she said to Cameron once, of a planned hiking assault on the Frying Pan Wilderness.

"How else are you gonna get any writing done? The apartment's *alllll* yours. Not like you care about nature anyway, Sam honey. You're the original city girl."

Samantha told her A.A. meeting: "Of course he didn't want me to go on their weekend expeditions. He was screwing Shari, or was trying to. And that's not true about my hating nature."

However much she shunned camping out in cougar country, a world of dehydrated trail food, latrines, mosquitoes, and bad hygiene, Samantha was nonetheless nourished by Aspen as natural backdrop: the towering summits peeking above roof cornices, a spring meadow with grazing deer at the end of a short residential street, black bears once playing at a neighbor's trash can; from the Co-Op grocery store parking lot, a spray of wildflowers scattered up the mountainside; from her car window on an impromptu September afternoon drive, the fragile reddening tundra of Independence Pass at 12,000 feet, the horizontal light and blue-violet skies of high altitude, the proximity of heaven.

"Well," she told Alcoholics Anonymous, "Cameron's and my relationship was over in Washington, if you want to know the truth. But we hung on to each other because there was no one else who'd have either of us. We'd stopped having sex, though we'd sleep in the same bed, and we made sure to keep alive all the vicious deteriorating-couple traits: blaming our reduced circumstances on each other, insane jealousies, all the twisted clever sadistic stuff."

Sam once put a clipping from the *New York Times* on Cameron's desk. It was about the Alsek-Tatshenshini Reserve in British Columbia, and how after all the efforts to wrench this pristine territory away from miners and timber interests, the place had become trashed thanks to improperly disposed-of rubbish from nature lovers—human waste, abandoned float rafts, ice chests, lost gear. The article featured other spectacular sites of tourist pollution due to backpacking, float-tripping yuppies who didn't mind screwing up a wilderness providing it was their discarded $500 imported Swiss propane camp stoves lying about and not some miner's sluice.

"What's the point of putting this on my desk?" Cameron asked, finding her in the kitchen.

"Thought it was interesting."

"Aw hell, Sammie, it's a piece of anti-eco propaganda probably copied right out of a Wise Use press release."

"It's by the environmental reporter for the *Times*—"

"By putting this on my desk you express your continual disdain for what I do for a living. That's what this is about."

He was right, but Sam argued anyway. "Look, I thought you'd want to know. Maybe if a similar situation was brewing in Aspen you could head it off at the . . . pass. No pun intended."

Cameron refused to be charmed; he crumpled the article into a ball. "I'm sure your buddy Shanker will take great solace in this article."

That had become a familiar ploy, raising the albatross of her servitude with Shanker. "Hey, I hated Frank Shanker enough to walk away from a powerful well-paid position in his office." That was Sam's official spin of 1993's events, offering a touch of nobility and uncompromised integrity. "If you have something to say to Frank Shanker write him a letter, but stop beating up on me."

"I'm just tired of the constant needling and sniping, Sam," he said, grabbing his coat.

"That's right. Go to Shari's now. She understands you."

"You know, frankly, she *does* understand me!"

Shari. Samantha Flint at her A.A. meeting sighed. "I suppose I should have figured that a man who would cheat on his wife would then cheat on the woman he left his wife for . . ." There, maybe she didn't need to get into any more nasty details. Screaming at each other, throwing things, making the neighbors call 911—over Shari? Yes, over Shari and over the fact that if Cameron left Samantha, she couldn't afford to live by herself in Aspen. She would have to land penniless in Florida. Well, she could seek out Mimi. But Mimi could never see Samantha in this decline; Samantha swore she'd keep her friend in the dark about how badly Aspen was turning out.

"Maybe there was something in the thin air of Colorado," Samantha told the group, her light tone fooling no one, "that kept me from thinking straight and leaving Cameron after two months. Clinical depression, most likely—not helped by the fact that a drink at 8,000 feet works like two at sea level."

Samantha was sitting in a village café full of ski-types, spending more money she didn't have, eating out for another meal with a notepad beside her—yes, another bourbon would be lovely, thank you—in case something significant for her novel occurred between drinks. Two women across the room were discussing everyone around them, thinking their voices weren't carrying. That waitress is wearing white stockings, which is such a disaster on fat legs. . . . Look at that woman with those little tiny rings cutting off her chubby stunted hands like sausages.

"Look at that bob. Would you have a round haircut when your face was such a big circle?"

"Chipmunk cheeks. That bad hair just frames her fat face. . . ."

Samantha stumbled off to the restroom and in shock stared into the mirror for fifteen minutes. But this . . . this was stylish! She'd been going for Miranda Richardson in *The Crying Game*—a timeless decadent '20s look that could fit in at a fancy ball or a punk club.

But those women said *my face was fat*. I've looked horrible for years *and no one's told me*.

The designation of "loser" had been patiently awaiting, Sam decided walking home from the café, tears escaping and freezing on her cheek—lying in wait, standing patiently by for me to pile bad decision atop bad decision, waiting for me to dazzle everyone in my twenties so they could gloat over my spectacular belly-flop in my thirties. Viewed from a great height, I am a fuck-up. I have no future. No career. No talent, as my unwritten novel is proving daily. No family I want to go back to, no money to go back to school to learn to do something else. And my youth is just about depleted too, which the drinking and smoking has helped along . . .

"I *told* you to come out here and work for me," Mimi calmly insisted, by phone.

"You . . . you aren't seriously thinking of *hiring* me—"

"I can pay you sixty thou. I'll take you to Donna Karan's, we'll get you outfitted, write it off as a business expense."

Mimi's *employee*? Would she be getting her coffee every morning? And yet, Samantha was weak. She knew she had passed from low-grade despondency to can't-get-out-of-bed depression. She would look at her laptop and force herself to sit in front of it, but hours would pass. She'd pour herself a glass or two—all writers drank, didn't they?—and then more hours would pass, wasted in front of the TV, paging through magazines. And then there would be the pathetic performance when Cameron returned home, later and later these days, where she would pretend she had written a little something and he would congratulate her.

"You have the money for a plane flight?" Mimi would ask.

"But, it's such charity—"

"No, ma'am. It is not charity. I don't trust one goddam person in my own organization. There are spies from CAA and ICM; there could be a palace coup at any minute. With *you* on the scene there'll be someone I can trust."

Mimi had left Ovitz's consortium of agents to set up her own management firm, imagining that CAA wouldn't see that as indirect competition. After all, by California law one's agent (who does the booking) and one's manager (who does the hand-holding and the career planning) cannot be the same person, right? However, some of Mimi's clients had been switching to Morris or ICM, dropping their former agents at CAA who, in turn, suspected that the upstart Mimi was somehow behind it, encouraging it.

"Do you know what it means to be on Ovitz's shit list? I'm sure CAA's fixing it so I can't eat lunch in this town again or anywhere else in the Western Hemisphere. Now are you coming to L.A. or not?"

Mimi rescued Samantha.

Drove through the night in her Porsche, across the wastes of Nevada and Utah. There she arrived, hair bedraggled, no sleep, wired on espresso, packing Samantha's bags before Cameron got back from a meeting in Glenwood Springs, dumping everything portable in her trunk to be sorted out later, leaving Cameron the furniture and kitchenware and no note. They sped toward the San Rafael Reef segment of I-70, pausing to gas up in Green River, Utah, properly disturbed by the sign: NO SERVICES NEXT 110 MILES. They filled the tank, bought yet another point-of-purchase snack, another diet cola to accompany the cookies, then got back in the car where Samantha cruised at a draggy seventy MPH, and Mimi faded into open-mouthed slumber.

"So," Mimi said, announcing she was awake north of Cedar City with Las Vegas on the mileage signs in ever-diminishing distances. It was night. "You're only doing seventy?"

Sam pulled over, they switched seats and Mimi brought their average up to ninety, except where city lights loomed ahead.

"What's this drinking business?" Mimi asked, barely paying attention to the trucks she skirted around a full forty MPH faster. "I'm not having you crack up, darling. You go to an A.A. meeting or two, if that bullshit will help—HEY!"

A Utahn in a rusted car packed full of kids cruised at a mere sixty in the passing lane.

"Goddam Mormon!" She blasted the horn. "California calling, asshole!"

"Which," Samanatha concluded, having entertained her A.A. meeting for fifty minutes, saying only half of what she could concerning the stresses of being Mimi's Hollywood lieutenant, "was how I got here in 1995." She had not been wholly forthcoming, and she wondered if her audience sensed it. All right, she would discuss something she hadn't confided to anyone: "I also ought to point out that, since Aspen, the simple things, getting up, going to bed, falling asleep—all of that has been . . . is pretty difficult for me."

Samantha should have taken this to Dr. Cline, a therapist Mimi found for her ("Please Sam, it's a status thing—everyone's analyzed out here"), but she shared it with A.A. instead.

"I lie down in bed, even after being awake for twenty-four hours, and I can't sleep. I almost lose consciousness and then an electric jolt goes through my body and I'm awake again. Sometimes I'm sure I'm not breathing and I shake myself awake. After a day or two, finally my body has had enough and I fall asleep for twelve hours and I really have trouble coming to. Now, this was sort of starting in Washington, where I drank so much to relax and did so much speed and coffee to get going—maybe I messed up the rhythms of normal life. Anyway, in L.A. I'm still paying for it."

They stared at her. They could spot a whitewashed confession.

"Actually, it's gotten worse. I still feel I need Xanax or Sominex, you know, to fall asleep and get some rest. And after taking those things, most mornings I need espresso and No-Doz and, if it's really bad, a tablet of speed to make it through a busy day. Clearly . . ."

Her A.A. allies listened intently; they understood the incapacity to deal with the agreed-upon conventions of life.

"Clearly . . . I can't continue to go pharmaceutical. I have to start trying to make it without all these crutches. Transference—isn't that what you call it? Trade in one drug habit for another. Well. I can't speak for tomorrow or even tonight, but right now, here with you guys, I'm doing just fine."

They clapped as she made her way back to her seat. William patted her knee adoringly, and Wolfgang kissed her cheek.

"Good job," Patrick said, touching her shoulder as he left the meeting room. "Seeya at Mimi's."

Afterwards, a studio executive's wife approached in the coffee-and-cookies mingle. "That Cameron fellow sounded like bad news," she sympathized. "But look how well it worked out for you in Hollywood, with that gorgeous husband of yours! My teenage daughter has a poster the size of a door in her room. Do you think I could get his autograph? I'd like to take a bite of him myself!"

And so back in her car. The only place, Samantha would attest, where she was really happy: her music, her air-conditioning, her bag of chocolate, her double-strength cappuccino in the console, her cigarette at the ashtray, her cellphone. If only all of life could be like her L.A. commute!

A lot of important agencies in New York worked out of holes-in-the-wall, like Sy Gold's operation; there was a smug Dutch-bequeathed frugality that seemed to say, "We run empires from this cubbyhole on West Twenty-sixth!" That wasn't the California way. The Mimi Mohr agency was at 9265 Sunset Boulevard, one building east of the line where the Beverly Hills world of manicured topiary and elegant, power-operated security gates began.

In the 1980s this stretch of Sunset almost became a second Rodeo Drive full of couture and hair salons, café and wine-bar perches for upscale lunching ladies, but the funkiness of Sunset had reasserted itself. Tower Records, the Whiskey, comedy clubs and their live cable broadcasts of expletive-spewing comics, get-your-maps-of-the-stars'-homes pavilions, Beverly Hills kids playing at being grunge lowlifes, authentic lowlifes working their way into Beverly Hills' youthful circles, prostitutes waiting at curbside . . .

"Sunset Boulevard," mused William once. "Where the sun sets daily on Western Civilization."

Let it set, Samantha reflected. She parked in the garage underneath the building, with a fee of $2 for every twenty minutes to discourage the nobodies who might pester the big agencies—

"Excuse me, Ms. Flint?"

Sam turned to see a young woman, very pretty, approach with a small portfolio.

"I am so sorry to bother you this way, but I didn't know what else to do. I got your name from Ruben," she recited hurriedly.

Ruben was one of the five guys in Tomorro Gs, the club-music group handled by Mohr & Associates.

". . . we were hanging out at the Romper Room, you know? And Ruben said you were real nice and I should come talk to you here, but your assistant said I couldn't have an appointment or even wait in the lobby to give you this."

Since when are people saying I'm *nice*? Samantha took the woman's portfolio. She opened it to the résumé. Sandra Blake, 26. Sam knew in a glance that she had shaved more than a year or two off her real age.

"Have I heard of you?" Samantha muttered, before scanning the résumé. Sandra was a daughter on *Gimme a Break!* with Nell Carter, one of those bizarre '80s shows where black people got on TV by ministering to straightlaced or wacky white families, providing all the warmth and soul and downhome wisdom, or by being freaky growth-retarded little boys farmed out to white homes. After that, Sandra had guest-starred on *Saved By the Bell* as a delinquent student, then *Sister Kate* as a runaway teen; there were one-offs on short-lived sitcoms *Still Here* and *Uncle Buck*. Her last TV gig was 1991. Back then her name was Winona Blake.

"What was wrong with 'Winona' Blake?" Sam asked.

"Oh. Well there's Wynonna Judd and Winona Rider now. Too many Winonas."

"Yeah, but now there's Sandra Bullock."

"I could change it again," she said slowly.

"But you've done some films," Sam mumbled, turning the page. Straight-to-video, low-rent titles, serial-killer-chases-blonde-around-deserted-sorority-house kind of films . . . Sandra's list included *Avenger 3*, *Key West Nurses* and, uh-oh, some of those soft-core porn films available on Pay TV in hotels: *Tracy's Wild Ride*, a hitchiker-in-hot-pants number, and *Boobwatch*.

"It's sort of a *Baywatch* takeoff," Sandra offered.

"Except they take off a little bit more, hm?" Sam said, closing her portfolio. "You might want to consider dropping those titles from your résumé. How naked did you get in these things?"

"I was never the main girl. I mean, I showed my tits, but that's about it. Rubbed some lotion on some guys, but no . . ."

"No screwing."

"Yeah, no screwing."

"Your agent let you do this stuff?"

"I don't have an agent anymore. I needed the money."

Sam gave a patented speech to all young hopefuls down on their luck. Never say die in this business, etc. Michele Pfeiffer was in *Grease 2*. Janet Jackson was on *Diff'rent Strokes*. Name the first ten pictures Sharon Stone starred in. Glenn Close started out in Up With People, for god's sake.

"Yeah, like, Traci Lords," Sandra said hopefully, "did porn and she was on *Melrose Place*."

"Yeah, but I think that can happen once and she was it." Samantha tried to escape with, "I don't know what I can do for you. Mimi Mohr decides on the client list and she's full up."

Sandra had expected a rejection. Maybe the night before she had fooled herself into thinking Samantha Flint was her salvation, let herself practice telling Mary Hart about how she cornered her agent in a garage and the rest was Hollywood history. Sam was new enough to L.A. that she sided with the underdog . . . No. It had to end here, before unrealistic dreams were put in motion.

"Well Ms. Flint, can you take my portfolio and just, you know, put it in a file drawer or something?"

"Sure." Sam closed the nicely bound leather portfolio package. Must have cost her.

Samantha took the elevator to the ninth floor. The elevator doors opened upon an opulent lobby; behind the receptionist there were raised, shining brass cursive letters against a mahogany plaque: MIMI MOHR & ASSOCIATES. Below, in lesser raised letters, were the names of subpartners and powerful consultants. Samantha was not among them. It was clear, as well, from her colleagues' condescension that everyone figured she was only there at the whim of the boss, Mimi's college buddy who needed a job. Samantha knew if she asked Mimi to add her name to the shiny gold display of "players" in the lobby that Mimi would roll her eyes, apologize for overlooking it, and have the artisan busy tomorrow correcting the situation.

But Sam would die before she asked for that.

Samantha handed Tiffani the portfolio. "Could you file that under Talent, Miscellaneous, please."

Tiffani saw it was Sandra Blake, the woman she'd effectively short-circuited for the last month. "Maybe I should throw it away?"

"Please file it where I asked."

Samantha ventured down the hall. She caught Mimi's eye and was waved inside her boss's plush office; Sam leaned against the doorway, pretending not to eavesdrop.

Mimi's facility with Hollywoodese had excelled in order to titilate her fellow deal-makers. Harley-Davidson slang: "I like it, Ben—we'll go into Sony together. You be hog daddy and I'll ride bitch." Topless bars: "Yeah, Miramax has got *lots* more money than they're stuffin' in my G; you and I gotta take 'em into the back room, Saul, for a lap dance." Porn films: "Norm, I'm giving you the money shot and you go and leave the lens cap on . . ."

Mimi was on the phone with Joel Goldblum, the agent for Amber Wentworth, whom Mimi managed. Mimi loved carrying on for Joel, who was utterly smitten.

"Oh really. Uh-huh. It's not *workin' my parts*, Joel. I thought Amber was going to be in the story of three generations of New England women, *Hallmark Hall of Fame* with someone like Jessica Tandy. Yes, I know Jessica Tandy is dead—now I need to be hearing names like Joanne Woodward, Shirley MacLaine . . ."

Mimi rolled her eyes.

"Coco Lane? Hundred-year-old Vegas whore Coco Lane? What— they backed the *Hollywood Squares* grid up to the studio and . . . Oh please—that shot-out piece of work? Her career's been *circling the bowl* for twenty years—jiggle the goddam handle, Joel!" Mimi listened a moment more. "Okay then. Get back to me, sweetheart." Now she turned to Samantha. "Tell me about Patrick."

"He didn't speak a word. It was my turn to speak—"

"Nothing happened then? That's good. Sorry Sam, can't do face time this morning, I am supercrunched, already late for Warners." Mimi stood, gathering papers in a Hermés-print folder.

"Meem, are we getting together this weekend?"

No, of course not, and Mimi rattled off a list of obligations, remembering the drinks meeting she had arranged at Friday midnight, for fuck's sake, but forgetting who with. "Blakely!" she yelled, sending him scurrying to her goddam calendar to see who the fuck she was fucking dining with. "Would you listen to my language? I've got to start doing something about that. Blakely, what weekend—"

He was instantly beside her, holding open a date book, allowing her to point to a free weekend for Samantha.

"That's a month from now," Sam said.

"And I'm *so* looking forward to it, sweetheart," Mimi said on the way out the door, clasping Sam's hands briefly and then departing. Blakely fell in behind with a briefcase, then Tony Vittorio, Tomorro Gs' promoter who made "deals" (bribing radio-station managers and program directors with loot for getting his single on their playlists—which is legal now, somehow), and then the firm's counsel. The parade of confident, striding associates, a blur of Italian suits and a mingled cloud of perfumes and colognes, disappeared into the elevator.

Samantha returned to her office and sat in it awhile. She looked at the phone and wondered if there was anyone from Smith or D.C. she might call long-distance and chat. "Tiffani," she called out presently.

"What."

"I think we'd better cancel the after-show meeting with Michael and T-Jack. Something's come up. Can you do that for me?"

No answer.

"Can you do that for me, dear?"

Still nothing, so Sam got up and peered around her office door. Tiffani was gone somewhere.

The label, at Mimi's insistence, had spent $20,000 on T-Jack Cole, a nineteen-year-old black deejay from Compton with juice. Club deejays were courted as passionately as high school basketball stars; for months a sullen, gang-clad entrepreneur-with-attitude would be plied with malt liquor (or Arrow's gin-and-juice cocktail, kept chilled in boardroom refrigerators) and Rolexes, gold jewelry, sports cars even—by a record industry in search of cool. And just as quickly, he'd be uncool. "Bunch of over-the-hill Jewish guys from

New York trying to second-guess the R and B market," as Mimi explained at the time.

Only six months ago Mohr Associates had met to invent a look and a marketing strategy for their yet-unnamed pop group:

"Is there any way," Michael the producer had asked, "that this group is going to have any black following whatsoever?"

T-Jack laughed. "Ain't no way—maybe if the brother's representin', know wha'mean? Ain't exactly mad talented. Shiht . . ."

Samantha watched the young man's hands strike a number of angles as he talked, ending up in the vicinity of his baggy-panted crotch. "Man, these lame muthafuckas don't kick back stoopid. My people just lookin' for a *phat* righteous groove on the hip-hop tip, know wha'mean? Lame-ass muthafuckas is *whack*."

"Eh," Mimi had said, yawning, "maybe we can get P-Dogg to kill his white wife or whatever it is that makes you a hero in the black community these days."

T-Jack started laughing, "That's cold fucked-up shit, lady."

"I try my best," said Mimi, flirting back.

"We're worried," began Christopher Tremaine, head of the label, Ganymede Records, impatiently "about the group's name."

This gathering threw a few names around, while Samantha's mind wandered. The one fact she knew about Christopher that trumped all others was that he paid people (men or women, irrelevantly) to let him take a dump on them. There was a Latin name for this fetish but Samantha couldn't think of it. Samantha found Christopher equally repulsive and attractive. He was as pale as a white person could be and hairless (she had seen him in shorts and a tank top at Michael's) except for on top; he had a head of dark black hair in a boyish cut, bangs hanging in his eyes. Mid-thirties? His eyebrows were shaped in semicircles, resembling a Caravaggio angel. Samantha often stared at his long, thin manicured fingers, imagining that he had his body hair removed pursuing some pedophilic notion of attractiveness. And then the excrement thing . . .

T-Jack suggested "Westside Gs."

"Doesn't G mean *gangsta*?" Samantha had asked.

"Lame muthafuckas need some'n stone-cold hard, dig?"

Samantha just stared at him, now suspecting he was an upper-class banker's son from Beverly Hills, playing at this.

"Let's go with Tomorro Gs," Christopher said, ready half an hour ago for this meeting to be over.

Tomorro Gs. "Tomorro" looking to the future when all men would be brothers before God, and "Gs" because they were bad gangsta motherfuckers who'd blow you scatterin' with their nines.

"Is there any compelling reason we have to misspell *tomorrow?*" Sam asked.

Yes, because it was def stoopid phat down, etc.

Cancel meeting with T-Jack and Michael, Samantha wrote on a piece of notepaper, placing it front and center on Tiffani's desk.

Might as well go home, thought Sam. Maybe Troy would be there and they could hang out, catch up.

As she wound up the Barranca Canyon, she spotted a crew trailer parked in front of the tall adobe gates, then another, then a catering wagon—some upscale Beverly Hills feedery, pâté and quiche and california rolls and bhajis for $4000 a day.

"Not these clowns again," she muttered.

In her front yard were the equipment wagon, a star's trailer, and a truck with poles and frames for lights.

"I'm sorry, ma'am, but entrance is by permit only. Are you on the list?"

"I'm on the fucking mailbox."

Sam floored past the clipboard-and-headset-boy, leaving him to sprawl on the lawn. In her garage, two techies were smoking pot, sitting on her washer-and-drier. They offered, she declined.

"But I may be back for it," she warned. She looked around for Troy's motorcycle. He was out.

Samantha and her newly acquired husband lived in a house in the Hollywood Hills that would lease for $20,000 a month. Inconceivable, that figure, but that was the rate. Mimi owned the house—or rather her company did—and Mimi rented out the location for TV shoots, film, poolside modeling, everything so far but porn films, but, Sam figured that was next. Mimi had recounted how she got this fabulous home:

"Herb Tuchner actually sued *my* ass when Patrick Fox left him for me. He libeled me, implied in *Variety* that I slept with Patrick. Anyway, I sued Tuchner for libel, figuring I'd just annoy him and get a settlement, but damn if I didn't win big."

"You took the man's house?"

"He shouldn't have libeled me. Sam, I've got the greatest lawyer, you gotta meet him. A very attractive—Blakely!"

Her assistant was in the doorway: "Yes, Mimi?"

"Get Robert Donovan on the phone for me, and set up a lunch at Chinois on Main. After Tuesday sometime, I don't care."

"Yes, Mimi."

"Sam, you'll love the guy, and if you get in trouble out here, he's your scumbag-for-hire. No one fucks with me anymore after the Tuchner thing."

"But," said Samantha, still a beat behind, "you took the man's home—"

"Myeh, he's got two homes. I took the good one. And God is punishing me for it too. The real estate market is in the shithouse— in fact my tax guy Stan Michaelson told me to—Blakely!"

"Yes, Mimi."

"Get Stan Michaelson on the phone and tell him I wanna do lunch at the Puck on Sunset sometime next week. Sam, you gotta meet Stan. Okay, he's not Mr. Conversation, but you'll be happy you know him when he's done with your taxes."

"You were saying about the house—"

"You can stay in the house," Mimi commanded, "until I get someone real to move in. You'll love it!"

But nobody ever moved in. Samantha had dwelled lightly in 1995, waiting for an eviction which never came; by 1996 her few accumulated things had gradually emptied into the vast house, and she'd begun buying furniture. Her stuff filled one little room of this two-story, six-bedroom, five-bathroom, four-fireplace, three-car garage, ochre Mission Revival hillside mansion with patios overlooking Los Angeles to the south and east, a jacuzzi and sundeck on the red-clay roof, a kidney-shaped pool tiled with hand-painted Portuguese *azulejos* that made the water iridescently aquamarine and inviting, all amid a landscape of ever-blooming tropical verdure, bougainvillea and jacaranda, palms by the pool that supplied a seasonal crop of luscious *medjool* dates.

Samantha was at first depressed by all the blank, furnitureless rooms, and her own drably furnished cell amid the spatial splendor. Not even Troy's moving in, after their marriage in December of '96, seemed to fill out the place, since he only brought a few boxes full of things from Laguna Beach.

But if she never felt entirely at home there, she never felt entirely *alone* either. Cleaning women, Mexican immigrants all, burrowed in and out with no discernible schedule. Sam would be awakened at 8:00 A.M. by a comprehensive second-floor vacuuming, or would be reading a trade magazine by the pool only to have Gabriela (the only domestic she learned the name of) approach silently from behind and scare the hell out of her:

"Will that be all, madam?"

After the heart-racing shock, Sam managed to say civilly, "Yes, that's fine, Gabriela." Sam had no idea what had been done or what she, when asked, consented to. "Maybe you can knock on the glass patio door next time and not scare Miss Flint to death?"

"Yes, madam."

Samantha had been surprised by workmen on the roof repairing the roof tiles, pool men and their assistants chlorinating and filtering, a small squad of illegal-alien personnel under the command of a master gardener who kept the grounds fertile and lush. She had learned not to walk around undressed or to leave her blinds open. And in time, she came to be comforted by all the comings and goings of the place and its innumerable dependents. It was downright aristocratic, really—Samantha's mother would approve—this constant buzz of servitude and anonymous upkeep.

Samantha had a new game. She raced the sun every Friday afternoon to Laguna Beach. She left Hollywood no later than 3:30, would do without food, would sacrifice a run to the restroom, anything in order to get on the freeways before the rest of California.

Beloved Los Angeles.

Has commuting ever been raised to such a pinnacle of self-expression? Los Angeles, Sam happily understood, was mercifully free of Washington's public transportation and taxi culture, New York's forced fraternization on subways. There's not the merest pretense of L.A. civic camaraderie. Poor dead, dwindling Washington and dated, increasingly irrelevant New York built great national monuments, skyscrapers of commerce, even replicated the cathedrals of their older-world counterparts, but L.A., the usurper, the last great city of the twentieth century, the capital now of American culture, has the interchange between I-110 and I-105!

Ramps for the carpool lanes to the left, ramps for the normal lanes to the right, the new metro line (like anyone's gonna ride that thing!) intersecting within the dual twelve-lane overlap, five, six levels high . . . Samantha, speeding through it at seventy-five MPH never ceased to marvel: never has so much concrete been poured so profligately in one place. These impossibly airborne exit ramps are our cathedrals' flying buttresses, the daily commute is our civic Mass, our cherished sacrament, the rush hour our penance . . .

I must write all this down, Samantha thought, leaving the Harbor Freeway for the 405.

She had dutifully rescued the brown accordion folder, THE COLLECTED WORKS OF SAMANTHA FLINT, from Washington and Aspen, and she intended at her first opportunity to add her own musings about Los Angeles to the reams of silly press releases she had penned and saved. Maybe a memoir—memoirs are getting big money now. *I Was a Cover-Marriage Bride* by Samantha Flint Chandler.

This particular Friday, the sun was turning increasingly orange in that mixture of smog, ocean mist, and Western sky that colored the world below a warm fireglow as early as 4:00 P.M. Then the sun reddened, bathing the strip malls and warehouses and the rusted long-haul semi in front of Samantha on the San Diego Freeway in a weak magenta, like a glass of Zinfandel rosé held up to the sky.

Samantha squealed the tires, hurtling through the curves on the Laguna Canyon Road, turning for the San Francisco–steep Third Street Hill and Skyline Drive. She would park on Michael's lawn if she had to—her reputation and unbroken track record were at stake! She parked in the driveway (where they had charitably left her a space), ran to the doorbell, shooed through the packed house of acquaintances and gorgeous, decorative men, and arrived with a triumphal flourish on the balcony.

"She made it! She made it!" Michael Gold screamed.

"I told you she'd be here!" Moe Silver declared, leading a chorus of cheers for her peerless record of anticipating the sunset. A margarita (nonalcoholic) was put into her hand.

"There it goes," Moe Silver officiated, out on the balcony in his silk dressing gown, drunk from an afternoon of tequila. All eyes turned to the west for the final parting of the sun, which shrank to a coal-red speck. Many times it was the afterglow that was the real show: a luminous play of magentas and pinks and burned orange, stirring the ocean-meets-desert air of the upper Southern California atmosphere, and last of all, miles away at Dana Point, long after it seemed anyone could possibly retain the sunset for themselves, a row of bay-windowed houses caught the final dull-scarlet.

Michael Gold and Moe Silver were the partners of Silver & Gold Promotions, producers and masterminds of Tomorro Gs (no, Silver and Gold were not their given names). This teenybopper boy–group had originally been conceived as another New Kids on the Block (once the biggest pop act of the year, whose third album didn't crack the *Billboard* Top 100), with a market of pre-adolescent teenage girls. Then Hanson went No. 1—real honest-to-god Oklahoma born-again teens—and Mohr & Associates decided there was no competing with that, so they decided to butch up the group and go for the urban dance-club appeal.

"Don't blink," Mimi told Sam when she heard Tomorro Gs' lame demo tapes, "or you're gonna miss the whole shootin' match."

All the "boys" were in their twenties, pretending to be teens, pretending to be heterosexual; all had signed shitty contracts that would give them more money than they'd ever dreamed of, but a mere drop compared to the label's and producers' take. The message of the group had something vaguely to do with racial harmony, so Samantha found it darkly instructive that all the members appeared to hate one another's guts.

As the launch date of May 1997 approached, drug-induced panic and pervasive second-guessing threatened to sink the whole project. Michael and Moe wanted to have it every which way: making the Chicano drummer and Asian bass player look plaid-shirt "alternative," the Navajo keyboard-player look like some kind of Duran Duran reject with big poofy hair, and the white lead singer, Troy, went from blond kid nextdoor to pouty, eyeliner and rouge, neo-Bowie gay club chic. P-Dogg, the black heartthrob, transformed himself from a clean-cut high school jock with a backwards Lakers cap and a large cross around his neck to full-fledged Crips insignia, flashing gang handsigns and glowering behind shades, grabbing his crotch for each photo opportunity, telling every interviewer within fifty feet how he was gonna mess up those disrespectin' East Coast muthafuckas and they'd better watch their fuckin' back.

"Tell you what," Mimi soon suggested firmly to P-Dogg, "let's see if we can not get ourselves shot before this damn single is released, whaddya say?"

"Okay babe," he said, initiating a series of complicated homeboy handshakes with Mimi, who somehow kept up. "What I'm hearin' you say is that I gotta keep it real where the music's concerned. Concentrate on my skills."

As if the boys could actually *play* those instruments.

As if they could sing a note.

Hundreds of thousands in studio costs, style consultants, choreographers, the best video team in the biz, promotion people—an exhausting effort designed to have the nation of 270 million humming Tomorro Gs' dance hit. Fortunately, the nation was easily led and the single, "Inside You," was climbing the charts toward the Top 10, with everyone associated with the CD sick to death of the hook now grooved into their cerebral cortices:

> Don't wanna be . . . beside you.
> Just wanna be . . . inside you.

Over and over. Must have taken them, gee, a whole minute to write this one, and yet there were four credited songwriters on this masterpiece, including Michael and Moe.

"Spice Boys," dismissed *Entertainment Weekly*, giving them a C−. Comparing them to their rivals, the Backstreet Boys, the *L.A. Weekly* trashed them as "the Backroom Boys," hoping the seedy gay-underworld allusion would fly over the heads of the libel lawyers.

Samantha at the time questioned the efficacy of releasing a debut single with such strong sexual content.

Tony Vittorio, the group's promoter (and only straight man for miles) just laughed. "Are you kidding, Sam? Bunch of teenage girls in TLC sing 'Rock hard or two-inches, I ain't too proud to beg.' 'I wanna lick you up and down,' is a number-one hit. Where you been? The American music industry is about providing a rhythm track for twelve and thirteen year olds to fuck to."

"Margarita time!" cried Moe, joining his partner Michael on the balcony in Laguna Beach, in a matching floral-print silk dressing gown. Michael and Moe were hefty, balding agreeably shallow forty-five-year-old men who got their start at Casablanca Records and had yet to shake off the magic glitter disco dust. They lived as lovers provisionally, a shared mountaintop house in Laguna Beach, a co-owned city apartment in West Hollywood, although this arrangement was fluidly unmonogamous, and they picked up (and shared) young men at will.

Their weekly bacchanals had a bit of the partying-on-the-Titanic feel: booze was poured, pot was smoked, drugs were inhaled in the back bedroom, and sex was had, although a trifle more discreetly. Brushfires, financial ruin, earthquakes and mudslides, AIDS and overdoses, records that wouldn't sell, heart attacks and middle-aged maladies—all were gathered and poised, lurking somewhere beneath the balcony to do the revellers in . . . but not tonight.

"Where's your husband?" Michael whined. "Why won't he come down anymore?"

Sam shrugged. "He's got that new motorcycle and all he does now is ride all over the San Fernando Valley."

Moe enthused, "We miss seeing his precious little tush around these parts!"

It was right here, at one of the Friday soirees, when Tomorro Gs was but a gleam in Michael's glassy, drug-unfocused eye, that she met Troy. One evening indistinguishable from any other at Michael and Moe's (just as all evenings are the same evening in seasonless Los Angeles), Samantha sat by herself contentedly on the sofa, when the most beautiful young man she had ever seen plopped down beside her.

"Troy. Remember?"

Troy was ripe to be groomed for stardom; he had been a longtime hanger-on of the Michael and Moe set. There was a rumor that Moe had put a few thousand into Troy's mouth—caps, bridges, bonding. Troy had the requisite teen-idol cheekbones, a mane of yellow-gold ponytailed hair, large sad green eyes that would one day stare out of many a poster hanging in nine-year-old girls' rooms nationwide. His distinction was his dark, sharp eyebrows, which belonged on an adult face and provided a range of intelligent, sensual expressions. He was visually perfect to play a damned nineteenth-century poet, or a romantic who dies for love in a duel . . . until he opened his mouth and revealed himself to be a lower-class slacker from a trailer park in Santa Ana. But people had a habit, as is common with the beautiful, of seeing what they wanted to see in Troy.

"Out with the old," Troy said when he met Samantha, "and in with the new." He nodded toward Michael's new "discovery" currently on display on the balcony.

Sam asked, "Were you one of Michael's, uh . . ." How to put it?

"Long time ago. Glad that's over with and I can, you know, pursue my music."

Sam hid a smile.

"Oh, I'da let Michael screw me anyway," he said.

Samantha wondered if Troy knew not to talk this way to the media.

"Now Ruben," he added, as they both appraised a buff brown Latino by the pool, shirtless, bandana on his head, tight jeans. "Ruben only does producers. He knew all about Michael and made a big play for him. Thinks he's gonna break out and be some kinda movie star, so he's taking all these kung-fu lessons."

Michael once confided to Sam that Troy was who they created

and constructed the entire group around. Casting the others proved to be no end of fun as well as frustration. P-Dogg was billed as coming from the mean streets of South Central (middle-class from Torrance actually), and Storm, a Native American found at great trouble and expense after open casting calls in Tucson, Phoenix, and Flagstaff. Storm, short for Storm Clouds Rising Over White Mountains (which Mimi fabricated during a staff meeting) was born John Sanchez. And there was Brad, a Korean-American, cast because he didn't look *too* Asian for mainstream sensibilities. Troy remained through all the personnel changes the token white, but the true hurt-eyed huggable heartthrob of the group.

And he was indestructible.

He had survived an abusive home, life on the streets, hustling and petty criminality, a short stint in a juvenile facility, a beating by a homophobic cop, a rape at knifepoint, the spectacle of watching others in his former "escort service" profession disappear and die of AIDS. Samantha had no idea how much if any of his history was true. But by any measure, he was indestructible, and indestructibility was a quality Samantha highly valued. The one time, last year, when it looked like he might have to be dropped from the group, Sam came to his rescue—going as far as marrying him. Something always kept Troy afloat. She had come to his rescue, and perhaps he would come to hers.

"How was Laguna?" Troy asked late Sunday night, home at last, tossing his helmet on a bedroom chair (though by the look of his hair, blown every which way, it was clear he hadn't worn it).

"They miss you," Sam said, reading in her bed.

He flopped down, bouncing on the mattress. "They miss doing me."

"Did you have sex somewhere?" He rolled over on his back, and Samantha pulled on his ponytail. "Tell your wife the truth."

"Some boy who wrote me a fan letter. Some high school guy in the Valley who's all queer and in love with me."

"You looked him up?"

"Showed up at his house, put him on the back of the bike, took him over to Malibu Canyon and, you know."

Samantha was astounded. "You don't mess with people's lives like that, Troy. That can have consequences."

"Naw, he understood. It was a onetime thing." He now rolled over on his stomach. "Went by Bob's Bottle Club too."

Samantha refused to say anything motherly or authoritative; once that started, Troy would pull away from her. She pretended to be caught up in her reading. "See any of your old customers?"

"I was looking for Mr. Ishima. He lent me all this money and I swore I'd pay him back one day. Thought I'd see him drop dead of surprise by showing up with a thousand dollars and paying him back."

Bottle clubs, Samantha learned from Troy, were an L.A. phenomenon. Open at midnight, closing at morning light, catering to men with their own bottles, just a dark place to sit and drink. One paid for one's glass and setups. Exclusively a male preserve; no one socialized, no one went looking for anyone there. Some clubs had a radio playing quietly, some had a TV running, but the purest offered complete silence to go with the shadows.

"Easiest trick in town was the bottle-club guys. They're not even queer, most of 'em. They just want something warm in their bed; they can barely walk to the taxi by the time I get to 'em. Only thing those guys ever done killed was their, you know, what's uh . . ."

"Their liver."

"Mr. Ishima," Troy said in his tone that announced that something truly unbelievable was coming. "He was with some Japanese bank downtown. Every night he drank a bottle of Jack Daniel's, left a hundred-dollar tip for the barman, who didn't do anything but get him a glass! I'd just stand outside and wait for him to come out and he'd see me and that'd be that. We'd go back to some high-class hotel in Hollywood and they'd have these refrigerators full of drinks and candy bars, and like chips and stuff. And you'd look on the little sheet that had prices? And it was like, a little bag of potato chips, *six dollars*. A ginger ale, three-fifty!"

This was the amazing part of the story.

"Anyway, he lent me some money to get some new clothes. I just wanted to thank him. Hope he's not dead." Troy hopped off the bed, ready to crash in his own bedroom down the hall. But sometimes they did sleep in the same bed, cuddling and talking.

He would say on such occasions, "If I could, I'd do it with you, Sam. You know that, don't you?"

"I like it the way we've worked things out," Sam would say.

BEEP. *Hello Sam-Sam, this is Mom. It's hot here like you wouldn't believe . . .* Mom's weather report from Clearwater. *Now Sam-Sam, we have to straighten out when I'm going to come visit you and your husband. I know, I know you said it was a showbiz kind of thing, but I still ought to meet the man that's married my daughter—and you swear to me he's twenty-six? I read in the* National Star *that he was nineteen—*

Oh god. Mom wanting to meet her son-in-law. Mom distraught and miserable that she wasn't invited to the sham wedding. Mom not knowing what to tell all her friends.

BEEP. *Samantha, this is Cindy from Dr. Cline's office calling. You haven't come in for some time—*

"Because I don't want to," Sam said, fast-forwarding.

Occasionally a sisterly check-in: BEEP. *Hey Sam, this is Kel. Nothing special, just wanted to see how big my long-distance bill could be— I'm goin' for my personal best. Chuck Jr. has gotten it in his head that he wants to go to Disneyland, even though Disney World, which we've been to a hundred times, is right down the road . . .* Out of habit she still calls her son, "Chuck Jr.," even though Chuck Sr. separated from her two years ago. Kelly now lived in Dunedin, within view of Clearwater, making a pretense of living independently of her mother and older sister, subsidized by government aid, a single woman with four children, no skills, no daycare—

BEEP. *Good day, Samantha, this is Wolfgang Wurzburger . . .* He always left such a formal message with his full name. Usually Wolfgang and William's messages arrived minutes apart, as if they were keeping tabs on each other.

BEEP. *Samantha, this is William. Wolfgang tells me you've dropped out of our A.A. group, and of course, I'm concerned. You know as well as anyone that you can't get anything out of it if you don't work your program. Your sponsor Tad wants to call you but the number you gave him doesn't work, so he wanted me to give—*

"I haven't dropped out," she said to the machine, erasing all the messages, half-listened to. "I'm busy busy busy."

Wolfgang was a bad influence; he loved American-style fast food, hot dogs, Winchell's twenty-four-hour doughnut stands. He would phone Samantha, insomniac at 2:00 A.M., make a request for a doughnut run, and she'd be in Hollywood twenty minutes later, to stay up with Wolfie eating doughnuts. If that made them hungrier, then it was off to the 7-Eleven for one of those microwaved burritos or the A.M./P.M. for hot dogs garnished with the delights of the condiment table, exposed to the elements all day. They would sit on the curb out front of the all-night convenience store.

"I'm quite sure," Wolfgang said, running a finger across the top of his overdecorated hot dog and licking it, "that no one will ever give me money to make a real film again. But one day, I will save my money, yes? I will make an independent film with low budget, something raw and original. There will be a Wurzburger renaissance." He bit into the hot dog. "I don't suppose I have to tell you about the kind of frankfurters you can get in Berlin, hm?"

"Why haven't you gone back?"

"No, no, I am here for this reason," Wolfgang swept the panoramic vista of the parking lot with the hand holding the hot dog. "The Golden Land. Sunny California." He laughed. "They say *laidback*, but this is the most ambitous, driven city in the United States—all the more so for nobody being able to admit it. You have to pretend that you are unconcerned with your career, your money, your status, your beauty."

"And you don't?"

"I am what becomes of a person who does not. I truly do not care. I choose to believe in the California-as-advertised, hot tubs and campfires on the beach, a mindless Summer of Love, yes? All winter long, for the rest of one's life." He finished up his hot dog, before turning to Samantha. "*You* care. You measure yourself against the others—she is thinner, she is richer."

"I can't help it."

"Trademark of the American woman, this constant taking measure. Constantly insecure. Mothers raise their daughters very badly here."

"You can be nonchalant," she insisted, chewing. "You've made films that will be taught in film schools in a hundred years."

He snorted, dismissing this.

"No," pressed Sam, "you've done something—I haven't yet. I should have written something publishable by now, by thirty-seven. Plenty of time to have written a novel."

"There is still much time."

"Actually," she said, slipping an arm around him, touching her temple to his temple, "I have an idea for a screenplay. You are free to make it your comeback. It's called *Ruin*."

"Ruin," he repeated.

"I have become fascinated by ruin. No mere setback, no run-of-the-mill failure; any of us can experience that. I mean complete and total career and social devastation. What's ahead for Tomorro Gs."

Soon dawn would appear, gray and uninteresting, and she would retreat to her fortress in the Hollywood Hills, to her hot toddy, a glass of milk warmed in the microwave accompanied by a Xanax, so the day's tensions wouldn't impede that drift into oblivion . . .

BEEP. *Samantha, this is William. Am I being officially avoided? I know you're not too terribly busy, because I keep hearing that you make time for Wolfgang and . . . and his little activities. Anyway, shall I make reservations for us somewhere. Thursday night? Thursday night, since your weekends now belong officially to those male prostitutes down in Laguna Beach . . .*

He knew. Wolfgang had somehow let it slip, the business a few months ago about Wolfgang buying Samantha a gigolo at the Beverly Hilton. Then again, William always talked bitterly and jealously about Sam's choice of company, the unworthiness of her male companions.

His name was Boyd-Scot. ("*Liebchen,*" said Wolfgang, "I endeavored to find a man without a hyphen in his name for you, but at this escort service, but this was to no avail . . .") Samantha sat nervously in the $256-a-night hotel room waiting for him to arrive, every few minutes or so swearing to herself she would get up and walk out. Finally, he arrived.

"I'm Boyd-Scot. I need the money up front and then we can begin. I don't do asswork."

Well, at least nobody was pretending this wasn't a business transaction. It was like dealing with a masseur at a spa—not that she'd ever done that either. "I don't know what you mean by asswork."

"Isn't there a man with you? I thought a man made the phone call."

"He did. That was a friend—he was placing an order. For me."

"Okay, then," he said, unbuttoning his pressed silk shirt. " 'Cause I don't do asswork."

He was worth Wolfie's five hundred bucks. Six-three, chiseled Chippendale-dancer body, unreally endowed, and proficient in all the lovemaking arts and tricks that Samantha had never experienced. All women should do this once, she decided. Just to set a standard, raise the bar a bit. But unlike some women—and one heard about them, scattered throughout Beverly Hills—this was not the first taste of something that would become a lifelong addiction. No endearments, no patter could persuade Samantha that he meant a word of what he said about her full breasts, her creamy skin; it was all too mechanical. She was left with some striking images though.

Boyd-Scot had slowly stripped naked and sat in a plush chair across from Samantha, also undressed, and the routine here was for each of them to arouse and stimulate themselves while looking at the other. But Boyd-Scot faced the turned-off television to Samantha's right, the dark wide screen that now reflected himself, while he moaned, "Yeah . . . you're gorgeous . . . you deserve the best, baby, and I'm it . . . see what you've done to me . . ."

Wolfgang was wrong about how excited she would be to hand over the money; there was no frisson of power, and Boyd-Scot didn't seem particularly humiliated or degraded. Paying for sex, Sam theorized, is a male turn-on, since men mix status, power and money more readily into their sexual tastes. A real turn-on for Samantha would have been if Boyd-Scot somehow found her phone number, called her, wanted just to talk, wanted to get out of that life and be with her. And when she fantasized about Boyd-Scot, it was this, not the hour of supreme lovemaking that he had given her, but this fantasy, the tortured man with sex as a career. . . .

Again, one had to be indestructible.

BEEP. *Hey Samantha, this is David Sutton again. I think this is the right number; it's hard to tell from your machine, but . . .*

David from Manhattan, now living near Poughkeepsie, married to a lawyer while he managed a bakery and coffee shop in the Village, three kids, all en route to Disneyland for their summer holiday. Could she join them? Wouldn't it be great to see each other again?

"No," she said quietly, wounded by his sweet voice, still high and boyish. She would resolutely erase the message, not sit compulsively beside her answering machine and repeatedly play it, not let his voice return her to some younger still vulnerable part of herself. Nor would she arrange to see him, feel an old attraction, probably make a successful play for him because he would be weak; I'm only entitled, Samantha thought with asperity, to one home-wrecking a decade. Her machine beeped, all messages had been erased. She had not even listened to his phone number, so David Sutton was safe.

BEEP. *Samantha, this is Blakely. It's such a silly call really. Mimi wanted me to make sure you were awake even though it's three P.M. You know this is the day you're to accompany Amber down to see Alex Rostov for her reading. . . .*

"Damn," Samantha muttered, still in bed. She allowed herself two speed tablets, which were necessary in emergencies like this one. She washed it all down with some orange juice, vitamin pills, bee pollen—hm, no blood-pressure pills left.

"Why didn't they send a limo?" were Amber's first words, pouting from the front steps of her bungalow.

"Because this is an audition, not a command performance before the queen. Get in."

Amber turned from Samantha's car, idling in her Westwood driveway, and went back inside. Time passed, the audition hour approached. Inside, Sam figured, Amber was calling Joel, her agent, who no doubt called Mimi, whose line was busy when Sam called Mimi for permission to bag this whole dog-and-pony show.

Finally, Joel's Audi sped up to Amber's house; he went within, talked his client into coming out, getting in Samantha's car, and going to read for the part of Daisy, the next-door neighbor's live-at-home daughter on *In the Family Way*, a pilot being readied for the replacement season of 1998, taking a cue from a *Newsweek* cover story about how kids today can't make it and they're all ending up back at home, with spouses and kids in tow.

Alex Rostov, the casting agent, was waiting for them outside a sound stage on Paramount's Melrose lot. "You're too late," he said, leaning into Samantha's window. "Jim's gone to dinner." Jim was the show's creator and omnipotent.

"Thanks a lot," Amber hissed at Samantha.

While Amber pouted in the car, Samantha hopped out and walked Alex back to the commissary. "Personally, I don't care if the little bitch never works again," she told him.

"I like your management style," he nodded pleasantly. Alex was thirty and energetic and on the way up in television. He had cornered the market as casting agent for five of Fox's sitcoms and few hip production companies didn't attempt to call him first. Rich. Dark-haired with goatee, handsome even if a little stressed. Samantha decided after the gigolo incident, she would aim for a real relationship with a decent man. Indeed, such a prospect had the very lure of the experimental and exotic, since it had happened so few times in her life.

"Is your wedding ring," she asked, walking beside him closely, "to keep all the young Hollywood starlets from throwing themselves at you, only adoring you for your casting . . . prowess."

He laughed. "No, Sam, it's an actual wedding-inspired wedding ring. Married two years."

"We'll fix that when my new law passes."

"Which law is that?"

"The Samantha Flint Southern California Polygamy Statute. In lieu of the shortage of available straight men, the straight men in the population have to do double and triple duty, giving us late-arrivals a chance at happiness."

"Hold it. Aren't you married to that guy in that, what are they called? TooMany Gs?"

Samantha shrugged. "Call it a marriage of convenience, Alex. Anyway, happy to hear you're happy. Darn it."

"We can still be friends," Alex said, which he probably shouldn't have if he was wholly uninterested in her. He stood ready to go into the commissary, rushed but polite, while Sam was illegally parked and Amber was calling god-knows-where on Sam's cell phone. "I'll call you if Jim decides to reaudition Amber," he said.

Samantha was desperate to lengthen this rather successful flirtation. "Oh," she said, fumbling, "do you remember . . ." What was her name? "Winona Blake on that Nell Carter thing—"

"*Gimme a Break!*"

"Yeah, one of the daughters? Older, not too plastic looking, good comic timing. You think her name could go in the pot?"

Tony, operating six months ago on the now-altered premise that Tomorro Gs were aiming for a nine-to-twelve bubblegum market, had booked them on a series of teen-appeal appearances (Moreno Valley Mall, a Tower Records in the San Fernando Valley, South Hills Mall in Costa Mesa, various pubescent wastelands) culminating in an appearance in the amusement park attached to the MGM Grand in Las Vegas, a second-rate theme park devoted to the ludicrous notion that a town of mafia fronts, whores, gambling addicts, sports books, alcoholics, and topless dancers could be re-created as a "family" environment.

"This is going to be *soooo* lame," said Troy.

"What the fock are we gon' do?" Ruben demanded. "Ride on some goddam roller coaster wid a big ol' smile on our fockin' faces?"

Ganymede Records had ordered a tour bus, another relic from the era when they were going to be pitched to prepubescents instead of clubmongers. The bus looked like a reject from *The Partridge Family*, a multicolored pseudo-groovy bus with their group logo.

Brad: "I'm not getting on that dipshit bus. Buses make me nauseated anyway—don't put me on that muthafuckin' thing unless you want me puking all over you."

Storm: "I'm not sharing no fucking queer-room with you assholes in Vegas." He grabbed his crotch. "I'm gettin' me some fucking pussy—"

P-Dogg: "Yeah, maybe some *ass*-pussy."

Ruben: "Nigger, I better get my own fockin' comp suite room in Vegas, homes, one with a bar, with a hot tub—"

P-Dogg: "Oh, like you gonna score or some'n?"

Brad: "Bee-atch is gonna connect after he calls 1-900-COCK. Pay some skeez to bust his nut—"

Ruben: "Fuck alla you fuckin' assholes—"

Samantha cleared her throat. "Boys. Some ground rules, please. You've got to start getting into the habit of cleaning up your language. You can't talk like this to the press or in front of fans. And in public no drinking, no smoking, no gambling—"

The group erupted: "*What??*"

"We're leaving L.A. for America, got that?"

The trip to Las Vegas was barely organized mayhem. The trip up Interstate 15 set the tone with the boys mooning passersby from the bus, pissing out the back window, and Brad, hungover and in some kind of withdrawal, throwing up as promised.

In early September, there wasn't much of a family crowd at the MGM theme park, and the kids that were there didn't seem interested in having hysterics over Tomorro Gs. The reporter for the *Las Vegas Times* didn't show, but that was evidence of a merciful god. Only Troy, Brad, and Ruben bothered to make the gig; P-Dogg and Storm went gambling, rented a car, went to see Busty Malone and her 76-inch bust at H.D.'s House of Ta-Ta's, drove drunk to Nye County for the Cherry Ranch to have two prostitutes enact lesbian scenarios while they jerked off—and that's merely the activities they chose to *share* with Samantha.

The phone rang.

Sam raised her head, thinking for a moment she was at home in her bed, except this bed was a king-size. She had closed the thick curtains and wasn't sure if it was day or night.

"Hello Sam, it's Mimi."

"Hey, you . . . you just caught me in."

"Aren't the boys supposed to be with you at some mall?"

That sounded familiar. "Uh, someone from Ganymede took them over." Not true, but Sam figured she had the day to make up a good excuse for why no one did anything they were supposed to.

"Go ahead. Tell me the worst of it."

Storm gambled at Bob Stupak's Vegas World and, against all odds, spun the big two-story wheel-of-fortune and got the $10,000 spot. He demanded his money, but the management said he had to be twenty-one to win it. He was twenty-six, he said, proving it with his driver's license, to which they said they'd be happy to give him the check before photographers and media, who would be interested to learn that he wasn't eighteen like Tomorro Gs' press kit said. Sam showed up at 3:00 A.M. to talk a drunken Storm out of making a scene ("For god's sake you're making hundreds of thousands off the single, and you'd blow that for ten thousand dollars?").

P-Dogg flashed his credit card at Harrahs and proceeded to gamble away $12,000, combining his heroin-snorting habit with a compulsion to sign chits while sitting at the $50-a-chip table, high roller for a night. When he couldn't hold the pen to sign the receipts, they got him a cab, which he threw up and passed out in. Sam came down from her bedroom at 5:00 A.M. to pay the furious driver, slipping him a C note for his trouble, and another $100 to help carry P-Dogg to his room. Then—

Mimi noted, "Ganymede ought to reimburse you."

Troy and Ruben went to the gay bar where the Vegas female impersonators and showboys frequented; there was a live show where a bunch of gay porn stars took everything off and got fondled by the big tippers in the audience. One of the strippers thought Ruben was cute and performed sex on him, kneeling at his seat, according to Troy.

"No chance the press was around, was there?" Mimi asked, nonchalantly.

"Guess we'll find out. That was Thursday night. Last night we had a rock-stars-trash-the-hotel-room episode—"

"I get the idea. How're you holding up through all this, sweetheart?"

"You know me. Indestructible."

Drugs was how. Before the Las Vegas adventure, Samantha asked for something in the amphetamine family and Ruben said, "Baby, why waste your time and money when there's *glass*?"

Sam had said that was a little hardcore—

"No, *chica*. Much speed as you do? You can take it, mama. I do it all the time. You wanna be up for two nights in a row gettin' the fockin' job done? Crystal is the way."

But isn't it addictive—

"I ain't gonna let that happen to you!"

Wasn't that sweet of him?

And in any event, crystal meth was all it was advertised to be and more. For seventy-two hours she had been the old Samantha, sharp, managing ten things at a time, clearing out a briefcase full of over-due work, bills and lease payments, writing postcards to friends she needed to thank or keep up with. She went shopping at the Forum in Caesar's Palace and obsessively purchased a whole new battery of kitchen gadgets and implements and had them shipped to L.A., vaguely remembering her current kitchenware was beat-up and in-adequate. Looking at her credit card receipt—$824.56—she re-solved not to go shopping on crystal meth anymore.

Mimi: "When are the kiddies back in L.A.?"

"I told them to make their own arrangements to fly back, since everyone, including me, refuses to get on the vomit-bus again. We still on for the weekend?"

Mimi seemed confused. "Um. Oh yeah, quality time at Malibu. I think I have one meeting, however—"

"I'll quit your firm if you cancel on me. I mean it."

"All right, all right."

"Can you transfer me to Tiffani so I can get my messages?" Mimi obliged. "May I speak to Samantha Flint please?"

Tiffani replied, "She's at the MGM Grand this week for a meet-ing . . . is this you, Sam?"

"Yeah, can't fool you." Sam glimpsed the table and saw a full ashtray and a nearly empty bottle of bourbon. That's right, she and Tony the promoter had stayed up smoking and swapping war stories the night before, but he did all the drinking. She quickly patted and groped the space beside her . . . nah, she didn't sleep with him, though that would have been all right. Her purse with her vitamins and Prozac was on the couch across the room, inconveniently—

"Sam?"

She had forgotten Tiffani was on the line. "Oh yeah, Tiff, can you uh . . . tell me what time it is?"

"It's four-thirty."

"P.M.?"

"I wouldn't be at work if it was A.M."

"Any messages?"

Some guy from Starbird Productions named Alex.

"Give me Alex's number . . ."

After a stumble to the bathroom, the taking of pills, and ordering coffee from room service, she fell back into the bed. This bed will be my office today, she decided.

"Alex," she said, finding the casting agent before he left his office in Los Angeles. "Samantha Flint with Mohr Associates. Any word on Amber from Jim?"

"Amber's out," Alex said. "But funny thing. I mentioned Winona Blake to Jim, just to show I was earning my paycheck. Guess what? Jim's first directing gig was *Gimme a Break!* and he remembered her. He'll let her read for the part."

Samantha set the phone down with a small cry of joy.

Ha, wait until the other associates hear about this! See Mimi? I'm acquiring working talent, adding to your roster. Samantha wanted to see ol' Tiffani's face, first thing the morning after this all worked out.

Sam fell back into her bed as lighthearted as she'd been in months. Maybe Sandra Blake would get to tell her ambush-in-the-parking-deck story to *Entertainment Tonight* after all.

She felt good enough to call her mother, an act that required great equanimity. Mrs. Flint had much to say about all the bodily deteriorations in the neighborhood, how Bethie's oldest was tarted up and skipping school, hanging out with the wrong sort. And of course, the weather, which was the preamble for her mother's hurricane paranoia, which led to her crime paranoia:

". . . and over in Tarpon Springs, Samantha, a woman *my age* was raped, with her neck snapped, just like that. It's not like I have anything to steal. Raping women of my age . . . This February, over the Presidents' Day weekend, a woman, sixty-seven, was raped in her trailer right here in Clearwater, at two in the afternoon.''

"Mom, what are you doing? Keeping a scrapbook?''

"It's just terrible being alone.''

"Where's Bethie?''

"Oh, she comes in so late, I almost never see her. And when I'm off to shop or get my hair done, most mornings I don't even see her. She's not much security for me anymore. And you know what?'' Mrs. Flint added, whispering. "She's had sunglasses on all week.''

"Is that so unusual in Florida?''

"I think she has a black eye,'' Mrs. Flint whispered, almost inaudibly. Though Bethie wasn't in the house, Mrs. Flint habitually whispered bad news to diminish its impact, i.e., "Poor Mrs. Landros has,'' dropping to a whisper, "cancer.''

"You think someone's beating on Bethie?'' As her mother talked on, Samantha fished around in her purse for a tablet of speed; the lulling monotony of Mom had tempted Sam to fall asleep again.

"I don't know what I did wrong to have my girls so unhappy,'' Mrs. Flint concluded.

"I'm not unhappy, Mother.''

"You're in a marriage that you say is all showbiz. Is your husband there with you in the hotel? Do you even share the same room?''

Samantha didn't know how to explain herself.

"I didn't raise you, Sam-Sam, to think so lightly of marriage, I can tell you that—''

"Mother, did you get my money order?''

Her tone changed completely. "Oh yes, Sam-Sam, that was so . . . much, can you afford to give away so much? I couldn't believe it, thought I'd read the number of zeros wrong.''

"Well, that's what being married to a rich 'little boy,' as you call him, will do for you.''

"I'll use the money for—''

"Mom, Mom, don't tell me what you're gonna do with it.'' Her patience was now slipping away; she couldn't find a tab of speed anywhere. It was time to hang up. "It's your money, just don't tell me what you're giving away to Bethie or Kelly."

Ta-da! Samantha got through a call with her mother without a breath of controversy or argument, and if serotonin-inhibitors were invented for nothing else, they had justified themselves.

She didn't want to sleep again. For exercise, she walked with her cup of room-service coffee to her suite's spectacular terrace that overlooked the long 5000-room expanse of the MGM Grand Hotel with its view of the silly pseudo-medieval castle of the Excalibur Hotel to the south, the faux-Polynesian skyscraper of the Tropicana, the vast pyramid and Sphinx of the Luxor Hotel, the fake New York City skyline across the street, the Chrysler Building replica spray-painted silver, and to the north the magnificent, profligate Strip of Las Vegas and its millions of blinking, flashing, pulsing lights, blazing although the sun had barely set.

The fanciful scene before her had no more reality than her life, her so-called marriage, now not even a year old. Troy and everything associated with the fame of his pop-music group, the pile of money, the concept of being married—it was all agreeably preposterous.

"Best decision I ever made," Sam said aloud to Las Vegas, sipping her strong coffee.

Yet she remembered how she was the one, just nine months ago, Christmas of 1996, who fought the cover-marriage idea, initially:

Two o'clock in the morning, Mimi in her silk dressing gown, having driven in straight from Malibu; Michael, Tony, Christopher all in attendance, Blakely taking notes at his laptop, and Sue Gant barking out suggestions about how to avoid the scandal. Mimi, hoping for a dramatic war-room effect, had dimmed the lights except for a table lamp on her desk.

"Clay Weedon," Mimi intoned, dead serious, "was picked up two weeks ago for solicitation on Santa Monica Boulevard. He propositioned an undercover cop. Selling his ass for just twenty bucks."

Michael put his head in his hands.

"Like all such offenses, it made the police blotter, public information. Clay Weedon," Mimi explained for those who hadn't gotten it, "is the original name of Troy Chandler who, fortunately, has yet to change his driver's license."

"Who knows?" asked Michael.

"I think no one in the media, yet. Troy called Ruben, who had a friend go down with bail money."

"You guys cut him a check last month for eighty-nine thousand dollars, so he wasn't doing it for the money, clearly," said Tony, stating the obvious.

"It's a matter of time," said Sue Gant, the flat-voiced, big-boned publicist with the high platinum-blond dye-job, who regularly referred to publicity crises of twenty years ago. "I was at PMK when the Richard Chamberlain-is-gay rumor started making the rounds. We made sure there were women for him to be seen with—"

"We'll just hook him up with some woman," Michael blurted.

"What I was saying," said Sue, bristling at being interrupted, which she rarely was in her peerless p.r. domain, "was that it's a matter of time before someone figures out that Clay Weedon is Troy Chandler. These tabloids have a staff that pores over the blotter each and every night—they feed in *every name* picked up on vice, drug possession, john-stings into their computers. If five years from now some actor makes it big, they run a check, there's his name and then they've gotcha. They may know about Troy already. Some troll like Cyril Demby might be holding it, waiting for the maximum time of embarrassment."

"Can we pay them off?"

Sue laughed. "In the olden days, yes. Hell, when I started out, they wouldn't even think of doing a gay exposé on Rock Hudson or Montgomery Clift—too discouraging to their housewife readership. But it's all fair game now."

As the others squabbled to find the best strategy, Sam, ignored on the sofa, experienced déjà vu: this could have been an afternoon in Frank Shanker's office. Or at any time, in any politician's office, in any boardroom, in scores of offices across Hollywood, across America where people, shills, flaks, yesmen, fixers, bagmen, water-carriers, smoothers, advisers and experts and pundits, scrambled to whitewash, cover up, put in the best light . . . A growth industry in late twentieth-century America: the ever-expanding demands of staff and resources to make sure something *true* doesn't leak out.

Michael said, "Why don't we drop Troy from the group, and replace him with an alternate."

So much for the allegiance of Troy's former mentor and lover. "That's not necessary," Samantha began.

"We've already shot two videos," Tony reminded them.

"We can't drop him," said Christopher icily to Michael with an accusing squint. "He might go to *Hard Copy* and tell them about how the boys were auditioned on your little casting couch. They might pay a lot for that."

"Troy's already got a TV movie lined up," Mimi informed Michael impatiently. "This is about more than just the group. Troy's the breakout star of the bunch—we've got product left on the shelves here with several years of earning power."

Tony shrugged. "Maybe the LAPD has a weak case."

This is a town of gangs, Sam thought.

Management gangs desperate to keep a client's dirty secret from the media gang. The tabloid gang desperate to find some dirt before the p.r. gang has time to cover ass. The LAPD gang (funded by her tax money) in sting operations to humiliate the gang of lonely older men and the desperate boy gangs who offer themselves as tricks. All of these sordid little tribes bound by the lure of unearned money, the lucre they could beat and extort out of each other—

"You know him best, Sam," Mimi prompted.

"I say we let him say he's gay. That the hustling business was a misunderstanding and the cop was a homophobe. But go ahead and let him say he's gay."

Stunned silence, before Michael muttered, "You're crazy."

Blakely: "It'll ruin the group's image."

Mimi shook her head. "I've told you a hundred times, Sam. America hates faggots."

"I'm saying," Sam marched on, "it's the nineties. They're already out-of-the-closet performers in alternative bands, so any day now some mainstream pop group is going to do it—why not us? It'll triple sales in a lucrative gay market. This is a young-adult club act—"

Michael: "That's precisely our objection."

"May I finish?" Sam insisted, annoyed at how adamantly the gay people at this meeting argued for the sanctity of the closet. "Gay men, a hefty chunk of the dance-single market, are not flocking to the stores to buy a Tomorro Gs remix, anymore than they did a New Kids or a Joey Lawrence CD. They *would* if there was a gay, gorgeous, out-of-the-closet hunk in the band. Rather than being dopey like New Kids, a gay member gives the band an *edge*. Yes, America is full of bigots but they're not *and never were* the pop-music market. Nobody under thirty cares if you're gay—"

Michael: "That's not true."

Tony, the only straight man in the room, defended her. "That Ty Herndon guy. Allegedly propositions a male cop, exposes himself. That's redneck country-and-western music, and he's still got a career."

Sam concluded, "Look, the whole point of this artificial little boy-group was diversity. Why not a gay guy?"

"We're not talking about U2 here, Samantha," said Christopher with a look of impatient distaste. "Speaking for the label, this is a one-off, okay? We get a few hits and the boys move on to other things." Translation: the skids. "If this product was going to be around in five years, it might be worth the risk."

Michael: "Christopher's right, Sam."

"What about Melissa Etheridge? Madonna plays at girl-girl stuff. I promise you, celebrity lesbianism is almost passé—"

Michael: "It's very different for gay males, you know that."

Blakely: "I don't know that you can appreciate what kind of persecution that gay men go through."

Samantha crossed her arms and said lightly, "So I guess Jesse Helms wins another round here tonight with all his allies in the entertainment community."

Oh the indignation! Young lady, I gave money to the West Hollywood AIDS Project, blah blah blah. Don't question my commitment to gay rights, blah blah blah. Liz Taylor knows me by name, blah blah blah. I was at the AmFAR thing at the Wiltern Theater—

"With a woman on your arm," Sam reminded Michael.

"Christopher's right," Mimi concluded, tired of the sidetracks. "We're not dealing with the next Pearl Drop here—"

Blakely interjected: "That's Pearl *Jam*, Mimi."

"Whatever. The last thing we need is Southern Baptist neanderthals burning the CD, putting pressue on Wal-Mart to not stock Ganymede Records and clouding up a simple, predictable release to the top-40 playlist."

"Pat Robertson burning the CD . . ." Sam paused to consider if you could burn a CD. ". . . would be the best thing that could happen."

Oh the arguments came fast, impeccably reasoned, lovingly constructed. Couldn't get Tomorro Gs on the air in Omaha. Couldn't expect support from *Tiger Beat* and *Teen Dream*. Parents would boycott. No boy would buy it because his friends would think he's a fag. Everyone's sympathetic to Sam's point of view—

"Yeah," said Sam, "I really feel the *love* in this room."

And if Troy had had the nerve at that time, Samantha reflected on her Las Vegas terrace, I wouldn't be Mrs. Troy Chandler today. Michael and Christopher and the other Gs harrangued Troy so thoroughly ("You've ruined everything we've worked for!") that he was near-suicidal when Samantha drove down to Laguna Beach to see if Mimi's prize client was all right.

"What am I gonna do?" Troy wailed, running to her car as she pulled up to park outside of his Laguna Beach apartment. He threw himself into her arms and squeezed her tight as no one ever had.

"It's gonna be all right—"

"I've messed everything up for everybody. Mimi's really mad, isn't she?"

Mimi, bloodsucking twenty percent from the kid's paltry take, and he's worried about *her*. "No . . . no she's not really mad—"

"Michael, I can't face Michael!"

"We're going to fix everything," she said, putting an arm around his shoulder. "That's what I'm here for, to straighten all this out."

Samantha had parked her car next to some trash cans in Cedar Alley with room for cars to get around.

"Everyone down here," Troy said, pointing to the neighboring houses, "wants me to move. They signed some kinda petition thing, 'cause of all the teenage girls who come looking for me and, well,

I've been, you know, having sort of parties and stuff. A lot of my old crowd from L.A. is living with me here now.''

Samantha pictured this rich-retired neighborhood and the effect of Troy—who had never had a dime in his life, now racing through his thousands of dollars—and his sad invite-everyone parties, the parade of hangers-on and crack-smoking riffraff. "You know Troy, you've gotta be careful,'' she said delicately, "not to let your old friends take advantage of you.''

"I mean, some of the guys don't have anywhere to go, and I said if I ever got rich enough, then they could come down and be with me. Like my friend, Rodger,'' Troy explained. "I think he, like, got high and went around with a key or something and scraped all these people's cars up and down Cliff Drive. I told the police I didn't know anything about it but they knew to come by here. Shit,'' he added, seeing something over her shoulder.

Speaking of the police, there was a Lexus (driven by a white, face-lifted, silver-haired woman with a carphone at her ear) and, behind her, a Laguna Beach police car with lights flashing.

"This your car?'' the policeman asked Samantha. He wasn't even twenty-five, a boy scout in a man's uniform.

"Yes.''

"You'll have to repark it.''

"What's wrong with how I'm parked? The woman,'' she motioned to the Lexus lady, prim and self-righteous behind tinted glass, "has plenty of room to get by.''

"You have to double-park behind the cars on the carport here.''

"But there would be even *less* room for her to get by.''

"Look, I don't want to write you a ticket—''

"All *right*, I'll repark it.''

As the cop pulled away, Sam started up her Acura, soon realizing that she couldn't back up because the Lexus lady was too close to her bumper. Sam got out of the car and went around to the lady's window. "Could you back up?'' she enunciated through the glass. The woman was furiously redialing the cop. "Why can't you back up a little bit?'' Sam slammed her hand down on the roof of the car. "You stupid Orange County . . . Can't you talk to me like a

civilized human being—stop calling the police, for god's sake . . ."
Samantha glared in exasperation at the pampered, jeweled, perfectly
coiffed woman in some animal panic of horror, the horror of dealing
with people who were not in her employ. The woman reached for
the electronic locking mechanism of her car with a trembling hand,
but having already locked the doors she unintentionally unlocked
them—

"Stupid bitch!" cried Troy, who in that second opened her
passenger-side door and grabbed her cellular phone, ripped it from
her hand as she yelped in terror, and began smashing the phone on
the cement wall near his house.

"Troy, that's enough!" Sam cried.

Troy dove back into the car and Samantha feared he would hurt
the woman. He got in her face screaming at the top of his lungs:
"What's your goddam problem? You know what a fucking stupid
rich-bitch you are? Go ahead call the fucking police!"

"Troy, get out of the car!" Samantha called, running around to
pull him out.

"Who the fuck does she think she is?" Troy said, swinging wildly
as Sam pulled him back and forced him toward his house. Next
thing Sam knew, Troy was on his motorcycle, tearing out of his
carport.

So they made a quick exit from Orange County.

And, for the moment, it seemed natural to move Troy into Samantha's big mansion with so much space. And then the marriage
ploy more or less accreted. Samantha couldn't precisely remember
who suggested it. Troy told the *L.A. Times* and *Us* magazine that
he was involved with someone in his manager's office named Samantha. Mimi thought it a sensational idea.

"Think of the moolah, sweetheart," she advised. "In a few years
when no one cares anymore and the kid's career is over, you get a
divorce and walk away with a little pocket change. Of course, the
time to walk away is before it all goes up his nose or he buys his
mother a house or some kind of bullshit like that."

Good old Meem, always looking out for the best interests of her
best friend Samantha. Mimi designed an obstacle course of public

appearances, from the grungey clubs along Melrose to the innumerable Billboard Ace Soul Train People's American Music Golden Choice Awards that happened once a week in Hollywood so everybody could win one. Samantha stuffed herself into a Donna Karan and Troy snuggled close for the cameras, and they "passed." They even began to toy with the idea that a real marriage wasn't necessary, that the tabloids had missed the scoop.

Until Cyril Demby called.

Samantha sat across from Cyril Demby of the *National Sun* on the open-air porch of the Mondrian Hotel on Sunset Boulevard. From this porch, one could see (on days when one could see) most of residential Los Angeles and West Hollywood down below.

"We'd like an exclusive wedding portfolio, of course," Cyril Demby said. "We'll set up the location, the garden, the hotel room, so there can be no other publications in on the action, hm?" The waiter happened by and Cyril tagged him for the third time to greedily order another Glenlivet. "You're paying, after all!"

Demby would have drunk himself to death in Fleet Street obscurity long ago if he hadn't been rescued by the American tabloids (and tabloid TV shows), who imported him to dispense his especial British-honed flair for innuendo and dirt. He had become so uncrossable, so impossible to strike back at that he could move around Hollywood lighting at tables, pretending he was beloved and welcome, needling his future celebrity victims ("Cyril knows where you were last night, darling, *yezzzz*, not with that *gorrrrgeous* husband of yours, I dare say . . ."). His hair was a rat's nest, combed unconvincingly to hide incipient baldness, he was generally unkempt in creased clothes, lapels and ties with food stains, greeting his victims with his toothy cigarette-blackened smile and booze breath. Sam noticed his beltline, how his shirt, missing a button, rode up to expose a triangle of pink baby fat.

"So," Sam reviewed, as she found something more savory to look upon, "we give you an exclusive to the storybook wedding, invite a few low-level celebs—"

"Try George Hamilton and Alana Stewart, dear girl. *Yezzz*, yes, they'll go absolutely any-bloody-where there's a camera these days."

The Glenlivet arrived and Cyril drank from the tumbler, his upper lip rising repulsively as he took a sip.

"And what will you do with the police-blotter story?"

Cyril smiled. "You mean our Troy-boy toy-boy—I think I'll use that phrase, *yezzz*, yes indeed—when is Cyril going to run it? When is Cyril going to tell Americker that their little heartthrob lets old geezers suck his cock for money? The Fall of Troy. Teen Idol for Rent. *Yezzzz*, that's about what Cyril will write—very tasty, that. Samantha darling, that raises an interesting point. Do you think at the wedding if I gave Troy-boy a twenty, he'd pay some lip service to 'little Cyril,' eh?"

He was provoking her, trying to get her to say something vicious.

"Hm? Is it just bloody curb-crawlers, or can the rest of us get in on the *ack-shee-on*, hm?"

"Cyril," she said calmly, "I was hoping we could make a trade here. You get exclusive wedding pictures, which your female tabloid readership would rather see than another gay-outing piece, and you decide not to run the solicitation story—*ever*. In addition, we will give you complete access to the other members of the group."

"I'm going to need, *yezzz*, yes indeed, another one of these— garçon! *Yezzz* . . ." He ordered another drink. He would mooch five drinks in twenty minutes at a bar where they charged fifteen bucks a Glenlivet. "Oh Samantha, Samantha darling. You want me to tell you that the story will fly fly away, be forgotten. Heh-heh, you must understand that all you buy is *time*. Cyril doesn't run it this week, Cyril doesn't run it next week."

"It's the week after that I'm concerned about."

"Then we'll have to have some more wee little preprandials, will we not, hm? And we'll see what else you've got for Cyril, eh?" His drink arrived and he sucked from it as before; it seemed he was just getting started. "I hear that little has-been Amber Wentworth wandered into our telephoto lens at one of Hollywood's abortion clinics, hm? We've got a nurse confirming she was riding high in the stirrups, eh? Get it? Amber Aborts Patrick Fox's Lovechild—Against His Will. Ooh something of the like, *yezzz*, yes, that's quite tasty. Cyril likes something along those lines, very nice, very nice . . ."

So you wanna be in showbiz, little girl?

You wanna move to Hollywood and meet all the nice people?

And yet, thought Samantha, Troy and I survived it all—the paparazzi, the impossible-to-explain phone calls with my mother—and I can only imagine what Sy Gold or Warren Proctor or the girls from Smith must think. Since Samantha kept finding herself on the edge of paparazzi shots, she began doing diet pills in earnest so she could fit into her designer dresses. And when the diet pills didn't quite kill off her appetite, the speed did. That's where that started in earnest.

Mimi was even stirred to a moment of sisterly concern last year: "You don't look so healthy now that you're thin, if I may speak frankly. You're not letting it get out from under you, are you sweetheart?"

"Letting what get out from under me?"

"Your life."

Well, of course Samantha's life was out of control. So was everyone's, actually, but Samantha's inability to steer was more obvious than others—but at least she was still *functionally* out-of-control, like most of Hollywood's elite. This was a barely controlled skid—each course correction only causing her life to fishtail and careen more dramatically. And what was the alternative to living like this, again? I'm sorry, Samantha thought, I didn't catch it the first time—what was Samantha Flint supposed to be doing? Living with her cranky mother or her beaten older sister or her divorced younger sister with four kids on welfare? No doubt, she was sure, my little complicated life is not *nice* enough for the viewers at home. Oughtta change this country's name to the United States of Nice.

The pretend honeymoon was in Hawaii.

Troy went out with a pack of condoms to ingratiate himself with the fleshy brown islanders, while she picked up a cute busboy in the tiki lounge. Michael and Moe and Mimi and everyone thought it was a hoot; even William got used to the cover-marriage idea once it was obvious Samantha didn't love Troy and there was still hope for him. But Wolfgang found the entire matter repulsive:

"For one thing," Wolfgang said as they cruised Santa Monica

Boulevard, "don't think you can save anyone. One can only save oneself, and often that rescue is not possible. Troy is a scavenger. I understand his type and you do not. He is where he is, of course, because he knows how to use people."

"You haven't met him. He's actually rather innocent."

Wolfgang raised his voice: "It is an *act*, Samantha. American boys are very accomplished at this. It has been the destruction of many an older foreign man, this nation of Tadzios. But it is an act."

The hollow-chested boy in the worn leather vest appeared again, more sunburned and battered than the last time. He didn't bother to fix his commercial stare; he watched them pass without emotion or interest, the manner in which he now endured the whole of life.

"Santa Monica Boulevard," mused Wolfgang, now returned to a pleasant tone. "*Heilige Monika*. Saint Monica, the mother of Saint Augustine. Young Augustine lived a life of debauchery and wrote of his passionate love for another man. But mother kept praying until Augie saw the light and the days of male orgies at the baths and opiates were at an end. Ironic, yes? A street of hustlers at the center of Gay America, to be presided over by this ever-fretting canonized mother of a gay son, hm?"

Samantha wasn't listening, still thinking about her mission. "I think there can be innocence amid the mire," she said.

"But it is not Troy's innocence that attracts you," he said carefully. No one but Wolfgang ever talked to her like this, in his combination of cold lucidity and provocation. "It is his being victimized. Innocence is very boring, really; it is simply lack of experience, a blank tablet, an absence of color. Why don't you admit what I can freely admit? We prefer the beautiful people we wish to love to be losers, discardable, not capable of mattering to us, hurting us. Everyone else has used Troy, taken their pleasure from him, given him twenty dollars or a recording contract—whatever—then tossed him back upon the pile. And now it is your turn."

Samantha was silent.

"Shall I recite Wolfgang's Rule for you again? What innocence obtains is projected by the john onto the trick."

On the MGM Hotel terrace in Las Vegas, she dismissed her pessimistic friend's assessment. Back inside her bedroom, she lay down on the bed for a minute, feeling the warm, fading poststimulant pulse, her body's deceleration. The only time she felt she could naturally fall asleep.

"Hey Sam," was the next thing she heard.

She turned in the bed and Troy was standing beside her. Though sluggish, she had a genuine sense of panic about being seen unmade-up, in such dishevelment.

"We're the only ones left," he said.

"Left where?"

"In Vegas. I stayed an extra day since you were staying too. Everyone's down in Palm Springs—Michael's rented a floor of a hotel. And then, like, Ruben told me he'd given you some crystal meth and I thought, shit, she's dead in her room. So I got them to let me in," he explained as he poked her, "and you're alive."

Checking her watch, she saw hardly any time at all had passed. It was 6:30 P.M . . . of the *next day*. "What happened to Saturday?"

"Came and went," he said, stretching out, glancing at her ceiling. "You gonna give me a ride back to L.A.?"

Samantha had rented a Mercury convertible, on some Elvis-movie-based whim, wanting to drive a convertible down the Vegas Strip and the canyon of neon. After she fixed herself up, she went to reception to face the management and pay the bills for every-thing—a broken lamp in Storm's room, a cut-up pillow in P-Dogg's room (he bought a knife at a gun-and-knife shop), and a gambling debt charged to Brad's room.

Samantha, chauffeuring Troy to Palm Springs, noticed she was going 80 MPH on southbound Interstate 15. "Jesus Christ," she muttered, "eighty and look how I'm getting passed."

Sunday night at 9:00 P.M. and Las Vegas was evacuating for Southern California, two southbound lanes full of the usual low-rollers trying to cross the Mojave in under five hours, going for the record. The inches separating the cars in front and back of her did not deter Sam from turning on the internal light and peeking at her ragged California highway map. She was investigating how to leave the highway for the untravelled two-lane roads most non-

Californians would never consider taking without survival supplies and guide.

"Look at all the stars," Troy said, hypnotized.

The spray of the Milky Way divided the heavens; one could tell that stars had colors here in the desert. It was quite chilly at the Mountain Pass turnoff, some 4,000 feet above sea level, but Troy was not to be denied the stars, so Sam blasted the heat so they could keep the top down while Troy, scrunched under his secondhand leather flight jacket, fished from his suitcase.

"Hope we don't break down," sang Troy, at heart hoping they might and an adventure would ensue. The two-lane road was desolation itself. Once or twice an hour an oncoming pair of headlights appeared, maybe thirty miles away, then the headlights disappeared, appeared again and then twenty minutes would go by before they passed Sam's convertible . . . then all was quiet and dark again.

"You can't see the stars in L.A.," Troy repeated.

Sam had anxieties about breaking down, vulnerable to whomever happened by, old desert tax-evaders with gun racks in their pickups (who'd as soon rape Troy as herself), strange Mansonesque cult members . . . She quickly glanced at Troy, so content and secure that the splendor of this nightdrive was soon contagious.

"Hey Sam, guess what? Like, I was at the Sands last night, just walking, and I stopped to look at that volcano go off at that hotel?"

"The Mirage."

"Yeah, and this car slows down at the curb, and the window rolls down and I hear this man go, 'Get in.' " He started giggling. "I mean, I'm just standing there and this guy picks me out like I'm working." Sam didn't respond, so Troy egged her on: "I'da gotten in the car, but . . ."

"*Ohhh* no, young man, we've had enough of bailing you out."

"Aw, I'm just kidding."

Samantha was curious. "The escort service is one thing, but the street is another. Why would you ever work the street?"

"Hey, it's not so bad once you learn what to look out for," he said, lovingly visiting the legend of himself, homeless at fifteen, a street dweller with an occasional meal from the Catholic mission, a sometimes-available cot within a state-run juvenile shelter. "See, I liked the old guys," Troy explained, " 'cause often they didn't want to do anything or take their pants off even—*whoa!*"

A coyote at the edge of the road had been briefly mesmerized by the headlights. It changed its mind about crossing and resentfully padded back into the brush.

"Wow, is that like a wolf?"

"Just a coyote."

"That's so cool!" His first nature sighting.

The next half hour brought the overpass for Interstate 40; a rusted, crooked rarely-seen sign announced the junction. The four-lane highway of transcontinental truck traffic thundering from Flagstaff to Barstow seemed an urbanized, overcrowded ribbon after their desert trek. "We could drop to Twentynine Palms on the Amboy Road," she suggested, plotting with the map.

"No interstates."

"Yeah, no interstates." Sam drove under the I-40 overpass and back into the night.

"I'm gonna tell Ruben about the coyote. Just like in the cartoon."

"Just like in a nature show," Samantha purposelessly corrected.

"You wonder what he's, like, doing up at this hour."

"All the animals come out at night in the desert. They sleep all day when it's too hot. Little kangaroo rats, coyotes, mountain lions, rattlesnakes."

"Cool," Troy said, thrilled at the notion of rattlesnakes on the loose all around him. He settled back into his star-viewing position. "Hey Sam. You know what I'm gonna do next big interview?"

"What?"

"Gonna tell everyone I'm queer."

"Hey now, you had your chance to tell the world. Too late now. Be a little embarrassing for me, don't you think?"

Concern for her reputation didn't dim the appeal of his fantasy, apparently. "You know, I'll wait until I'm picking up some award on TV."

At least that wasn't much of a threat. "Just remember *you* have to go in and face Mimi."

"Man, Mimi is, like, pure evil."

"You don't mean that."

Samantha faltered. But Troy went on, "We'll be at the top of the dance charts next week—that's what Tony's saying. And they'll have us on the cover of *Us* or some'n, being incredible fucking role models. And they'll say isn't it great you guys have so much in common, and I'll say yessir, we all had to screw our producer."

"Troy, you're not gonna say any of that."

"Everyone gay always tells the press before they're about to, you know, die of AIDS. You gotta do it before that."

Sam reflected. "You don't have AIDS, do you?"

"I dunno, and I ain't gonna get the test neither. But if you're queer, you're gonna die from it."

"That's very wrong, Troy. If you—"

"First all the queer people will die, and then all the girlfriends of guys who cheated on 'em with other guys—which is, like, a *zillion* guys—will get it, then all the straights, starting with the girls, then the men. Everybody eventually. I heard some guy on TV say the virus is gonna grow and . . ." Troy couldn't think of the word.

"Mutate."

"Yeah, that's it, *mutate*. And soon we'll be getting it from, you know, people sneezing and stuff."

Sam stared at the road. She remembered Frank Shanker's tirades against gays and people burdened with AIDS, his favorite groups to beat up on. And, Samantha thought simply, I worked for Frank Shanker. I helped his career live another day, helped him make it to the next mean-spirited vote.

"You wanna hear stories," Troy was saying, "I got lots more stories!"

It won't do to say I *compromised* my moral core, Sam thought. Moral cores can't be compromised, they just disappear. You can't be a little bit virginal, can't have committed only a little bit of a murder—

"You think Christopher paying people to let him take a dump on them is weird. This one guy, like, wanted me to go back to his house, and I said no, 'cause I never did anything risky like that, but

I did go in the back of his van. He was wearing *diapers*. All he wanted was for me to change his diapers. . . ."

Samantha Flint was struck with the concept of morality; it never had seemed quite so clear and obvious to her: we shouldn't let children tell lies or copy someone else's homework; we shouldn't cheat on our taxes or on our husbands on a business trip. Because once it starts getting away from you, once the *habit* of morality is unlearned, even just set aside for an afternoon tryst or parked out back for a business deal, even within easy reach, it doesn't come back readily at all.

Maybe it never comes back.

"There was the time these two black guys—"

"About what you said," Samantha interrupted. "Telling everyone you're gay."

"Maybe at the Billboard Awards. Like right on TV."

"You ought to do it," she said. "You know, give me time to work up a supportive press conference for the both of us."

"Right on." Illumined by the dashboard lights Troy's face was soft and juvenile. He smiled at Samantha, pleased with their conspiracy, showing the big *Teen Beat* grin. "Let's not tell Mimi, 'til we do it."

"Yeah, let's definitely not tell Mimi."

Then slowly ahead: Amboy, California.

Eerie in the moonlight, seemingly two-dimensional like a painted backdrop, a town with every building painted white. Population ten, tops. No lights on anywhere. The pumps at the one gas station had been removed; there was a boarded up motel, a weathered white curtain barely stirring in a glassless window. Sam rolled the car to a stop and then flipped off the headlights, turned off the motor. Utter silence.

"Do you think anyone lives here?" Troy asked.

"Not anymore." She paused. "Maybe a few ghosts."

That made Troy pull the jacket around him tighter. "Weird," he said, adding with an edgy smile, "Turn the car back on."

Samantha, a little spooked as well, obeyed. As they coasted forward, the headlights found the old route marker—U.S. 66.

"My god, look at that," she said.

Troy didn't respond.

"Get your kicks on Route 66? This was the original way to drive west, from back in the 1920s. The roadtrip was invented right here," she emphasized, hitting the steering wheel. Sam stared at the faded, rusted sign. "Before the interstates. This very road used to go through Springfield, Missouri—where I'm from. I remember my daddy and me driving along 66 and singing that song."

Troy stared at her like she must be incalculably old to precede the interstate system. "This is, like, the first highway, huh?"

"They must have forgotten to take the sign down."

Troy appeared confused.

Sam explained, "They decommissioned the route when the interstates came through. The greatest highway since the Oregon Trail, and they just . . . they just took it off the map." She looked at the relic, the dated design of double sixes, a defiant milepost refusing to die, speaking from the black-and-white newsreel past of Ma Joad and Neil Cassady and Nat King Cole and Broderick Crawford, maybe having survived for this last moment, two kids with the top down, lost in the American night.

"Route 66 might as well be gone," she said, slowly letting the car roll past the sign. "Sixty-six was for when the West was new. California's full up."

"People, like, fly everywhere now anyway," Troy said solemnly, having partaken of Sam's nostalgia that regrettably, even for her, had to be half-borrowed from her parents' generation.

Samantha and Troy rode the final leg of their trip through the bizarre stone sculptures and rock pagodas of Joshua Tree National Park, moonlit and desolate. Soon they passed the closed Cottonwood Springs ranger station and arrived, some miles later, to Interstate 10 in the middle of nowhere. Within minutes, filling the valley 3,000 feet below them, were the lights of Palm Springs, and beyond that a dim silhouette of the 10,000-foot San Jacinto Range, a glint of moonlight on the snowcaps two miles above the desert.

"Man, that's just . . ." Troy was in awe.

Samantha pulled over to the emergency lane so Troy could relieve himself and she could get out and look. The interstate was dark for the most part, only the trucks out now, passing with their siren wail, crescendo and diminuendo.

"It's a lake of fire," he said, transfixed.

"What?"

"A lake of fire."

Samantha joined him, leaning against the hood. "And you told me you hadn't been to church once in your life."

"Huh?"

"The Lake of Fire," she repeated. "It's in the Bible, in *Revelation*."

"Hmm, I thought I made it up," he said, turning back to the twinkling, sharp glitter of the lights from afar, quavering orange as if lava were trying to seep up from the foot of the San Jacintos. A sudden protective panic came over Samantha, and she stepped forward to give Troy a secure hug, and somehow he must have felt her intention, because he, lightly, gently, released himself from her grip and took a step away, loyal only to the shimmering lights below.

Palm Springs.

As promised, Michael and Moe had rented the fourth floor in the Hacienda Orpheus hotel; the Laguna Beach and West Hollywood gang was at the bar, already tipsy, waiting for Samantha and Troy.

The Hacienda Orpheus was, Michael declared with some justice, the greatest orgiastic fantasy constructed since Tiberias's pleasure palace on Capri. Naked male models roamed the poolside, sauntering through the bar in only a towel; a porn film was in production in one of the rooms on the third floor and a few privileged spectators were welcome. It was $225 a night, so the clientele was rich, though no shortage of riffraff made it through the door on the arms of older, monied gentlemen.

The folks in Springfield, thought Sam, have no earthly idea what goes on out here.

"Samantha, you look *fabulous*," Moe was saying.

Samantha had not intended to be the token straight girl in the Michael and Moe social circle, but it had worked out that way. Sam's 1997 calendar showed "M & M" written down over most weekends. Her race to the Friday sunsets had long now been established. Michael and Moe's circle adored her, praised her average dress sense, her nothing hair, her so-called beauty. Vainly, she had begun to fix herself up spectacularly for each plunge into this circle, so as not to disappoint.

"Can I get anyone anything?" Troy asked, standing.

After the obligatory sexual suggestions, the gang declined.

"Nothing for me," said Rider, Tomorro Gs' tough-as-nails stage manager, who sat nearby with one of her girlfriends from the roadie crew. They both were staring holes through Samantha, so Sam smiled back pleasantly.

Hamming it up, Troy shrugged cutely and exaggeratedly tiptoed toward the elevator with Ruben, toward his stash of illegal contraband upstairs. Ruben had become the king of pills, the middleman for Tony, who was doing more drug-supplying than promoting lately.

"How 'bout you, Sam?" Ruben asked, before grabbing his crotch. "Anything I got you want, mama?"

"My usual CARE package, I guess." She would leave it to fate. Ruben kept her supplied with diet pills, speed, Valium, and Xanax, but if some crystal meth found its way into her brown paper bag . . . then so be it. She certainly had no intention of getting hooked on that stuff.

Michael returned from the bar with a club soda for Samantha. "Honey, go out to the pool and see some genitalia!"

"How long's it been, Samantha," said one of the Laguna Beach strangers, "since you've actually *seeeeen* one erect?" Samantha laughed with everyone else to be polite.

Samantha had seen innumerable gorgeous gay male bodies, more nude men than she could count, overheard more pissy drama than she could recite. These guys are great, Sam would tell anyone who asked, but privately she had been subjected to one too many nights of men arguing over the relative merits of various divas, unforgiveable things being uttered about Streisand, unhealable breaches . . .

"I couldn't believe it," said the man to Michael's right. "When they gave Carol Channing her lifetime Tony, the crowd didn't even *stand*. After a while someone stood up to get everyone else on their feet, but can you *imagine*? Oh, I would have been so offended.''

Samantha watched the opinionated men overrule and correct each other around the table. Someone enraged the Broadway regular, saying, "I found Carol *particularly* effective in her handling of the baboons crawling between her stick-legs on CBS's curiously named *Circus of the Stars*. . . .'' Michael tried to smooth everything over, but Sam saw the seething, unrequited injury in the eyes of the man who'd made Carol Channing his personal deity.

"Do you like Judy Garland?" Samantha asked Troy when he returned, giggly and glassy-eyed.

"Who?"

Maybe this stuff is generational, she thought. Twenty more years of this crowd and I, too, Sam thought, could be Tallulah or Bette or Joan. Some women receive gay-male veneration and some don't. Diana Ross (did she really cancel a show because they sent the wrong color limo to her hotel?) is a cult figure; Gladys Knight and Aretha Franklin, greater talents, aren't. Poor Judy, veteran of sad, degraded, blotto live-TV performances, is unequaled in gay hearts, while Ella Fitzgerald with decades of flawless singing and unblemished decorum has next to no gay cult. Obviously the bitcheries of these women were a draw, but there was something else: public disarray, the barely holding it together, the inability to retire and get off the stage before self-parody set in, flailing and desperate.

Ruin, she said to herself. Something would come of that title.

"I don't know," Michael was screaming, "we'll ask Samantha about that one!" Someone had mentioned being "on the rag."

Samantha wondered if it was her fate to become a drag-queen version of herself, gutter-mouthed, smoking cigarettes and firing off bitchy ripostes. It was weary to perform her own act: tough, cynical, always joking about how she didn't have a man, hadn't been laid in years, wished the gorgeous queers around her could be "straight for a night," ignoring the misogyny and "fish" references and the whole drag sensibility—which was *in no way* a loving homage to women, but a dissection and obliteration of female attributes, a final revenge on their mothers and crazy aunts and diva heroines.

I want out, Samantha decided. "I'm off, boys!"

There was a chorus begging her to stay: "Samantha," Michael pleaded, "this whole week we're here celebrating Troy and Ruben and . . ." He seemed to forget who the other boys were. "..all of us and our number-one song! I've only been a part of three number-ones in my whole life. So it's gonna be the biggest, raunchiest, nastiest party you've ever seen!"

"I'll try to get back Saturday, but I have tons to do back in L.A."

Sandra Blake and her comeback awaited. Or should we stick with Winona?

"Tiffani," Samantha said, striding into her office at 2:30 P.M., Tuesday afternoon. "Can you find for me the portfolio and résumé for Sandra Blake? I had you file it under Miscellaneous."

Samantha went into her office, bare of any amenities except the computer and a telephone, a few half-filled file cabinets. Samantha was a little self-conscious about those vacuous file cabinets. Ever-malicious Tiffani, under the guise of being helpful, would ask, "So that I can, like, better help you do your job, Samantha, like, *what exactly do you do around here?*" Samantha prepared a tall double-shot latte she'd bought from the concession downstairs, and began to tear two Sweet 'N Low packets and stir them in. Heck, she did plenty around this place. For two straight years she wrote virtually every press release issued from Mimi Mohr & Associates. The warm-hearted charity work engaged in by that paragon Amber Went-worth. That moral titan Patrick Fox and his time spent at a gang community center. Not to mention planting stories in the trades about her marvelous boss—

"I'm sorry, Samantha, that file doesn't appear to be there."

"Look harder. I put it into your very capable hands. Perhaps it's under *B* for Blake."

Some moments later, Tiffani had checked all the files. Then Samantha stormed out and checked all the files herself. "You threw it out, didn't you? Against my specific orders."

"I don't know what you're talking about."

"You have the rest of the day, darling, to find Winona Blake's telephone number, or you're fired."

Samantha walked down to Mimi's office and was waved inside.

"I want Tiffani out of here," Samantha began. "She schemes against me, she throws out things I tell her to keep, she pursues her own projects on company time—"

Mimi: "I can't fire her, sweetheart. Tiff is very well connected."

"I cannot believe we have to scurry around our secretaries because they have some important relative somewhere—"

"Well, sweetheart," Mimi cooed. Mimi had, at last, adopted her mother's placid serenity for dealing with anything unpleasant. "If you can get me inside dope on what CAA is up to and have a boyfriend well-placed at ICM and have a mother who drinks with Clint Eastwood in Carmel, then we can fire her. As it is, I'm late late late . . ."

Mimi scooped up her papers and a Gucci satchel, and stood against her window. The light poured in behind her and Samantha was stunned by Mimi's figure. "Have you had work done, Mimi?"

"It's just a Wonderbra darling, but thank you! We'll talk about Tiffani," Mimi promised, "next week sometime. Maybe we can trade around. Joanne's looking to get rid of Blossom."

"What do you mean next week? I thought we were on *this very Friday*. Your place in Malibu!"

"Oh. Yes, let's do it then. We'll leave at seven. I'll drive."

Samantha, not wanting to see the office another moment, drove back to Barranca Canyon . . .

Who was the impediment in her driveway today?

A man with a headset approached: "Excuse me, you're not authorized to be here." Then this fellow said the magic words that were supposed to make her melt, make her touch herself, make Angelenos delirious about having their neighborhoods being torn up, their landmarks blown to smithereens, their traffic tied up for hours: "I'm sorry, we're making a *movie* here."

"This is my house. I'm perfectly happy to call the police and have you evicted, if you like."

Headset-man went limp and disgusted, put on his best why-me expression and began yelling into his cell phone. "Julian, Julian . . . could someone get . . . Can you come down here?"

Julian informed Sam that this was a Movie. Didn't she know a Movie was being made? Surely she didn't intend to get in the way of a Movie being made.

Yes, she did.

After Julian, she got Willow. "Hello, Ms. Flint? I'm Willow, Mr. Ellis's personal assistant. Is there a problem here?"

"Yes, there's a problem in that your filming was only to take place during the weekend I was gone. It's Tuesday, I'm back, now clear out. . . . Hold it, what are they doing with the paint?"

Willow blanched and looked at a number of others before looking back at Samantha. "Yes. Yes." Such a mewling, harmless voice. "Yes, we had to redo the living room. Our art director had more of an ecru in mind."

"The walls were already beige."

"Yes, but there were colors that were coming out that," she winced, as if Samantha would now sympathize, "weren't what the script and the art people called for. It wasn't *working* for us."

"So you're repainting my living room. You intend to paint it back when you're done?"

"Of course, we will have the one little wall painted back—"

"You've painted *one* wall? Now, when you repaint that one wall, that one wall will look different because the . . . the *ecru* is underneath it. I want all four walls painted ecru and then all four painted back. Now, I'm allergic to paint fumes." She wasn't, but here was where some pocket cash might be made.

At this point, the director was called in his trailer. He was apprised of "a little situation we have here," then he said he'd come, kept everyone waiting for ten minutes, then appeared. He was young and good-looking and looked right through his personal assistant as she recounted a tiresome synopsis, then cut her off: "We're truly sorry, Ms. Flint, for this inconvenience and our running a little behind here but we will need the week . . . Do you like the Mondrian on Sunset?"

"I think I'd prefer Palm Springs for the weekend."

"Yes, Willow—petty cash please?"

In Sam's two years in this house, she had seen the yard dug up, the upper-bedroom window blown out with an explosion, trees cut down and new ones ordered whole and replanted. She had watched film crews photograph a scene with the view of Los Angeles behind them, while the art director said, "Don't worry about the city, we're going to use a matte. . . ." For god's sake, why pay Mimi $20,000 to use my balcony then if you're going to fake it with a process shot?

No wonder average movies were costing $40, $50 million to make.

Friday. And, unbelievably, no cancellation from Mimi.

Samantha strapped herself in the Porsche's passenger seat, ready for action. This was likely to be their last such conclave of 1997, so Sam was ready to enjoy Mimi's Malibu beachfront townhouse; she felt as if she'd been there many more times than she had, thanks to a hundred TV shows and movies in which people lived just like Mimi on the Pacific.

"Birth canal in five, four, three, two . . ."

That's what Mimi called the end of the Santa Monica Freeway. Interstate 10 boasted twelve lanes through downtown, but at its western terminus its lanes disappeared with dwindling utility, from eight to six to four, before plunging into a tunnel and reemerging in a different world along the Santa Monica strand, the magical Pacific Coast Highway. On the city side of the tunnel was a smoggy, hot, dry riot zone distressed by rush hour; on the other side, ten degrees cooler thanks to the ocean, the more beautiful California of cleaner air and unobstructed sunsets, volleyball courts, surfers in wetsuits, milkshake and hot dog shacks nestled beside the beach homes of the super-rich, the cliff towns of Pacific Pallisades and Malibu.

The P.C.H. followed the coast precisely, and for the next twenty miles Mimi hugged the tortuous course—like all Malibuites, taking it heedlessly at 60 MPH—often inches from Mercedeses and Lincoln Town Cars and Lanzias speeding in formation on either side. Mimi entered her driveway at speed, cutting across lanes of oncoming traffic, stopping on a dime and rearranging Samantha's internal organs against her seat belt.

"I've got all this gourmet deli crap," Mimi said presently from the kitchen, gathering up some cheese and crackers from an expensive Italian crisper. "Now, help yourself. I have plenty of sparkling water and some diet drinks."

"I brought one of William's Gary Farrell 1987 Russian River Pinot Noirs for you."

"And you're not gonna have any?" Samantha shook her head no. "You got willpower. So this A.A. cult-thing is doing you some good, huh? Hey, whatever happened to that Dr. Cline lady?"

Samantha balanced a piece of Stilton on a Scottish tea biscuit. "She was all right but it got embarrassing."

"Therapy's supposed to be embarrassing."

"No, telling my personal life wasn't embarrassing. I meant sitting there indulgently going *on and on* about myself and paying that woman $150 an hour to listen was embarrassing. I mean, millions die in Rwanda, and here I am going on at length about my miserable adolescence." Samantha didn't mention her diet-pill and speed habit to Mimi, or her once-or-twice flirtation with crystal meth.

The woman, Dr. Cline, was intensely devoted, taking copious notes, scribbling furiously while one said the blandest of things—it made Sam wonder if she was working on a short story. Samantha distrusted the premise of psychotherapy because, as with the daily horoscope columns, anything at all could sound pertinent and applicable. Daddy too distant? That's why you are so distant in relationships, why you never invest yourself fully. Daddy too smothering? In your struggle to break free of his oppressive intimacy, you have become distant in relationships and don't want to invest yourself fully. Anything could be interpreted to explain everything, mix and match.

Sam would blab for an entire session with no input from Dr. Cline, who, suddenly, would erupt in a torrent of questions:

"You had asthma as a child?"

"Yes," Sam said.

"Asthma inhalers contain ephedrine, which can be addictive. It can give you a rush if you overmedicate with it. Did you do that?"

Samantha stirred. "Yes, sometimes. I thought the little rush you got was from having clear lungs, though—"

"So from a young age you associated health, the ability to breathe without distress, the cessation of panic, with this rush, which you still look for. What's the best thing about being on speed?"

"Control. We all want to be able to turn life on and off when we feel like it, and short of having a handheld remote for Life Itself, the pills are the next best thing." That was Sam's smart-mouth prepared answer, but Dr. Cline wanted her to investigate her compulsion further: "Desire," Sam listed next. "Makes me horny as hell. I suppose the blood rushes to all extremities, erogenous zones included. Back in Aspen before lovemaking, I would sometime take a No-Doz." She laughed. "Wouldn't Cameron love to hear that? I had to take a stimulant before having sex with him."

"But you also need tranquilizers to get to sleep."

"Look, I have a pill problem because I have a sleep disorder. For me, without medication, to lie down and try to get to sleep is impossible. Just lying down and thinking is when my adrenaline starts pumping—I'd be awake all night without a Xanax."

"No," Dr. Cline emotionlessly corrected, "you have a sleep disorder because you have a pill problem. Despite having high blood pressure, you take diet pills, drink caffeine all day, the occasional amphetamine. This is quite dangerous. Shall I take this as a death wish?" She folded her arms and waited for a serious answer.

"Of course not. Take it as a thin wish. Otherwise, I'd be the size of . . ." Dr. Cline, forty-five, a mother of two little girls, was not thin herself. ". . . a barn or something."

"And you would hate yourself then?"

"No, of course not. But I wouldn't be pleased I was big."

"When you were 'big' your life had no sexual value then?"

"It, yes, was probably less—"

"No man could love you if you were big like your mother and your sisters?"

"My sister Kelly's husband left her for another woman, presumably thinner—"

"You don't know that for sure."

"And my sister Bethie is pretty chunky too, and she'll take anything home with her from the country-and-western bars."

"That's what happens to heavy women, isn't it? They have no self-respect, so they prostitute themselves. How are your relationships any different, Samantha? A cabdriver you never see again, a paid-for gigolo, a busboy in your Hawaiian hotel. It doesn't sound like any of this is getting you any more happiness than your sister."

"But my sister goes out and gets drunk and takes anybody she can, because she *needs* someone. She does it every weekend."

"And you merely do it once or twice a year."

"I don't *need* to pick up strangers. I do it to amuse myself. It's intellectual, it's to make myself feel something, feel . . . different."

"To escape from yourself."

"Something wrong with that? I'm with myself the other twenty-three hours of the day, three hundred sixty-four days of the year."

Then Dr. Cline would go silent again, and Samantha's rambling monologue, having revealed more than she intended, would continue.

It took Sam a long time to learn the first rule of therapy: stonewalling—reveal nothing, not even insignificant trivia that seemed of no evidentiary use whatsoever.

"What was your first boyfriend's name?" Dr. Cline asked, looking through dog-eared pages of legal-pad notes. "In high school."

"Paul O'Connor."

"He had broken his ankle, you told me."

"Well, yes, when I first met him. I held the bus for him."

"He was on crutches? With a cast?"

"Yeah. So?"

"He was an emblem of male helplessness, vulnerability. It drew you to him, made you love him." Samantha was divided between finding something to her theory or dismissing it as preposterous. "You have maintained a pattern of preferring to love 'damaged goods,' have you not? Starting with your father."

Jesus, thought Samantha, if I wanted evisceration, I could stand up at A.A. and do it myself. I'm paying $150 an hour for this!

Mimi poured herself glass after glass of the wonderful wine.

"Swell guy, that William, giving us this baby." It was a mark of Mimi's relaxation that her fax beeped, her cellular and home phone were both ringing off the hook, and she took no interest.

As the night continued, girlishness settled in. The two amused themselves by trying to light a fire in the fireplace. Mimi had purchased cedar logs in a bundle at the store, but they wouldn't stay lit, so they finally resorted to pouring expensive brandy on them. Then, when that inferno quickly burned itself out, they went searching in a neighbor's recycling bin for newspapers, giggling tipsily and sneaking around *ssshing* each other as if their escapade was a grand, illegal caper.

"Now see if that does it," Mimi said, having stuffed two days' worth of the *L.A. Times* under the logs. It erupted and filled the house with smoke, setting off the smoke detectors.

"The flue!" Sam cried, soon realizing that Mimi didn't know what a flue was. After taking the batteries out of the smoke detectors, Mimi put out their small fire with a foam fire-extinguisher intended for chemical fires. Sam reached up into the chimney to open the flue, covering her arm in soot while Mimi laughed.

"Forget it!" Mimi yelled, laughing as she hadn't in years. "Goddam fireplace probably added thirty K to the goddamn price of this place and it doesn't fucking work!"

"It works if you open the flue!"

Samantha cleaned herself up and then escaped the smoky living room to join Mimi on the outside terrace. Sam stared at the nighttime sea, coordinating her own thoughts to the rhythms of the waves, enchanted by the moon to the south and the hazy orange glow of L.A. that faintly warmed the eastern horizon with a string of twinkling city lights twenty miles away.

Mimi brought out the remaining brandy. "Might as well use this for its intended purpose. Oh, there was something I was going to show you . . ." She ran back into the house and returned many minutes later with a small file folder that Samantha had seen somewhere before. In college maybe? "Know what this is?" Mimi teased, waving it before her. "It's our old Venice file."

"From New York?"

"Yep. Full of travel-page clips I thought were interesting." Mimi sifted through the yellowed clippings. "Lots of little hole-in-the-wall hotels they recommend. Probably aren't there anymore, or at least not as cheap."

"We're never gonna go," Sam said lightly.

"The hell you say."

"We haven't gone in the fifteen years we've talked about it. Hell, you can barely spare me an evening. When do you foresee having two weeks to go to Venice and putz around with me?"

Mimi didn't answer, but held up a faded clip about the *Ospedale degl' Incurabili*, a civic convent for the terminally ill. From the Renaissance on, Venice had "hospitals" for women in desperate straits, orphans, illegitimates, the unmarried poor, even the *convertite*, the reformed prostitutes, a profession Venice numbered in the tens of thousands. And in each palatial hospital there were orchestras and choirs and chamber music groups—ensembles so superb that Vivaldi and Mozart wrote for the women there. They sang behind screens, like the great beauties of an Ottoman harem, so that no man might fall in love with them and lure them from their redemption . . . or perhaps so no one would see the sores and diseases of the dying, but rather hear only the angelic harmonies soaring in the serene, candlelit halls of the Venetian Renaissance.

"Can you imagine?" Mimi asked, her attention now wandering back to her own ignoble century and her own republic. "Imagine if we had a National Persons With AIDS Choir. What poignancy it would give the religious music . . . Don't hold your breath waiting for Newt Gingrich to propose that one. Let's fly to Venice tomorrow."

Samantha, long after Mimi had tuckered out and gone to bed, stayed up on the patio reading their Venice File. Most of the clips Mimi had cut from the *New York Times* concerned artists, once her consuming passion. Tintoretto in the School of San Rocco (Rocco wasn't even a real saint, apparently) painted the upper chambers as a young man, did the same for a council room as a middle-aged man, and in his nineties, supervised the downstairs murals. Oh, to be able to spend eight decades nurturing one's talent, let alone living in a city and society worthy of such a monument . . .

Monuments. There was still no statue of Edith Wharton in Central Park.

She couldn't get to sleep that night.

In her consternation with the movie folks, Samantha had forgotten to pack her tranquilizers. She had enough Xanax lying in the bottom of her purse to get her through Thursday, but for the visit to Mimi's, Sam decided not to drive all the way back to Hollywood to get her pills. Why, it would be an experiment. Something to report to Dr. Cline. She trusted the rhythm of the ocean and a late night of talking with Mimi would make her properly tired . . . It didn't. The thought of Venice enticed and agitated plans in her head, as did the thought of writing. Was there still time? Maybe in Venice, she thought, as she was tossing and turning. I'll get a small apartment where I can write, where maybe going to sleep and waking up can be beautiful and natural . . .

Saturday morning Mimi was gone, back at meetings and power lunches and the full social schedule to which she was addicted. Samantha reckoned she'd had two hours of sleep, none of it REM-worthy. Samantha called Troy's hotel room in Palm Springs where they'd been celebrating their No. 1 record all week, in between L.A. media appearances. No answer. She tried Michael's room and Troy was there:

"Come on down!" he screamed, as some furniture crashed in the background. "Ruben, what . . ." Then Troy was convulsed. They were smashing the TV the way P-Dogg did in his room at the MGM. "We got, like, tons a money!"

"I'll be down in a bit." First, she would swing by home, dodge the movie people, get her stash of speed.

Gabriela was waiting for her, pointing out how the painters trod paint into the carpet. "And the walls they no look right, madam," she said, leading Sam to the beige-ecru-beige of the living room.

Samantha searched around the bedroom, newly cleaned and organized by the maids, but she could not find her 20/20s anywhere. "Gabriela," Samantha said insistently, "did you accidentally throw out those pills in a brown paper bag?"

She shrugged. "Maybe the other girls . . ."

"I need those medicines."

"They no medicines, madam. They drogs."

Samantha knew there'd be no shortage of narcotic ordnance at Palm Springs, so she let it go. Gabriela however stood, all five feet of her, in the doorway, a moral presence. "You and Mr. Troy both do too much drogs. No ees good!" She then pretended to dust where there was no dust. "In the *USA Today* they say rich people get hooked on pills like street people do crack."

"What can I say, Gabriela? Hollywood has corrupted me."

"Hollywood don't corrupt nobody," she said plainly.

"Excuse me?"

"You heard what I say to you, Mees Flint. *Hollywood don't corrupt nobody.*"

The money must really have been flowing, because any other hotel in the world would have shown Michael and Moe's crowd the door:

P-Dogg had smashed two TVs, Ruben and Troy one apiece, which they sent flying four stories down to the pool deck, to the annoyance of the other customers. Storm had thrown up *in* the pool, which had made for a long filtering and draining episode to the bother of the naked gym-buffed male models paid to adorn the poolside. The porn film being filmed last night was now ready for its outdoor scenes by the pool, where the one-in-a-million bodies would perform.

Ruben, Troy reported, had been assigned "chief fluffer." What was a fluffer? Did she really want to know what a fluffer was?

One of the porn stars wandered in to sit beside Samantha in the bar, waiting for his scene to start. Sam and he talked for fifteen minutes; how long he'd been doing this, how many guys, do you actually enjoy it, is it true a lot of the gay porn stars are straight. He was a really nice guy, an artist in his way.

"I choreographed the final fuckpiece," he said with mild bitterness, "but you'll never see *my* name in the credits."

"Same with what I do," Sam nodded.

By nightfall, Samantha decided things were too crazy for the suburban middle-class likes of her. "Palm Springs is all full," she protested to the gang at the bar. "Not a hotel room for miles. And *no*, I'm not staying in this place."

"I have an extra bed in my room," said Rider.

Rider was a fixture on the tour, managing her roadies and techies with an iron hand. It was too simple to describe her as "butch," for she rode the line between conventionally feminine (full lips, makeup, and eye shadow) and conventionally tough-girl lesbian (a nearly shaved brunette head under a man's fedora, several earrings and ear-piercings, tight black denim jeans and a tighter T-shirt that showed off a developed, athletic frame, born of lifting amps and speakers).

Samantha knew that refusing this invitation might be attributed to homophobia. Besides, L.A. from Palm Springs was the dullest, longest hundred-mile drive on earth.

"Gimme your keys. I'll drive you over," said Rider.

Rider wasn't staying in the gay-male strip on Warm Sands Road; she was ensconced in one of Palm Springs's twenty lesbian hotels, Radclyffe Hall (get it?), a mecca around Dinah Shore Golf Classic time.

"You know that bigot sportscaster they had to fire at CBS?" Rider said, on the drive over to the Radclyffe. "The guy who said ladies' golf was nothing but dykes. He was right. Shoulda mentioned tennis while he was at it. This town has an extra hundred thousand dykes on hand on Dinah Shore weekend. Gotta come down for that some year."

"Was Dinah Shore gay?"

"She hung out with Burt Reynolds," Rider remarked, turning into the palm-lined parking lot. "How about you?"

"Hm?"

"Troy is queer so everyone figures you must be too. Standard cover marriage," she suggested, naming a few of Hollywood's most famous couples who were pulling the same thing. "I always thought you were Mimi Mohr's . . ." She elongated the phrase: "Secret lover."

"We're close but not *that* close."

Rider pulled into a parking space in front of a palm tree lit from underneath by a blue light. Sam had the sense of being in a dream-world, the cool after the day's heat, the bad sleep followed by the dregs of stimulants rummaging around in her system, and then this Palm Springs nightworld of hotels and never-closing bars with never-sleeping people, colored lights on palm trees, Rider's hand upon her thigh . . .

Rider leaned in, smiling, a few inches from Samantha's face. Sam smelled her sweet gin-and-tonic breath, looked into the woman's large blue eyes, which were in command. "You wanna?"

"You're very attractive, but—"

"You think? What do you like best about me?"

Samantha felt Rider's hand work its way to her waist. "You've got nice eyes."

Rider smiled and shrugged. "I'm just messing with you," she said, withdrawing. "You don't have to worry about being molested in the night, honest." Rider hopped out of the car and got Samantha's things out of the trunk, while Sam took a full breath and undid her seat belt. Her heart had beat a little faster. Not exactly arousal, but not exactly repulsion either.

Samantha lay down in the room. The sliding door was open to the outside and the desert air was turning cool and crisp; Samantha on her bed, her hair brushed by the dry breeze, seemed to float . . .

"So what are you gonna do now?" Rider asked, flopping onto the other bed across from Samantha.

"Watch some bad TV." Sam picked up the remote and began looking at the racy cable movies on at this hour.

"Is it just me," asked Rider, glimpsing some straight-to-video bomb, "or does every other movie on HBO after one A.M. star Corey Feldman?" Rider then got up and reflopped on Samantha's bed, took the remote from her hands and turned the TV off.

"I thought you weren't going to molest me," Sam said, rather resigned to it now, maybe looking forward to it.

"That was when you were sitting in the car. Sprawling on the bed is a whole 'nother matter. You look wired," she added, pressing Sam's wrist to her cheek as if she were taking a pulse. "What do you do?" Her meaning was clear to Sam.

"Took some speed an hour ago, I . . ."

"Can't do 20/20s myself. All the blood in my body goes to

my clit and I can't be responsible for my actions." Rider's sweet breath was now an inch from Samantha's face. "Ever had oral sex performed on you while doing speed? I'd like to do you, Sam. Right now I should be at a party where they'd be falling over themselves to get to me, but here I am hangin' out with you. If you're unadventurous, you could just . . . just let me do everything." Rider touched the side of Samantha's neck, under her hair. Rider unfastened and slipped off her tight jeans; she was wearing boxer shorts underneath. Her legs were smooth and sturdy like a swimmer's.

"You must work out," Samantha said, hearing herself be banal.

Rider hopped up and turned off the overhead light; the next moment she was on the bed in Samantha's face again. "Yeah, I work out. Earlier you said I had nice eyes. What else do you like?" Rider took Samantha's hand and placed it on her collarbone, then lowered it. "I'd say my breasts are my second-best feature."

The adrenaline was racing through Samantha's head, pulsing in her ears; her body throbbed.

"You'd have run screaming by now if you didn't wanna do it," Rider declared softly. "I gave you a good five-minute escape hatch there, so now you're mine, Sam," Rider said, slipping off her undershirt.

"I have this control thing," Samantha stammered, breathing unevenly as Rider pressed against her. "I always . . . I mean, it bothers me not to be in—I mean, not to know what's going to happen."

Rider hopped up again and went over to her suitcase and returned a moment later with a cannister of amyl nitrate, to make Samantha relaxed and loose, and a pair of handcuffs.

"Rider, I couldn't possibly—"

"They're for *me*. So you won't be scared." Rider slipped them on one wrist, then another. "Now. *You* are in control, Samantha. No need to be afraid. What do you want me to do to you first?"

Rider sure knows how to work the parts, Samantha thought; the whole thing reminded her of the gigolo at the Beverly Hills Hilton. Nothing like a professional. Yet Samantha watched their lovemaking as if she were watching a wildlife special, detached, clinically curious, amused. Sam reached down to guide Rider's head at her waist—Rider's close crewcut grazed and tickled her thighs.

Maybe this would be love.

Sam had looked so many other places that anything new brought with it the ancient hope, the old nearly dead longing for something passionate that would obliterate the drudgery, the wearisome effort her life had become. Maybe she would spiritually surrender to Rider, or finally to someone, anyone, providing that someone could take her away from the futility of intoxication and recovery meetings, from the empty follies of career and social life—

The phone rang. And rang.

Rider picked it up. "Hello, Troy. Your wife's busy right now. Call an ambulance, if you think you're dying."

"Is something wrong?" Sam whispered.

"Fag shit," Rider whispered back, before ushering Troy off the line. "That's a good boy. Yes, go hang with P-Dogg. Bye-bye."

In ten minutes, the phone rang again:

"Goddamit," snapped Rider, picking it up awkwardly with her hands in the cuffs. "What? I can't understand . . . She's sort of busy right now."

"Troy again?"

Rider dropped the phone into the bedspread they had kicked back. "He's having some bad trip, all crying and snivelling. Says P-Dogg hit him." Rider sat upright on the bed and hung up on Troy, called the office, and requested a hold on all incoming calls.

Ten minutes later there was a knock on the door. A woman from management, dreadfully sorry about interrupting, said an emergency call had come in—could they plug the phone back in?

"I don't know why you're going," Rider said, as Samantha dressed. "It's like a kid wanting attention."

"Look, if it's nothing," Sam said, tenderly touching Rider's cheek, "I'll rush right back."

"Don't race back on my account," Rider said coolly. "I'm going to the party." Rider had satisfied her curiosity and now Sam could be dispensed with. "Seeya," she said, leaving.

Samantha stepped into the bathroom to straighten up; she wasn't sure if she could drive . . . but that turned out not to be an issue, since Rider had taken her car to the party. Sam went to the lobby and ordered a taxi.

"Hacienda Orpheus?" the driver checked. "The fag place?"

"That's the one," Samantha said, too tired to send the ugly man away and order another taxi.

As she rode over there, she became lucid, clear-thinking, as if she had found the eye in the hurricane of depressants and stimulants. What exactly was the long-term plan here with Troy? Stay married while he goes to treatment, while I go to treatment? When exactly do I bail out? After the big money comes in, presumably, but what does that make me? Did I see myself married to him ten years from now? That nice couple who lived high in Laguna Beach near the canyon, ol' Samantha and Troy. She writes books, he did some movies a few years back, had a few dance hits—

"Here we are," said the driver.

"Can you wait for me?" Samantha decided not to preview that she would be carrying out a drugged-up pop star.

He said yes, but abandoned her as she entered the darkened lobby of the Hacienda Orpheus. There were the sounds of partying, men yelling, someone screaming, but none of it was nearby. No one was at the pool, which looked like a war zone. No one was at the front desk. She rang the bellboy buzzer. Nothing. Finally, someone in a T-shirt leaned out of the door as if he didn't have pants on: "What?"

"Sorry to bother you—"

"We're full-up. What the fuck do you want?"

"I need to find a guest, Troy Chandler."

"We're closed," said the man, closing the door hard.

Where did Michael say their floor was? Samantha went to the elevator, and thinking she remembered the suites were on the fourth floor, pressed 4. The fourth floor of the hotel was dark, though there was plenty of noise from blaring TVs, pumping stereo speakers blasting a metallic techno track to an imposibly fast rhythm. The smell of pot smoke, cigarette smoke, and something more acrid, tweaked Sam's nostrils and stung her eyes—was that what crack smelled like? From one room emerged a group of laughing, intoxicated shaved-headed boys, shirtless with countless body-piercings, lopsided tattoos—was that a swastika? One was hysterically laughing while stumbling away from the other, holding a bottle where his friend couldn't get at it.

T-Jack and his crew were in a hotel room with the door wide open. T-Jack had his own bottle of gin-and-juice he was swigging from; so did his buddy. They sat in chairs with their pants down, being serviced by some bony white girls who barely were contained by their skimpy outfits, girls with shiny red or luxurious blond wig-hair . . . and falsetto voices ("You the man, baby.") Oh, drag queens.

"You like what you see, bitch?" T-Jack asked Samantha.

Further down the hall, she heard mumbling in one room, and cracked the door to peer inside. Two men, one at least fifty and the other in his thirties in a tank top, prodigiously muscled, had laid a young boy, who didn't look sixteen, over a stack of pillows atop a footstool. The boy's pants were pulled down and he was either about to be sodomized or probed—

One of the men: "Gotta problem, fish?"

"I just . . ." She found her voice. "Looking for Troy Chandler."

"Haven't seen him."

"This is all consensual, isn't it, boys?"

"You havin' a good time, Jerry?" said the oldest. The tank-top man lifted the boy's head by his hair and nodded it yes for him, while the boy moaned half-unconscious, "Susan . . ."

"Yep, he's having a good time." And then some fourth person behind the door slammed it in Samantha's face, and she heard the door lock tight.

Then she heard Troy's giddy coked-up laugh from down the hall. She knocked and feebly called out, "Troy?"

No answer. Then Michael's voice, "Is that you, Sam?"

The door was unlocked and Samantha pushed the door open a little. The room smelled rank with sweat and the reek of some kind of medicinal lubricant. She could detect the smell of urine. Michael Gold, sitting on the bed with his shirt off—not a winsome sight, really. He was hairy all over his body, his shoulders and back, and he weighed in the neighborhood of three hundred pounds. He held out some ecstasy. He wanted to love the whole human race. He held out his arms to Sam: "Samantha, my favorite woman . . . welcome!"

Christopher Tremaine stood beside a glass-topped coffee table where lines of coke had been delineated with a razor blade. Christopher was wearing a silk dressing gown, naked underneath. Samantha, barely able to stand the smell, was further revolted by his chemotherapy-like hairlessness. "Something we can help you with?"

Then Troy, completely naked, entered the bedroom from the private bathroom. "Shit!" he staggered, returning with a towel wrapped around himself. "Sam, Sam, Sam . . ." he said dreamily, insensibly high on something. He stumbled toward her to nuzzle his face with hers.

"Troy," she whispered, "maybe we oughtta go."

"Samsamsam . . . it's gonna, gonna be all right, just just—"

"Let's go home, huh?"

"Sssssh. Just just just, chill, be cool," he said, shushing her though she was done talking. Michael reached over, still laughing, and swiped Troy's towel, then fell over to the side of the bed in hysterics. Troy looked down at himself, then up at Samantha, his gaze swimming, his pupils dilated. "I don't have anything on," he said.

Samantha backed away.

"Hey, don't go!" He put his arm around her neck, and put his head on her shoulder. She automatically reached around to steady him, aware she had never before touched his bare back. "Michael and I," Troy said, leaning into her. "We're gonna make this whole new big CD, with me solo. I'm gonna make us a million dollars, and we can . . ." But he couldn't keep track of a thought as complicated as the future.

"Troy, I'm going to L.A. now."

"No, I know you're gonna, like, move out," Troy was near tears again, "and divorce me and everything, but you can't do that!" He clung to her wrists.

Michael: "Aww, now don't cry!" Then Michael started laughing again, and flicked him with the towel.

"Cut it out!" cried Troy, suddenly reduced to a preschooler. Then he suddenly remembered he was naked and covered himself, stepping back, as Christopher closed the door on her.

Samantha froze, unable to knock upon the door again, or to retreat to the elevator. She didn't know what to do.

Samantha had sworn to protect Troy. Her head throbbed with the smells, with the speed, with her panic, yet through the murk she detected a sickening flash of desire, shining, as she contemplated Troy's accidental, undeserved beauty—a beauty degraded by narcotics and circumstance, still sufficient for the carrion-pickers like Christopher and Michael to fill him full of drugs and lies so they might feed on him again. But was she any better than them?

It came to her: what I do next actually matters, for a change. I save him here or . . . or I save myself.

She turned and walked down the hall, past the sounds of sex and blaring TVs and music, someone blasting a porn video so the sounds of sex, *do it baby, eat that thang, you're so hot*, pulsed through the door . . . or maybe it was real sex . . . or maybe it was sex being filmed, which wasn't real . . . A nausea came over her, and the thought of returning to Rider's hotel room across town was oppressive, just as the parched desert air was oppressive. Right now, she thought, stumbling through the darkened lobby and out to the parking lot and down the block to a convenience-store pay phone, right now I must make contact with a real human . . .

In that moment of confusion, she thought of William.

Dawn was just breaking as William drove Samantha past the wind farm—the square miles of high-tech rotor blades that caught the gusts and produced electricity, sitting in the low mountain pass between Palm Springs and the Los Angeles sprawl. William was lecturing, peppy and energetic at 5:00 A.M., as Samantha only half-listened. "Franklin Roosevelt ran the White House, through the Great Depression, the New Deal, fighting World War Two, with a White House staff of *fifty*. Fifty, Samantha!" William laughed his baritone laugh. "Michael Jackson has fifty people in his press office, for god's sake. And you're part of this media cancer too."

"Part of what."

"Part of this growth industry. We don't *make* anything anymore in this country. The TV, the VCR, the computer chip—we invent them and then we let foreigners build them for us. The only growth industry in this country is media. You make a product. I hire ten people to advertise it, twenty lawyers to defend it against the lawsuits of twenty other lawyers, thirty people in a press office to issue p.r. lying about the product—cigarettes, breast implants, cars that explode on impact—and then I hire twenty consultants to meet with twenty focus groups and marketing surveyors to better tailor my p.r. From top to bottom, a service economy in which the service is bullshitting each other, making nothing of *value*, just endless media-generation. That's where our country is headed. That's all there is for anyone bright to do anymore—fight for a place in the parade of press conferences and lawsuits."

Samantha smiled weakly. It was beautiful in the pass, even with all the otherworldly windmills spinning and whirring. San Gorgonio peak on one side and San Jacinto on the other caught the pink dawn light. Speaking of service economies, only William, among her friends, could be awakened at 3:45 in the morning and asked to drive out to Palm Springs to rescue her from a bad situation.

"Damn," he was saying, not able to get his jazz station any longer on the radio. He happened by a rap station from San Bernardino. He laughed again. He couldn't be happier, talking effusively, Samantha—who needed him, who called him and only him!—by his side.

"Rap music is the minstrel show of the '90s," he began again. "Back in the '20s, some blacks played out the worst negative stereotypes of colored folk for a white audience—laziness, drunkenness, stupidity, lechery. Now a new round of black men play at being rapists and crooks and cop-killers and big-dicked thugs for white amusement. The bulk of rap bought in this country is bought by white people."

The Valium was kicking in, and the edge of Samantha's speed-induced paranoia was dwindling. She felt safe again. Now if William would just let this stay what it is—a friend doing a friend a favor. If he would just keep it like this and not try to run his game.

"Told you about that club-scene crowd, didn't I?" he said.

Los Angeles was coming to muted life on a Sunday morning when they reached his house off of Wilshire Boulevard. He had lowered the blinds and his bedroom was dark and warm.

"You always give me a call, don't you?" he said lightly, already deep into his self-doctored version of this episode. He was jaunty, arranging her pillows, tucking her in, placing a wastebasket beside the bed in case she became sick. "No matter what goes wrong, you know you can depend on—who?"

"On you, William."

"That's right, baby," he chuckled. This was how newlyweds bantered with each other, familiar and cutesy-pie.

"You're gonna be on the sofa if I need you?"

William emerged from his bathroom. His bedclothes were a T-shirt with the athletic number long worn away, and some loose terry-cloth gym shorts. He turned off the light and she felt the bed depress on the other side. "No, don't be daft. I'm going to be right here."

"I might be sick," she discouraged, though she wouldn't be.

"Not like it's our honeymoon, silly-millie," he chuckled again, stroking her shoulder ineffectually. "You just have a good sleep." He snuggled in closer.

She felt William rub one of his legs against hers, then press closer. Maybe she should let him screw her. No, even if that solved today's problem there would still be months of consequences, the declarations and emotional scenes. Samantha was lying on her back and she moved her hand slightly to her left, to judge how close William was, and she brushed against his shorts and what, possibly, was his erection. She sighed and rested her other arm across her face.

But I don't have anything left except my consent.

It's the very last thing I have. I can't trade away my last thing, can't barter it for a safe place to stay. I've been entered from every orifice, every illusion, every principle raped and poked and prodded, everything and everyone I've loved whored and violated or, like Mimi, ruined by Hollywood.

Hollywood don't corrupt nobody.

William, all at once, rolled toward her, taking her shoulders gently in his hands, sliding a knee between her legs. "I've waited for so long for you to come to me," he said, barely able to find words to keep pace with his emotions. "I love you—but you know that."

"I know that, William. Not sure why, but—"

"No no no, shush. None of that kind of talk."

She reached back in the direction of his face; she stroked his cheek. "Tomorrow, William. I'm going to pass out," she lied, "and that's not how I want it to be."

He silently withdrew.

She asked, "You understand, don't you?"

And, for a moment, she had a surging feeling of panic. He was stronger and bigger; maybe he would take what she denied him. If he forced himself on her, then maybe it would be over, and he would consign himself to some damned place, to live out the rest of their time together in remorse and guilt. But at least that would end his pursuit. Whereas if she offered to make love to him, there'd be no denying him ever again . . .

But then William rolled away and sat on the edge of the bed; then he went into the bathroom. She heard a low groan and she pictured her friend—a picture she never could imagine before—relieving himself at the sink. Then he left the bedroom for the kitchen. Samantha was almost asleep when she heard a glass break, a light glass, maybe a wineglass. He was drinking. And so she allowed herself to drift away to sleep, sure now that he wouldn't assert himself further, couldn't do so. His violence, as always, done to himself exclusively.

The brutal slaying in Palm Springs was all over the papers the next day, all over the TV, but Samantha didn't realize it. Nor did William, who had gone to his office (or somewhere) to brood, leaving out orange juice and instant coffee next to a fresh croissant, his car keys so she could get around, a little pile of money so she could function . . . it was total overkill, but sweet, so sweet and pathetic. So she decided to drive back to her home in Barranca Canyon—

What's the circus today?

But this circus looked different. Police cars. Media vans. Has my house been broken into? That wouldn't make the news. And then she let her mind return, her sense that something wrong had happened, suppressed since last night.

Samantha turned around in someone's driveway and drove up and over the mountain, fumbling on the radio for the all-news station, the one Angelenos listened to for O. J. and earthquakes. Ah, here came the headlines on the radio news:

Troy Chandler, dead in Palm Springs.

Details sketchy. Throat slashed. It appears that he was struggling against handcuffs. Fellow group member, Clarence Graham, known as P-Dogg, taken in by authorities for questioning. Producer Michael Gold says that P-Dogg had threatened to kill Troy in front of everyone, in the wild goings-on of a celebration party for their number-one hit, "Inside You"—in all record stores and now available in cassette and CD maxi-single, taken from the album *Bruthas with Skillz* by Tomorro Gs, Ganymede Records, distributed by Warners— and it seems a fight broke out. There was some broken glass; P-Dogg slashed his friend's throat. Police confirm that Clarence Graham tested positive for PCP. Lawyers for Mr. Graham say he does not know exactly what happened the night in question.

No tears, you'll note.

Mild surprise, yes, although not that great a shock. It was to be expected given all trajectories, Samantha sighed, and given her past, her track record: her inability to save anyone, her incapacity to redeem any situation with all her love and all the gifts of her heart. So, no. No tears, no drama. I will play-act a bit for Mimi's sake, she decided, for William's sake. Samantha aimed the car for home.

Top-40 Heartthrob Dead.

Teen Idol Boy-Toy of Lecherous Producer Killed in Gay Drug-Induced Rage.

Cover Marriage to Overaged, Haggard, Played-out Samantha Flint (Who Needs to Lose Thirty Pounds) Revealed as Cynical Drug-Crazed Sham.

Three police cars. Five TV vans. Bright TV camera lights on minicams and all waiting for our Sammie, waiting for the grieving widow.

Right before her bend of Barranca Canyon was a cul-de-sac, High Rock Court. Not ready to face the cameras, Samantha drove up the dead-end sidestreet and drove around the small loop at the end. I could go to any of these houses and no one would know who I am, she thought. I could drive back down to Los Angeles and go to the most public places and enjoy another few hours of my old life, my anonymous life . . . but to go forward to the mansion, that was where the earth would open and the Furies would be released and nothing ever after could bring back this precious anonymity. She pulled over and parked for a minute.

Just a minute more.

She watched her glowing digital clock tick off five minutes, 4:36 P.M., 4:57, now ten minutes more; it was like racing to the bow of the sinking ship to avoid the icy waters one more minute, one more increment of life. Samantha felt her old self lessen and pass through her hands even now, with each breath, with every heartbeat, going away, almost out of view . . .

There she is!

Mrs. Chandler, over here!

Were you with him when he died?

What were you doing at a separate hotel?

Did you know that the Hacienda Orpheus is primarily a gay hotel, Mrs. Chandler?

"Well, the production team is gay and it's not so unusual for us music-biz people to go to a place like that to celebrate—"

Did you see the body, Samantha?

What about the brutality?

Have you talked to Palm Springs police yet?

BEEP. *Hello Samantha. This is Trisha Blaine from KCLF Channel Six, and I know this is a horrible time for you. . . .*

How the hell did she get this unlisted number?

I don't know if you saw my piece on Easy-E, the rapper who died of AIDS? Well, we had the exclusive conversation with the family and I think you'd agree it was delicately, sensitively handled. Now I know, being in the business, that you eventually will have to make some kind of comment and I just want to make sure that what you *have to say comes across—in* your *words. You could sit in on the final edit, if you would give us an exclusive—*

This afternoon *Live at Five* brings you an exclusive interview with Brad Cho, a member of the group Tomorro Gs. "I knew something bad was going to happen," said Brad in a sound bite. "Too many drugs and too much kinky stuff going on. Not that I'm gay, you understand . . ."

BEEP. *This is William. I want to apologize for what must seem to you like an attempt to take advantage when you were vulnerable*

Mrs. Chandler, do you have a comment on the Santa Ana woman who claims that Troy Chandler, when he was known as Clay Weedon, fathered her child?

Mrs. Chandler, Trisha Blaine, KABC News. Did you have any clue to your husband's secret life?

Have you had an AIDS test, Mrs. Chandler?

There are stories that you watched while he engaged in sex with other men, do you have a comment?

These scars from handcuffs—did you engage with him in any kinky bondage sexplay while he was alive?

TEEN-IDOL VICTIM WAS
ONCE A MALE PROSTITUTE

by Cyril Demby

The *National Sun* has exclusive proof that long before Troy Chandler broke young girls' hearts in the Top-40 spotlight, he was taking old men's money for sex on the mean streets of Los Angeles. Troy Chandler was arrested in Christmas 1996 for male prostitution, under his given name, Clay Weedon . . .

Sam furiously turned through the *National Sun* to the jump page. Yes, at least, they'd run an attractive picture of her, taken at the wedding.

Says his wife, the lovely and powerful Samantha Flint, a Hollywood manager, "This news comes as a complete shock. I thought I knew Troy better than anyone, and to find it's all been a sham makes me feel like a colossal fool."

People close to Troy report that when she was away on meetings and high-powered trips to New York and Europe, Troy would turn her posh Hollywood mansion into a *palace of homosexual orgies.* The gay elite of Hollywood would flock to his mansion for things that one source said, "rivalled the goings-on of ancient Rome."

Troy was insatiable, reported one close friend, and would have two and three hustlers brought up to the Barranca Canyon mansion high in the Hollywood Hills and force them to perform sex acts on each other and on himself. Once, when someone asked him about what would happen if his wife found out, Chandler just said, "She'll never find out. She's too in love."

"I am devastated," Samantha Flint said last week through a spokesperson. "I had no idea that he had a secret life. The sad thing is that he might only have married me as a cover, and to help his career. While I really loved him with all my heart!"

Mrs. Chandler, did you have unprotected sex with your husband or his clients?

Did he bring his customers back to your house?

Channel Two special series. *Teenage boys: Trading Sex for Careers.* "This is West Hollywood, where the party never ends. And for some boys, homeless, underage, with a drug habit, it's the last chance at stardom . . ."

BEEP. *Samantha, this is your mother. I suppose you're not at this house anymore, but you have to get in touch. If anyone who is listening to this can get a message to my daughter, if you would tell her that she has to call home*

Former 39th District congressman Bob Dornan called today for the closing down of West Hollywood's gay bars and chided his rival, Representative Loretta Sanchez, for being soft on sodomites. "These miscreants and perverts shall not any longer be allowed to engage in their unlawful, ungodly acts in the City of Angels!"

Well, Jim, it seems Mrs. Chandler is no longer at the Barranca Canyon address. We have here a Gabriela Gavia Rosales who has said she hasn't seen Samantha Flint Chandler in five days. "She take her suitcase and go."

Action News Two caught Samantha Chandler in an A.M./P.M. on San Vicente as this exclusive video surveillance picture shows:

Mrs. Chandler, there were reports out late last week that you may yourself have been involved in his male prostitution operation. Were you getting a cut of the profits just to keep quiet?

They're calling you the Barranca Canyon Madam—

Ms. Chandler, Ms. Chandler! Over here! Did you know that the sex clients serviced by your husband include some of the most prominent names in Hollywood?

Will you name names?

We cannot confirm or deny reports at this time that Samantha Flint has received death threats from Hollywood moguls that might be exposed in the upcoming court case—

Was there a diary, Mrs. Chandler—

"I go by my own name, Samantha Flint."

Can you confirm or deny that five years ago, Troy Chandler was a guest of Michael Jackson's Neverland, when he was thirteen?

Do you think one of the powerful studio execs had your husband murdered so he wouldn't reveal his name?

Do you know if your husband was engaged in any blackmail?

At what time, to the closest hour, did Madonna leave the party?

There have been reports from some of the party-goers on the night your husband was killed that some young men used his blood to paint satanic slogans on the hotel walls. Was your husband into any kind of cult?

There have been tales of ritual satanic abuse. . . .

Hard Copy has obtained the first interview with Clarence Graham's hosebag white-trash girlfriend, Gabi Johnson. "It's like, this cop from the L.A.P.D., like, they were really roughing up P-Dogg when they came to arrest him."

Uh, you mean, the Palm Springs police.

"Huh? Yeah, them."

Were there any racial epithets used?

"Whuh?"

Did they call P-Dogg any names?

"Oh. Oh yeah, like they said 'Nigger, blah blah' and like 'Okay, like nigger, you're under arrest now'."

BEEP. *Samantha, this is Mimi, out in Malibu. For god's sake get in touch, sweetheart. I'm concerned about you. Rumor has it that you're holed up in some hotel in Santa Monica. I hired a detective to hunt for you. I swear, this Troy thing—you can't escape it, no matter what channel you're on. Of course, now their album is number one. . . .*

In a Channel Two KCBS exclusive, we talk to Troy Chandler's long-lost mother. "Troy ran away when he was fifteen. I loved him very much but he wanted to go make his own way . . ." Mrs. Weedon has retained Gloria Allred in her suit against Mimi Mohr & Associates and Tony Vittorio. "My son'd be alive today if it weren't for those people, and I'll be damned if they get to keep my son's money."

"But," Sam said numbly to the motel TV, three in the morning, "you . . . you put cigarettes out on his backside. Troy told me when you were out looking for a fix, your boyfriends tried to screw him!"

This is Ray Mtumbe, reporting live from City Hall, for KCAL News Nine. All attention has turned to Palm Springs Detective Melvin Crotts, who will give a live news conference . . . oh, I understand he's coming in right now to the Riverside County Courthouse: "Good afternoon. I want to make it clear right from the get-go: I have never used any racial epithets in any of my nearly twenty years on the force. This girl's accusations are unfounded . . ."

ABC's *20/20* has learned that there was a previous incident with Detective Crotts in 1988, when a Mexican-American suspect named Raul Jebebe filed a complaint against the Palm Springs P.D. for the use of homophobic and ethnic epithets in his drug possession arrest.

Senator Frank Shanker will be our guest later today speaking, of course, to the problems of a Hollywood so out of touch with the mainstream values of the rest of America. Be here with me and Family Frank himself, nine o'clock Eastern, eight o'clock Central—

We're here, Bree, with one of the over one-hundred teenage girls who have brought flowers to lay on the sidewalk in front of this hotel in Palm Springs, which has begun to resemble Kensington Palace after the death of Diana—

CBS Evening News: "Dan, the credibility of Detective Melvin Crotts would seem to hinge now on Raul Jebebe and if he can shed light on Detective Crotts as a fair and impartial enforcer of the law." Ron, perhaps you can tell us, does anyone have any idea where Mr. Jebebe is? "Uh, no Dan. It seems no one knows what became of a very important individual in this case."

Channel Four: Two people have come forward to discredit Raul Jebebe before he is even found . . .

Channel 5 KORC-TV has learned that Raul Jebebe worked at this hardware store in Garden Grove . . .

Breaking news. Channel 7 KABC has learned that the much-sought-after Raul Jebebe is now living as Juanita Juarez ("No comment! No comment!" says a large Hispanic woman, running from the cameras) in San Bernardino, according to Raul's sister, Carmelita Jebebe Gonzalez: "Yeah like, he din' want no mo' to be a woe-man trapped in a man's body, is like it is. And he went down to Mexico where they switch yo' self over real cheap-like? Tha's wuh happened."

Sixty Minutes has learned that the group got their drugs from this man, Tony Vittorio. (Tony was holding his hands in front of his head, slipping into his car in the parking deck.) "It's how it works all over showbiz, man," said a silhouetted head with an electronically disguised voice. "Stars aren't gonna go down to Melrose and buy their own drugs, right? Too risky. So they get it through their agent or their manager, or someone in their office. . . ."

KCBS is *live* on the scene: "Good afternoon, ladies and gentlemen. The district attorney's office wishes to affirm that we are going ahead with an investigation of three entertainment firms: the Hill and Hagen Agency, Beal Studios, Limited, and Mimi Mohr and Associates. We have evidence that all of these firms have been engaged in the distribution of drugs to favored clients. Question?"

Mike Menzies, Channel Two *Action News*. "This practice is

thought to be widespread in Hollywood and has been going on for years. Why choose now to make an example of these firms?"

"Yes, we do intend, as you put it, to make an example of these firms so maybe Hollywood can clean up its act. These firms take young talent, prey on their insecurities and the difficulties of show business, and offer these kids—'cause we're talking about kids, here—drugs to make them dependent. It's hard, you can imagine, to fire your agent or your stage manager if he or she is your source for a drug you're addicted to. We can't keep going to drug-related funerals like River Phoenix and, um, Kurt Cobain and Troy Chandler . . ."

Inside Edition showed slow-motion videos of a vulnerable Troy: "First River Phoenix and now Troy Chandler—is young Hollywood awash in drugs?"

Samantha saw her own blurry photo, zoomed in upon:

"And who was the woman—now under indictment for drug possession—who provided a front for his masochistic homosexual exploits. . . ." More angelic *Teen Beat* pictures of Troy. "Forced to sell his body on Santa Monica Boulevard for the drugs he craved . . ." The music swelled into the opening credits before the video went into freeze-frame and the British announcer read the title in bold letters: TEEN IDOL FOR RENT.

Whoa, there was Tiffani: "Samantha Flint was pretty drugged-out herself. Did she love him? Uh, I don't think so. She was a pretty hard woman. In it for the money, probably. And the drugs."

Tiffani, can you confirm that the night Samantha Flint's husband was being murdered that she was staying at a lesbian hotel in Palm Springs with Cynthia "Rider" Black?

"I think it was just, you know, typical Hollywood—she was a dyke, he was a queer. Not that there's anything *wrong* with that . . ."

KNBC-TV Channel Four has just learned that Clarence Graham, known to millions of his fans as P-Dogg, has been formally charged in the slaying of Troy Chandler!

I think it's ironic, Barbara, that a group formed to promote the harmony between races, to represent the new generation of colorblind American kids, ends up a symbol of the racial strife in America during the '90s. For some response on the street, let's go to Hildegard Perez in Compton where she's found some angry angry African-Americans . . .

"The autopsy shows that Troy Chandler had cocaine in his system as well as crystal methamphetamine, Adovan, phenobarbital, and marijuana. In the neck wound itself—and here, Jim, is where it gets really interesting—was powder cocaine, traces of semen, and traces of excrement. Back to the studio and to you, Jim." Well, that's quite a mystery, isn't it Kristie? "Sure is Jim, and now, speaking of excrement, with the Santa Anas on the rise, it's 'Constipation Season' for L.A. according to Dr. Blum . . ."

Samantha watched Geraldo Rivera interview a "secret" guest silhouetted against a dark curtain. Even silhouetted and with the voice electronically altered it could only be Blakely.

"I knew the boys in Tomorro Gs," Blakely was saying. "They often came to me and asked where they could get help for their drug use, but Mimi always stopped me from helping them. Mimi told me that the boys only were looking at a two-year career, max, and if they had drug habits they would need her agency to keep them working. Guest spots on low-rated sitcoms, dinner theater in Arizona, rich kids' birthday parties."

Samantha said to the TV: "That's the only thing you've said so far that actually sounds like Mimi, you little piece of shit."

". . . there was such pressure to do drugs if you worked at Mimi Mohr," Blakely said tearfully. Before the next ad break, Geraldo Rivera revealed that Blakely had accepted a $100,000 figure advance from St. Martin's Press in New York for his story *Inside the Downfall of Tomorro Gs*, which promised to tell of life within the "agency that used young men's lives for all they were worth, and threw them aside like Kleenex." Blakely broke down: "You see . . . Troy and I were more than colleagues. He was . . . we were *lovers*."

"Oh, brother," Samantha said, finishing off her Mounds bar, some of the only solid food she could get out of the motel vending machine. It was important to be thin for the trial, so she wasn't eating a lot, not counting diet pills and some things, you know, some crystal, just to keep herself awake so she didn't miss anything on TV. She had to make sure nothing was reported that she didn't hear.

She was gonna bust this case wide open!

"Detective Crotts, please. Tell him it's Samantha Flint."

The detective was on momentarily, out of breath, as if he'd run to receive the call. "Where are you?"

"At a pay phone near a taxi rank in front of a hotel, so I wouldn't bother tracing the call. It's not P-Dogg, and it's not that Nazi kid you rounded up a week ago either. Do you know who it is? Do I have to tell you?"

"Mrs. Chandler—"

"Ms. Flint! For the hundredth time, I kept my name."

"Ms. Flint, if you have information that could lead us to the murderer then you must tell us. You don't want to be charged with conspiracy, do you?"

It was hard on meth not to babble everything she knew at once. "The key is the glass coffee table. If you ask around, as you've probably done, you'll learn that Christopher Tremaine is into . . ."

"We know what's he's into."

"They had Troy handcuffed to the legs of the glass coffee table, naked underneath. Christopher takes a dump on the glass, which I think was as far as Troy was willing to go. Masturbation, I suppose, all around. What went wrong was Michael Gold. He's two hundred eighty, two hundred ninety pounds at least. He's getting off on the whole scene and sits on the other end of the coffee table and rests his weight with Christopher's. The table shatters, and a shard of glass goes into Troy's neck. Now I don't know if they dragged him to P-Dogg's room, I don't know if Troy got up in a panic and ran there . . ."

Samantha had told the story, fearful that in visualizing such an absurd, hilarious, wretched, damned ending to her husband's life she might feel something, be carried away with the emotion of it.

But nope, there was nothing.

"And then I think they tore the place up to confuse everyone, breaking windows, destroying furniture. Made it look like a skinhead riot broke out. I bet P-Dogg was out cold through the whole thing—and remember, Michael pointed the finger at P-Dogg to begin with."

"That scenario, Ms. Flint, fits our lab work, our facts. Just one problem. We won't get a conviction without a witness putting Troy Chandler in a room with Michael Gold and Christopher Tremaine."

There's the punchline!

No, of course, it was foolish to think that she could avoid the worst of it: the trial, the center stage and spotlight, the glare of national publicity. There was no stopping that flow of sewage, nothing to hang onto in the maelstrom, as the gutter approached, the abyss . . .

"You saw your husband, Gold, and Tremaine together?"

"Yes."

"Saw them engaged perhaps in this act."

"The moment before. It was two A.M. or thereabouts."

"You'll have to testify to this."

"But . . . but it's not a murder now, is it? It's a death by misadventure, or whatever you call it—"

"No, it's a conspiracy. Because Christopher Tremaine and Michael Gold told police and a grand jury that they saw P-Dogg attack Troy. Maybe manslaughter since illegal drugs were involved. And because of the handcuffs, perhaps rape and assault charges—"

"It wasn't rape, detective. That's one thing it wasn't."

We're here with Johnny Cochran at the Maranatha African Methodist Episcopalian Pentecostal Church in Torrance with some very angry angry African-Americans

Clarence Graham, formerly known as P-Dogg, now preferring to go by his Muslim name, Abdul Muhammed Mustafa

KABC has just learned that, like Michael Gold yesterday, Christopher Tremaine, president of Ganymede Records, now has been charged with manslaughter in the death of pop idol Troy Chandler, with counts of conspiracy, obstruction of justice, soliciting, and drug possession. His attorney, Alan Dershowitz, said in a prepared statement today that he was confident that his client would not spend one single day in jail for this offense

"It all comes down, Jim, to the testimony of the state's surprise witness—get this—Troy Chandler's *wife*. Who saw Michael Gold and Christopher Tremaine and her husband right before they engaged in the kinky sexplay that led to his tragic death." You know,

Pedro, even if it was a cover-marriage for the money, why didn't she, as a concerned human being, do something to stop such a dangerous round of sexplay?

Samantha ate her Almond Joy mechanically, saying to the TV, "I think *sexplay* is to this trial what *sidebar* was to the O. J. trial." Sexplay. Fuckpiece. Asswork. So many fun words in California.

What kind of woman could watch her husband

The trial will reveal how Samantha Flint could have seen this young man, so dependent on her for drugs and friendship

All eyes now turn to Samantha Flint

In an exclusive interview with *Live Action News*, Christopher Tremaine talks for the first time! "Samantha Flint—who is a total junkie—and the lawyers of Clarence Graham have manufactured this terrible libel that

The question our viewers want to know is: Where is Samantha Flint?

And now back to Greta Van Susstern and CNN: "The case comes down to whether the jury believes the elaborate and rather unseemly tale of Samantha Flint Chandler

The testimony of Samantha Flint, which begins this week

You know, Regis, it seems no sooner had Los Angeles gotten its fill of O.J. and Monica Lewinsky than, durn if we're not right back in the middle of another mess in the courts. I feel like I have to put my hands over little Cody's ears so he won't be exposed to all this tabloid trash. And like I told Frank this morning, the thing I don't understand about Samantha Flint

The whereabouts of Samantha Flint are still unknown right now, Chuck, but *Action Nine* correspondents are investigating reports that she has been moving about between Santa Monica motels, and has been seen wandering the streets

With the late Michael Gold out of the picture and not around to defend himself, it would seem Samantha Flint becomes all the more important in constructing the events of that fateful evening

It all comes down to Samantha Flint

Samantha Flint Chandler, the

Troy Chandler's not-so-grieving widow, Samantha Flint takes the stand in two days

Samantha, hair dyed red and pulled back in a scarf, sunglasses, an old man's large denim shirt with paint stains, and a pair of old jeans, walking unnoticed down Santa Monica Boulevard at six in the morning, past 23rd Street, 34th Street, circling back around to 29th Street, lest anyone be following her this morning. If she had to leave for the Riverside County Courthouse, then she'd at least get there with no one on her trail.

She passed newsstands that showed her picture. Much plumper than she was now. She looked good now, right? Good that she had lost so much weight because she was going to be on TV this afternoon—this was the big day, yes it was—everyone was going to watch. They would hang on her every word. What was on that last newspaper?

CHANDLER TRIAL FIGURE MICHAEL GOLD
KILLS SELF AND LOVER

LAGUNA BEACH—Orange County authorities report today that the body of Michael Gold and his partner Moe Silver, founders of Silver & Gold Promotions, were found at their shared home in Laguna Beach last night. Neighbors reported hearing gunshots at 6:30 P.M. and police were called to the address soon after.

Laguna Beach police found drug paraphernalia and the presence of cocaine

"You buy the paper?" asked the foreign-born merchant.

"No," said Samantha, scooting away quickly, turning her face from him. She'd already had too many close calls today, people taking notice of her, squinting, trying to see who she was.

And now Michael and Moe are dead—killed by Christopher so they wouldn't turn state's evidence on him? Gotta keep running before anyone finds where I am. She was full of energy (considering she hadn't slept in two days), passing dilapidated motels, barrooms, topless/bottomless peep-show parlors, pool halls, immigrant tacky-souvenir stores . . . Look, you could buy a Route 66 placard there, in the store with the hand-lettered sign: LAST TEN MILES OF THE MOTHER ROAD. Right here? Santa Monica Boulevard? This was where the old Route 66 made its way to the Pacific? Samantha knelt down on the sidewalk to touch—

"Ma'am, are you all right?"

People were noticing her. Samantha stood up and counted them, spinning this way and that—people were watching her, from across the street and from passing cars. She needed a bus right this moment—the buses are the only thing you can trust! Leaving a shoe behind, she began to run toward a distant bus stop.

The press hordes were at the front door of Mimi Mohr & Associates's office building on Sunset Boulevard, and at the parking deck entrance, the two places they wouldn't be charged with trespassing. Samantha ran the gauntlet:

Mrs. Chandler, did you hear about Michael Gold's death, and do you feel responsible?

Did you and Troy Chandler ever consummate your marriage or was it just a sham?

Were you in the room when Troy died?

Is it true you were covered in Troy's blood when the police found you wandering around Palm Springs?

At the coroner's, can you describe the state of Troy's body?

Was his head attached to his body by a thread?

Were the eyes gouged out?

Samantha—yes, please, over here! When you saw him on the coroner's slab, did you want to climb on top and fuck him like one of his tricks?

"Excuse me . . ."

"Come inside, Ms. Flint," said Lance, the beefy security guard, trying to separate her from the mob of microphones and TV lights.

"Did you hear . . . Lance, did you hear what that woman just asked me? Did I hear her right?"

The security guard led Samantha, momentarily confused, within the building's reception lobby, the limit of the media. Samantha stumbled against a cold marble wall and touched her face to it. The woman holding the camera, which seemed to have an actual eye in it, an eye with a film over it—the woman was deathly white with blood, fresh wet blood instead of lipstick

"Lance, did you see that woman who grabbed at me right before we got in the door?"

"No ma'am."

Samantha went back to the glass door for a second look, which set the camera crews and microphones into a flurry again. ("She's coming out, boys!") Samantha, like when one goads a dog, feigned moving forward with a small jerk, and the mob stirred and roiled and scrambled, then she was still and they froze motionless. She moved another inch, and the crowd beyond the glass exploded and clammered and recombined, then she froze still and so did they

"Ms. Flint?"

Samantha found she was still standing against the cold marble wall.

"I'm going to my office," Sam said to the security guard, pressing the side of her head. Mimi's floor was a ghost town: no receptionist, no Tiffani, no Blakely. Samantha wandered past the empty offices.

"May I help you?" Another security guard associated with the Riverside D.A.'s office appeared.

"I'm looking for Mimi."

"Are you Samantha Flint?"

Samantha couldn't find her voice, her heart beat wildly with fear. She was in too much of a panic to speak, and so quickly moved to Mimi's office, and locked the door behind her. Mimi's was the only office still furnished, her desk piled with papers and newspaper clippings. Samantha sank into the brushed leather sofa and . . . and almost instantly the crystal methamphetamine rush was broken. Perhaps hours passed. She was now very tired, nodding into an almost sleep when she heard a loud knocking on the door:

"Sam, this is Mimi. Are you in there?"

Mimi! Samantha staggered to her feet, toward the small mirror on the wall, and checked herself. She didn't want Mimi to think—

"Sam, open up!"

Samantha opened the door and Mimi walked in, dressed in black suitable for mourning, taking off her wraparound sunglasses and setting them gently on her desk. "Security had orders to call me if you showed up," Mimi said, sitting in her high-backed chair behind her desk. "You're all right?"

"I'm not giving out where I'm staying because . . . because it's getting crazy out there—don't make me tell you where I'm staying because I can't tell you—"

"Calm down, Sam. Calm down."

"If something happens to me, go get my journal. I've got instructions that you're to have my journal—it can't fall into their hands—"

"Sam, it's gonna be all right. Calm down. No one's going to get to you in my office."

As Samantha fell silent, Mimi slowly creaked around in her swivel chair to look, for one of the last times, out her window upon Century City to the west.

With so much to say, neither of them said anything.

Samantha was scared to be too curious, but of Mimi's own volition the details soon came pouring out. Patrick Fox was gone, so was Amber, so were two or three other cash-cow clients; last week she had laid everybody off. All her files and bookkeeping records were with the police and the Riverside and Los Angeles County d.a.'s offices; they were going to crucify her for something, having said they'd make an example out of her. Now they were looking for just what.

"You won't go to jail, will you?" Samantha asked weakly.

Mimi shook her head slowly, depending that her lawyers would keep that from happening. "Tony is toast, though."

There were, between them, no cries of how unjust it all was. There wasn't, after all, in the whole of Los Angeles an entertainment concern where similar drug-distribution charges couldn't be pursued. They both understood:

No-talents get $20 million a movie because they could. The police made a publicized celebrity arrest because they could. The media was generating slander after slander because they're allowed to. Peripheral riffraff like Troy's junkie mother and the trailer-park floozy who claimed Troy fathered her child were suing because they could. Mimi's rivals were moving money into the d.a.'s reelection if they'd "get that bitch Mimi Mohr," because they could. And there was money in it for everyone, except the person who was "it" for this round: Mimi. Samantha and Mimi understood Hollywood opportunism because they had been dispensers and recipients of it.

"I was walking down Santa Monica," Samantha said, a tear now running down her own face, "and I passed this joint."

Mimi sniffed, reaching in her desk for a tissue.

"It was a topless bar—well, more than that, because it advertises 'totally nude.' Bobby Midas's Show World. Looks like an old movie theater. Have you seen it?"

No.

"And outside on the marquee, they had a list of girls . . . glossy photos of women, you know, with little pieces of black tape over the crotches and tips of their breasts . . ." Samantha, not entirely stable, laughed deeply. ". . . like, like they were really covering up something and you couldn't get the idea. And there was this display in one of the windows. Come see Winona Blake, it said. 'You re-member her as Maggie on *Gimme a Break!*, but she's all grown up now!' "

Sam stared at Mimi as if this might mean something to her.

"And did you know—did I tell you? That Winona Blake—well, she's Sandra Blake now—gave me her résumé, and I even got an audition for her but Tiffani threw her résumé away and . . . and now, there she is, working at this topless-*bottomless* place."

Mimi leaned forward, still looking at Samantha with tenderness.

"I mean, does Winona Blake think that . . . what is she thinking? That's been bothering me all day. . . ."

Mimi marvelled, *"That's* what's been bothering you all day?"

Sam felt her eyes fill with hot tears. Ah, so here they were: while national humiliation, the death of her father two years ago, the death of her pretend husband, the slipping away of her health, her life, her soul, had failed to bring them, poor Winona Blake dancing at Bobby Midas's Show World had brought the tears forth.

"Why is she doing that?" Samantha demanded. "Why can't she just walk away?"

"Because. Nobody ever just walks away."

Just as nobody can really save anybody, Samantha decided. I shed tears for Winona Blake because I could have helped. But the world is filled with Tiffanis. And it has not been my fate in this world to save anyone I cared about, starting with myself. Not Cameron, with whom things could have been very different if I had returned a love equal to what he gave me; not William, whom I could have rescued from a life of loneliness.

Not Troy, whom maybe no one could have saved.

Mimi looked out the window at the phalanx of media vans. "Some fourteen-year-old boy had a crush on Winona Blake when she was on TV and living *her* fantasy, and now he's twentysomething, hasn't been laid in three years, and it's his turn for *his* fantasies to come true. He can give her a twenty for a table dance." Mimi slid the tissue box to her friend. "It brings people out. Someone who once had a career, someone we once envied. People want to see 'em brought low. People want to see other people go *splat* at the end of a long nosedive." Mimi had been thinking a lot lately about falls from great heights.

Sam reached for a tissue and blew her nose. "Why can't she just go home or do something else? Be a secretary or sweep up somewhere . . ."

Mimi deadpanned: "What? And leave showbiz?"

Samantha stared at Mimi, and realized that no one would save her either. After a lifetime of Mimi's help and guidance, Samantha thought, this should have been the moment when *I* was strong and uncompromised. When Mimi needed me, I should have been the one to help her pack the U-Haul for the ride back east—find Route 66 and throw 'er into reverse!

"Let's get out of here," Mimi suggested.

Mimi and Sam hunkered down in Mimi's Porsche and escaped the parking deck, leaving a fantail of cameramen and reporters following the progress of the car. One or two broadcast trucks gave chase, but when Mimi found the 405, she took it up to ninety MPH and lost all the tailgaters.

"I'm sorry, Samantha. Sorry for dragging you to L.A., sorry for the A.A. meetings and that stupid idea about the cover marriage. I haven't exactly been a lifesaver, huh?"

"I'm the one who's sorry, Meem. I've been a shitty best friend—I was supposed to be looking out for you too."

"Nyeh," Mimi waved this aside. "We made some mistakes, but

basically the big boys wouldn't let us play in the game. We got screwed this round. But we'll be back."

"We will?"

Mimi left the 405 for the short 90 Freeway, headed toward Marina del Rey and the shore. They were halted at a stoplight, and Mimi turned to Samantha with a gentle smile under the Ray•Bans. "Red hair looks good, Sam. Wouldn't have thought it, but it suits you." She patted Samantha's knee. "We're gonna get you straightened out, sweetheart. That's . . . that's the first thing."

Samantha warmed to hear Mimi take charge!

"Get our teaching certificates," she continued, turning onto Lincoln. "We may have to legally change our names and lie low for a little while, but life goes on, right? You'll teach English, I'll teach History of Western Art, some little college somewhere in New England. Maybe start our own private school for girls, a prep for Smith. Be some money in that."

"I don't care about the money," Samantha said, as she motioned for Mimi to pull over a few blocks short of Santa Monica.

"That was reflex, what I said. I don't care either." Mimi pulled into a bus stop on Main Street and idled. "You want out here?"

"I've been taking city buses everywhere," said Samantha. She opened her door but Mimi pulled her back and leaned across the front seat, clasping Samantha tightly. Samantha squeezed back with all her weakened strength, burying her face in Mimi's neck, inhaling her perfume . . . Issey Miyake, $110 a bottle, reminding Sam of childhood summertimes in Missouri, lilacs and honeysuckle.

"Once your testimony's over give me a call, and we'll skip town," Mimi said, before looking down at her floorboard, not wanting to look Samantha in the eyes for this: "You're not . . . you're not going to take anything for this afternoon, are you sweetheart? You don't want to come off like . . ."

"No, don't worry. No pills or anything."

"Promise?"

"I promise."

Mimi's voice was hopeful again. "It'll all be over soon. After the trial, we'll head back to New York maybe. Reconnoiter."

"And you promise you'll take me with you, Meem?"

"I promise, sweetheart." She revved her car. "Hey? Don't I always work something out?"

Samantha's friend tore away in the sports car she would soon have to sell, on her way back to Malibu and her house that would soon be put on the market.

And what a bunch of bullshit, those promises.

Mimi could never leave L.A. after it handed her this defeat. She's planning her comeback strategy this very second. She always wanted to be a household name, Sam thought, and that's what she is. Mimi could no more leave L.A. than Samantha Flint could get through this afternoon's testimony without a crystal. Can't even remember my own goddam name right now without one.

Where was her brown bag with that crystal? She searched her purse and her pockets, realizing her packet must have fallen out in her earlier scrambles through Santa Monica. No, wait. She snorted it already, didn't she? One can always score near the beach. Where the hell did Mimi let me off?

Corner of Main and . . .

Venice. Venice Boulevard. To her left, a short two blocks away was the ocean. Venice Beach.

Venice, where any amateur could score some crystal, just a tiny little rock is all it would take anyway. Not like she was looking to buy a shipment, just a little glass—or dirty powder, she wasn't choosy. But she was sort of panicked. Why didn't the earlier crystal she sniffed work? It's like everything is goddam *normal*, like my mind is mush—where is the acuteness, the clarity, that hearing my pulse all over my body, in my neck, in my eyes, that delirious surge that makes you think you could bite through steel. . . .

Why were people backing away?

"Hey, aren't you . . ." began someone.

"Excuse me," she said, businesslike. "Looking for a connection . . ."

Samantha stumbled along the Venice Promenade, the ocean and the palm-filled park beckoning beyond. On her left and right were the few Italianate buildings attempted for this civic folly back in the 1910s, the St. Mark's Hotel with its arcade of Venetian columns.

And yet the city fathers filled in most of the canals, abandoning their notion to re-create the City of Canals here at the edge of California

"Over here, lady."

A scruffy kid with acne—always ask the lowlifes with acne, their skin breaks out because of crack, and they know where to get what you want. "I might be able to help you."

"I need to hook up with some crystal. In a hurry, before I come down all the way. I can't come down because today, you wouldn't believe what I have to do—"

"Whoa, bitch. Let's go walking, okay? See if I can find Donny. Hey, C. J.!"

A girl approached, halter top, pale, unhealthy skin, stringy hair dyed oil-black, nose ring. "What, man?"

"Where's Donny? Got someone lookin' to hook up."

"He's over at the pier where he always is. You can tell him *fuck off* for me. You can tell him I don't wanna suck his goddam two-inch cock he can't even get hard!"

But in Venice there are Ten Thousand Courtesans

"Donny! Over here, man. Got some business for you, bro."

But in Venice the great artist Veronese killed a man—over love, over art!—and he was on the run so this priest said, yes, I will hide you here, if you paint the ceilings of my church, San Giovanni Cristosomo

"Yeah, I got what you need lady. Damn, she's fucked up!"

"Don't talk about her like that—"

"Shut the fuck up, C. J. Whyn't you ugly on out of here?"

"Screw you, asshole! Tried to rape me—"

"I wudn't fuckin' touch your dried-out shit for anything, you crackhead bitch. Like I want AIDS drippin' off me and shit."

They have a choir here, a choir of people who are dying, and this choir has all these orphans and sick people and people with AIDS and they sing these beautiful heavenly songs. Samantha could hear the music, the high soprano of a boys choir, ethereal, soaring above the traffic noise and the noise of Venice's vendors and hawkers

"Hey, lady—don't snort it right here, for fuck's sake. Shit. There're cops all over!"

But in Venice, the nobles never used the walkways, moving around only by gondola and magnificent bedizened barges—the first floor was for servants who used the streets and brought in the food; the nobles lived from the second floor upwards, that's why the second floor is called the *piano nobile*

"Hey, Donny, she's passin' out or some'n."

"C'mon, Donny," cried the girl, "you don't take her purse!"

"Aww, that's just major fucked up, man!"

"Let's just see what she's got," Donny snarled, tearing at Samantha's right arm to get the purse.

Samantha felt her head hit the sand when she fell, some grains spraying up into her mouth. The fall didn't hurt. Nothing hurt except her head which seemed to have burst and was flowing outward, draining into the sand. Had she been shot in the skull? With her working hand, she reached up to check. No, but she had sand in her hair. Bad thing, having sand in your hair. It was at once the worst imaginable pain in her head, and yet a warmth there too, spreading

"What . . ."

She tried to speak. This was not very bright, upon reflection, to buy one's methamphetamine from this undependable young man she didn't really

"Got some Xanax," Donny announced, dropping unwanted items out of her purse onto the sand. "Just bullshit Tylenol in here, fuck it."

"Stop it, give it back to her," the girl said, scrambling to retrieve the purse. Donny pushed her into the sand.

"Fuck you, Donny!"

The younger boy with the bad skin just laughed at her predicament. "Shit, C. J., you shoulda seen yourself go down, just like, *bam!*"

"Credit cards, man! She's got a hundred of 'em!"

Samantha informed them crisply that no good would come of trying to use them, since many were cancelled and others were full to their limit. Except no sound came out of her mouth

Then it was later.

You'd think lying on the beach like this someone might have found me. Wait, she wasn't where she started. She'd been dragged behind a supply shack for the lifeguards, next to the pier. It's dark. She heard the ocean, in and out, a splash and a long hiss in retreat, and she heard the wooden pylons of the pier creak and groan. There was a light on the end of the pier, hallogen blue-white, that reflected like a moon, a streak across the black, still Pacific.

And soon, there were no other details, just the light.

"There she is!"

When I get out of the hospital, Samantha figured, I'll track down that good samaritan who called 911 and, I dunno, take him out to dinner. The paramedics, the stretcher, then the big ride in the ambulance. Don't understand the jargon. Now the emergency room, where I'm conveniently hovering over my body on the table.

"Where's the CT-scan?"

"Have we got the tox-screen yet?"

"I'm gonna put a five on cocaine. Dilated right pupil . . . no response to light, possible coma."

"Grade two or three?"

"Maybe our little overdose has had a stroke."

"Got the CT-scans."

"About time, Jackie. Did you see if the pizza has arrived yet, by the way?"

"Tom, it's been out there for the last twenty minutes. There's one slice left, I think."

"Shit Francine, go claim that slice for me while I look at the . . . whoa nelly. Get neurology down here."

"She came in with a pulse of 95, b.p.'s 250 over 160, and she was out cold. Gotta be some high-grade crystal we're dealing with here."

"Slice is gone, Tom. Sorry."

"Fuckin' A. If I collapse from hunger in the next half hour you greedy bastards will know why."

"You want us to get an IV ready for you?"

"Ha-ha. How long did the paramedics say she was down for?"

"Tox-screen! We've got amphetamine, traces of Valium."

"Valium and crystal? Make up your mind, sweetheart—what's left of it. Do you wanna go down down down or up up up?"

"Whatta we got here? This the 'found-down'?"

"Hi, Earl. Sorry to get you out of Hatcher's little soiree cocktail party—"

"I was just getting a buzz. Of course, a case of the shakes, Tom, is the key to good neurosurgery. Whatta we got here? Uh-oh."

"Pulse is dropping, as is b.p."

"Hell of an aneurysm. Cerebral cortex is fucked—pardon the French, Jackie."

"Oh, Earl, we speak quite a bit of French down here."

"Looks like the brain stem is taking up residency in the spinal column."

"Well. Can we . . ."

"No."

Look at the neurosurgeon, the guy looks like Marcus Welby. He could be anyone's grandfather. If anyone could save me, he surely can. And yet everyone's just standing around.

"You wanna call code? By the way, who's the attending?"

"Ha, she's all yours, Tom. You're two for three this evening. Hope no one I want to survive comes in tonight."

"Heart's still going. Barely."

"You mean . . . Dr. Higgam?"

"Yes, son."

"You mean we gotta just sit and wait until she . . ."

"If we'd gotten her five minutes after it happened, maybe we could have gotten oxygen to her brain, so there'd be something left if she ever woke up again. Even then, she'd be relearning the alphabet for the next ten years. I hate pulling people back just for that. Though I do it a few times a month."

"Shame. She's so young."

"You're the first-year? See the X ray here . . . there's your classic herniated brain stem. Once the aneurysm explodes, the blood builds up pressure in the skull, it pushes the stem down the spinal cord, and since the stem tells your heart to beat, well."

Aw no. You're kidding.

That's it?

"Bad dye job but otherwise she's sort of pretty. You think it was a suicide?"

"An accident, probably."

"Looks like that woman who was married to that—uh, Troy Chandler guy who got killed."

"She's a little too old, I think."

Such a tormented, spectacular raging and flailing is life, so much glorious noise and light to bask in, so much truth and beauty each life might contain, yet how lightly we hold it, a cigarette here, an unsafe dash against the stoplight there—how loosely grasped it is, how muffed and fumbled away, rolling toward the storm-drain before we've had time to clutch at some meaning, adorn ourselves with purpose, or forge redemption from the passing years

"No I.D.?"

"Heh-heh, Francine, your and Jackie's evening entertainment will be to find out who the hell she is. But that can wait until you get me something to eat. Manuel, how many slices did you have?"

"You pickin' on me again, doc?"

"It's sad. Just waiting for her heart to stop."

But the light is still there. At the end of the pier.

"There she goes . . . nope, another beat. Let her sit here awhile so we can tell her family we had her on the table for twenty minutes trying to save her."

"Time of death?"

It was a summer evening and Samantha Flint, nine years old, had been taken by her father to visit the Boatland showroom, where they happened upon an impromptu cookout provided by one of Mr. Flint's partners and his extended family. Sam and her father had been expected back in Springfield for dinner but her daddy phoned and told Mom they'd be staying, and Samantha, like any child, was giddy at the change of schedule.

There were other children whose names she never learned, but her own age, from less citified places in the Ozarks, intoxicating with wicked words in rural accents, hyperactive and fun. It was one of the few times she remembered "playing" as hard as she could, chasing, tagging, hiding in the woods, crouched down dirty and sweaty, tackling, being tackled, part of an aching jumble of bodies and ticklings and punishments and, for Sam, crushes on each of the scrawny anonymous Missouri boys who allied with her rather than their wild-haired sisters and cousins.

Amid this inexhaustibility of body and lengthening of time known only to children, Sam looked up to sense the oncoming evening, the thickening of the moist night air, the way the haze gathered above the dark green waters where they met the pines—not quite fog, but a softening of shoreline and treetops native to the Ozarks when the lake turned cool and still. With the smell of barbecue smoke and honeysuckle and the rich plush grass they'd wrestled in, rooted up by handfuls for the fun of it, Sam waited in the purest dread for that call of her name, that sign that it was time to leave for Springfield. But the voice didn't come, this August night rich in childhood hours.

Then the other kids began to beg to go swimming in the lake, though no one had bathing suits. The other kids stripped to their underwear, which Sam viewed with confused feelings of desire and abandon, before she begged her father to let her strip to her underwear too. If Mrs. Flint were around this would have been grounds for divorce and exile to the orphanage, because, like all refugees from hillbilly country, Mrs. Flint was keenly aware of the proprieties, ever-vigilant for telltale signs of her children's inferior breeding. But Daddy said, "Don't tell your mother, Sammie girl. It'll be our secret, y'hear?"

"Okay, Daddy. The brunettes against the blondes."

"That's right, darlin'."

So the normally shy Samantha, peeled down to T-shirt and panties, ran headlong down to the rickety pier. Yes, that pier, which had been preserved in memory with iconic force, illumined only by a blue-white streetlamp, orbited by hundreds of insects; Sam would always be able to recollect the light's steady hum. Oh how her playmates screamed and splashed and laughed with her. Did one of the boys try to make her lift up her shirt (god, she was flat as a board! What could those boys have gained from that!) . . . Did she really paddle to the shore and roll with the boys in the mud while the other girls squealed? Wasn't there a playful fight in the shallows, one of the boys whispering something naughty in her ear as he attempted some liberty—nothing adult and sordid, just a proposed glimpse of something forbidden, a touch upon something private, the tamest breach of innocence?

No, no breach of innocence: innocence itself!

"Samantha!" called a boy from the end of the pier. "C'mon and jump with me!"

"Samantha's in love, Samantha's in love," mocked the boy's girl-cousin, leading her muddied playmates in the chant.

Samantha ran to the top of the trail and turned for the pier, her limbs loose and free, a joy inside escaping with each laughing stride, hurtling herself fast down the child-trampled hill, the spiky grass prickling her bare feet, clasping the beautiful boy's hand before they flew through the air, out ever so far, out above the warm black water, for an airborne moment part of the night and the stars and the summer heavens, indulgent and immane.